SECOND STAR
TO THE
LEFT

MEGAN VAN DYKE

SECOND STAR TO THE LEFT

MEGAN VAN DYKE

CITY OWL
PRESS

SECOND STAR TO THE LEFT
Reimagined Fairy Tales, Book 1

CITY OWL PRESS
www.cityowlpress.com

Cover Design by MiblArt. All stock photos licensed appropriately.

Edited by Heather McCorkle.

For information on subsidiary rights, please contact the publisher at info@cityowlpress.com.

Print Edition ISBN: 978-1-64898-139-5

Digital Edition ISBN: 978-1-64898-140-1

Printed in the United States of America

PRAISE FOR MEGAN VAN DYKE

"Packed with steamy romance, adventure, and an unforgettable cast of characters, Megan Van Dyke's clever reimagining of Peter Pan, centering Tinker Bell and Captain Hook, is an absolute treasure. The writing is effortless and draws you in immediately, leaving you fully immersed in a fantastical world that feels both familiar and fresh."
— *Paulette Kennedy, International Best-selling Author of Parting The Veil*

"Megan Van Dyke's story resets the balance of Neverland, turning an imaginary playland into a world that lives and breathes through every scene. Highly recommend!"
— *K.J. Harrowick, author of Bloodflower*

"A delightful, sexy romp set in a fresh, yet familiar fantasy world. Perfect for anyone who has shipped Tinker Bell and Captain Hook!"
— *Jeffe Kennedy, award-winning author of Dark Wizard and The Forgotten Empires*

"Fast-paced, witty, and romantic."
— *Christy Dirks, book reviewer*

"Keep your hands and feet inside the ride at all times. Ladies and Gentlemen we are going to Neverland. But not the Neverland you remember from your childhood. Hook and Tink are amazing in this new twist on a classic."
— *Melody Caraballo, author of Unhinged Witch*

"A must read with magical, unforgettable characters!"
— *Abby Glenn, book reviewer*

To Mom
Thank you for believing in me before I ever believed in myself.

1

*N*othing attracted attention like free booze. The Lazy Mule wasn't usually this popular, or so the locals said, but the promise of free drinks lured every shopkeeper and down-on-their-luck sailor into the dirty, ramshackle building near the docks. Tropical air, thick with humidity and the promise of rain, filled the bar as tightly as the patrons crammed into every nook and cranny.

Tink pulled her braid over one shoulder, careful not to dislodge the sections covering her pointed ears. She rubbed the loose ends between her fingertips, feigning nervousness as she glanced over her shoulder.

Men and women alike clamored toward the far table where a large, blond man regaled the crowd with tales of his crew's success. He was attractive, with bulging muscles, towering height, and a chiseled jaw. But if he made one more crude joke about plundering something, Tink was going to toss her drink at him. *Stupid pirate.* Soon enough he'd stumble and fall, or the rotting table would finally give way. She grinned. That alone would be worth the cost of the trip.

But the blustering first mate of the *Jolly Roger* wasn't her target. No, to get what she needed, only the captain would do. Tink licked her lips as her gaze caught on the equally tall but leaner man with one shining black boot propped on the seat of a nearby chair. He shouted colorful additions to the first mate's tale and called for another round of drinks for all his "friends."

The poor ale Tink sipped turned sour on her tongue before she forced it down. The captain's arrogance knew no end. He traveled from one pirate-friendly port to the next so he and his crew could rave of their accomplishments. At least it made them easy to track.

Tonight, they bragged about their theft of the Heart of Fire, a stunning ruby set in gold. A half-grin pulled at her lips. What would they say when she stole it from them?

Captain Hook, so named for the distinctive metal weapon that replaced one hand, raised a pint in the air. Dark ale splashed over the side. Mugs clinked, rising with cheers from the crowd who joined in the toast.

Finally, *finally*, the captain glanced her way.

Her heart gave an involuntary leap as sinful lips twitched on a strong face. Or perhaps it was his coal-dark eyes that twisted her up inside. He raised his mug, taking a long swig, but his attention never left her.

Perfect.

One look and she'd hooked Hook. A small laugh burst from her lips that she covered by biting her bottom lip in feigned embarrassment.

Before he lowered his drink, Tink twisted around back to her mug warming on the bar. Warm ale and filthy pirates. Every girl's dream night.

She snorted. *Sure.*

Her stomach turned as she rubbed the mug between her palms. This wouldn't be her life. Not anymore, not after tonight.

A woman squealed as a drunkard yanked her onto his lap, nearly sending them both tumbling to the ale-soaked floor. How did she ever enjoy these horrid human bars? She and her cousin Lily used to slip through the pixie doors—the circles of trees, stones, mushrooms, or whatever the elders of old selected—for a little fun in the human world all the time. They'd drink, dance, flirt with whichever handsome human caught their eye, then sneak back home before the elders were ever the wiser. They'd done everything together for as long as she could remember. The elders frowned on such elicit exploits. But really, only allowing them out to trade and gather goods not available in their homeland was, well, boring.

Her chest grew tight. *Had Lily made it home? Was she okay?* The bracelet around her wrist with its broken gem weighed her down. Tink had committed an unforgivable sin—selling her pixie dust—to save Lily from that wretched Captain Blackbeard and his crew. A nastier man never drew breath. *Filthy pirate bastard.* That act got her banned from her homeland, Sylvanna Vale, rendering her unable to pass through the magical doorways. Pretending to be human and hiding her wings was a pain. *By Durin's beard, binding them hurts!* Without the cloak around her shoulders, someone would notice where she'd lashed them to her back, and that...well, best they didn't.

"Hey there, lovely lady." A man brushed against her at the bar, smelling of sweat and sour ale—or something even fouler.

"Hello." *And please go away*, she added silently, barely giving the man half a glance. If he had any wits, he'd leave.

"You here with anyone?"

Somehow his breath was worse than the stench clinging to him. Hanks of greasy hair lay against dirty skin. When was the last time he bathed? Humans were disgusting in general, but this one was something extra.

Tink glanced back at the pirates and stiffened. The captain was gone. *Shit. Where did he—*

The intruder slid in front of her. "I'll put the wind in yer sails if ya raise my mast."

Tink gaped. He did *not* just say that to her.

A burning flush rose from her chest to the tips of her ears. Her lips thinned. She needed to ditch this slob and quick. If she lost her chance to get the Heart of Fire because of this fool, she'd... Her nails dug into her palm. She didn't even know, but something horrible.

His filthy hand latched onto her arm. "Come on." Grime-crusted nails dug into her skin. "I can pay ya."

With one quick move, Tink *accidentally* knocked her drink over. Ale splashed across the man, some of it splattering her as well.

"You bitch!" He stumbled back. The man behind him barked in outrage.

Tink slid off her barstool, aiming to flee, but the man grabbed her arm again. She wrenched it back, her other hand sliding under her cloak, searching for her hidden dagger.

"I'll—" The man paled as a hand closed over his forearm. Clean, black cloth and fine stitching caught her eye.

"You'll leave the lady alone," the velvet voice rumbled just behind her.

Unexpected heat raced up her stiff spine. Captain Hook pushed the man away and wedged himself between them.

"You...you're..." the man stammered before turning and shoving his way through the crowd in haste.

"Good riddance." Hook faced her, glancing over the splatter of ale on the billowing tan shirt tucked into her tight breeches. "You all right, love?"

"I can take care of myself."

His eyes widened.

Shit. She was supposed to seduce him, not brush him off. "But..." She licked her lips before glancing away, then back. "I really appreciate the help."

He tipped an invisible hat, the motion as natural as if he rarely went around without one. "Always happy to help a lady in distress."

"How very gallant of you." It took everything she had to keep the sarcasm out of her voice.

"Can I buy you another drink..." He cocked his head, waiting for her name.

"Tinker Bell." *Oh, Beryl's wings.* She hadn't planned to give him her real one. She grinned through her error and slid closer. "And I do believe you already ordered another round for everyone."

His fingertips, with nails painted a midnight black, grazed the edge of her shoulder before he pulled back. The touch, so brief and fleeting, sent a thrill down to her toes. It shouldn't have. He was a pirate—a notorious one. Worse, her target. But if he was interested, it made her job so much easier. Stealing the ruby was a test, and she couldn't fail, not if she wanted the merfolk's queen, Titania, to trust her. She needed her trust before the queen would even discuss a trade for the black pearl—the only object known to fix anything broken, even her bracelet.

"Tinker Bell." He took his time with her name, and the way he drew out the words melted her more than any drink.

"Just Tink is fine," she added, suddenly warm.

"Aye. Not that swill, Tink." He gestured to the nearby drinks. "The barkeep has a few more pleasurable options."

"Well…" Tink ran her hand down his sleeve. "I think I might enjoy that."

2

*H*ours or minutes later—Tink couldn't tell—Hook and Tink spilled out of the rancorous bar into the still night air, their clothes sticking to the humidity dewing their skin. Barely a sliver of moonlight slipped through the cloudy night sky, but Tink hardly noticed. Her vision blurred at the edges. Each step contained a little wobble.

Damn, the dark rum he'd procured had been strong. She'd only taken little sips compared to him, but still, it clouded her head. *Stupid, stupid, stupid*—getting drunk like she was just out for a good time. The only bright side on this dark night was that Hook downed more than enough to make his gaze heavy with lust and his step just as unsteady as hers. He didn't even blink an eye when she suggested he show her his ship.

"Pride of the seas!" he proclaimed, flinging an arm toward the docks and splashing half of the drink he still carried over its rim. "You won't find a more impressive ship than the *Jolly Roger*. Not in all of Neverland."

"I've heard it's quite big. Strong. Fast too." She giggled, not at all faked, and brushed against his arm. No, more like stumbled into him. A lesser man might have tripped and fallen into the nearly empty streets, but not Hook. Tink may as well have hit a tree for all he moved.

"Careful there, love." He steadied her with his hook, somehow delicate and careful despite his drunkenness. "Wouldn't want you to miss out on such a sight."

"No." She looked him up and down, taking her time as they stumbled along. Tink licked her lips slowly, carefully. "We wouldn't want that at all."

The hooded glance he shot her, shadowed by the night, stirred her blood more than it ever should. *Filthy, stealing, double-dealing, no-good pirate, that's what he is.* It didn't matter that he could charm the fins off a fish and had a grin that could melt iron. He stole the Heart of Fire. He deserved to have it stolen from him. Not to mention a pirate had gotten her into this mess, so it was only fair she used another to help get herself out.

Tink twisted the bracelet around her wrist. She'd find a way home. Saving Lily, the closest person she had to a sister, was worth the cost, and she'd make the same choice again in a heartbeat. *Durin's beard, I'd do anything for her.* But she'd be damned if freeing Lily from that wretched Captain Blackbeard would cost her a place in the Sylvanna Vale. It had been a night similar to this one, beautiful and peaceful. Tink shivered.

"Are you all right?" Hook asked.

Tink glanced up at the roguish pirate with a start. When had they stopped walking? Worse, he sounded almost as sober as she suddenly felt. That wouldn't do. "Just cold for a moment." She gave him her best honey-and-whiskey smile and trailed a hand down his arm.

Okay, that was a terrible excuse. Tink silently cursed herself as she kept her grin frozen in place. No one living could be cold in the tropical humidity they practically swam through.

Hook plunked his cup on a random windowsill—an interesting present for the lucky owner—and wrapped his good arm around her shoulders. "I could take you back."

"No!" she replied, a little too quickly. "No, I want to go with you. Weren't you going to reenact your theft of the Heart of Fire for me?"

"Interested in my jewels now?" He laughed, his tone warmer than the night.

"Well, you know they say the fastest way to a girl's heart is pretty things." She leaned in, letting her body brush against the heavy fabric of his coat. A massive ship loomed at the dock just ahead. It had to be his, and damn if it wasn't as impressive as the rumors said.

"Well, what do you think?" He gestured to the ship. His arm slid down her cloak, tugging her closer. "Is she all you—" He halted.

Tink froze. Nessa's flute, her wings. He didn't know what she was, didn't know about them. But he felt them. *Holy elders, why hadn't I thought of this?*

"You're a…" He trailed off, waiting for her to answer.

"Pixie," she responded, barely a whisper. The last thing she needed was more people to know about her. Humans were greedy. *Never tell them what you are if you venture into the human lands, because they'll want your dust.* It was one of the first lessons every pixie learned before they came of age and were allowed to leave. A pixie could give some away. A little here. A pinch there. Blessings for folks who were kind. But never sell it. Not one coin or they could never go home. And didn't she know it.

"I'm sorry." Genuine panic laced her voice as she waited for him to pull away and leave her standing at the edge of the dock. "I enjoyed being with you. I worried that if I told you, you might…" She shrugged and stared at her feet.

Hook's calloused hand tipped up her chin, forcing her gaze to his. "You thought I might not be interested?" She could just make out the arc of one dark eyebrow.

She nodded, swallowing her apprehension.

"I'll admit, I've never been with a pixie before, but that's not going to put me off." He leaned in, his warmth lulling her in like a gentle tide. "That's what this is for?" He tugged at her cloak.

"Not everyone is so kind to pixies." Especially not pirates. Is this where he asked for her dust? To shower him with the drug humans couldn't get enough of?

He slid his arm up, careful not to press on her already folded and bound wings. "You're safe with me, love."

Her stomach twisted. There he was being all kind and courteous, and she planned to rob him blind. Doubt twisted around her, tugging her back from the boat. She stumbled, blaming it on the strong drink they'd shared, but it wasn't that. Captain Hook had a reputation, all right—ruthless, skilled, rich. He'd plundered a number of royal ships that she knew of, not to mention it was rumored he participated in some more *above-deck* business dealings. Because he hoped for someone to share his bed? Yes, that had to be it. Rum and resolve straightened her back and steadied her step. She slipped her hand in his and let him lead her aboard.

Masts towered into the night above, their sails pulled in and tied up while at port. The deck was clean, orderly, lacking the stench of fish and even more unsavory things that had dominated a few smaller vessels she'd been on. The intricately carved door they passed through into the heart of the ship could have easily belonged on a fancy manor.

Hard as it was to admit, his rooms were nice too. A lush, comfortable-looking bed with crimson coverings dominated one wall. A sturdy desk of carved dark wood—*mahogany?*—stood across from it. Various objects and treasure were tied to the walls or secured on shelves with books crammed between. Thick glass windows let in natural light—or they would during the day. This night, only candles illuminated the room, ones Hook lit as Tink took her time admiring the sights.

"So who was Roger?" Tink asked.

"Roger?"

"You know, of the *Jolly Roger*?" She canted her head to the side.

"Ah, that Roger." He placed the last candle back in its stand. "Would you believe I don't know?"

Tink's brows rose, and she stumbled a half-step. "You, the great Captain Hook, don't know who your ship is named for?"

Hook rubbed at the stubble on his chin. "The great Captain Hook. Now I like the sound of that."

She glanced away. The blush on her cheeks wasn't even faked.

"So do I get to see the fabled Heart of Fire?" Tink asked over her shoulder as she trailed her fingers along the edge of his desk.

"Ye are after me jewels," Hook replied with a smirk, letting a lilt into his voice.

Oh, if only he knew. Queen Titania asked for that jewel, and only she possessed the enchanted pearl that could fix Tink's bracelet and get her home. Whatever she had to do to earn her trust and get one step closer to home, she would.

Tink settled on the edge of his desk. "You did promise."

"Aye, I did." At some point, he'd lost his jacket, leaving just a loose shirt tucked into his breeches. "And I always keep my word. But first, close your eyes, love."

Apprehension coiled in her gut, but she complied. Of course he wouldn't want her to see where he kept the treasure. It was so hard not to peek.

Shuffling, a few clicks, and the scrape of wood met her ears. Time seemed to stretch forever. Her back went stiff as the captain's footsteps trailed across the carpet to where she stood.

"Can I look?"

"Aye."

Her eyes snapped open as he set a thin box on the desk. "May I present..." He lifted the lid. "The Heart of Fire."

A gold necklace dotted with rubies the size of her thumb stared back. It would be a lie to say her mouth didn't water. The object she needed, the first step in her ticket home, was finally within her grasp.

Hook leaned over her, his chest nearly pressing against her back. From his deep inhale of breath, she could have sworn he sniffed her hair. *Weird pirate.*

"Would you like to try it on?"

Her breath caught. She nearly vibrated with joy. "Yes! Um...I mean, who wouldn't want to? Something so beautiful."

"Indeed." The edge of one finger grazed her cheek as he took the necklace from its box, lifting one end of the chain with the tip of his hook through a link.

The mermaids wanted this stunning necklace back in their hoard, and soon she'd get it to them. Teeth dug into her lip as she tried to hold back her grin. Weird, filthy pirate or not, he was playing right into her hands. When the heavy weight settled onto her chest, Tink faced him, making sure to *accidentally* brush against his crotch in the process.

Hooded eyes raked her form as Hook took a seat in his wide chair and reclined against the red velvet, legs spread, hands on the armrests like a great king. "Lovely."

Merrin's teeth, it is. Was this how the great queens felt, with their hoards of jewels? She wouldn't know. Pixies weren't supposed to like such things. Perhaps that part of her broke when her bracelet did, sealing her banishment. Or perhaps she was doomed to be an outcast from the start.

"Is it better like this?" She gestured to the necklace. "Or..." Tink released her cloak, letting it fall to the floor. Next, she undid the ties at the top of her shirt, pulling it open until the necklace rested against her skin, just above the bindings concealing her breasts and wings. "Like this?"

Hook nestled further in his chair, rubbing at the stubble on his chin but never taking his searing gaze off her. "That. Yes, I like that."

Heat coiled deep in her gut as she climbed onto his lap, straddling him in the chair. "I thought you might."

The captain momentarily went rigid before relaxing and wrapping his arms around her backside, pulling her close. Damn, the feel of his hand on her made everything blurry. It would be so easy to forget what he was and why she was there. To give into those coal-darkened eyes, honeyed words, and deft touches. He'd be a skillful lover, of that she had no doubt. She could enjoy him, accept whatever he had to offer. Steal his jewels in the morning and be off before he even woke.

No. Too risky. More of his crew might come back to the ship. They could leave port before she woke, and then she'd be in over her head just like she'd been with Captain Blackbeard. She stiffened at the thought—the memory of what she'd sacrificed.

"Love?"

Shit. There she went again, falling back into memories and forgetting why she was there.

Coarse whiskers scraped her palms as she took his face in her hands. She gave a coy grin. "Captain?"

He let out a soft groan, clenching her tighter as she rubbed against him. The hard bulge pressing against her core sent a thrill up her spine. He was ready, right where she wanted him. Hook placed his forehead against hers, leaning in until they shared the same breath. Tink's hands slid down his neck, his chest, savoring the hard muscle underneath.

"I'm going to kiss you now," he whispered.

Her heart leaped, breath catching in her throat. "Finally."

Demanding lips crashed into hers, consuming, conquering. Stubble scraped against her skin. He cupped her backside, grinding her against him. Tink's hands wove through his short, dark hair, holding him to her as his tongue flicked against her own. Hints of rum teased her as she arched into the embrace, giving as much as she took. An earring scraped her palm as she slid her hands down to his shirt, pulling, tugging, wanting it gone.

Tink let out a squeal as the captain stood in one fluid motion, lifting her into the air with him. Her legs wrapped around his waist, her arms circled his neck. Hook drew back, just enough to give her a scalding, hungry gaze as he carried her to the bed. Her toes curled in her boots, her body going liquid at the heat in that look. He wanted her. All of her, even though she was a pixie. How long since someone wanted her like that? A renowned captain, no less.

A long time. Too long.

Rather than lay on her on the bed, on her wings, he sat on the edge before laying down and pulling her onto his chest.

Nagging guilt swelled up like a wave, threatening to swallow her. He gazed up at her as if she were a treasure, a precious gem plucked from obscurity. And she was going to rob him.

Tink swallowed, letting her gaze travel from his face and down his torso while she warred with herself. Even so, she tugged at his shirt. "Now how are we going to get this off?" The thickness of her own voice surprised her. She wasn't supposed to want him, not really.

He yanked his shirt up and over his head faster than any one-handed man should be able. Damn, but he was a sight—all coiled, tanned muscle.

Tink slid her fingertips into the pocket on her breeches, just far enough to touch the contents of the little pouch she had hidden there. It was now or never. A step farther and she risked going too far, falling under the spell of this wicked pirate.

She ran her finger along her lips, pretending to enjoy the view. *Okay, not totally pretending.* Or not at all. The sight of him spread out below her would fill her erotic dreams—pirate or not. Tink rubbed against the bulge in his pants as she leaned over his chest. That was for her. Another conquest of the night.

Pressing her lips to his was easy as breathing. Maybe easier. It really was too bad she only had him this once. He wouldn't want her again once he woke and found out what she'd done—the theft, or the means of it. There was a reason humans weren't kind to pixies. Either they wanted their dust for themselves, or they accused pixies of using their magical dust to bewitch them. Just a small amount, consumed by a human, hit them harder than any drug. They'd be off to dreamland, "flying on the pixie dust" as some called it, for hours, only to awaken without a hangover and the echo of fanciful dreams. Many craved it to escape their lives, if only for a little while.

Tink drew back, admiring the strong jaw under her palm. This close, she finally noticed the shade of Hook's eyes, dark grey like stormy seas.

"Love?" He brushed hair back from her face. "Are ye...glowing?"

Already her dust, her tainted kiss, addled his senses. "Glowing?" She slid her pixie dust-coated finger across his lips for good measure.

He didn't fail to disappoint, that wicked tongue flicking out to lick at the tip. "Aye... Ya..."

That twinge of guilt swelled up again, a hint of loss accompanying it. He went limp under her, his breath soft and even as he slipped into a deep slumber.

Glowing? For him? What nonsense.

Tink slipped off the bed. The necklace lay heavy against her chest as she admired the sleeping pirate. One last look for her memories.

"Farewell, Captain."

3

Three months later

Solid ground always made him unsteady. It wasn't right—something so hard, firm, and unmoving. Hook frowned down at the dirt marring his leather boots. The things he did for his crew. He'd take the sea any day—wind in his hair, sun on his back.

He glanced back at his ship moored in the harbor. A wry grin painted his features. The *Jolly Roger*'s masts towered above the other ships in port, a commanding presence that no one would miss. Sunlight splashed across the sail, lighting the skull and crossbones painted there. At least the weather was fair—it always was in Tortuga. Old witch magic the locals said. Spells worked into the soil to ensure safe haven for pirate, merchant, and fisherman alike. Little wonder the land felt wrong.

He shook his head as he pushed open the door to the Rusty Anchor—Tortuga's most notorious bar and brothel. He'd promised his men one night on shore before returning to sea. With casks of ale and food on their way to the ship, he could finally join them. But Hook had a different aim than drink or pleasure. Ale and rum loosened the tongue, and a loose tongue was a pirate's friend. Slip a few coins into pockets, and well, he'd have a new treasure in his sights by nightfall.

Or a way to break the bloody curse on him. For that, he'd give every scrap of treasure on his ship and then some.

Laughter and pipe smoke billowed out from within. A cave would have been brighter than this shithole. It had nothing on the colorful rays of sunset sparkling off the sea at his back. Sweaty scoundrels and buxom barmaids filled the crowded room. A few of his men already lounged among the patrons, wasting their hard-earned coin on piss-poor ale.

He tipped his brimmed hat as he wove through splintered furniture and sweating bodies. He gave one a grin, another a wink

Smee sat at a table near the bar, his sandy head leaned over the back of the chair. At first glance, he looked asleep, peaceful as a babe. Another step showed the rest of the scene. A bouncing brunette straddled his lap, skirts bunched around her waist. Smee's groan carried through the room. His arms tightened around the woman's waist, urging her on. She squealed in delight, biting her painted bottom lip.

No one looked. No one cared about the woman's conquest of his first mate.

"Captain," a barmaid crooned. "Care for some company?" Her come-hither look promised an adventure despite another man's arms around her. The sweaty sailor was so lost in his cups he didn't notice his catch's wandering eye.

"Not tonight, love." The phantom memory of his hand twitched where his namesake hook now resided. It'd been too long since he had a woman. Too long since that wench Tinker Bell drugged him with her kiss and stole his treasure. Worse, she'd cursed him twofold. One look at another woman, and all he saw was her. The dimpled cheek. Pink lips. Tousled, blonde hair. Eyes as clear blue as a shallow reef. His cock betrayed him, stiffening as her face taunted him from his memories.

The bar beckoned, tearing him away even as the woman called out to him again. She'd been right in front of him, but all he saw was Tink.

Worse than ruining him for women, she'd turned the sea against him. Nothing else could explain why the summer storms tore his sails and blew them off course while leaving their rivals untouched. Hook slammed the point of his hook into the wood of the bar. He was better than that, damn it. Blessed by the god of the seas, born of his potent seed from the waves themselves.

He liked that rumor best. Far better than the truth.

"Rough seas, eh, Captain?" the barkeep asked, barely sparing a glance at the new divot.

Hook grimaced. That wasn't the half of it. "A mug of your best." He fished in his coin purse with his good hand until he found the piece he sought and slammed it upon the wood. Gold shimmered in the dim light. He had a reputation to maintain after all.

Curious glances roved over him from around the room. He stared down each in turn, a smile for friends, a hard look for strangers. Each face he memorized as he waited for his ale. No one approached, yet.

The barkeep returned, his countenance bright—the coin's work, no doubt. Foam clung to the rim of the generously filled mug. Hook downed a swig as Smee's woman climbed off his lap, giving the bar a show of his satisfied manhood. Thin, sour liquid washed over Hook's tongue.

"Horse piss!" Ale sloshed onto his hand as he slammed the mug down.

"That 'er is fine stuff." The man gestured to the spilled liquid pooling on the counter.

Hook leaned onto the bar. "Not worth half what I paid you, mate."

The barkeep leaned in, only the twitch of his pinkie giving away his fear. Everyone had a tell. The bulky man might heft a barrel farther than him, but Hook would wager his skill with the saber any day. "Best I got, Captain. Swear it."

Hook's metal hand scraped another gouge in the bar. "You don't keep special stock?" He turned the point of his hook up, letting it catch the dim gleam of the oil lamp. "For…discerning customers?"

The burly man's throat bobbed as he loosened his shirt at the neck. "Did, b-but Captain Blackbeard, er, made a-a special request. Might be here any day…"

Hook nearly shook with anger as he pushed back from the bar. *Captain Blackbeard. That bloody bastard.* He'd had the edge on him since he lost the Heart of Fire, and now he'd even taken his drink. That old croc had it coming. He'd worked too hard to become the youngest pirate captain of the Cerulean Sea in history. Prince of the Waves, they called him.

And the things Blackbeard had done to him... His hand tightened into a fist. But he was coming here soon? That was interesting. And unfortunate.

"Er, Captain," the barkeep said. "I do have sometin' else may interest you."

A deep breath dimmed the fiery coal of revenge lodged in his heart. *Information. Right.* That's why he came. Hook's brows rose as he leaned in. "Captain Blackbeard's date of arrival?"

Maybe he could catch him unawares, finally pay him back for some of the misery he'd caused.

"No. Soon, but I..." The man's gaze darted.

A disappointed sigh slipped from his lips. "A new schedule for the merchant ships?"

That could be handy, especially if any were bringing more of that fine silk from the southern isles. He'd gotten a hefty sum for the last chest he *acquired*.

"No..."

Such a disappointment. Hook stroked the dark stubble along his chin. "You try my patience. Return my coin and those of my men, and maybe we'll forget this little incident."

The man's eyes widened. "Wait, ya want this." He drew out a leather bag, laughably small in his worn hands. "Promise. Just a smidge and all your worries disappear." He leaned in across the bar and whispered. "Pixie dust."

"Pixie dust!" Hook's bellow cut through the room. Men and women froze. Conversation ceased as all eyes snapped to him. Smee unsheathed the dagger at his side, scanning the room for danger.

A groan caught in his throat. "Can't a man shout, you scallywags?" Hook gestured with his hand. "Back to it, you barnacles. Drinks on the house." He lifted his mug and took a long swallow.

Cheers rose. Mugs clinked as sailors followed his lead. Hook wiped his mouth on his sleeve and slammed the mug down again, trying to banish the taste from his mouth. People resumed their play as if he'd never spoken.

Bloody, vile substance, pixie dust. One pinch in a drink, and a man could lose hours in a world of his imaginings. A spoonful? The whole day. There was only one pixie he'd heard of in recent months who stooped so low as to sell her dust to humans—the same one stuck in his head. Tinker Bell.

Hook shoveled a handful of coins onto the bar. "Now, barkeep, tell me everything you know about this pixie dust."

*H*ook fumed out of the Rusty Anchor into the dimming twilight, Smee close on his heels. "She's here."

"She?" His first mate tucked his shirt into his pants.

The look Hook cast him over one shoulder was flatter than the calm sea.

"Oh, *she*!" He adjusted his belt before smoothing out his hair. "Of course, how could I forget."

Hook rolled his eyes. They'd been friends since childhood, and Smee was loyal as a hound, but sometimes he had more brains in his cock than his head. "Said he bought the pixie dust a few days ago." His fist tightened. "Got it from a blonde woman in town."

Smee rubbed the back of his neck. "Yeah, but that doesn't mean he got it from *her*."

The captain skidded to a stop, hook raised. His mouth opened and closed. Blast it, Smee had a point. Tinker Bell had become notorious in recent months—the only known source of pixie dust on the Cerulean Sea. At the moment, anyway. But tracking her down? That was the rub. He'd yet to get such a promising lead. No matter how much gold he offered, they couldn't say much about her, or they'd bought the stuff weeks ago. She must have a fortune tucked away.

"Still." His long, black coat flapped behind him as he took off toward his destination. "We'll check each tavern. If she's here, someone will know something."

The next one loomed on the cliffs ahead. A rope bridge hung in the air over the beach, stretching out to the Crow's Roost. Drunkard's Doom, they called it. More than one man had taken an ill-fated spill. A massive, ancient tree clung to the cliffside at an impossible slant, its branches reaching toward the distant horizon where sea met sky. The bar, two stories high, wrapped around its trunk and lower branches.

"There's something else," Hook said as they neared. "Blackbeard is due in port soon. Reserved stock with the bartender—all the good stock." Of course he did, bloody crocodile.

Smee stumbled a step. "Blackbeard?" His voice rose an octave as he glanced toward the *Jolly Roger* moored at the docks. "Should we make for open seas?"

Should they? That was the question. Tortuga was neutral ground, even the old croc respected that, but they might catch him before he arrived. Hook rolled his shoulders. "Not yet." First, he'd get that thieving pixie and deal with the curse she'd put on him.

Lively conversation mixed with crashing waves and gull cries as Hook and Smee made their way along the bridge. The slight sway and creak of wood didn't faze the two men who lived upon the waves.

"Nice tune," Smee said as they stepped from the bridge onto the landing porch.

Conversation and laughter warred for dominance over the music spilling from cracks and high windows. A mandolin, perhaps. He rubbed the stubble on his jaw with his hook. Well played. Too bad he didn't have time to enjoy it.

The Crow's Roost boasted a lively crowd. With the storms abated the last few days, merchants and sailors were about their trades again. Coin for them meant more for his crew. Often the local merchants paid him for protection on their route, or assurances their ships wouldn't be raided by him and his crew. Their prosperity brought a natural grin to his face. If not for Captain Blackbeard poaching ships in his waters or whatever blasted pixie curse Tink had placed on him, life would be easy.

"Look what the tide dragged in!" A slim brunette pushed men out of the way as she neared them.

Not *them*. No, her smile wasn't for Hook.

"Brielle!" Smee shone like the sun. He spread his strong arms wide as Brielle stopped, giving him a once-over.

"I wondered when you'd step back into my bar." She winked.

Smee drew her into a hug before lifting her off her feet and twirling her around as she squealed in delight.

Brielle nodded to Hook as she regained her footing. "Captain."

He tipped his hat to her. Times like these, he was glad Smee had a woman—or three—in every port. Brielle didn't own the bar, but she might as well have. The owners were childless and treated her like their own. If Tink had been around Tortuga selling her bloody dust, she would know about it.

Even so…Hook wrapped his arm around Smee, giving him a hard pat. "Don't forget why we're here."

It wouldn't take both of them to find out what Brielle knew. Smee would likely fare better without Hook anyway. Somehow, she preferred his jovial first mate. Her loss.

Hook grinned as he spotted the crew of the *Skipper* near the short stage. They still owed him this season's payment, and from the number of drinks on the table and girls in their laps, they could afford to pay.

"Gentlemen." Hook's booming voice carried over the table. Glazed, widened eyes stared back at him. One man with his boots propped on the edge of the table practically fell out of his chair. Hook swept his hand toward the men in a grand gesture. "And here I thought a sea dragon took you all down to the depths. Why else would you be late on my payment?"

Their captain stood and smoothed greasy hair back from his face. "Well, ya see, sir, we—"

"That's *Captain* to you, mate." He angled the point of his hook toward the man's face, savoring the small quiver in his lips. "Captain Hook."

The mandolin stopped abruptly, but Hook ignored it as he stared the man down.

"Aye, Captain Hook, sir," he stammered. "Didn't know you 'er in port."

Cries of frustration rose up behind Hook. Furniture clattered. Someone backed into him. Who would dare? Hook whirled, shoving the offending man toward his companions as he scanned the flustered crowd. The musician had fled the stage.

"Grab that brat!" A man yelled, pointing toward the door. His dirty, wet shirt stuck to his chest, the victim of spilled ale.

A figure hurtled for the door, sliding between patrons or knocking them aside. A hooded cloak hid their form from behind, but they stopped briefly at the door and looked back to the room.

The air charged and prickled like the moment before a lightning strike. Hook's breath caught in his throat as the rest of the room blurred. Tink stared back at him. It was her. It had to be. Nothing else explained the wide-eyed stare or the way one look at her strangled him. The moment vanished as she slipped out the door, mandolin in tow.

She'd pay for stealing from him, cursing him.

Hook bolted toward the door.

4

*T*ink sprinted across the rope bridge, not caring how it creaked or swayed. Her pulse pounded in her ears, each beat urging her to run faster. Falling onto the beach below would be better than getting caught by that arrogant pirate.

That look—she shivered as she raced through the twilight. No, he certainly hadn't forgotten that she'd stolen from him. It didn't matter that she needed the Heart of Fire to earn the merfolk's trust and get one step closer to her real goal—home. Pirates only valued gold, and she'd taken something worth a heap of it.

Filthy, rotten, no-good pirates.

Her wings ached, straining against the bindings she'd wrapped around her torso. She shouldn't have come to play at the Crow's Roost that night, not with so many ships in port after the storms. But she needed what money she could get, and drunk humans tip pretty ladies well...when they think they are human. Sure, she got plenty of unwanted looks and offers, but those she could deal with. If they knew she was a pixie, they'd want the dust she no longer had. She'd had plenty of it once. It came naturally and plentifully in the vale. Here though, she'd only managed to make a little after she'd shed all she had to save Lily from Blackbeard, and even that was weeks ago. Nothing about her wings worked well outside of the vale.

She stumbled a bit as she left the bridge and veered onto the path running through the edge of town toward the forest. One glance over her shoulder sent her heart racing even faster. Hook crashed through the bar's door. His gaze found her in the dimming light without error. *Shit.* The crimson lining of his jacket fluttered as he lunged toward the bridge after her.

Tink could lose him in the forest. She had to. Of all the rotten luck...

Bad enough it was rumored Blackbeard might be in port soon, and now Captain Hook out of the blue? The very last two pirates she ever wanted to see again.

She propped her mandolin against the back wall of the last building. It wouldn't aid her flight, and Hook wasn't after an instrument.

Leaves and underbrush crunched and crashed as she sprinted down various animal paths. When she looked back over one shoulder, the toe of her boot caught on a root, sending her tumbling to the ground. Tink's arms and chest slammed into the packed dirt. The impact rattled through her bones and knocked the wind from her chest. Beyond the buzzing in her ears, the unmistakable sound of someone hacking their way through the brush reached her. Pain faded in a rush of adrenalin as she pushed to her feet and took off again.

Soon she'd be to safety. It wasn't the Sylvanna Vale, her real home, but it'd do. For now. If that greedy pirate caught up to her, she might never see the vale again. Tink nearly cried in relief as rays of moonlight touched her treehouse—ramshackle boards and branches that made a twisting house of connected rooms in and around the massive, near-hollow trunk of the old tree. She could take credit for the retractable rope ladder, a catapult to shoot fireworks, and other defenses her tinkering had conjured. The original structure was someone else's abandoned creation though, one she'd fixed up and improved.

"Finally!" Tink grabbed the rope ladder and scrambled up one rung at a time. If Hook found her treehouse, he wouldn't get in. She'd see to that. Worst case scenario, she'd unbind her wings and fly away when he wasn't looking. They didn't work well outside the Sylvanna Vale, as if the very air was different and caused them to struggle through it, but they could get her away. Maybe.

Heavy, racing breaths echoed in the dark room as she pulled up the rope ladder and secured it within. She slammed the door shut. Her cloak found a home on the floor before she pulled off her tunic and started to unbind the fabric from around her torso.

Movement in the shadows drew her eye. Tink froze, half-undressed, as she peered into the darkness between stacks of supplies she'd hoarded away. Only a thin slat of light spilled into the room from the lantern she'd left lit in the adjoining one. Her hands froze.

No. She hadn't left a lantern burning, she wouldn't. Her wings fought against the remaining fabric, pushing free and sending it sliding to the ground as she entered the room. "Who's there?" The snapped question was met with silence. Did Hook beat her here? He couldn't have, could he?

She turned away from the lamp, back toward the room she had vacated.

"Wings?" someone whispered.

"A pixie!" came another voice.

She'd barely turned toward the voices before a blanket cloaked her in musty darkness. Tink screamed and clawed at the cloth.

"Don't let her go!"

Hands grabbed at her. She screeched as someone yanked a delicate wing.

"Tie her up!"

Panic bubbled up her throat as she struggled against the attackers. From their voices she guessed at least four, maybe more. If only she had some dust left. Without it, she was no better than a human with wings, possibly weaker.

Something pulled around her chest, forcing her struggling arms against her body. The blanket drew tight over her face. Air became thin. Her wings cramped as they were forced down against her back.

Tink willed her body to go limp, to give in, even as her lungs yearned for air. If they didn't let her go, she'd suffocate.

Someone pulled the blanket from her face. She gasped mouthfuls of precious air, head spinning and eyes squinting against the lamplight as she took in her attackers. Short. Male? Scrappy clothing. Five of them that she could see.

These weren't gnomes. They were too big, the proportions all wrong.

"You're kids?"

The red-headed one put his hands on his hips as if to say that should be obvious.

Human kids.

Tink nearly laughed at the absurdity of it all. By Beryl's wings, human children had tied her up in her own home.

"Is she really a pixie?" the shortest—possibly the youngest—said. He gazed at her with wide, brown eyes as if she were a kraken or some other monster.

"She's got wings, don't she?" The one with long, blond hair poked at her right wing with a stick.

Tink hissed at him, "Don't you dare."

The boy jumped back, but she didn't let up on her hard stare.

Red stepped forward. He was still a boy, but his wiry build and features marked him as the oldest, possibly almost a teenager. "Give us pixie dust, and we'll leave."

Dust? What could they want with—

The youngest grabbed onto Red's shirt. "But you said we could stay," he whined.

"This is my home, and none of you are staying," Tink said. "You're not getting dust either. Now untie me and go back to your parents."

"We ain' got parents," Blondie replied.

No parents? A sharp ache slipped through her chest. Five children in torn and poor-fitting clothing stared back at her. Various expressions from pursed lips to pouts met her look of confusion. She knew what it was like to be separated from family. How much worse would it be to have none at all? Still, it didn't explain their request. "Why do you want dust?"

The little one tugged at Red's shirt. "Dan said it makes you happy."

Tink groaned and strained against the ropes. "Dan is an adult?"

The little one bounced. Red put a hand on his head before answering. "Yeah, works at the bakery. Gives us bread sometimes."

She'd have run her hands down her face if she could reach it. These kids had no idea. Pixie dust wasn't magic—not the kind she could see written all over the hope in their faces. It could get a man drunk faster than a whole bottle of rum, and all they'd remember was whatever happy thought it conjured.

"You're too young." She shook her head. "Besides, it's not what you think." Humans couldn't use it to aid nature either—not like the pixies did by working it into the ground and helping plants to grow.

"We're not too young!" the freckle-faced one yelled.

"Yeah!" the others chimed in. One even stomped in indignation.

She sighed, rotating her shoulder as the rope loosened a bit. *What a mess.*

"Tinker Bell!" The deep, roaring yell seeped in through the cracks of the treehouse.

Her heart dropped. *And getting messier...*

The boys raced to the window. One leaned out so far, Tink reached for him on instinct. Not that she could move her arms or get there in time to pull him back.

"He looks angry," Freckles said.

"That a hook?" Blondie asked.

"Cool!"

"Kids?" The disbelief in Hook's voice was impossible to miss. "Is there a young woman up there with you?"

"No," Red said, "but there's a pixie."

Durin's beard. Can these kids not shut up?

"Well, now." Hook's tone shifted to one of pleasant surprise. "How about you hand her over to me?"

"Don't talk to him, he's—"

"She's our pixie!" Red shouted back.

Well, okay fine, maybe it wasn't so bad if they talked to him. At least they were all distracted. Tink twisted her arms and flexed her wings, wincing at the pain. If she could just get free, she could fly away and leave this all behind.

"I could pay you."

The boys looked at each other. "How much," Red asked.

"But the dust…" the little one whined.

The skinniest kid—who'd yet to utter a word—grabbed at his stomach as it let out a loud rumble.

They were hungry. Even if she had dust to give them, they needed Hook's offer. *Damn him.*

"Catch," Hook called.

Blondie grabbed at the small object, nearly dropping it back out the window before he pulled it in and held it up to the light. A gold coin sparkled and glittered. The other kids leaned in. Freckle's mouth gaped open.

"It real?" Blondie asked.

Red took the coin and bit it. "Real enough."

"I've got more where that came from," Hook called.

Red called the other boys together. They whispered in a huddle, though the words were loud enough to know they spelled her doom. She nearly screamed in frustration when the ropes refused to budge. If only she had some dust left, maybe she could buy her way out of this. She tried to stand but slipped and tumbled to the ground.

"Well?" Hook asked.

Red nodded and broke away from the huddle.

"Wait," Tink said, craning her neck up to look at the lead boy. "I can get you dust. Not this minute, but I'll get some and come back."

He looked between her and the window.

"You can sell it," she added. "It's worth a lot to the right buyer."

Red knelt in front of Tink and held up the gold. "Maybe you're a pixie, maybe you're not. And maybe you're telling the truth, but maybe not. This. This is real." He turned to the window. "You'll have to come up and get her."

"Let me in then, mates."

Rope dug into Tink's side as she wiggled on the floor. "Don't."

The boys ignored her as they exited toward the room with the rope ladder.

Shit. Tied up, half-naked in her own home, and about to be sold to a pirate who no doubt wanted to see her punished for her theft against him. Maybe she shouldn't have stolen the Heart of Fire, but what option did she have? It would have taken ages to save money to buy it from him, if he'd sell it at all.

Everyone knew mermaids were fickle creatures. Would they wait that long for their gem back? *No*, she sighed, they wouldn't, and the only whisper of a way home she'd found would have been lost. Stealing it was a test to earn their trust, to prove herself an ally to the merfolk and worthy of dealing with them for what she really wanted—the mystical black pearl that could fix anything, even her. Angering Hook was worth it. Queen Titania wouldn't even discuss her pathway home before, but now she knew what she really wanted in exchange for the precious pearl: the scale of Leviathan. *Greedy witch.* As if stealing the Heart of Fire wasn't hard enough on its own. She ground her teeth. The merqueen was taking advantage of her, no doubt, but Tink didn't have any other options. She'd come this far. She couldn't give up now.

Getting the scale...well, she was still working on that part. But if Hook threw her in a cell, she'd never get it, much less return it to the merfolk in exchange for her prize. Worse, what if he made her walk the plank, arms bound, weights on her ankles? Her chest squeezed tight. Hysteria bubbled up her throat in a humorless laugh.

He wouldn't even need the weights or the ropes. She couldn't swim in a still, shallow pool.

The thump, thump of heavy boots within the treehouse sealed her doom. Tension sizzled in the air.

One glance over her shoulder sent her heart leaping and shirking at once. The dim lantern highlighted the planes of his face, catching the gleam in his eye. It was that look that had nearly made her forget her mission when she crawled into his lap, pixie dust upon her lips, ready to steal the necklace he'd so recklessly draped around her neck in an effort to seduce her. Not that he needed the help.

"All tied up like a gift." Hook knelt before her, a wicked grin upon his face. He rubbed at the stubble on his chin. "No wonder you didn't fly away, love."

Tink scowled. "I'm not your love."

"Aye. Pity that."

She swung a leg, attempting to knock him down, but the blanket and bindings stifled her movements. At least they covered her, though. If Hook had found her in just her breeches and underthings, she might have flushed pink from navel to nose. The boys didn't need to see that either, even if they were house-stealing, backstabbing little thieves. Besides, she was sure that any desire Hook had for her fled when she'd left his ship, treasure in tow.

"Now, love." Hook knelt in front of her, just far enough away to avoid what little thrashing fury she could conjure. "Where've you hidden the Heart of Fire?"

5

*H*er scowl held more fight and fury than a brewing hurricane. He grinned in return, savoring the press of her pink lips and the way her blonde hair spilled across her face and exposed one pointed ear.

"Why would I tell you?"

The question yanked him back to the moment. A few seconds in front of her and already her curse crept under his skin, trying to distract him. "Maybe we can make a deal?" The sooner he got what he needed and left her behind, the better.

"Hah." She wiggled on the floor. Part of the blanket slipped down, revealing a bare shoulder. "I should trust the word of a pirate?"

"I may be a pirate, but I'm a man of my word, love."

"I. Am. Not. Your. Love!"

He sighed. *Does she always have to be so difficult?* "If you'd rather I haul you off to my ship and toss you in a cell…" He shrugged as he stood.

The children looked on, unwilling to miss a moment of this encounter. But it was curiosity on their faces, not fear or worry. Had she adopted these children? He suspected they weren't hers by birth. Not one bore the faintest hint of pixie traits—not a wing, pointed ear, nor spark of magic about any of them. Blood relation or not, he wouldn't deprive a child of their protector. He was a pirate, not a villain.

"Tell me where in this..." He gestured around. "...dwelling to find the necklace, remove the curse you put on me, and I'll let you stay here with your dear children, savvy?"

Tink's eyes widened, but before she could respond, the tallest child, the one with red hair, spoke up. "We're not hers."

"Oh?" His brows rose as he looked between the two. "She's not your mother? Protector?"

"We don' need no parents," one boy said.

"Yeah!" two others agreed.

He could have sworn Tink groaned before she let her head thump against the floor.

"She wanted to toss us out," Red said. "Wouldn't even give us pixie dust."

Well, now, this made things even more interesting. Hook leaned back on the edge of the table as Tink pushed to her knees.

"No generosity for these poor kids, eh?" Not that they needed pixie dust at their age, unless they planned to sell it. He rubbed his chin. *Smart kids, tracking down a pixie for her dust.* He might be able to use such savvy young ones from time to time. And by the looks of them, they could use the work. Their clothes were barely stitched together, and sunken cheeks spoke of too many missed meals. Fragmented memories of his childhood tried to creep back into the shadows of his mind, but he blocked them out. No time for that.

Tink tried to blow the hair out of her face, but it fell right back, trailing down to the edge of the blanket just below her bare collarbone. He'd had only a brief glimpse of her before she fled the bar, but Hook could have sworn she'd been more clothed. "They invaded my home, attacked me, and tied me up," she said. "You really expect me to welcome them?"

Not her kids then. Nor even friends.

"How about I sweeten the deal for you then?" Hook replied. "Give me the necklace, get rid of this curse, and I'll leave you in peace. I'll even take this lot with me."

Her whole body slumped. "I can't." The reply was so quiet, he nearly missed it.

Red stepped forward, hands on his hips. "We're not going anywhere."

Hook ignored him and knelt in front of Tink again. She looked at the floor, not meeting his gaze. Even with them both on their knees, her head just reached his neck. She'd fit perfectly against him, sharp little teeth grazing his neck while her tongue... He coughed, shaking away the unwanted thought. "What did you say?"

"We're not—"

"Yeah, yeah." Hook waved at the kids. "Heard you the first time."

Tink took a deep breath and finally tilted her head up to look at him. Her normally alluring gaze had turned somber. He almost felt bad for the tricky woman. The vulnerability vanished as she notched her chin higher. "I can't give it to you. I don't have it anymore."

Bloody hell. Hook swayed, blown over by her words. She didn't have it? *Hell storms.* She surely hadn't spent the sum the Heart of Fire would fetch on this ramshackle treehouse. Which meant she still had the money.

He grazed the underside of her chin with his hook, just enough for her to flinch against the cool metal but leave her unharmed. "Who'd you sell it to? Where's the gold?"

"I didn't sell it. I gave it back to the mermaids."

Hook shook his head. "The—"

"Mermaids!" the littlest boy yelled, drawing their attention. "I want to see—"

"Hush," Red said.

Bloody kids. And bloody mermaids. They were a curse-mongering lot— among other things. "You didn't place the curse on me, did you, love?"

Tink's frown wrinkled into a snarl. "Pixies don't curse people."

No, he didn't think so. But it was hard to be sure where pixies were concerned. Most kept to themselves in their hidden cities. A lot of what people knew of them came more from rumor and legend than personal experience. "No, but you gave the mermaids my name, huh?"

"They wanted vengeance and asked who'd stolen their necklace. Why wouldn't I give them an answer?"

Nothing good ever came from angering the merfolk. Their queen,

Titania, had a short temper. No wonder it was the sea—the queen's domain—that ailed his crew. She'd likely tacked on the extra curse of desiring the pixie who stole from him just for fun. He could almost see her cackling from her favorite rock. His hook scrapped a gouge in the table. *But bloody hell, if she was going to curse someone for the theft, it shouldn't have been me.* "Because I didn't steal it."

Tink straightened, her eyes blinking rapidly before her head tilted to the side. "Whoops."

"Whoops?" The boys jumped as the tip of his hook smashed into the wood.

The blanket shifted as she attempted to shrug. "You still stole it."

Hook stiffened. "It's not the same." He wasn't fool enough to steal from the merfolk. Stealing from Blackbeard, though, that was a joy he couldn't pass up. Hook's missing hand itched. That crocodile deserved the mermaid's wrath. He'd string him up the mast one day, but first he needed to deal with the spitfire in front of him. Tink blew at the hair falling across her face again. The motion stirred something low in his gut. Those pink lips... His mouth watered thinking of her taste.

Blast. He needed this curse removed—fast. A pretty distraction and rough seas were a pirate's greatest weakness. One he couldn't afford.

The kids whispered to one another. One bounced on his feet. Another complication, but maybe they could be useful after all. Hook stood and approached the gaggle of them. Red pushed the little one behind him.

"What's your name, Red?"

The boy stuck his hands on his hips and straightened his spine. "Peter."

"Well, Peter, you look like a smart boy. Since our friend Tink here won't make a deal with me, perhaps you will." He reached into his pocket and fished out a few coins. "As promised, and a few extra."

The blond boy's mouth gaped as he swayed toward the coins.

"Thank you..."

"Hook, Captain Hook." He lifted his hat and gave a dramatic bow to the boys. "Now," he said as he replaced his hat, "you're all welcome to live here and enjoy this fascinating home while I take this meddlesome pixie with me."

"What?" Tink screeched. "This is my house."

Hook looked over his shoulder at the fuming beauty on the floor. *Blast, she's lovely when she's furious.* "It was your home, love."

"I'm not your—"

"But seeing as you stole a very valuable treasure, I think this is a more than fair trade. You and the boys will watch after the place, right, Peter?" He winked at the boy.

"Of course." Peter grinned in return.

"And...if you happen to find a beautiful necklace—chain gold and a ruby bigger than that coin I gave you—hold on to it for me? I'll make it worth your while." He tossed another coin to the lad, who grabbed it out of the air. They wouldn't find the necklace, if Tink was to be believed, but perhaps they'd find some other lovelies for him. With another wink to the boys, he turned back to the woman on the floor. "Time to get back to my ship. The crew'll think you bespelled me again."

Cloth rustled on stone as she thrashed against the rope still binding her arms. "I'm not going anywhere with you."

"Oh, on the contrary. We're going to find us some mermaids."

In moments, he had her hoisted over his shoulder, barely dodging a kick to his own treasured jewels.

"You cannot just...just steal me!"

"Pirate, remember?"

"Insufferable, lousy, no-good, thieving pirate!"

His chest rumbled with laughter. "Who's the thief?"

She screamed in frustration and thrashed in his grip.

"You'll want to stop that," Hook said. "It's a long drop down that ladder of yours." She stilled like a sack of grain. *Smart girl.* The climb down would be difficult at best with his good hand occupied holding her steady.

He tipped his hat with his hook. "Boys." Without another glance, he headed for the exit, ready to be rid of this place for good. No sooner had he left the room than the boys let out excited whoops and cheers. Soft, rapid thumping echoed as they took off to explore their new abode. Tink sighed—more frustration than resignation. He could almost picture her pout. Too bad he couldn't see her face, or any of her with the blanket tied around her. He'd remedy that. Soon, very soon.

6

*T*his was it. He was going to drop her, and she'd die from the fall. Such an embarrassing end for a pixie. Tink did everything she could to remain still as Hook descended the swaying rope ladder with only his namesake to hold him steady. His other arm—one she had to admit was rather strong and solid around her legs—kept her from spilling to the ground.

At last, Hook's boots thumped onto solid ground. *Praise Holy Flora.* He'd made it down without killing her. Still, she'd gut him like the slippery fish he was for abducting her like this. And giving her home to those little rascals? Unacceptable. Maybe she'd drug him with pixie dust, if she could ever make more, and drown him in his precious sea while he lived in his happy dreams. Just thinking about it made the corners of her lips curl.

"It's a long walk back, I'm afraid," Hook said, though he didn't sound the least bit sorry.

Something crashed above. Boys whooped. The silhouette of one shone against the thin curtain over a window. She sighed. There'd be nothing left of her home if she didn't get free soon.

"It's a fair night. Calm sea. Nice breeze. Would be perfect with fine rum and a beautiful woman in my arms. Oh wait." He patted her legs. "I seem to have one. Too bad she's a trixie pixie."

Tink rolled her eyes, trying not to focus on Hook's coat-covered ass looming in her view. Shapely, but not too much so. She could almost picture the way his breeches stretched across the firm backside underneath. Or the corded muscle of his back that her fists had smacked against without avail.

"Trixie pixie," he mused aloud. "I'll have to remember that one."

A groan slipped out into the night. "I'm glad you find this *so* funny."

He laughed. "Not in the least. What I wouldn't give for a clear head and skies."

Clear head? Tink's brows wrinkled. The mermaids vowed to turn the sea against whoever stole from them, but had they done more? She sighed. Probably.

Abruptly, Hook came to a stop. He adjusted her bound form, sliding her to her feet. It was impossible to miss the hardness of his chest, of all of him, as he lowered her to the ground. "I'd love to carry milady all the way to her ship but…" He shrugged.

"Such a gentleman."

He gave a dramatic bow and swept his hand over the rough path toward the shore. "Ladies first."

Tink could move her legs below the knee, but not much. Did he really expect her to waddle all the way to the ship? "You know, if you untied me—"

"You'd spread those gossamer wings and fly away."

Snarky bastard. She scowled at him before turning with a huff. *Fine. Let him laugh, but as soon as I get these ropes loosened up, I'm outta here.*

Hook whistled one lively tune after another, a mocking accompaniment through the dark woods. He didn't even stop when Tink fell and scraped her knees, just lifted her up and urged her along. Nessa's flute, what she wouldn't give to slap that horrible grin off his face. She couldn't even see it where he lurked on the path behind her, but it was there. *Lousy pirate.*

She did need to see the merfolk…eventually, once she had the scale to trade to them. Showing up empty-handed though? Not great. Though delivering the Heart of Fire had "proved her a friend to the merfolk," Titania had said. They wouldn't even consider trading with her prior to that. Perhaps they'd help her out of this mess, for their benefit if not hers.

Tink took advantage of the darkness to wiggle and stretch against her bindings as they walked. A roll of the shoulders here, stretch of wings there. Slowly, oh so slowly, they began to loosen. A little more and she'd be free.

At length, the trees thinned. The soft crash of waves and distant sounds of evening fun tickled her ears, peaceful, pleasing sounds, so unlike Hook's whistling.

"Captain!"

She groaned inwardly. And unlike *that*. Escaping Hook wouldn't be easy. Him and another pirate? So much harder.

"Smee!" Hook called. "About bloody time!"

A large man bounded their way through the underbrush. With all the racket he made, he might as well have been a charging bull. He was tall, muscular, and just big in every sense of the word. All brawn and no brains —that had been her impression of him in their brief encounter before she'd stolen the necklace from Hook. He did that impression even more justice now.

"You found her!" Smee yelled as he trampled a bush.

"No thanks to you," Hook grumbled, though his tone lacked bite. "Where've you been?"

Smee ground to a halt in front of them, breathing hard.

This was it, her chance to flee. Tink stepped to the side of the path and pushed her arms against the bindings.

Smee rubbed the back of his neck. "Sorry, Captain. I...well, I—"

"Tell me later." Hook clapped him on the shoulder with his good hand.

Her wings screamed in pain as she used them to push against the blanket, stretching the rope. Just a little more... One shoulder inched free, an elbow almost pulled loose.

"Mind carrying our precious cargo?" The captain gestured in her direction.

No. No. Not again. Tink lunged for the brush, but Smee caught her around the waist. She screamed in frustration as he slung her over his shoulder like a sack. Sweat, ale, and cheap perfume—a woman's no doubt —flooded her nostrils. Did this man never bathe?

"Feisty one." Smee adjusted her over his shoulder, cupping her backside in the process.

"Watch your hands, you beast!" She swatted at him ineffectually.

"A real tiger shark," Hook agreed with a smirk. "Now then. Let's find our ship."

*Tink yelped as Smee sat, or rather dropped, her onto her ass on deck. "Bastard."

"My ma and da were married," he replied, a look of pride beaming off his features in the moonlight.

She rolled her eyes.

Other members of the crew gathered, eager to see the captain's newest prize—her. Two barely kept their feet, drunk as they were.

"Gents, you may remember Tinker Bell." Hook sauntered around her. "She'll be with us for a while. Until she repays her debt."

"Debt?" Tink gaped. How in all of Neverland did he expect her to do that?

Hook ignored her. "Rest up tonight, men, because tomorrow we set sail for the Azure Lagoon!"

Murmurs of bewildered excitement filled the air.

"Untie her, but don't let her spread those wings."

Tink stared him down, but her thin lips melted into a sigh of relief as the ropes around her were cut. To be able to move again… She closed her eyes and nearly moaned at the pleasure. Wings stretched. Shoulders rolled. A warm breeze tickled bare skin.

"Ya didn' tell us she was *that* kind a' guest!" a man said.

Heat flew to her cheeks as her eyes snapped wide. Merrin's teeth, how had she forgotten? She pulled her arms in front of her chest, hiding the thin undergarment that barely covered her breasts. Her wings flickered as a shiver raced down her spine despite the inferno burning her up from within. Had it been daylight, they'd have seen her skin flush pink. Back at home in Sylvanna Vale, she'd never been the shy or modest sort, not around her kin, but to be nearly bare in front of these filthy humans was a new low, even for her.

A solid form blocked the men from her view. "She's *not* that kind of guest." Hook's words held a sharp edge she did not expect, especially not directed toward his own men. "Nothing to see here. On your way."

Tink grabbed at the fallen blanket, pulling it toward her, but as she did, something heavy and warm settled around her shoulders, draping over her. The scent of man—hot-blooded, swarthy man—consumed her.

Hook, his white shirt catching the moonlight and ruffling in the breeze, turned to Smee. "Gather up the crew. We leave at dawn."

"Aye, Captain."

His coat. Durin's beard, he covered me with his long coat. Supple leather and silver buttons embraced her in their shell.

All at once, the ship became too quiet as the crew found somewhere else to be. The *Jolly Roger* was a beauty, even she had to admit that—sleek yet sizeable, well-kept with clean, polished wood. She'd spotted carved railings she'd ogled the last time she was aboard. And rumor said it was one of the fastest ships on the sea. Tink had loathed the drunken men eyeing her harder than she'd inspected the ship, but now that they had vanished, leaving her with only the captain, she longed for them to return.

Desperately.

"Well, milady, we should get you inside." Hook stood over her, an imposing man if ever there was one, with his arms crossed and brimmed hat hiding his face in shadows. He unlaced his arms and offered his one hand to her in a gentlemanly flourish. Always putting on a show, even now.

Tink's nails dug into her palm as she fought the urge to slap his hand. But he had ordered his men away and given her his coat... Her fist loosened. Her shoulders drooped as she set her fingers on his. In a moment, he had her on her feet, her small hand in his too warm and calloused one. Her other kept the coat in place, leaving the blanket in a heap on the deck.

Her wings fluttered behind her in the opening of the coat, which nearly dragged the ground at her booted feet. A few flaps and she could lift off this deck and flee. Hook's hand tightened on hers.

No. He had too firm a grip, and she didn't have the strength to fly off with him if he fought her, which he would.

With practiced ease, the captain used his hook to open a door and led her up a flight of stairs and into the heart of the ship. A lone lantern lit the hall, casting dim light against the smooth, weathered wood. What would her cell be like? Filthy? She shivered. Pixies loved cleanliness and nature—grass, trees, flowers. A dirty prison would be torture. Did he know that? Her nose wrinkled. *Probably.*

Apprehension clouded her vision until Hook released her hand. Little of the room was visible from the meager moonlight filtering in the thick-paned windows, but the size alone said it wasn't a cell. A key clicked in a lock behind her. Moments later, a lantern flared to life.

They'd gone up, not down.

Tink's face heated as realization of the room she stood in took hold. A stately desk loomed near the windows with a red velvet chair gilt in gold. Sprawling bookcases were built into the wall. Various baubles, maps, and amusements were displayed with pride upon their shelves. And, of course, the lush bed with crimson coverings dominated one wall.

She'd been here before. How could she forget?

Captain Hook's private quarters.

7

"*N*ice cell." Sarcasm dripped from Tink's voice as Hook circled around her.

He rested against the edge of the desk. Bold words, but easy to read between. Her wings twitched and nose wrinkled. Tink's clear-eyed gaze darted this way and that. He'd made her nervous. Hook removed his hat and set it aside. "You don't want to be locked up down there tonight, love."

Her lips thinned as she clutched his coat tighter around her. "I'm not staying in here with you."

"Yes, you are." He wouldn't have her out of his sight, and not only because she might find a way to escape. "Half of my crew is drunk. The other half will be when they get back to the ship." He grabbed a cloth from atop the desk and polished his hook as he spoke. "A few of them may have found a lovely lady, or man, to share the evening with. Most won't. They lack my charm." He grinned.

Tink rolled her eyes.

"When they come back, swaying on their feet, eyes blurred from the ale, they might see a pretty thing like you and think you chose to be on this ship. Many have." He stroked a cloth up and down his hook in slow, rhythmic motions, not so much cleaning or polishing it, more out of habit. The practiced move calmed him, distracted his thoughts from the woman lingering so close to his bed. "Perhaps they'd think you took a wrong turn, got stuck in a cell by accident while trying to make a little extra coin giving comfort to some lonely pirates."

"I'm not a whore." Tink gaped. "They wouldn't dare."

"I'd like to think not. If one of mine did such a thing…" The cloth stopped. "…they wouldn't be on my crew anymore. But best not to risk it. For your sake."

His crew would *never* treat an innocent woman so. But if she used her cursed kiss on one of them the way she had on him, would they force themselves on her in the dreamy haze of the pixie dust? Could they? Wasn't a chance he could take.

The wrinkles between her brows smoothed out. Her entire face lost some of its sharpness.

"In fact, I think you should stay here until you've repaid your debt."

The softness vanished into pressed lips. "How exactly do you expect me to repay my so-called debt when I'm stuck on this ship with you? Swab the decks?"

"Mmm," he mused, "I would enjoy seeing you down on your hands and knees, working up a sweat." *Bloody hell, the vision that conjures is a curse of its own.* How would he get that out of his head? Tink on the deck of the *Jolly Roger*, white shirt stuck to her skin with sweat, hair pulled back behind her head, looking up at him.

"Rotten pirate," she snapped.

So much fire. His lips quirked up at the corners as Hook crossed the room to her. "Thieving pixie." Harsh words, but no bite.

"You stole it first." Tink notched her chin higher, her blue eyes staring him down along her slightly pointed nose.

"I did." He grinned. "I'll be taking this back now." He tugged his jacket off her, leaving her bare from the waist up other than the cloth wrapped around her chest. *Fuck.* Her pert nipples beaded against the fabric. Blonde hair had come loose from her braid and draped across her creamy skin. Hook turned away before he could give in to the temptation to seek a closer look.

"Hey!" Tink yelled after him, but no footsteps followed as he made his way to the wardrobe.

Open the door. Hang the jacket. Don't think about the half-naked beauty in the room. It wasn't enough that her curse filled his mind with visions that left him longing for her taste, but he'd happened to bring her here half-naked. Of all the shit luck. She needed clothes. Now.

He bunched up a pale shirt and tossed it toward her across the bed. "Here." It would be too large, but it would do.

"My wings…" The gossamer things fluttered behind her like fine transparent silk in a rainbow of pale colors. Her face flushed pink, turning almost red near the tips of her ears. The color spread to her chest, even though she tried to hide it behind her lean arms.

He tossed a second shirt near the first. "Bind them."

The blush vanished as her eyes flew wide. "You can't ask a pixie to bind her wings! It isn't right."

Pixies and their rules. He sighed, leaning against the wardrobe. "You had them bound earlier this evening. What's the difference?"

Her face flushed again, adding more fuel to the fire of his wicked thoughts. He couldn't help but wonder how far down her petite form the blush traveled.

"You know nothing about pixies." She pulled the shirts to her chest but made no move to put them on.

He shrugged—an empty gesture. He cared more than he should. "I know a little."

"Not enough…"

As he was quickly learning. There was one thing he was certain of, though. The main reason he brought her onboard, or so he told himself. "I know you make something very valuable. Something that could go a long way toward paying for your crime."

A humorless laugh bubbled out of her. She hunched over, pulling his shirts tighter to her as her shoulders shook. When she straightened, her features had gone cold and sharp as stone. "I can't just make pixie dust whenever I want."

"No?" He asked it aloud, but the question was more for himself. There was more to her words, he'd wager a hefty sum of gold on it. But what?

"No."

He closed the distance between them, coming around the bed until he stared down at her. "Care to explain?"

"No."

"You must have made a fortune selling so much. Care to tell me what happened to that gold?"

Her brows drew together, as if she had no idea what he was talking about.

She had sold it, though. He'd met no other blonde pixie selling dust, and he'd looked—far and wide ever since her drugged kiss. She'd had plenty of dust then. The whispers he'd heard of someone selling pixie dust fit her description perfectly—well, from the few who had gotten a decent glimpse of the seller.

"Well, then, we're at an impasse."

She stared back at him, unblinking. A bubble of tension hung heavy in the air, ready to burst. If he didn't get away from her, he might do something stupid. But he couldn't leave her free to roam...or shirtless.

"Give me one of those," he said.

"What?" Her brows scrunched until she noticed his outstretched hand. "Fine." She shoved one shirt toward him, nearly dropping the other onto the floor.

At least she held on to the nicer one. Still. Hook frowned as he held up his shirt. He dug the point of his hook into the cotton and pulled it downward. The shirt ripped, leaving a long hole in the back.

"You—" Tink stared at him, bewildered.

"For your wings." He tossed the shirt back.

Tink fumbled it out of the air, lips slightly parted. "Thank you."

She wouldn't thank him for what came next. As she turned away and examined the shirt, he sought out the item he needed within a heavy trunk. Once he had it, he took his time making his way back to her. Tight, black breeches hugged her backside, sinking down into boots laced up her calves. If only she craved him the way her curse made him feel. His shirt slid over her head. Too big, too long, but perfect all the same. Tink fumbled with the slashed opening, working her delicate wings free. Their color was hard to describe—almost a rippling pale rainbow against sea foam. Damn, she was turning him into a poet.

And now a villain.

Hook clasped the iron handcuff around her wrist.

"Hey! What?" Tink jerked away. Betrayal, worse than when he'd taken her from her treehouse, flashed across the face of the woman wearing his clothes.

"Can't have you flying away in the night. Or slitting my throat." A thick, corded rope hung between them.

Her mouth opened and closed, but words didn't come out.

"You'll have room to move, to get to the chamber pot, that chair, the nightstand." He gestured quickly to the items as he snapped shut the other end of the cuff around a thick post on the headboard of the bed.

Tink flushed pink. "Filthy, lousy, no-good pirate!"

Aye. That he was.

But a pirate stole treasure; he didn't let it run free. If she truly no longer had the Heart of Fire, there'd be no getting it back from the merfolk. He'd risked much stealing it from that bastard Blackbeard. He'd done it for sport, more than value, but still...he could have sold it, spent that coin on his crew. Or given it back to the merfolk in exchange for something else of value.

Speaking of...

"What did you get from the merfolk for my treasure?" Part of her payment was clearly a curse on him, but no way she took that risk just to ruin him. He'd been a perfect gentleman to her. Bloody hell, he'd have given her much more than that if she hadn't drugged him with her kiss.

"Your treasure?" She fumed at the edge of the bed, barely looking at him below her lowered lashes.

Tink in his clothes, on his bed... *Fuck.* Furious or not, she was a sight to behold. He shook himself. "Aye, *my* treasure." He'd stolen it, so that made it his. "Such a valuable jewel could have gotten quite a sum. I might be willing to ease some of your debt..." He trailed his pointer finger along his jaw. "...if you were to hand over whatever you got in exchange."

She crossed her arms and turned away from him. *Why?* It wasn't a bad offer.

"Their trust," she said at last.

"And...?" He waved his hand for her to continue.

"And what? They'd never dealt with a pixie. Said I could earn their trust if I returned their missing treasure."

He blinked at her. No way had she given it back for nothing. "You lie."

She stood with a huff. "I do not!"

"Bloody hell, woman. What could you possibly need their trust so badly for that you'd give away a fortune?"

She pursed her lips and turned away again. "Not your business."

A treasure for trust? Ridiculous. "Got enough gold selling your dust, eh?"

Her wings twitched, but she refused to answer.

When the silence stretched, he realized she wasn't going to. With a sigh, he pushed off his desk and adjusted his breeches. It was going to be a long voyage to the merfolk with her on the ship, and in his bed. No matter that it was just a few days. He scrubbed his hand down his face.

Being stuck in close quarters with her might be the worst curse of all.

8

*T*he ship rocked, nearly tossing Tink from the bed. Thunder cracked. Lightning flashed outside the windows. Tink curled in on herself, begging every holy, revered elder the pixies had to keep the little food she'd eaten in her stomach. Hook wasn't here. She hadn't seen the irritatingly handsome pirate since she'd fallen asleep the night before last…handcuffed to his bed.

He'd slept, or played at sleep, in the window seat across the room—far from the reach of her short chain. When she'd awoken, he was gone. Though a day and a night passed, he didn't return. Where, or if, he slept, she could only guess.

Just like so many other terrible humans, he'd asked for her dust. Well, too bad for him. And he thought she'd made a fortune selling it? Hah! What a joke. Fortune indeed. Wouldn't that be lovely? She had sold some of it, what little she had left after saving Lily from Blackbeard. A bit here and there for food and supplies, to buy passage to see the merfolk, but not enough to generate any real wealth.

As for creating more…she could have at home. It had never been a problem there. But here, her wings just wouldn't do it, and now they were plum out of dust.

With a sigh, she wiggled down into the inviting sheets. It was the best rest she'd had in months. Not that she'd ever admit it. The comfortable bed cradled her far better than the stiff cot in her treehouse and many times better than the forest floor and other unsavory places she'd slept before she found her temporary home.

The storms came during the second night, tossing the ship as she plowed on toward the merfolk's Azure Lagoon. Tink slept little since then, though she tried. Food and water had been more of a challenge. Everything she took down wanted to crawl back up her throat.

She screeched as another wave rocked the ship and pulled the sheets over her head with her free hand. Wood cracked in response, a sound like the ship being torn apart.

"Stop screaming like a wounded harpy!"

She gasped and jerked the sheets down. Hook loomed in the doorway, strong and steady despite the rocking of the ship in the storm. But his expression was anything but calm—thin lips, stiff jaw, hard gaze. He was the spitting image of the fierce pirate rumors claimed him to be. Dark hair clung to his face while rivulets of water streamed to the floor. If he'd been wearing his hat, it was long gone.

Another swell made her stomach drop and slosh. Tink clapped her hands over her mouth. Durin's beard, she couldn't get sick in front of him. She wouldn't.

Hook's harsh expression vanished, smoothing out into something like pity. "This is your bloody fault." He slammed the door behind him and approached her. "Cursing the sea against me." Though the ship bucked, he walked with practiced ease.

"I didn't—" She braced herself as another swell rolled the ship. Ugh, she'd get nowhere arguing with him. "Are we almost there?"

"Yes."

She nearly cried with relief. Surely the merfolk's curse wouldn't call a storm down on their own land.

"My crew think you're torturing yourself. Say it's bad luck to have a screaming woman on board." He stood right in front of her now, rain-soaked clothing dripping onto the elaborate rug.

"And whose fault is that?" Tink rose up on her knees, a poor attempt to make herself intimidating. "You brought me here, you—" A scream swallowed up her tirade as the ship canted to the side. Before she could steady herself, she careened off the bed, right into the captain.

They toppled to the ground. Hook groaned as he smacked against the floor. Tink's face smashed against his wet shirt and the hard chest underneath. For a moment, a blur of color swarmed her vision. Buzzing rang in her ears. All at once, her senses returned. She straddled Hook—hard, wet, and very much a man. Tink shoved her now damp hair out of her face as she sat up.

He made a sound low in his throat as she moved. Not in pain, no, she'd heard this sound before, the moment she'd crawled into his lap the night they first met. Tink went still as her gaze caught his. Hooded, stormy grey eyes stared up at her. The captain made no attempt to move as his lips curved into a slow smile.

A strong hand slid up her leg. Heat blossomed low in her belly. The wetness growing between her legs had little to do with the rain soaking into her breeches from Hook's drenched clothing. Her wings fluttered as his thumb rubbed a slow path up and down her thigh. She forgot where she was, the rocking of the ship, the shackle on her wrist, everything but the man below her. For the briefest moment, she even forgot who he was and why she loathed him.

His gaze traveled over her, and his eyes widened. "Your wings are shimmering, love."

He may as well have dumped her into the sea.

She shoved off him, leaping away as if burned. The rope binding her to the bed held firm as she tested its limits.

Hook groaned again as he sat up, a wet heap of man on the floor. "Care to tell me what that means?"

Tink turned away as her cheeks flamed. "No." Absolutely not. Never. She chanced a glance back at her wings. *It isn't possible, is it?*

She rubbed her hands down her face, a poor attempt to scrub all thought of him from her mind. Only then did she notice the ship had stopped rocking. "We cleared the storm?"

"Aye, feels like it. We should be near the Azure Lagoon by my estimate."

She bobbed on the balls of her feet, not caring about the way her stomach still flipped and flopped. It would settle soon. She'd be out of this room, back in the fresh air. On land! Blessed land.

A hard rapping on the door made her jump. She whirled around to find Hook on his feet. A brief flash of annoyance faded from his features.

"Captain!"

"What is it, Smee?" he called back.

"Another ship anchored outside the lagoon. Looks to be the *Siren*."

Tink stiffened. "More pirates?"

Hook nodded. "Run up the flags. Anchor farther out."

"Right away," Smee called back through the door.

Great, just what she needed—more greedy pirates who'd undoubtedly want to use her for their own supply of pixie dust.

"It's best if they don't know what you are." He gave a meaningful glance at her wings.

For once, they agreed.

. . .:·: ::·:·.. ..

ink followed Hook onto the deck, savoring her freedom. She'd bound her wings and tucked Hook's billowing shirt into her breeches. A cloak over her shoulders further hid her wings, and a bandanna over her hair kept her ears tucked away. To anyone they encountered, she'd look like a simple deckhand.

Thunder rumbled from the storm nearby, a mass of dark clouds and pounding rain at their backs. The island was a peaceful oasis, as if they'd sheltered in the eye of a hurricane. Beyond it, more dark clouds loomed in the distance.

Rowboats stood ready to be lowered into the calm sea just outside the merfolk's lagoon. Hook gave orders to his crew, pointing them this way and that. "You four, with me."

Tink straightened. Two of them were female. She slid closer to Hook. "You were worried about my safety with your crew, but not theirs?"

"Anne and Sage?" He chuckled as he looked over at the two women climbing into the boat. "They can take care of themselves. Besides, Sage's one of the ones who might have pulled you into her bed." He winked.

Tink notched her chin higher. "And I can't take care of myself?"

"Can you?"

"Give me a dagger, and I'll show you."

He looked her up and down, the rounded edge of his hook tapping against his chin. "I'll keep that in mind."

Laughter and joyful squeals rolled across the calm swells to their rowboat, a sharp contrast to the crack of lightning at their backs. Tink kept looking over her shoulder, expecting the storm to draw closer, but it never moved, as if an invisible wall held it at bay. An element of the merfolk's curse, Hook said, protecting their lagoon from the effects of their own wrath.

Crystal blue, clear skies stretched above, with the sun shining down bright and hot on their backs. As they edged around an outcropping of rock, the merfolk came into view—lounging on the rocks, playing in the water. A few leaned on the wooden dock that thrust out from the beach, where several humans gathered with them. Crew members of the *Siren*, no doubt.

A mermaid, or possibly a merman—it was hard to tell the difference with so much of them hidden under the water—popped their head out of the water near the boat. Pale-pink hair decorated with small shells trailed down over dark shoulders. A high-pitched giggle chimed out between pointed fangs. "Come to play?"

Hook stood up and edged to the side of the boat. "Captain Hook." He tipped his hat to the mermaid. "Come to see Queen Titania."

Tink blinked away her surprise. Hook wasted no time.

The mermaid let out a dramatic sigh. "We shall see." Without another word, they vanished into the sea, barely a ripple in their wake.

Sailors gathered near the end of the pier as the rowboat approached carrying Hook, Tink, Smee, and a handful of Hook's crew.

"Captain Hook!" a woman bellowed from the end of the pier. She wore a wide-brimmed hat with dark curls billowing down around her shoulders. A few streaks of silver colored her hair, but the woman stood with all the strength and confidence of youth. "I hear it's you we have to thank for this storm."

"Happy to oblige, Cressida." Hook thumped a booted foot onto the edge of the boat and swept a dramatic bow in her direction.

"That's Captain Cressida. Don't forget it." Her reminder wasn't a true threat, more a good-natured jab. It was clear Hook had a reputation with this other crew, and not all of it bad. Even without the title, her stance and lavish attire marked Cressida's rank on the *Siren*. Her boots were polished until they shined, and her breeches lacked any holes or patches. Even the jacket she wore over a billowing shirt cut a flattering shape, as if it had been tailored specifically for her—gold buttons, silver stitching, and all.

"Wouldn't dream of it, love."

Tink frowned. Just as quickly, she shook the expression away. Who cared if he called every woman in Neverland "love"? He didn't mean it. Not when he said it to her, and likely not to anyone else.

Cressida's crew lounged in the sun or flirted with the merfolk, mermaids and mermen alike. A few others lingered onshore. Common behavior, she supposed, though one thing struck her as out of the ordinary.

"Is all her crew women?" she asked.

Smee smiled, a wistful, faraway look in his eyes. "Aye. The *Siren* boasts the fairest crew on the seas."

Hook turned away from the dock as they neared and lowered his voice. "Do try *not* to get too friendly with them this time."

"And the merfolk?" Smee gazed toward mermaids at play. Both male and female dressed alike—no clothes to speak of other than shells or seaweed as decorations. The mermaids often chose not to cover their chests as many races did.

Hook slid a narrow-eyed look at Sage. "I do believe last time two mermen got a little upset…"

Sage messed with the end of her brown braid. "Don't look at me."

He let out a dramatic sigh.

"Captain?" Smee asked again.

"Fine. If you must."

Smee's countenance brightened considerably.

Cressida appraised Tink as she climbed onto the dock. "Adding more women to your crew." She smiled. "About time."

Hook edged in front of her. "Don't go trying to recruit her away from me now."

Cressida laughed and tossed her curly, dark locks behind her. "Protective. How...unlike you."

The mermaid who'd met their boat popped their head back out of the water. "She'll meet you."

Tink's gaze traveled across the lagoon to a lone outcropping of rock in shallow water. Bright-colored coral in pinks and oranges clung to its base, peeking out from the water each time the tide receded—Queen Titania's audience rock. Tink had met her there weeks ago to deliver the necklace she'd stolen from Hook. An odd fluttering filled her chest. How many pixies could say they'd met the merfolk's queen at all, much less twice? Perhaps they'd write about her in the pixie histories, if she could ever get the scale of Leviathan, return it to the merfolk, use the enchanted pearl they offered, and fix her bracelet so she could return home.

Right, easy enough. She sighed just thinking of the many obstacles before her.

Hook nodded to the mermaid before turning back to Cressida. "A truce while we're here?" He held out his good hand.

She grasped it. "Of course."

Smee had already garnered the attention of some giggling merfolk before Tink and Hook reached the beach.

"It seems like you're on good terms with Captain Cressida," Tink said as her boots sunk into the sand.

"Cressida and her crew are mostly friendly...unless you cross them," he replied, but his focus was on the queen's rock, still empty despite the mermaid's word that the queen would meet them. "They prefer to earn money protecting merchant ships, recovering lost goods, and other upstanding services."

"Like you?"

"Yes."

She'd meant it as a joke, but his response held utter sincerity. Sudden nerves twisted tight within her, but it wasn't the queen she worried about. Her gaze slid sideways to Hook. Had she misjudged him? Yes, he had a fearsome reputation—a man one should not cross. But she hadn't heard of him doing anything truly horrid, not like Captain Blackbeard or some other pirates who preyed on the innocent and unsuspecting. On women like her.

Oh, wait…

"Let me do the talking," Hook said as they neared the rocks.

Her lips thinned. "So I'm just here to look cute?" He'd gone through a lot of trouble getting her there just to tell her to keep quiet. *Stupid pirate.*

His lips quirked up at the corners. "To confirm that you were mistaken when you said I stole the Heart of Fire and ask the queen to remove her curses from me."

"You did steal it," she reminded him.

"But not from them."

"And they'll just believe me?" Tink frowned. Most likely they'd believe the pirate dragged the witness there against her will. Which of course, he did.

"They can tell when you lie to them, you know. You told them I stole it, and they believed you because you believed it. If you tell them differently now, and I do as well, they'll hear the truth."

Most interesting. Tink skipped a step and nearly stumbled in the sand.

"So once we clear this up, you'll let me go? Take me back to Tortuga?" The sooner the better. Every day spent stuck with this lousy pirate was one more away from home. She needed to be searching for information about the scale, not spending her days chained to his bed. Most sailors she'd talked to said it didn't exist. A legend they called it. One old man, though, had told her stories about a woman hiding it in a cave and leaving a trail of clues for her descendants. "Hid it somewhere normal folk wouldn't look," he'd said. It was a start, only a matter of time before she came across someone who knew more.

Hook's jaw stiffened. "That was a valuable jewel you stole…"

Nails dug into her palm. "You can't seriously—" A large swell rose from the deep and sped toward the queen's rock. Tink's eyes flew wide.

Hook pushed Tink behind him as the wave grew in the otherwise calm waters, rising high as their heads. Water crashed against the rocks. Tink ducked behind Hook. A gasp wrenched from her throat as cold water swirled up around her calves. As it retreated, the water tugged at her, begging her to come with it, but she grasped onto the man in front of her instead, who stood firm against its grasp.

Musical laughter chimed through the air. Tink peeked around Hook to see the water recede from the rocks, leaving a sandy path from them to the shore. On the largest rock sat Queen Titania. Violet hair spiraled down to her iridescent, navy tail. Like other merfolk, she wore no human clothing, though pearls of cream and pink accented her hair, and a crown of bone-white coral graced her head. The merfolk queen cocked her head to the side as she took in her small audience. "Not a combination I expected."

Elongated, sharp teeth peeked out from between her lips. Those things could bite a fish in half. Or a pixie. Tink shuddered. Was the queen amused or annoyed? If the latter, they were in a heap of trouble.

9

Saltwater dripped off Hook's face and slid down into his boots as he stood before the queen of the merfolk. Given her reputation, she'd probably splashed them on purpose. Tink released her hold on his coat and stepped out from behind him. She'd had no trouble letting him take the brunt of the wave. The petite pixie gave a wobbling curtsy, her boots sinking into the wet sand. Even with her wings bound, it seemed the queen recognized her.

Hook removed his hat and swept a bow. "Queen Titania."

"Captain," she replied, her tone flat.

Bad sign. Best get to it. "I've come to ask you to remove your curses."

She crossed her arms, brows rising. "You waste my time, Captain."

He swallowed. Of all the times not to be able to lie and charm her. Cressida's crew in port only complicated things. They were friendly—most of the time—but further angering the merfolk wouldn't do any favors for him with them either. If the laughter and frolicking on the beach were any indication, the merfolk were quite enamored with Cressida's crew.

"It was my error," Tink said, stepping closer to the queen. Hook shot her a sharp look, but she ignored it. "I heard him boasting of the theft, and

I believed he stole it from you, but that was wrong. Captain Blackbeard stole the Heart of Fire from you. Captain Hook took it from him."

Titania slid her sapphire gaze to Hook. "Still a thief."

He should have known Tink wouldn't keep quiet. Did she have no idea how thin the queen's patience was? "Tink stole the necklace from me shortly after I acquired it." Hook straightened, doing his best to keep his tone calm and easy. "I couldn't return something no longer in my possession." Not that he would have, but she didn't need to know that.

Tink's cheeks flamed. "And if not for me stealing it from *him*," she accented the word, "I could not have returned it to you as you asked of me."

Titania tilted her head this way and that. "Whatever shall I do with you two thieves? Both of you ask favors of me."

Both of them? Hook glanced at Tink from the corner of his eye. She'd said she traded the necklace for their trust. What could a pixie want from the merfolk so badly?

The queen's tail flicked an arc of water toward their boots. "And yet, you both made offenses against me. You," she said as her sparky gaze slid to Hook, "boasted of your theft instead of vowing to return our sacred treasure. And you, little pixie, caused us to turn the sea against the wrong pirate."

Tink stiffened next to him. "We beg your forgiveness for our errors. What can we—" Hook grabbed her hand and squeezed. Offering anything to a mermaid was risky. The queen already had her decision, he could see it in the glimmer of her eyes and the hint of a grin on her lips. How had Tink survived a prior encounter with this vicious queen?

The queen's attention slid to their joined hands. Hook released Tink, lest the mermaid get the wrong idea. It took everything he had not to wipe his hand on his coat. Though even that might not remove the memory of her soft skin against his.

"I would ask a favor of you both," the queen said. "Do what I ask, and I will reward each of you. For the pirate, the sea will no longer rage against you. For the pixie, you will have the pearl you seek, no further payment required."

A pearl? All this nonsense for a bloody pearl? He had at least a dozen of them somewhere in his cabin, not to mention the long necklaces he'd acquired years ago. She could have taken those. They *would* look stunning draped around her neck.

Tink swayed on her feet. Whatever it was, it was important, valuable enough that not even the Heart of Fire had been sufficient payment. Or Queen Titania was taking advantage of her naivety, as she was known to do. Still, it couldn't be any normal pearl, but he'd get to the bottom of that —later.

"What favor?" Hook asked. To offer such a prize, it wouldn't be simple. No, the queen was crafty as a pirate. Craftier.

Titania's fangs glinted in her serpentine smile. "I want the scale of Leviathan returned to me."

Bloody hell. The thing was no more than a legend. A myth. The dragon god Leviathan was said to be so large it could swallow a ship whole or stir up a tidal wave with a flick of its tail. Hook had lived on the sea most of his life and never seen anything like it—or met anyone who had. There were worse monsters on the sea that occupied his thoughts—namely the old, bastard crocodile who'd taken his hand.

"I already vowed to return it to you in exchange for the pearl," Tink protested, her voice cracking.

His head snapped her way. This pixie planned to find a mythical treasure. He nearly laughed. She was bold, all right. And desperate. So very desperate to attempt something like that. If he hadn't known her, he'd say daft, but there was too much cunning behind her crystal blue eyes for that.

A pixie in human lands, alone, desperate for help from the merfolk... There was much to her story he didn't know and couldn't guess at. Curiosity tugged at him like a pulled thread. Something else too—an ache in his chest he studiously ignored.

"And now you'll have help." Titania grinned, exposing her fangs.

"Where is this scale?" Hook asked, turning his attention back to the queen.

Water splashed in an arc from a flick of her tail. "If I knew, I'd have it already."

So, it existed after all. Hook rubbed his jaw. All he had to do was find something most of Neverland didn't believe existed. But just as Titania could taste a lie in the air, she couldn't utter one herself. No merfolk could. Legend said that long ago the dragon god Leviathan had come to Neverland. There it fell in love with a human woman—or a mermaid as the merfolk liked to claim. Duty called the god away, but it left with its beloved a scale from its body, a way to call it to aid if ever she or her descendants needed. The legend was true, it seemed, at least part of it.

Tink looked between the two of them and swallowed. "I was told it's hidden in a cave, somewhere normal folk don't go."

"Determined." Titania leaned back on the rock, her breasts proudly displayed in the sunlight that glimmered across her pearlescent skin. "And bolder now. You should have asked me more about it the last time we met."

Tink's cheeks flushed.

"I see why you like her," Titiana said to Hook.

He stiffened. The comment knocked him off-balance worse than her request. But Tink didn't notice. Instead, she hung on the queen's word.

"The Shrouded Isles." The mermaid's gaze turned dark as the misty cluster of islands themselves. "I can feel it, my ancestor's treasure calls to me, but the water there is...unpleasant."

This was bad. Hook turned, his boots squishing in the sand, and stared past the sandy beach to the surrounding forest—inviting, lively, colorful, full of trees laden with ripe fruit. Paradise, his crew called it. Everything the Shrouded Isles weren't.

"The Shrouded Isles," Tink repeated, as if committing it to memory. "We'll find the scale. I'll make sure of it."

Hook whirled around. "Wait one minute." He waved his hook at the women.

The queen's gaze narrowed at him. "You're a pair, and she has agreed." Another flick of the tail. "I look forward to having the scale in our possession once more, where it belongs. Do this for me, and you'll have what you asked for."

Bloody pixie was going to get him killed, literally. First stealing from him, then cursing him, now agreeing to find an item no one knew the exact location of in a place everyone avoided. Worst of all, she haunted his every thought, another curse he needed to rid himself of. Now.

"If we're done…"

"Wait," Hook said.

The queen grinned. She knew, blast her. What would she demand to remove his second curse, his other hand?

He turned to Tink. "I need to speak with the queen. Alone."

"You're not worried I'll fly away?" She balled her hands on her hips.

He glanced at the horizon and raised his brows. "In this storm?"

She only shrugged before turning back to the mermaid. "Queen Titania." She curtsied before walking down the beach.

"You desire my company, Captain?" The queen leaned forward, her long claws adding ripples to the rolling tide.

To say no would offend her, but yes would be a lie. There was a reason he avoided these shores. The lusty merfolk sought to seduce any who ventured near, but only if one impressed them, made them feel desired. They couldn't be courted with pretty words. His best compliments earned him only scorn and dismissal, shunned for the lies they were. It wasn't his fault he favored the feel of a woman's legs wrapped around him, holding him tight. "I want the second curse on me removed."

A lavender brow lifted. "Oh? And why do you think you're twice cursed?"

He flicked a half-glance toward Tink. Sage wrapped an arm around the pixie's shoulders, leading her over to where a few merfolk lounged on the beach with members of Cressida's crew. His heel ground into the sand. "There's a woman. Can't get her out of my head."

Titania laughed. "That's not a curse. It's called infatuation. Some might even call it…love?"

Hook ground his teeth. A thieving pixie who got the sea turned against him? Not a bloody chance. He might call her love—hell, he called a lot of women that—but it didn't mean he was *in* love with her.

The queen hummed. "No, not yet. But maybe someday? It's certainly lust."

"I'm not some green in the gills boy."

"No." Sharp fangs peeked out. "You're not."

Frustrating mermaid. "Look. The sea is my only wife. I don't get attached to women." Lovers came and went. They didn't linger in his bed, much less his thoughts. There wasn't time for it, not that any'd caught his eye if there had been.

"You're lying, Captain."

"I'm…it's this bloody curse. What do I have to give for you to get this woman out of my head?"

"So desperate," she hissed. "Too bad you're not afflicted by such a curse. Oh, the things I could ask of you if you were."

Not afflicted? He blinked. It wasn't possible. "Magic then."

She shook her head. "None that I can smell. Desire is a natural thing. Give in. Let it sweep you away. Perhaps that will clear your mind of this woman…or is it a pixie?" Her sly gaze slid down the beach.

His fist opened and closed. *Bloody merfolk.*

"I await my scale, Captain. A scale of the dragon god of the seas should belong with the people of the seas."

Waves lapped at his boots. "That's the only reason you want it?" he asked. But he already knew the answer.

"A queen can never have too many weapons at her disposal. Surely you'd agree." She cocked her head to the side.

Of course he did, which she already knew. Though… "And what's to stop me using it? Or Tink?"

Titania bared her fangs.

"Accidentally," he added.

"Do you know how?" she practically snarled.

No, he didn't.

When he didn't speak, she responded, "Then you have your answer."

"You ask too much of her," he said, refusing to let the queen have the last jab.

Titania glanced down the beach. "So desperate… I couldn't help myself." She shrugged. "But now she has help." A slow, wicked grin spread across her face. "You see, these things have a way of working out."

His teeth ground together. *Bloody mermaid.* She had been taking advantage of Tink's naivety. Not that it should bother him.

"Don't keep me waiting, Captain." Titania glanced at the storm clouds.

"For your sake, if not hers." Sunlight glinted off navy scales as she flipped off the rock and disappeared below the water.

10

*T*ink fanned herself with a giant leaf, fighting a losing war against the heat racing under her skin. But the sun disappearing behind angry storm clouds wasn't solely to blame. Pirates and merfolk frolicked in the crystalline shallows, most without some, or all, of their clothing. Rum flowed freely from tapped barrels that Cressida and Hook's crews had brought to shore.

Fish roasted on a fire for the humans—the merfolk ate them raw and wiggling, sometimes while still embracing their partner of the moment. The scent turned Tink's stomach. She didn't eat fish, or any meat— something Barley, one of Hook's crew, discovered the first morning on Hook's ship when he'd brought her salted codfish. If she'd had anything left in her stomach, she'd have lost it over that disgusting sight.

"Care for another?" Barley offered her a ripe mango where they lounged in the shade provided by lush palms on the edge of the beach. Of all the crew, he was a calm anchor in the storm, level-headed, soft-spoken. Honestly, not at all like most pirates, which raised him higher in her esteem.

The creamy sweetness of sugar apple still lingered on her tongue. "No, thanks."

Squeals split the air. Tink couldn't help but look, drawn by curiosity that teased her more than the breeze blowing strands of her golden hair. A naked man—Smee—hefted a mermaid from the sea. The first mate twirled her around above his head as the swell of a wave lapped at his chest. Moisture grew between Tink's legs as she drank in the revelry before studiously looking away back toward the forest. Pixies were not always the modest sort, but neither did they lust so freely and openly. Their pleasure was in one's company, their trust, not only the feel of another's body entwined with their own.

But she'd lost that company, the companionship, her home. She sighed, and her shoulders hunched. A pixie without that was nothing more than a pretty wraith with wings.

"You could join them, you know," Barley said.

Tink rolled her eyes. "That's the fourth, no fifth, time you've said that. You could too."

"Someone ought to keep an eye on you." He grinned as he brushed long, brown hair back from his face. "Besides, these won't fix themselves." Barley lifted the garment in his hand for emphasis. A basket full of assorted clothes occupied the sand next to him. He was the quiet sort, saying little and content to linger in her company while he worked.

"Captain's order, eh?"

"No. He didn't need to ask."

Of course not. Ever loyal to his captain, Barley favored more creative ventures than hoisting sails or navigating by the stars. The crew was lucky to have him.

Said captain had disappeared into the forest shortly after his private meeting with the queen. Tink shivered, remembering her fang-filled grin and dark claws longer than a jungle cat's. Whatever they'd discussed, Hook didn't like it. A dark cloud loomed over his mood like those still rumbling on the horizon. Tink overheard brief words with some of his crew, informing them of their destination, before he'd stomped off without another glance.

Instead of dimming the mood, the news spurred the pirates to party harder. One last fling in case the treacherous waters of the Shrouded Isles dragged them down to the depths. Sage and Smee had literally dragged her into the water with the merfolk until she shook them off and traded the sea for shade. They'd laughed and smirked as a wave nearly knocked her down during her retreat, yelling all kinds of things about how she owed them for getting them all cursed.

Maybe she did, but she wasn't about to join their romp. Honestly, she was amazed they didn't hate her for what she'd done. They had every right to. When she'd ventured the question to Barley earlier, he'd merely shrugged and said Hook had told them it was an accident, one she was going to help fix.

Tink pulled at the sleeve of her shirt, stuck to her skin by a sheen of sweat and heavy humidity. *His* shirt. He'd covered for her to his crew when he had no reason to. A part of her wished the captain had joined the revelry. What did he look like without his shirt? His breeches? Another part of her, a dark, secret, treacherous chest she kept locked away, loathed the idea of him caressed by mermaid claws or wrapped up in one of Cressida's crew.

"I can't sit here anymore." Tink pushed to her feet, brushing sand from her pants.

"Oh?" Barley glanced toward the revelers.

Tink put her hands on her hips. "No. I need..." *To relax. To think. To get away from filthy pirates.*

He pointed his sewing needle at the dirt path behind him. "There's a hot spring a little way down that path."

A flicker of joy bubbled up from the hazy murk within. She flexed on to her tiptoes, body already loosening at the prospect. Warm, soothing water in a bath that wasn't salty. No mermaids. No orgy. Just— "Can I go alone?"

She feigned modesty, staring at her boots like a child. Barley was a tolerable companion, for a pirate, but stripping down in front of him was out of the question. Sharing a bath with him? *Hard pass.*

The shirt he mended found a home on top of the others in the basket. "I should go with you."

"Not a—"

"Fine. I'll just watch the path," he said, raising his palms. "Make sure no one disturbs you."

She clasped her hands in front of her and gave him her brightest smile. "Perfect."

⋅⋅⁖ ˙˙·˙·⋅.

*M*oss-covered rocks tickled her bare feet. Large pools of water trickled down like a giant's staircase, one to the next, from somewhere high on the steep hill above. Birds sang. Tree branches laden with fruits dipped toward the ground. Others formed a canopy above, bathing the springs in muted, dim light. Soon the sun would sink below the storm clouds, and the only light would be from the luminescent moss hanging in clumps off the rocky hillside.

Tink sighed as she unwrapped the binding around her wings and dropped it on her pile of discarded clothing. They stretched and fluttered, lifting her toes off the ground, as she worked out the aches and kinks from keeping them bound. No amount of stretching could compensate for the soreness the bindings inflicted—a necessary evil living among humans. When was the last time she hadn't felt pain performing such a simple lift? Hook feared she'd fly away? *Hah.* She'd be lucky to fly the short distance back to the beach before her wings groaned in agony. Misuse and living outside the magic of the vale were cruel punishments to any pixie.

Steaming water enveloped her foot, her calf, her thigh, then higher as she drifted down into the spring's embrace. She groaned in mixed pleasure and pain, savoring the sweet burn that distracted from her abused wings. Smooth boulders lay below the water's surface, providing the perfect seat, as if someone had long ago built this hot spring stone by stone for human use. Perhaps they had.

A contented sigh joined the fading bird calls. It was peaceful, comforting. Such a pleasant change from the ridiculousness on the beach. Every step she'd taken into the woods away from it had lifted her spirits. Tink let her head rest against a mossy rock as she sunk into the water up to her neck. A thread of homesickness stitched its way into her heart. If she closed her eyes, she could be there, resting in the springs beyond her little village with her cousins. Did they think her dead? Mourn for her?

And Lily… She had to have made it back, she had to be safe. But then why had no one come looking for her if Lily had told them where she'd gone and what had happened? Perhaps they really did consider her a lost cause.

"And now I'm stuck with these filthy pirates," she lamented.

A deliciously deep voice broke the peaceful night and vibrated along her skin. "Who's filthy?"

11

$\mathcal{T}$ink screamed. Her eyes flew open as she leaped toward the center of the pool and away from the voice at her back.

Hook stood on the bank next to her pile of clothes, a bemused expression on his devilish face.

"You!" She covered her breasts with her arms. "You—"

Flora's petals! Her heart pounded in her chest as she took in the smug pirate. Wet locks dripped water onto his bare chest. A fine smattering of dark hair adorned lean, chiseled muscle that even the dimming light couldn't hide. Something hung on a string around his neck, landing over his heart. Her mouth dipped open as her gaze traveled lower, taking in toned abs and a dark trail disappearing into damp breeches.

He dropped the boots and clothes he carried on the ground next to hers. "You were saying, love?"

"Ugh!" She splashed water in his direction. "Don't you know it's rude to sneak up on women while they're bathing? Or ever, for that matter."

"Is it?" He scratched at his chin. "Last time I interrupted a lady in the bath it turned out quite nicely for the both of us."

Her cheeks burned, and she swatted at the water. "You're disgusting."

He sniffed at his arms as he sat on a large boulder, legs spread and elbows propped on his thighs. "Actually, I'm clean as I've been in weeks."

Tink turned her back on him. "Leave."

"We're to be allies now. A team. Shouldn't we get to know one another?"

"Allies don't lock each other up," she snapped over one shoulder.

"They don't steal from each other either."

"Tink!" Barley's shout carried to them through the trees.

Great. Just great. She sunk lower in the water. Even more of an audience. So much for a relaxing soak before more days of misery on board the *Jolly Roger.*

"Barley."

"Uh...Captain."

Tink glanced over her shoulder. Barley's gaze traveled from her to Hook and back, lingering over her upper wings that stretched above her head.

"All's well," Hook said. "Go on back—"

"Like hell," Tink said. "Take him with you and leave me be."

Hook stood. Not the easy, lithe movements of earlier, but the stiff posture of a captain. Tink hugged her arms tighter around herself. All at once, he seemed taller, stronger, menacing in the specks of twilight and glowing moss.

Barley looked between them again, clearly on edge. "I'll go back to the beach." His attention shifted to Tink. "Yell if you need anything."

Tense silence threatened to chill the waters as Hook watched Barley retreat into the forest. "You've made a friend."

Tink huffed and blew the hair out of her face. "Not all of your crew is as irritating and unreasonable as you."

"Perhaps. But let's get one thing straight." Hook crouched by the edge of the water. One step closer, and he'd fall in. "No one commands my crew but me."

"Aye, aye, Captain." Sarcasm laced her voice, but if Hook noticed, he chose not to comment.

She turned her wings to him. Maybe he'd finally take a hint and leave her be. He was silent so long, she almost thought he had until he spoke again. "What do you need a pearl for? Can't be a normal one. You could have stolen that from me instead of the Heart of Fire."

The bracelet on her arm suddenly felt like a lead weight, dragging her into the depths. "You're not going to leave until I tell you, are you?" When he didn't respond, she sighed. "It's a black pearl. *The* enchanted black pearl. It fixes something that is broken. Anything."

"That's worth all this trouble? What do you have that needs fixing?"

She glanced back at him through the steam. "Perhaps I'm broken, Captain."

"You don't look broken." He'd perched on the edge of the pool. Deft fingers trailed across the water, stirring up little ripples.

Beryl's wings, will he not just leave?

"Oh really? Besides the fact that I'm stuck here and can't return home?" *Insufferable pirate.* "No, not broken at all. Wouldn't you want to be whole again?"

He stiffened.

Instant regret coiled through her belly. *Why, oh why, did I say that?* Mentioning his hook of all things...

"Captain Hand wouldn't have the same ring to it." She caught the hint of a smile, but his voice lacked playful mirth. "No. It's part of who I am. I wouldn't change it."

Figures. He wasn't the type for self-pity. No, the great and glorious Captain Hook likely had a higher view of himself than the gods. Though his comment stirred a question she couldn't help but ask. "What did they call you before you gained your hook? Surely you weren't born with that attached to your arm."

"Might have been unpleasant for my ma. Let's make a deal, love. Tell me what it is you want to fix so badly, and I'll answer your question."

Not a fair trade. Not even a bit. Tink frowned at the water, cursing the way his voice, smooth and rich as caramel candies, enticed her to play along. She was naked for goodness sake! With night descended and water cocooning her in its embrace, she could almost forget it. Almost. Reluctantly, she raised her arm out of the water and jingled the broken bracelet.

"I wasn't lying when I said I was broken." She glanced back at him again, taking in the way the moss glowed against his tanned skin. "When pixies come of age, we're given a bracelet. It lets us travel from the

Sylvanna Vale to the rest of Neverland through our pixie doors. You might know them as flower rings or stone circles." She turned away, studying the variations in the rock through the haze of steam. "There are many guidelines we're to follow when we visit human lands, but only a few strict laws, ones established by the ancients to keep us safe. If you break one, your bracelet breaks, and you're banned from using the doors."

"You can't go home." His voice held something she'd never heard —sorrow.

Tink bit her lip and shook her head. "Can't see my family. Can't even tell them I'm alive."

"What did you do that's so horrible?"

"Does it matter? It's done. I'm an outcast. Banished. Condemned." The words spilled out like a torrent, unstoppable as the ache in her chest. "I don't belong anywhere anymore."

Her hands fisted in the spring's heat. She dropped her gaze to the tendrils of steam rising from the pool. "But if I get that pearl, I can fix this. I can become a real pixie again. I can go home. I—"

Water splashed behind her.

Tink gasped and whirled around to find him chest-deep in the spring. "James."

The name cut straight through her panicked thoughts. She blinked, sucking in air. "What?"

Hook waded through the water until Tink craned her head back to look into his solemn, steady gaze. "My name is James."

James.

His hand brushed her side, just over one hip, warm as the waters around them. That touch, so brief and gentle, broke the tethers that locked her in place. James, he was James—not a merciless pirate captain, not someone she'd stolen from, not someone who'd taken her captive for revenge. No, he was just a man, bare-chested and breathing heavily. In his eyes, she saw the mirror of her own desire, a hunger she could no longer deny.

Tink stepped closer until the sodden fabric of his pants brushed her bare leg and his strong form blocked out the glowing plants beyond.

Without another moment of hesitation, she wrapped her arms around his neck and pulled his face down to hers.

Soft, moist lips crashed against her own. A hint of the sea teased her tongue. Their first kiss had been tentative, deceptive—at least on her part. Her only focus had been getting her dust across his lips, in his mouth, and letting it work its magic on him. She'd barely had time to savor the strength of his body under hers, the coarse stubble of his shadow of a beard as it scraped her delicate skin.

This time his kiss consumed her, drowned her like a tidal wave and pulled her down into the depths of the sea. By all the revered elders, she couldn't focus on anything but Hook. *No...James.*

Skin met skin as he wrapped her in his embrace and pulled her close. *Durin's beard, his chest is hard. Smooth. Warm.* It was like embracing a marble statue in the heat of the midday sun. Tink leaned against him, desperate to feel, to sink into his kiss. All her worries washed away, lost with the flick of his tongue against her own, his breath in her lungs.

Her legs wound around him, eliciting a groan that rumbled deep in his chest. Strong fingers cupped her backside, pulling her tight against him in a daring, intimate way that set her core aflame. If only he'd stripped off his breeches. She had half a mind to rip them off, reveal his cock, and slide down onto it. Her core clenched tight as she nipped at his bottom lip and imagined his girth. He'd be well made, he had to be. And it'd been so long...

What did it matter if he was a lousy pirate? Tink ground against him, savoring the bulge that teased her taut nub. Her hands fisted in his hair. *Holy Flora, he wants me too.*

A delicious tingle trailed down her wings and along her spine. Tink let her legs go loose, sliding down his body. Her hands followed in a seductive caress as she continued their kiss. Down his neck, over strong shoulders, down his chest to—

Her fingers stilled over the pendant on his necklace. It's wasn't a pendant. It was a ring. Too small and dainty to be his.

Tink jerked away, severing their kiss and sliding from the arms of the man holding her.

Water sloshed around her as Hook straightened, a lusty moan slipping into the air between them.

A ring, he was wearing some woman's ring, and still he looked at her like that, like he might devour her or bring her to climax over and over and—

"Love, your wings are shimmering." He rubbed at the stubble on his chin. His eyes hooded further. "For me?"

"Ugh!" Tink swept her hand across the top of the pool, sending a wave of water splashing toward the filthy pirate.

"Hey, what?" He straightened.

She twisted around and placed her palms on the edge of the pool, shoving out of the water with a flutter of her wings. A soft glow surrounded her, illuminating her form. Her wings were shimmering. A good thing, if only he hadn't caused it.

"What did I do?" He sounded dumbfounded, like a child slapped on the wrist after misbehaving. And oh, he had. Did he have no shame?

All the senseless desire coursing through her veins turned leaden. The glow of her wings dimmed as she scrambled into her clothes. Behind her, water splashed as Hook climbed from the pool.

"Did you drug me again? Is that it?" Bitterness laced his question.

Tink twisted to glare at him over one shoulder. "If I had, you'd already know."

The momentary hardness in his expression broke. "Then what..." He gestured between them. "You kissed me. I thought you were enjoying yourself?"

She twisted and tugged at the shirt until her wings pushed free. "Then you, Captain, know nothing." Stepping into her pool, kissing her like that... *Ugh, filthy, thieving, dirty pirate.* She should have known better. How had she expected more?

Without a backward glance, she stomped off into the jungle.

12

*T*he storm passed in the night, leaving calm waters and clear skies in its wake. Finally. Bloody mermaid curse whipping up unnatural storms had tossed them around like dice in a cup. At least they'd been smart, leaving wealth and goods with their families or tucked away in troves. They'd been dipping into those reserves since these storms hindered their business—and thievery. But really, that was just a different kind of business. Anyone who crossed the Cerulean Sea knew the price. It was no different than paying the Gamoreans, or other kingdoms, for passage through their lands.

Hook nudged his first mate with his boot, trying to rouse the man where he sprawled half-naked in a hammock on deck.

"Adella?" he mumbled around a yawn.

"Try again," Hook replied.

"Captain!" Smee snapped up, suddenly wide awake. The hammock twisted until it spilled the larger man onto the damp deck below. "Ugh, sorry, I—" Smee rubbed at his head.

"Yeah, yeah, but you'll turn red as a lobster sleeping out here like that." Hook gestured to his lack of shirt. His first mate was a hairy one, "a cuddly bear" he once heard a woman proclaim. Well, he had the size to fit that description, if not the claws. Really, he was more like a big dog—

loyal, trustworthy, and not above sniffing around the skirts of every woman he passed.

He loved the man, though—his brother, even if they weren't related. He'd had his back since they were boys. If not for Smee, he probably wouldn't be alive. Certainly wouldn't be the captain he'd become.

As long as Smee kept his eyes, and hands, off one particular woman, he could do as he liked with any of the others. Tink sat in the shade of the sail, pulling needle and thread through fabric. Barley must have put her to work. Fair—he should have some return for watching after her yesterday. His lips pulled thin as he eyed his crew preparing the ship for departure. Though considering the condition of the rest of them, he decided he might be thankful for skipping the festivities. They'd right themselves soon enough.

He, on the other hand… While his crew partied with the merfolk, he'd replayed his encounter with Tink over and over. The agony in her words had pulled him into the water. Bloody hell, he'd even given her his real name, one he hadn't used in years. For a moment there, he'd deluded himself into believing her kiss had been true this time. That she wanted him. The way she'd wrapped her legs around him and rubbed herself against him… He groaned. She was a seductress, that much was certain. He didn't need a curse for those memories to haunt him. Too bad her kiss had been another twisted game.

He wiped the back of his hand across his mouth. She hadn't drugged him this time, probably because she didn't have any pixie dust left, or so she claimed. But she'd pulled away fast enough. Was she embarrassed about her wings glowing? Truly, he didn't know pixies could do that, but then he really didn't know much about them at all, except that humans rarely saw them and their dust could demand a sizeable amount of coin. He'd *acquired* some once. Nasty stuff. Knocked out half his crew for a day.

"Give in to your desire," Queen Titania had said. *Hah.* Much good that did. Thoughts of the little pixie kept him up all night, even after he'd pleasured himself to visions of her after she'd stormed off. Gods above, he'd gouged a new groove in the wall with his hook when he returned to his cabin to find her sprawled across his bed, sound asleep.

His fault. He'd locked her in there—once, and now she'd claimed it as her own. Wouldn't need to lock her up anymore, though. She'd be a fool to try and escape now. Pixie or not, she wouldn't be claiming the scale of Leviathan without help. How she'd thought to get it before was beyond him. A pixie, alone in the Shrouded Isles looking for a scale? He shook his head. A death wish, that was. A fool's errand. He rubbed at his chest, trying to ease the slight ache there. She wanted to go home. Couldn't blame her for that, but the queen's price was too steep for her to pay alone. Impossible—maybe. Which raised the question again, what had she *done* to get herself banned from home like that?

"Uh, Captain?" Smee nudged his arm.

"What is it, Smee?"

"I've been talking to you for over a minute, but you're just staring off at the island, this grimace on your face." He rubbed the back of his neck. "I know I drank a lot, but..."

Bloody hell. How long had he been staring Tink down? At least Smee didn't notice that part, but who else... He glanced around, watching his crew. Sage winked at him, but knowing her that could mean anything.

"To your post." He swatted Smee on his back. "Let's get some wind in these sails."

"Ah! Wind in the sails!"

A sharp whistle screeched above. "Captain!"

His fist tightened. *What now?*

One of his crew waved frantically from the crow's nest, spyglass in hand, signaling at something offshore. Hook hustled across the deck. If another storm was rolling in—

A ship sped their way on a convenient breeze. Big one from the looks of it.

"The *Kraken!*" the crewman called from above.

An icy chill surged through Hook's veins. *Of all the bloody ships...* "To your posts!" he called. Hook grabbed Smee's arm and ordered, "Ring the bell, get everyone on deck."

Of all the times for Captain Blackbeard to show his ugly face. Doubtful he was here for a frolic with the merfolk. He'd likely caught wind of their recent departure the moment he pulled into Tortuga and followed course.

Bloody hell. He'd been so distracted with Tink and his curse, he'd forgotten the bigger threat roaming the seas.

Across the lagoon, Cressida's ship was a similar flurry of activity. They'd just spotted the same thing in their efforts to depart.

"Let out the sails," Hook called. Thank fuck they'd already hauled in the anchor. If they could shove off, perhaps they could avoid an encounter. Captain Blackbeard wouldn't have forgotten about a certain necklace Hook stole off him—or any of the many other things they'd done over the years. It was perhaps his worst theft ever for all the mess it started. The man thought himself the king of the seas—he would show him.

Hook turned for the wheel but crashed into the woman standing behind him, a frozen pillar in the chaos. Tink had gone white as a seagull, staring off toward the horizon.

"Did they say the *Kraken?*"

He could barely make out her words over the bell starting to peal, the rush of boots across the deck, and various shouts and curses.

There was no mistaking a look like that. She knew the ship. Knew it and feared it. Not the kind of fear inspired by reputation either. What had that bastard done to this pixie trapped far from home?

"Get below deck. It'll be safer there."

She blinked, unmoving.

He clamped a hand on her shoulder. "Tink."

A shiver echoed through her body as movement returned. "Right," she said, voice barely audible. Without a glance at him, she took off for the stairs, braided blonde hair trailing behind her. Hook pulled at his collar, savoring an odd brief moment of relief as she disappeared below. One less thing to worry about. That was all.

The *Kraken* would come upon the *Siren* first. It might give them time to run...but he couldn't do that to Cressida and her crew, especially not when Blackbeard was involved. No one needed to be left at the mercy of that crocodile. Two against one, they might stand a chance, even with the *Kraken's* notorious firepower.

"Roll out the cannons!"

Fuck. They weren't ready for a battle—nothing prepped, little room to maneuver.

"Sails secured!" Smee called up to him.

'Bout bloody time. Hook grabbed the wheel. Wind caught in the sails. The *Jolly Roger* lurched away from the dock. Poor girl, he didn't like to treat her so, but they had no choice.

He spied the *Siren*—judged the angle of their sails, the direction of the wind. With any luck, they could get the *Kraken* between them.

"Cannons to starboard!"

The crew rushed to obey. Pride swelled in his chest. They knew their posts, their roles. Each member worked together like gears in the fancy pocket watch he'd *acquired* a few months back.

The breeze tugged at his hat as they raced toward the advancing enemy.

A deep boom sounded. A cannonball whizzed in their direction, falling short and splashing into the sea.

"That came off the front!" Sage yelled from below.

Hook grimaced. *Aye.* Leave it to the old croc to have a trick up his sleeve.

More shots followed. One grazed the port side.

"Damage?"

"She'll fix," Smee called back.

The *Siren* neared the enemy, drawing their fire. *Perfect.*

Adrenaline surged through Hook's veins as he turned the wheel, bringing them in closer for a shot.

"Should we fire, Captain?" Smee asked halfway up the stairs to his deck.

"Hold." His body hummed as they drew closer. One good shot would be worth ten poor ones. This close, he could almost picture that bastard at the helm of the *Kraken*. Bloody croc deserved a slow, painful death for all he'd done to him. His phantom hand tingled where his hook curved over a handle on the wheel.

Each victory against him fueled the coals of revenge lodged in his chest. Every time someone praised the *Jolly Roger* or spoke of the great

Captain Hook was one less voice boosting Captain Blackbeard. Someday...someday he'd bring that bastard low.

"Captain!" Smee called again.

He shook himself. *Focus, man.*

"Aye! Disable them. Now!" he called back, sure Smee would pass on his orders. They had only one chance, a few minutes before the guns were focused back on them. One well-positioned blast of the *Kraken's* cannons could wreck them—or worse, give Blackbeard the chance to draw close and board them. He wouldn't surrender his ship and crew to that bastard. Never.

The best chance they had was to land a solid blow and flee, for now.

Sea breeze filled the sails. The ship lurched, ripping across the water. In moments they'd slide straight past the *Kraken.* Too close for comfort, but necessary. He only prayed the *Siren* kept their focus for one more bloody minute.

Cannons boomed. The *Jolly Roger* rocked from the force of the blasts sailing toward the *Kraken.* One cannonball hit the deck, sending boards splintering and men running. Another clipped the mainsail, ripping it. A grin spread across his features. *Perfect.*

More blasts echoed across the water. The *Kraken* returned fire. He gritted his teeth as one blast crashed against the hull. *Better not have hurt my bloody ship.*

His crew rushed to action. They'd handle it. He had to put some distance between the ships.

Hook's hand froze on the wheel. His chest tightened. There, standing at the helm of the *Kraken,* stood Blackbeard. His black attire and full, dark beard were unmistakable. Acid burned Hook's throat. The things that man had done... He'd half a mind to steer closer, climb the rigging, swing aboard, and end things one way or another.

A strong gust blasted him in the face. Hook shook himself. No, his crew, he couldn't risk them like that, not now. Not yet. He tore his gaze away from Blackbeard and focused on the task at hand.

The *Siren* sailed in the opposite direction and showed no sign of turning. Was she fleeing? He couldn't blame them. Even from a distance, he could see the damage to one side. It was not enough to sink them, but they'd need repairs. Hopefully his ship had done just as much to their side of the *Kraken*.

As for their sails...

"They're lagging!" Smee whooped, throwing his hand in the air.

Aye. A grin spread across Hook's face as he righted the wheel. The split sections of the *Kraken*'s mainsail fluttered in the breeze, completely ineffective. The foresail bore a rip too, likely compliments of Cressida. Such a big ship needed all its sails to be effective.

"We got 'em!" Hook yelled.

The crew let up a cheer.

"Should we try to circle back?"

The bastard deserved to see his ship at the bottom of the seas, but that would have to wait. Cressida's ship showed no sign of slowing or turning. She'd helped them, at great risk to herself, and would do no more. Even weakened, the *Kraken* was a formidable foe, especially when it caught them unawares and still reeling from one storm after another.

No. The tip of his hook dug into the wood of the wheel. Another day Captain Blackbeard would get what was coming to him. Hook found the ring around his neck and rubbed it between his fingers. He'd get his revenge. One day.

"Stay the course."

As the *Kraken* faded from view and the crew recovered from the battle, Smee edged closer to his captain. "Um...Captain, sir, when should we turn back?"

Ah, right. With the appearance of Captain Blackbeard, he'd forgotten to fill him in on the plan he'd concocted in the late hours of the night. The few he could spare between his unfulfilled lust.

"We don't. We head for Rochland."

"Rochland? But the Shrouded Isles are east," Sage said, pushing her way into the conversation.

Hook raised his brows. "So we can poke about and get ourselves killed finding the scale of Leviathan? Much good it'll do us."

"But we have to get it!" Tink stood on the stairs, hair in disarray. Balled fists were planted on either hip, though she looked for all the world like she might hurl her guts out over the deck at any moment.

"Bloody hell, what are you doing up here?"

She wrinkled her nose but refused to back down.

"We're going in with a plan, and guidance," Hook replied, staring them each down in turn. "And if anyone doesn't want to venture the journey, they can stay on land."

Smee was the first to break the silence, pushing closer to his captain. "You can't mean to see…her."

"Aye, I do." If anyone could help them navigate the Shrouded Isles and find the scale, it was the Green Witch.

13

Holy revered elders. Tink would never get used to the sea. Always rocking, moving, swaying. She gagged, holding in her meager breakfast. Okay, the stiff wind was better than the last few days of idling along in the current and hoping for the slightest breeze to fill the sails. Faster meant closer to their destination, which was one step closer to the scale of Leviathan and to home.

And away from Captain Hook.

He'd spared barely a word to her since they left the merfolk and evaded the *Kraken*. Not that she wanted him to, of course not. She rubbed her chest at the memory of the dainty ring. Did it belong to this Green Witch they planned to visit? Some other woman who would greet him the moment he stepped on land? Blast him for filling her thoughts. She couldn't count the number of times she'd replayed their kiss. Kisses, to be more accurate. And how many times was he going to stare at her just to turn and walk away moments later? *Annoying, weird, bloody—*

"Hello?" Sage waved her hand in front of Tink's face, snapping her back to the moment. "Little miss pixie is turning red in the sun, or is it something else?" She winked.

Tink rolled her eyes and adjusted the hat Barley had given her—a lifesaver under the scorching sun. Humans didn't understand how lucky they were that their emotions didn't color their skin so vividly as pixies. At least his crew were kind to her, though. They had no right to be— she'd gotten them cursed after all. Even so, they'd mostly accepted her as one of their own, a temporary member of the crew on this expedition.

"If everyone we did business with held it against us, I'd have died before I grew my first chest hair," Smee had proudly proclaimed. A visual she could have done without. Not to mention their very different definitions of business.

"What do we do next?" Sage asked, gesturing to the ropes they had laid out.

The least she could do, Tink decided, was put her skills to use. Her mind whirled with possibilities for improvements to the ship. Honestly, she couldn't help it, she was a tinker pixie after all. Carrying goods up and down the stairs when these pirates could use a pulley system to haul up multiple crates and barrels at once was just silly. She'd offered a few days ago, but the crew had been on edge when the wind stilled, always scanning the horizon for sails, especially those belonging to a certain pirate. Even without the waves, their concern had been enough to turn her stomach. But today they'd finally loosened up, and she'd jumped on the chance to explain her ideas and put them to use.

"Loop that end of the rope through there. Then we need to get some nails to attach the beam to the spot we marked over there."

Sage beamed with delight. "We should have pressed a pixie into service long ago if they're all this clever."

A nervous laugh bubbled out. She couldn't be serious, right? "Not all pixies are so inclined. We all have our own talents and skills, just like you."

Sage slid her attention to two of the less than impressive crew members. "Some of us."

Tink hid a grin.

"Land ho!" Someone called from above.

"Finally!" Sage leaped to her feet.

Tink cringed as their hard work clattered to the deck. But land, now that was something she could get excited about. The breeze snagged at her hat and hair as she stood and caught sight of a speck of land stretching out on the horizon. Still far away, but close too. Oh so much closer than they'd been in days.

"Home sweet home!" Sage threw her hands up in the air.

"Home?" Tink's brows drew together.

Barley reached her side, carrying the length of netting he'd gone to fetch for their project. "No one told you?" he asked.

A knot tightened in her throat. No, they most certainly had not.

Home.

The place she longed for but couldn't reach. Tink twisted the bracelet around her wrist. Not yet anyway.

⋯⋰ ⋯⋰⋯

*T*his couldn't be the Port of Rochland where they said the Green Witch kept her shop. Tink had never been there, but everything she'd heard about it described it as a bustling city. The cove in front of them sported few buildings that she could see. And though the dock was sizeable, big enough to allow the *Jolly Roger* to tie up, only two small fishing boats were moored to it. Worn, dirt paths wove into the hills from the clearing near the dock, undoubtedly leading to more buildings, but this couldn't be a city.

Smee was one of the first ones down the gangplank, rushing to greet a gaggle of blonde women.

"He really does have women in every port," Tink said, as he lifted one girl into his arms and swung her around. He was nice enough, handsome, if not the cleverest of men. But still, so many...and they didn't seem to care that he embraced them all.

"He does," Hook agreed, leaning on the railing at her side.

She jumped, nearly flying out of her skin. With the hustle to get to shore, she didn't think anyone listened to her musings.

"But those," he said, gesturing to the women with his hook, "are his sisters."

Heat rushed to her cheeks. Of course. That made so much more sense, especially with their similar coloring. This really was their home, wasn't it? Sage said as much, but until that moment, it hadn't fully sunk in. This dock, it was made for them, for the *Jolly Roger*. And the handful of others walking down to the shore...they must be family too.

Her stomach tossed and turned as it had during the storms. Tink turned away, unable to watch the happy reunions. Without thought, she grabbed at her bracelet, twisting it around her wrist as she sucked in one deep breath after another. Hook watched her, his back to the shore. When his gaze dipped to her wrist, she slid it under her cloak. She'd chosen to hide her wings again once land was spotted. A shirt alone might do, but a cloak couldn't hurt, and the very last thing she needed was more attention on her. The sooner they got this done with, the better. Speaking of which...

"I thought we were going to Rochland to meet your Green Witch?" The words came out in a rush, fast as her racing heart. "This can't be it."

"We are." His lips quirked up at one corner. "By land."

By land. Her mouth opened and closed, but the words didn't come out.

"You thought we'd just sail into the Port of Rochland?" He rubbed his hook, an act that could have been menacing if not for the seductive grin on his lips. "We damaged the *Kraken*'s sail, but they'll have mended it or hoisted a new one days ago. You think they won't come after us? Blackbeard saw which direction we sailed. Rochland would be one of the first places they'd look."

She'd met Captain Blackbeard only once, and that was still enough to know Hook was right. He'd hunt them down. The mood of the crew of the *Jolly Roger* all the days they'd barely crawled along the water was proof enough of that. "So this is another part of the island."

"Aye." He glanced to shore. "Coconut Cove is a small fishing village, not even worthy of markings on a map. Just how we like it. Besides, the Royal Navy of Gamor likes to pretend this island is under their jurisdiction. They don't always look favorably on us mooring at the Port of Rochland. We like to leave them to their false beliefs. Do you know why?"

Her brows scrunched and head tilted to the sea as she looked at the world through his eyes. "Because if they have one port of refuge on their passage through the sea, they won't likely seek another?"

Hook nodded slowly. But that wasn't all. There was more, she could tell by his expression.

She thought she might know what it was. "And...if they don't want you to dock there, they probably wouldn't welcome other pirates either."

He grinned, looking proudly over his domain. "Exactly. We stay right behind their backs, the one place they never look."

The one place Captain Blackbeard wouldn't go sniffing around too closely either, but he didn't need to tell her that. She could see it in the hard set of his shoulders, despite the wicked smile he tried to hide behind. Blackbeard might sail close to port, look for their ship, but if he didn't see it, he'd keep going.

"You have a home here? Family?" The question twisted something tight in her chest, but for once, it wasn't the memory of her own family, of her lost home. No, this was something else. A subtle fear that another lovely lady would run down the docks, but this one wouldn't be a sister—at least, not to the captain. It was the same reason she couldn't ask about his ring.

Hook's hand wandered to his chest before he pulled at the lapel on his jacket. "Once." The warmth in his voice seeped away. "The sea is my home now." He shoved off the railing and stalked toward the gangplank without a backward look.

Gulls cried overhead. Soft waves lapped at the narrow beach. This cove was calm, mostly hidden by the surrounding cliffs. It was peaceful here—she'd give him that. A perfect sanctuary for anyone who enjoyed being far from others and at one with nature. Hook's crew didn't seem that type, though. By all appearances they loved people, parties, the open sea...everything this place wasn't. Perhaps there was more to them than she'd seen.

Tink followed after Hook, and though there were many joyous greetings for the captain, no young woman ran to meet him. *Thank all the revered elders for that.* Not that Tink had any right to be grateful, far from it, but one of the knots in her chest smoothed out. The others...not so much. Once again, she was a stranger in a strange place. And their joy...it should have made her happy, but all she felt was ill.

Nearby, Anne hoisted a young child, no more than four, into her arms. The boy burrowed into her neck, clinging to her as she opened her arms to embrace the man who'd limped along with the kid, his wooden leg thumping on the boards.

Funny, even as she wove through people on the dock in her aimless wandering toward the shore, she'd never felt more alone, more out of place. People in port towns, especially ones like Tortuga, didn't look twice at a strange face. Travelers and traders were always coming and going. What was one new woman? Here though, everyone was known —except her.

Shit. She should just go back to the boat, hide below deck, somewhere out of sight. Tink turned on her heel, dipped her head, and reversed her path.

A startled yelp slipped past her lips as an arm wrapped around her shoulders, pulling her to a stop. "Friends," Hook called out.

Of course it was him. He practically ignored her for days, and now he picked this moment to call attention to her? She wiggled against him, but he held firm.

"This is Tink, our newest crew member."

She couldn't meet anyone's gaze, especially not as they drew quiet, listening to the captain.

"Show her welcome here. We'll stay the night and be off to Rochland in the morning."

"Such a short stay," someone murmured.

Now Tink did look. Faces of strangers stared back, yet many held a hint of the familiar. Parents, grandparents, siblings. The likenesses were easy to see. No wonder they lived here in this hidden cove.

Long ago, she'd asked one of the elders why the pixies lived in the Sylvanna Vale. Why couldn't they all come and go and live with other races throughout Neverland?

"To keep you safe, my dear," he'd said. "To keep us all safe. If the other races know who you are, what you are, you'll be in danger."

"But why?" she'd asked, tugging on his robes, staring up at the pixie who seemed so tall—he was shorter than her now.

"Pixie dust is essential to our way of life. It's part of everything, our very way of being. But those outside see it as magical, a tool to wield as they see fit, if they even know how to use it."

Her little brows had scrunched together. "A tool?"

The elder had knelt before her, his weathered palm on her shoulder. "I'll explain when you're older. For now, know that we protect those we love by keeping them hidden."

Hook pulled her ever so slightly closer to him, and she let him. He was talking, saying something about their journey, but she barely heard it over her racing heart and thoughts. "That's it, we leave at dawn."

Conversation resumed. People headed toward shore. Hook's arm slipped from her shoulders. "You'll stay here while we're gone, there's a—"

"Wait, what?"

She spun to face him as the peaceful bubble of hope she'd felt a moment ago shattered. "I'm going too."

"It's safer—"

"No!" She stamped her foot. "Queen Titania said we're to do this together. You're not leaving me behind." No way she was going to just sit here and twiddle her thumbs. Plus, she couldn't risk Hook sneaking off and retrieving it on his own, or the queen saying she hadn't helped and thus didn't earn her reward. Tink shoved her fists to her hips and stared up at the pirate captain.

"As my lady commands." He swept a mocking bow. "But be warned, the Green Witch can be...interesting."

High-pitched squeals filled her ears. Blonde women flooded in around her, blocking sight of Hook's retreating form.

"Oh, she's so small!" The taller woman—*one of Smee's sisters?*—strung an arm through hers.

"You'll stay with us. It'll be so nice to have another woman around," a second, slightly shorter and stockier one, said as she took her other arm.

"Girls," a third reprimanded them, the oldest sister, by the looks of it—and heavily pregnant. Barley stood with his arm around her.

Tink gaped like a fish. "Your...wife?"

He grinned.

"I hope he's been kind," the woman said. Her arms settled over her rounded belly. "Now, let's get you settled."

Before Tink could protest, the women hauled her down the dock.

14

*T*here was always a feast when they returned. Food roasted over the fire. Kegs of ale tapped and poured until they ran dry. The best bottles of rum brought out from cabinets. Music wove through the night. People danced.

Pulling his crew away from home so soon grated against his heart, a black heart some called it. It still hurt to see the homesickness they tried to hide—smiles a little too broad, laughter a touch too loud, sudden silences. Maybe no one else noticed, but he did.

It couldn't be helped. There'd be no time for them to rest until they'd claimed their reward from Titania. Once the storms were off their heels, he'd have another problem to worry about—the *Kraken* and its bloody captain.

Smee's sisters swarmed around Tink like bees to a flower. It was hard to tear his eyes from her. For some reason, he wanted her smiles, her joy. He wanted her to be at peace here, but that was the very last thing he saw. Her back was straight and stiff in the chair she occupied. She'd flash one of the sisters a smile here or there, but he'd wager they weren't genuine. She tried maybe, but something held her back. Her gaze kept darting around the room, barely landing on him for a moment before moving on.

Those pretty wings were still bound despite the assurance that none here would threaten her.

She'd barely spoken to him since they left the merfolk. He couldn't puzzle her out. Why kiss him so passionately, then spurn him? Women didn't spurn Captain Hook, not after a kiss like that. He'd even told her his bloody name.

It was impossible not to watch her when she was on the deck of the *Jolly Roger*—sun slanting through her wings, shining from her hair. The way she laughed with some of his crew... Never him, though. Each time their gazes locked, she'd turn away faster than a minnow from a shark.

A distraction, that's what she was. Even so, the thought of her running off again caused a heaviness in his chest he couldn't quite place.

A lean form blocked his view. "Take me with you to the Shrouded Isles!"

Smee's youngest sister, Rell, stood with her hand on her hips. Unlike her sisters with their fancy dresses, she preferred breeches and a tunic—sailor's clothes.

"No." The gangly teen was eager, but that didn't make up for a lack of experience, and the Shrouded Isles was the very last place he'd take a new crew member.

"But you said I could join the crew on the next adventure," she pouted.

He tried to look past her, beyond the fire blazing in the hearth of the greatroom and the many bodies between him and Tink, but Rell moved with him.

"Captain, please, I'm ready!"

"Aye, you are, but we're not. This is a dangerous mission. It's not the time to learn the ropes."

The girl fumed, her fists balled and lips pursed. "You'll always treat me like a little kid."

"On the contrary," he grinned. "I have an important task, one I need you here for."

She beamed. "Tell me."

"We ran afoul of Captain Blackbeard on the way here."

Her nose wrinkled. "That bastard."

"Language," he reprimanded. He wouldn't have her talking like a sailor before she was one, however eager.

"Keep an eye on the horizon. Watch for his sails. Any trouble, you're in charge here while I'm gone."

Her eyes flew wide. "You mean it!"

"Aye."

She squealed, a shrill and terrible sound, before bouncing off into the crowd.

"Be careful what you promise," Barley said, taking the chair next to him.

Hook sipped at his rum. "If it keeps her from following after us in a rowboat, it's worth it."

Barley snorted. "For you. Reya's going to have my head if she has to take orders from her youngest sister."

A grin stretched his lips. Smee's sisters were as proud and loyal as their brother, quite a good bit savvier too. But Reya would need help with a little one about to make an appearance any day now. Keeping her overeager sister occupied couldn't hurt. "Speaking of Reya, you should stay here when we leave port."

"Captain—"

"It's your first kid, man."

"Aye." Barley sipped at his own drink. "But I can help him best by getting these storms off our backs."

Hook nearly groaned. Stubborn lot, pirates. "Think on it." He glanced across the room, catching sight of the empty chair Tink had occupied. Where did she—

"Reya had some news too," Barley said, pulling him from his thoughts. "The Royal Navy set up an intelligence post in Rochland."

His shoulders hunched. Could they never catch a break? "Looking for us?"

"Worried that too, but it seems they're after Blackbeard. Searching for his hideout."

The place where his hand used to be tingled. Blackbeard's hideout—one of the most closely guarded secrets on the Cerulean Sea. Seemed the old croc had finally pissed off the Gamorean royals enough for them to stretch their reach into the free waters. Didn't bode well—for any pirate or free folk. "If we could acquire what information they have…" He stroked at the stubble on his chin with his hook.

Barley grinned. "Aye. We could finally track down the bastard."

Taking care of Blackbeard might get the Gamoreans to back off too. Hook clinked his glass against the other man's. "Excellent."

He'd be sure to thank Reya and her sisters personally before the night was done. They kept home running smoothly for everyone while the crew was away and never failed to pick up some helpful information when they went into town. Which, hopefully, Reya wasn't doing in her condition. He'd have to ask after that as well, make sure she stayed home—her sisters too, so they could look after her and the babe.

Speaking of… He resumed his search of the room, unable to find the petite pixie.

"I do believe she went outside, Captain." Barley grinned.

Heat coiled in his chest. "Right, well." He coughed. "I should make sure she doesn't try to flee."

The other man sipped his drink, his grin never fading as Hook went for the door.

<hr />

Tink sat on the edge of the porch on the far side of the house, her legs dangling in the air and her wings unbound. The gossamer things floated behind her, catching the tiny bits of moonlight that slipped through the palm and lofty fig trees to land upon her.

A small sniffle slipped into the air, barely audible over the crash of waves on the shore and mass of conversation seeping from within the building. Somewhere near the beach, people laughed. A splash echoed up the hillside. Hook grinned. An evening swim in progress, perhaps?

But the grin faded as he watched Tink sitting there in the shadows. She rubbed at her face. *Homesick? Bloody hell, she'd scream at me for sure if she knew what I saw.* Still…something nagged at him, her words from the hot spring and her desperation to find the black pearl and fix herself. He frowned. She didn't seem broken.

He slipped back around the corner as quiet as a thief—he'd had a lot of practice over the years. A safe distance away, he made a show of stomping in her direction. A whistled tune accompanied his heavy steps as he rounded the corner to where she sat.

Tink startled and twisted in his direction. "What are you doing here?" she blurted. Dainty hands wiped at her face, then took their time tucking hair behind her ears, as if that's what their purpose had been.

"Can't a man get some air?" He stretched his arms over his head, a casual gesture in contrast to the tension running through his stiff muscles.

She pulled her legs up and hugged them against her chest. "I want to be alone."

The hollowness of her words wrenched his heart. Hook claimed a seat near her—close, but not too close. "No one wants to be alone, love."

"I'm not your love," she spat back.

He grinned. That word never failed to spark her temper. "You're homesick."

"Go away." She turned her head away from him, pointing that perfect little nose toward the palms above.

He stifled a yawn. "Care to tell me how you got banished?"

"No."

A tough one to crack, but if they were to be allies, he preferred to know what danger she might be dragging along with her. "You knew of the *Kraken*."

She shivered and hugged her knees closer.

Oh yes, she knew that ship, and not just by reputation. "I'd wager you've had a run-in with it before. Maybe even had the joy to meet its delightful captain?"

Tink whirled on him, her eyes wild. "Delightful? He's the nastiest, most horrid, disgusting, awful pirate who ever drew breath!"

Aye, she has that right. He leaned back on his hand and hook. "Worse than me, love?"

"Yes! You're..." She sucked in a breath and turned away.

Intrigued, so very intrigued. He scooted closer until her wings nearly brushed him. "I'm what?"

When she turned to him this time, he had to hold himself back, letting the tip of his hook dig into the wood. A deep flush painted her cheeks, visible even in the dim light. Her chest rose and fell. Those perfect lips begged him to close the gap between them, and he never left a woman wanting.

"A kidnapper. Just like him." She accentuated each word.

Hook gaped as she got to her feet and stalked farther into the darkness of the porch that wrapped around the massive house. She may as well have slapped him, but even so, he was on his feet following her in a heartbeat. "What did he do to you?"

If he'd hurt her—

She stopped abruptly and shoved him in the chest. *Do it again*, he nearly begged. His boots almost touched hers. Heavy breaths filled the space between them.

"He kidnapped my cousin, all right? My favorite cousin, who is like a sister to me. I went after him to get her back. He demanded my dust in exchange. I gave it to him. All of it. Selling my dust for her life..." She held up her arm and looked away, all her fire gone out in a rush.

A bracelet hung from her wrist. The sapphire gem bound in thin strands of metal was cracked—shattered—yet none of the pieces fell free, as if magic held them in place. She sold her dust to save her cousin and got banned from home for it. For a brave, noble act. His shoulders drooped as something heavy settled in his chest, next to the simmering coal of a need for revenge that lived there. She wasn't some criminal, some peddler of pixie dust for gold or riches. She just wanted to save someone she loved. And Blackbeard... That bloody, fucking crocodile had forced the choice on her.

"Did he hurt you, love?" A soft growl rumbled in his chest. He nearly vibrated with rage. If he hadn't already sworn vengeance upon him, he would have in that moment. To treat someone that way, to do that to this fierce, beautiful woman was unthinkable.

"Not really. But demanding my dust...what that cost me..."

He took her upheld hand in his, savoring the way a shiver rolled across her at his touch. "We'll get you home, love. We'll find the scale, return it to Titania, and you'll have your reward. On my honor as a pirate."

"A pirate's honor?" she asked skeptically, as she peeked up at him through the fall of her long hair, half-blocking her lowered face.

"Aye. A pirate's honor, his word, is one of his most valuable treasures." Without thinking, he raised her hand to his lips and placed a kiss upon its back. Her skin was warm, soft. The faint scent of flowers clung to her.

She jerked her hand away and slid it behind her back with her other. More color raced across her cheeks. Sharp little teeth chewed at her lip.

"Aye, well…" he said into the silence that lingered.

Tink stared at her boots but didn't flee.

One thing nagged at him, though. "You gave him all your dust? You didn't sell any later?"

"Some," she whispered. "At home, it comes back easily. Here…well, I haven't made any in a while, but some came back after my deal with Blackbeard. I sold it." She spat the words like a bad taste in her mouth. "To get by. I needed food, shelter, ship passage… But that ran out months ago. Playing the mandolin and selling my little inventions didn't make near so much."

Months ago? His brows drew together. "The bartender I met in Tortuga said he'd bought pixie dust from a blonde woman only days ago. That was the night I found you."

Pink lips parted. Her head cocked to the side. "In Tortuga…"

"It wasn't you?"

She shook her head.

Then who was selling dust? One of Blackbeard's crew? But why? Maybe it hadn't even been her dust, but it had still led him to her by some twist of fate.

The back door cracked open. Laughter spilled out into the night along with a few of his crew.

"Captain!" Smee slurred as he hoisted a mug in the air. "Brought ya a drink!"

He nearly groaned. *Bloody, terrible timing.*

"I should get some rest," Tink muttered.

Hook reached for her, but she'd already twisted away and slipped between his crew members. He could do nothing as those gossamer wings disappeared around the corner.

15

A handful of his crew accompanied Hook and Tink when they left after dawn, trekking into the hills behind Coconut Cove and traversing the worn paths toward Rochland. The rest stayed behind to tend to family and ship repairs. The first hour was full of yawns and weary sighs. Since then, though, they'd never shut up.

"Still can't stop laughing at Reya's face!" Sage said behind him.

"Hey now," Smee warned.

"Yeah, yeah, but seriously, the look she had when Rell told her she was in charge?" Sage cackled. "If she wasn't so pregnant with my future niece, she'd have probably tackled her to the ground."

"Your...wait, what?" Tink said.

"My niece. It's going to be a girl. You'll see."

"B-but..." She sputtered. "You're one of Smee's sisters?"

Almost there, love. Hook grinned.

Sage's burst of laughter likely scared off any wildlife for miles. If it didn't, Smee's guffaw surely did.

"Barley is my brother," Sage said when she recovered.

"Oh."

He could almost picture the flush creeping up Tink's cheeks as she and the others followed along the path after him.

"She might as well be my sister, though," Smee said. "Been hanging around since we were young."

"Ouch!" Tink yelped.

Hook whirled around, ready to run to her side. But Sage already helped her up from the ground where she'd stumbled over a tree root on the path.

"Merrin's teeth, that hurt."

"All right back there?" he asked. His fist squeezed around the machete he used to hack away pesky branches.

"We're fine," Sage assured him and waved him on.

It took effort to turn his back on them and focus on the path ahead. Times like these were some of the few he resented being captain. Command meant duty, leadership. Not stalking near the back of the line to watch Tink as she hiked with his crew through the jungle.

"Been meaning to ask," Smee started as they continued on their way. "Who's Merrin? And the other ones…"

"Durin. Oh, and Flora, I think," Sage supplied.

Aye, he had half a mind to know too. But Tink would never have told him. His crew, however…

"They're our revered elders," Tink said. "They watch over us from the spirit plain and bless our way of life. Durin is the elder of weaving and tinkering, Merrin of farming, Beryl of flight…"

She rambled on, listing off various names and things about them. Oh, to be able to write them all down. Perhaps then he'd understand even half the unique curses she loved to spout.

"So Durin's beard…" Sage began. "It's…unique?"

"Just big and bushy." He could almost picture Tink's shrug. "At least, statues of him portray it that way. And that's what the elders say too. The living ones who are in charge back home, not the revered ones in the spirit plain," she clarified for Smee, whose confusion he could almost feel in the air, especially as he "hmmed" and mused aloud at her words.

"Well, that's…a lot," Smee said.

"Sorry," Tink replied. "Guess it is confusing to outsiders."

"Life's simpler in the cove and on the sea, that's for sure."

"How long has your family lived here?" Tink asked.

"Oh, forever," Smee replied. "I grew up fishing these waters as a boy, mending nets, sneaking down to Rochland every so often to, er, examine the goods coming in."

"A pirate from the start," she said.

Her light giggle annoyed him. Not the sound, he loved that, but that it was directed at Smee. How could she talk and tease half his crew and ignore him? She'd answered all their questions, asked a number in return, but he might as well have been invisible. His back practically shivered from her cold shoulder. No sane woman ignored Captain Hook. That was half the reason he didn't want her to come. He couldn't think with her around, couldn't focus. And the other half—trouble followed her like a shark after blood.

"Aye, the captain and me use ta' get into all kinds of trouble."

The back of his neck burned.

"You grew up together too?" she asked.

Hook hacked a fallen branch with a machete, clearing the way for those behind. "That's enough of that. We're too close to Rochland for that kind of talk."

Best no one overhear something that could tip off the locals to who exactly lived on the other side of the island. He probably shouldn't have let her talk about her homeland either, but damn if he wasn't curious. The locals of Rochland knew most the residents of Coconut Cove, especially Smee's sisters, Anne's husband, and some of the others who often came to town to gather goods and information. But the less they connected them to pirates, the better for all of them. It was a risk, him coming into town with his distinctive hook, but some risks were necessary.

Sweat drenched his shirt, especially where he carried a small pack on his back. They all carried one, just the necessities. The branches overhead blocked out some of the noon sun, but nothing could hold back the humidity. The sea was kind, letting the wind blow across it to cool a sailor and fill his sails. But the land hated him as much as he loathed it. It always had to remind him of it too.

As they cleared a rise, the port city came into view below. Rochland had an orderliness to it he appreciated, with its buildings laid out in neat rows as if someone had bothered to plan it. *Suppose they had. Once.* The edges of town were less precise where it grew past its original borders. The witch kept her shop at the edge of the east quarter.

"There she is," Smee said.

"Wow!"

He looked over his shoulder in time to catch Tink's wide-eyed stare as she took in the city for the first time. He supposed it was impressive to someone who'd never seen it before. It was the opposite of Tortuga's haphazard wood buildings with its multistory stone structures and cobblestone streets. Which was probably why the royals of Gamor set their sights on it for an outpost.

"Remember what we discussed," Hook said, his voice low so only his crew could hear.

Nods greeted him. *Keep a low profile. Just a bunch of traders and craftsmen in town for a few days.* They even had a hoard of shell and fiber jewelry Smee's sisters had made to sell in town as part of their cover. His crew was used to this ruse, and it was the reason he'd brought only a few. Still, a reminder never hurt.

he blazing sun overhead beat down on the simple hat he wore, bringing out the smell of fish that clung to nearly everything in Rochland. His normal hat was so much nicer, stiff but supple leather, accented with red and gold stitching. *Lucky too.* But it was too nice, too recognizable to wear around the city. He pulled his cloak tighter around him despite the heat. His hook was a giveaway for his identity, but one he might need depending on the witch's mood, or the innkeeper's, or anyone else who came looking for trouble in this gods-forsaken city.

"Francis and Davies. Take our packs and go find an inn. Try the Gilded Pearl first," he ordered. They served a good ale. Better yet, it stood only one block from the orderly rows of streets and houses of the old city, not too far from the edge of the forest. That made it perfect for sneaking away if it came to it. Plus, they turned a blind eye if the customer paid well.

Both men trotted off with their packs in tow.

Just ahead, a two-story house painted a burned cherry red faded into the buildings around it. In all his years, the witch's storefront never changed. Time herself wouldn't touch the Green Witch, nor the men of Gamor whose patrols skipped this street, best he could tell.

Hook drew them to a stop outside the front façade. Unlike the other buildings, no windows gave a glimpse inside. The shop had no sign either, just a poor old bird's skeleton, wings stretched out in flight, above the door.

"Poor bird," Tink muttered.

"You can't mean good ol' jolly Roger?" Smee replied with a wry grin.

Hook's back stiffened.

"Like the boat?" Tink's fair brows rose as her nose wrinkled.

The boat, he mouthed.

"Yeah, you see this one time—"

"Smee?" He crooked a finger at his first mate.

"Uh…" Smee looked between them before stepping closer to Hook, who threw his arm around his shoulders, letting his hook gleam near his face.

Hook dropped his voice to a low whisper. "When I lost that unfortunate bet, did you really choose to name my *ship* after that bloody bird?" He pointed his hook toward the eerie skeleton, its bones bleached by the sun.

Sage snorted. "You didn't know?"

A sideways glance did nothing to dim her humor, nor Tink's, who bit her lip and looked away. Any idiot knew she listened to every word.

"Aye, aye, I did."

Hook sucked in a deep breath, drumming his fingers on his taller friend's shoulders. His ship, his pride and joy, was named for a bloody, dead bird on a witch's door.

"Could be worse," Sage offered.

Could it be? He pulled away from Smee, his good hand in a fist. "We'll discuss this later."

"Smee, Tink, with me. Sage, watch the street."

The first time he'd pushed through the witch's black door, he'd been a few new whiskers shy of a boy. She'd told him true what he wanted to know. Not that it helped. The ring sitting against his chest grew suddenly warm, heavy. Hook swallowed down those dark thoughts and entered the dim entrance hall.

Crimson drapes separated the room beyond. The moment he stepped through them, darkness and sharp, woody scent swallowed him. Thick, hot air, worse than the steamy day, buffeted his skin.

"Welcome, welcome," a melodic male voice called.

It took a moment for his eyes to adjust to the darkness. Only a few low candles illuminated the tight room. Shelves overflowing with bottles, jars, papers, and all manner of things boxed them in. Herbs and drapery clung to the walls. It was less space than he remembered, far less than expected from the outside.

The shopkeep struck a match, lighting additional candles on the tall table he stood facing. Tink stepped closer to Hook's side, and he fought the urge to wrap his good arm around her. This shop set his teeth on edge —how much more would it bother a pixie? Smee guarded her other side, and Hook lifted a brow. Every time his first mate scraped his nerves, he did something to soothe them again.

"How can I help you today?" Interest glittered from the man's tanned face, swaths of green and gold makeup painted around his eyes.

"We've come to see the Green Witch."

"Have you now? Perhaps I can assist? We have quite the variety of potions and tonics here for all your needs. You don't look ill. A love charm, perhaps? Something to help the lady choose between you two?"

Tink stiffened at his side. "That's not—"

"Oh, silly me," he rambled on. "You two must be related. Same coloring and all." He waved a dainty hand toward Smee and Tink.

Ridiculous. Anyone could see they weren't related.

"We're not here for any of your..." He bit back the words *worthless swill* and gestured to the room. "We need the witch's insight."

The man's cheerful expression turned hard. Spindly fingers nearly covered by lacy sleeves drummed on the counter. "An exacting customer, I see. But the witch is very particular about whom she meets with."

Hook's fist tightened at his side. This painted boy had no idea who he was dealing with.

The man's eyes coasted over each of them, nose wrinkling with distaste. "I'm not sure the everyday rabble can afford such—"

Hook tossed a pouch onto the counter. It landed with a jingling thump in front of the man, silencing him. His namesake arm slid from under his cloak as he advanced, coming to lean on the counter until the shopkeeper took a step back, swallowing.

Much better.

"Tell her Captain Hook is prepared to pay." He slid a coin from the pouch and sent it rolling back and forth across his knuckles. Light from the candles gleamed off the gold, casting sparkles of light against the stuffed shelves. "She won't find this *everyday rabble* lacking."

"Ah, yes..." The man coughed, shaking himself as he pulled his gaze away from the coin. "Yes, one moment, please."

With a snapping twist, he turned on his heel and disappeared through the heavy drapes behind the counter. Hook's eyes narrowed. So they weren't all walls after all. He'd assumed as much.

He glanced over his shoulder toward his companions. Smee had his arms crossed, a grin on his face. He nodded in acknowledgment. *Yes.* This was going better than he expected. *So far.*

Tink, on the other hand, looked like she might run back out the curtained entrance. Her arms hugged her chest under her cloak. Her gaze darted around the room as her shoulders hunched in. Suddenly, she twisted to her right, a soft gasp echoing into the quiet.

"What—" Hook pushed off the counter, crossing the room to her before he registered what he'd done.

Her blonde head shook. "I felt something. And now I smell—" She clapped a hand over her mouth, capturing a sudden sneeze.

There it was. A hint of bitterness in the air he hadn't noticed before. She turned away and sneezed again. He adjusted his stance and reached for the blade at his hip. What devilry was this?

Something moved behind the shelves. The softest thud whispered from the curtains behind the colorful rows of bottles and jars. He advanced, trying to see beyond the clutter. If someone spied on them—

"Thank you for waiting."

Hook snapped back toward the counter as the shopkeeper returned, his honeyed smile back in place. He adjusted his blue velvet hat as if the drapes had knocked it askew. "She'll see you."

Tension slipped from his shoulders. *About time.*

"Tomorrow," he continued. "Come back at noon."

He froze. Hot fury surged through his veins. "Tomorrow?" he spat. They couldn't afford to spend a day waiting around. "We're here today. Right now." And so was the witch, he had no doubt of that.

The shopkeep lifted the pouch of coins as if it were a dead animal and dropped it on the edge of the counter. "Tomorrow or not at all."

Bloody hell. He stepped to the counter and snatched up the coins before slamming the tip of his hook into the polished wood. "Tomorrow."

A forced smile greeted him, accompanied by another dramatic bob of the man's throat.

The witch's information better be worth it. So help him, if they wasted all this time for nothing... Hook turned on his heel and headed for the door, gesturing for Smee and the still sneezing Tink to do the same.

"Ta-ta," the man called after them.

Blinding sun and thick humidity had never been so welcoming as when they stepped back out onto the too-quiet street.

Tink sneezed again and rubbed at her mouth. "Merrin's teeth, that was awful!"

The hint of a grin twitched on his lips at the odd curse.

"One jar had these things floating in it. Looked like eyeballs..." Smee paled and turned away.

"That bad?" Sage shoved off the wall where she'd reclined against the storefront.

A shiver wracked Tink's slight form. Hook fought against the sudden urge to comfort her. She'd made it abundantly clear on the mermaid's isle, and every day since, how little of him she wanted. But what happened in there, and why'd it only affect her?

Sage stared between them, brows raised in question.

"Cap—"

He cut Smee off with a raised hand. "We have a meeting tomorrow at noon."

She shrugged. "It's a meeting."

Did none of them understand the urgency to be away? The bloody curse could set a storm upon them any day now. And if Captain Blackbeard caught wind of where they'd made port, a storm would be the least of their worries.

"Well, if we're done here, I'm going to Market Street," Smee said.

"Fine," Hook sighed. Not like they could do anything more today. Plus, he needed to look into that rumored royal outpost, see what he could discover. Perhaps he'd even see about pocketing a few interesting papers, if there were any to be had.

"Actually, I'd like to go to the market. Maybe buy some new clothes… that fit." Tink gestured to herself and the too-big shirt that she still wore. His shirt. A knot tightened in his stomach. With that cloak wrapped around her, he could almost forget.

"And since you kidnapped me, half-naked no less, I think you owe me coin to pay for some." She held out her hand like a child asking for a treat.

Damn if that doe-eyed look didn't make him want to give it to her. "You stole from—"

"From you first, yeah, yeah, but you still kidnapped me."

A passerby gave them a look but kept going. Wise on their part. "You're not a kid."

She groaned. "Adult-napped? Whatever."

"Fine." He fished out a small bag of coins and passed it to her.

The blinding grin she gave him in return—had he ever seen such a genuine one?—was worth it.

"Shall we?" She turned to Smee.

He grinned, offering his arm like some kind of gentleman, and led her away down the cobblestones.

The back of Hook's neck burned. Of course she'd prefer his first mate's company. Didn't every woman? Gods, how he loved and hated that man.

"Careful, you'll turn green with envy." Sage smirked at him, one hand on her hip.

"It's not…we're not."

She rolled her eyes and slapped him across the back—hard. "You've always been a poor liar. She's nice, though. Maybe be kind to her?"

"I am—"

Bright laughter cut off his words. "Sure, sure." She shook her head. "Half-naked, huh? You left out that little detail. Must have been a nice sight."

"Don't start." Bloody hell if another one of his crew tried to take her from him.

Sage smirked again and raised her brows. "See. I joke and you get that look like you're going to cast me off into the depths."

"She stole from us, got us cursed and into this mess. I can't want her. I should hate such a thieving little—" He snapped off his words before he could spill her identity to the streets. Last thing he needed was for her to cause more trouble.

"Well, for the record, I think she feels the same way about you." She winked and knocked her hip against his before sauntering off down the street. Hook was left to gape after her, unable to muster an argument or even a quip in response.

16

*W*ith gold in her pocket and the freedom to walk around town, Tink's wings twitched with the urge to fly. She'd be able to today, and well, even her footsteps were lighter. Whatever that bitter scent had been in the witch's shop that sent her sneezing, it'd passed without any ill effects as soon as they stepped outside. *Thank Holy Flora for that.*

"Come, look and see these pieces crafted with love and care, sure to brighten any lady's day," Smee called in his best salesman's voice.

Tink smiled at the passing customers and held out her hand, decked out in bracelets and rings Smee's sisters had made from carved shells and asked them to sell in town. Okay, so she wasn't totally free, but she didn't mind helping out—for a while. Not to mention that with the strapping sailor nearby, no wise person would bother her. Plus, it gave her time to get accustomed to this...city.

Many a sailor had clamored about the beauties of Rochland, but the homes and storefronts craning their façades over the cobblestones rankled against her very nature. The constructs of stone and wood were painted garishly bright colors and crammed one on top of another, with tiny alleys between their neat and orderly squares. Rare window boxes provided the only breath of nature, and even the flowers in those were often wilted and pitiful. Pixies were one with nature, and their homes were no different—built in and around great trees, taking advantage of what the forest had to offer. The treehouse she'd acquired had been a perfect example. The closest to home she could find. Here, humans had scrapped the land clean, destroying the beauty and wonder of the island in favor of their horrendous craftsmanship.

Her stomach turned over, and it was a battle to keep her grin in place. At least the cove had been better, its homes at one with the life around them—mostly. Still, they were nothing like her home in the Sylvanna Vale. Her mind whirled with possibilities as she stood in the sun, wings bound. Ideas for improving the homes in the cove presented themselves one after another.

But she wouldn't be with these pirates long enough to craft the designs, even if they wanted her tinkering. Her smile faltered for the briefest moment. Perhaps she could leave designs for them to put to use after she'd gone.

A gaggle of well-dressed ladies rushed toward her and Smee, chatting with one another and waving lace fans. Their dresses sported as many colors as the nearby shops. No doubt the grinning Smee blowing them kisses caught their attention as much as the jewelry. Tink forced her smile wider as she showed off the last of the goods—well, for a minute, until Smee instructed her to let the women try them on themselves.

"You made these yourself?" The dark-haired woman, clearly the leader of the pack, admired the new rings on her hand.

"No, my sisters did. But I like to help them out, you know." Smee winked.

"You have such talent," the woman exclaimed, turning to Tink. Smee was about to speak when she said, "I'll take the lot of these."

"Ah...all of them? Yes, oh, that's perfect, and they fit you so well." He took payment from the woman and kissed the back of her hand.

"If your sister doesn't mind, perhaps you can escort me home? I'd love to commission a piece to match a dress..." She trailed off, glancing down the street with a wry grin.

"I...as my lady wishes." Smee didn't spare so much as a backward glance at Tink, who waved and promised to see him at home.

Ridiculous flirt. A solid gold piece said there was no commission waiting for him, but a different sort of special request, one he'd happily oblige. Either way, at least she was free of him and her obligation to his sisters.

Now to backtrack to the tailor she'd spotted a few blocks ago.

Or...make a run for it. This was her chance, probably her only one. The coin Hook had given her was enough to buy passage. She could hop on a ship and go... A humorless laugh rose up in her chest. Where exactly? On to the Shrouded Isles to hunt for a hidden treasure in a place known to swallow people up without so much as a footprint left behind? She'd inquired about passage there after her visit to the merfolk. Only took twice to know that no sane sailor would take her near there without a whole sack of gold for payment. Where else could she go? Back to Tortuga and the kids who'd taken over her home? They'd probably wrecked it by now. *Little scamps.*

Tink stumbled as someone knocked into her.

"Sorry, miss!" the boy called, waving behind him as he rushed down the street.

She felt frantically at her pockets, then sighed. Not a pickpocket. Just a clumsy little... That red hair. His voice. Tink took off after the boy. What was the brat's name? Peter? His skinny form wove between bodies on the street, then turned left. When she rounded the corner herself, he was nowhere to be found—lost in the mess of horse carts, merchant stalls, and noisy humans.

It couldn't have been him, though, could it? She squinted at the people nearby. He looked so similar, and just for a brief moment she was sure, impossible as it was. It wasn't far to Tortuga. But what would an orphan boy be doing hopping from port to port, especially since he'd robbed her of a perfectly nice home?

Robbed her with Hook's help. She frowned. That man drove her mad. As often as she thought of their kisses—and Durin's beard, that was often —she couldn't forget that he'd adult-napped her too. Though now that he was helping her get the scale of Leviathan, albeit for his own purposes, his past transgressions didn't sting so badly. Whatever token he wore didn't belong to someone here, or it didn't seem so. Would it be so wrong to indulge in whatever pleasure he had to offer?

"Excuse me, miss?"

Tink gasped and whirled around at the voice just over her shoulder. She'd been so lost in thought she hadn't heard anyone approach. Curiosity twinkled in eyes painted with green and gold over their lids. Breath caught in her throat.

The witch's shopkeep.

"You..." He wore a hood pulled tight over his head and clothes. Hiding his appearance, but from whom?

"Executus," he accentuated his name, as if he were a great king reigning over all the people of Rochland. "The witch would meet with you, Miss..." He canted his head.

"Tink will do," she replied.

"Tink." He tasted her name and pursed his lips in distaste. "Well, Miss Tink, the witch will meet with you. Now, if you please."

Now? Her nose wrinkled. Something didn't smell right. "I'll have to find the others. It may take some time."

A soft shake of his head accompanied a small smile. "Only you."

Meet the witch on her own? She swallowed. Okay, yes, she knew vaguely what Hook planned to ask, how to find the scale of Leviathan or its exact location in the Shrouded Isles. Supposedly, the witch could discern such things with whatever twisted power she possessed. But was there a trick to it? Something else he hadn't told her? "I'm not sure I can afford it," she hedged. Hook had given her some gold, but not near what he'd offered the witch.

"This meeting is free. If you come now. Alone." He tipped his open palms up. "Her request, not mine."

Tink glanced up and down the street, hoping, praying to spot a member of the crew, but none were to be found. Her bound wings twitched as a shiver slid down her spine. *Blast it all.*

"Fine, take me to her."

Not even the slightest grin or hint of surprise touched his face as he replied, "Very good. This way."

The short blocks to the witch's shop passed by in no time at all. She could have sworn the market was farther away, but no matter how deliberately slow her steps, Executus never left her side, nor did she spot any familiar faces along the way. By all the revered elders, she must be desperate, hoping to see Hook's face. So many days she'd longed to leave him in the past, but right now, he was all she wanted.

The shop was dark and cramped as before, though not so hot, and the horrid, bitter smell that caused her sneezing was blessedly absent—or masked by one of the myriad pungent scents that suffocated the room. Some were familiar: vinegar, sage, dried spore root. Others…not so much.

"This way, don't keep her waiting," Executus said, a splash of annoyance coloring his words, as he led her through the heavy curtains behind the counter and up a set of creaking, musty stairs. Dark-paneled walls closed in around her like a coffin as she ascended to the second floor. Why, oh why, did humans prefer such cloistered homes? Everything in this place was dead, wrong. Even the bundles of herbs hanging from the ceiling in the main shop were dried and crumbling.

All that changed when Executus pushed back another set of heavy, crimson curtains. Plant life filled the room, climbing along the walls, pressing up against the ceiling, overflowing clay pots, and spilling off tabletops barely visible beneath the mass of greens and browns, some spotted with colorful flowers or with leaves tinted unusual shades like violet or pale blue. Tink's body hummed with the thrum of life echoing here, so different than the rest of the place. For a moment, she could delude herself that she'd stepped back into a glen in the Sylvanna Vale. Even a few birds called out in squawks and chirps where they perched among the tropical indoor forest.

A room so full of life, yet the sun didn't touch it. Only well-placed oil lamps lit the shadowed greenery. *How in the name of—*

"Thank you, Executus."

Tink yelped, jumping back and nearly bumping into the shopkeep as she struggled to place the voice. Her heart thundered in her chest when she caught sight of a short woman standing among the plants. Silky locks, dark as midnight and steaked with silver like rare falling stars, flowed down her body, nearly concealing a dress of dark green. But it wasn't the sight of her—how had she missed her before?—that caused a reply to catch in her throat. A brown snake, longer than the woman was tall, twined around her arms and over her shoulders.

"Have a seat, my dear." She gestured to a simple wooden chair facing the table in front of her. "That'll be all." With a wave, she dismissed Executus. Only a light flutter of fabric signaled his departure.

Everything in her rebelled against taking that seat. *Nope. No.* This was a huge mistake. That snake would eat her alive inch by precious inch, and no one would ever find her. Hook would assume she'd run away to retrieve the scale on her own despite their promise to the queen. He'd follow, determined to break his curse, only to run aground in the Shrouded Isles, Captain Blackbeard's cannons hammering the hull, and—

Tink shook herself. Why was she worried about him? Shouldn't she worry about herself? Her parents, who likely mourned her as dead? Lily, who would never know what happened to her missing cousin and how much she cared?

"You're an interesting one." The voice wrapped around her, echoing through her mind.

She twisted toward its source.

The witch grinned at her as she stroked the snake's head with motherly affection. "Take a seat. Or aren't you curious why I asked you here?"

"Why did you?"

"It's not often I find another of my own kind."

Tink gaped. "You're a—" Her mouth opened and closed, the word lost.

"A pixie. Yes." She rolled her shoulders, and dull wings previously hidden fluttered behind her. They were sad, dim things, like dusty spiderwebs. "I know," she said with a frown. "Not what they once were. But you...I'd wager yours are still quite bright."

"How do you know that?" She crept to the chair, lured by the witch's knowledge.

"Time teaches many things." The witch took a seat on her side of the table—too close, with the snake flicking his tongue in the air between them. "Sit."

Tink swallowed and sat, her palms clutching the wood for dear life. "The sneezing fit."

The witch grinned. "Very good. Yes, the dried draka kelp confirmed my suspicions after I saw you enter the shop with, well, I wouldn't say your friends. No, my dear, you seemed rather uncomfortable, am I right?"

That was the shop's fault. *Mostly. Maybe.* "Why did you ask me here?"

The witch sighed, a slight pout to her lips. She was a beauty, one who carried her curves with style and elegance. Not even the tell-tale marks of age that touched her skin and hair could diminish that. "So eager to leave. I thought it might be nice to have some company. Why linger with pirates?"

"I..." Tink lifted her arm, letting the broken bracelet slide down to her hand. "If I help them, there may be a way for me to get home."

"The elders are still close-minded, I see." She rubbed her wrist, right over where her own bracelet may once have been. "I could use the help of a fellow pixie. My wings grow weak, and I won't be able to make pixie dust much longer. It's essential for my spells, you see. But you, with the touch of the Sylvanna Vale still upon you, could help me with that. Surely the rumored Tinker Bell would sell her dust to a fellow pixie."

Tink's brows drew together. Dust for magic. How? A touch of home— "Wait, how do you know my name?" She'd given Executus her name, but only Tink, not her full name.

The witch laughed, a scratchy, high sound. "You've earned quite the reputation recently, selling dust. So rebellious, industrious, and yet you want to go back to the vale?"

The chair might as well have fallen out from under her. She had a reputation? How? Sure, she'd sold dust, but almost all of that was to Captain Blackbeard to free Lily. The rest she'd sold in little batches, mainly to innkeepers for coin to stay afloat and buy passage to see Titania. It shouldn't have been enough to earn a reputation. Unless the innkeepers were looser with their words than she thought. *Ridiculous humans. Couldn't trust any of them.*

Even so... "I'm sorry. I can't sell you any. I'm out of dust."

The witch's head tilted, her nose wrinkling in an all too familiar motion. "Poor girl, they taught you nothing before they sent you out into this world, did they?"

Fire raced along her cheeks and up to the tips of her ears. They had told her little—far, far too little. She stirred in the seat.

"You can make more dust, my dear. Honestly, I'm surprised you haven't." She leaned over the table, her snake flicking its tongue at Tink, way too close for comfort. "Especially with those two delicious men you were with, even though they are pirates... Or maybe you prefer women?"

"I..." Beryl's wings, she needed out of there. Fast.

The witch fell back in the chair laughing. "Oh, my girl. All you need are happy thoughts, pleasure, enjoyment. Let the world fade away and enjoy yourself."

Enjoy herself. Right. Like anyone could do that trapped far from home, trying to make it on their own with nothing, then getting abducted by a pirate. She had *so* much to be happy about.

"Once your wings start to glow, the dust is sure to follow."

Your wings are glowing, love. Tink sat up straight in the chair as Hook's words echoed through her mind.

She had glowed. For him. More than once.

"Ah, I see you have some experience in the matter."

"But I didn't..." Tink's wings strained against their bindings. "I still have no dust."

"How long did the glow last?"

"A moment? Not long."

"Not long enough for the dust to form."

She could make pixie dust. No wonder the elders didn't tell them. If a pixie enjoyed the pleasures of the human world, they could make plenty of dust, use it for themselves, sell it. What havoc that could wreak if humans had more access to dust. A sudden chill stripped the heat from her body. What if the rules weren't to protect them from humans, but humans from pixies?

The witch's serpentine smile answered that question better than anyone could. "Opens up a world of possibilities, doesn't it?" The snake slithered up her arm. "I could train you. Teach you things the elders would never believe possible. Why go back to that sheltered life when you could have the world at your fingertips?"

"I'll...I'll think on it." It was a certainty, though maybe not in the way the witch hoped.

"Do." She rose. "Executus!"

The shrill call set Tink's teeth on edge.

Time passed slower than molasses before the shopkeep slipped through the curtains and bowed at the waist.

"See our guest out," the witch ordered. "And dear, I do hope to see you tomorrow. Try to enjoy *all* that Rochland has to offer." The meaning behind her words was clear. She wanted her dust, immediately.

Tink forced a fake smile to her lips. That was easier said than done. If she could make any dust, it wouldn't be for the witch.

17

*H*alf a bloody day spent lurking near the royal outpost, and he'd yet to find a good way in. The building itself was easy enough to find—all he had to do was follow the Green Coats. But they'd gotten smarter. There were fewer windows and guards posted outside the doors. He'd learned more sipping ale in a nearby pub than watching the building. The guards liked to drink after their shift. Though today, all they'd blabbered on about was their newest romantic conquests—or lack thereof. He'd have to try another tactic tomorrow. The streets had already thinned, and being out alone at night would attract too much notice.

Hook sighed as he pushed open the main door to the inn where they'd stay the night, the Gilded Pearl. The common room bustled with life. The scent of fatty roasted meats wafted over him, setting his mouth to watering. One advantage of land was the varied food, and the cook here was known for it. Even Hook could only handle so much fish stew and half-stale bread.

"Aye! There he is!" Sage's familiar voice pulled his attention. She waved.

Half-empty tankards of ale littered the table. He grinned. No surprise there. At least they were all well. Though Smee had lost his shirt. Francis stripped off one boot and thumped it on the table.

"Not there, you dimwit!" Sage swatted it onto the floor and scooped dice off the table.

Ah, strip dice.

He hadn't played it in months. He slid his arm further under his cloak. And he wouldn't be playing tonight. Though watching, aye, that could be a pleasure if they rounded up a few more players to—

He froze half-way to the table. He hadn't seen her, her slight form blocked from view by Smee. The blonde braid was unmistakable, but the look on her face—pink cheeks, slightly glassy eyes—that was the look of his nightmares.

And, if he were honest, his dreams.

Tink looked just like she had the night they met, except she still wore his shirt. *Bloody hell.* He ran his hand down his face.

Hook slid into an empty chair and leaned over the table. "What are you fools doing?"

"Dice." Smee replied at length, barely audible over the racket behind him. Tipsy faces blinked at him, even Tink.

Thank all the gods it wasn't only his crew occupying the large room. Plenty of others crowded at tables and near the bar, making just as much racket. The game alone wouldn't draw much attention. It was one of the reasons he liked the Gilded Pearl. People didn't ask questions—it was the inn's one unspoken rule. But if Tink rolled poorly and someone saw her wings, that rumor would never stay quiet. They'd be running for the forest before dawn. Not to mention they'd need to avoid port, maybe even the cove, until the rumors calmed.

"And you let our *guest* play?" He didn't bother to keep the edge out of his voice.

"She wanted to," Smee said with a shrug.

"I'm right here," Tink snapped.

"And you should know better."

Tink shrugged. "I'm winning. Are you joining us or not?"

Everyone looked at him. *Terrible, bloody idea.* "You know I'm not." Even here, flashing his hook about was too much of a risk.

Davies dumped the two die onto the table, and their game resumed as if Hook didn't exist. He rolled a five, letting him pick someone to lose a piece of clothing. If Davies picked Tink... His hook dug into the table.

"Smee."

"Me again?" But his first mate's grin showed he wasn't annoyed. Far from it. Smee had half undone his belt before Davies named him.

Another roll and Sage gained a piece of clothing.

Tink took the dice and shook them in the wooden cup before spilling them onto the table.

A three. If she dropped that cloak...

"What was that about winning?" Sage cackled.

Tink stuck out her tongue and stood, swaying in the process. She thumped one booted foot on the chair, unlacing it to the whoops and hollers of the table and a few other patrons nearby. Hook couldn't pull his gaze away, couldn't see anything but Tink fumbling with the laces before sliding one tall boot off her foot, then the other. She stumbled into Smee as the second one pulled free. Not for the first time that day, he loathed his first mate. It should have been him she relied on to steady herself. Her hands sprawled across Smee's bare chest.

"Woah there." Sage gave a pointed look at the table. He'd gouged a deep groove with his hook.

He needed more ale for this. The ones from earlier weren't doing their job. He was too tense. Too...everything.

"Sure ya don't wanna roll?" The dice made their way to him.

He waved them off and aimed for the bar on the opposite side of the room. Women stared at him unabashedly as he waited for his drink, coy smiles shot his way, winks, unspoken promises. Gods he'd loved it once, having his pick, luring them in like fish to bait. And he always hooked his prey. But every damn woman looked the same to him now. He saw only one face no matter who he looked at.

Titania said it wasn't a curse. She couldn't lie, but she had to be wrong.

Ale had never tasted so good as he tipped back the mug, gulping half of it in one swig.

A brunette slid up next to him. "Hey there, stranger."

Hook flinched back as she reached for him. *Bloody hell, what is wrong with me?* Those warm, brown eyes and that painted smile should have any man on his knees.

From the corner of his eye, he caught a flash of blonde. Tink stood, fumbling with her cloak. What had she rolled this time?

"Hey!" the woman called as he fled, drink forgotten.

Hook slammed his hands on the table, causing his crew to jump and look his way. Tink's hands slipped from the knot she pulled at—but it wasn't her cloak. She'd undone the ties on her tight breeches, revealing a glimpse of pale skin. And that look on her face...lips pink and parted, a deep blush coloring her cheeks, tendrils of hair fallen free from her braid to brush the sides of her face.

With effort, he pulled his gaze to the table. Snake eyes. She'd rolled snake eyes. The odds were—*fuck the odds.* She couldn't strip everything off, especially not here.

"Stop," he said, his voice hoarse. "Stop right now."

"Sorry, Captain," she slurred, while tugging at the waistband of her breeches. "Rules are—"

Tink screeched as he hefted her off the ground and tossed her over his shoulder. The whole bloody room turned to stare at them. *Great. Just bloody great.* He hadn't given two seconds thought to anything before he rounded the table and scooped her up in one swift move.

Fists smacked against his back as he adjusted her weight. The blows were mild at best. Either she didn't want to hurt him or she was too drunk for anything more. The prior—hopefully.

"Put. Me. Down!"

Davies fell onto the table in his efforts to avoid Tink's flailing legs. Others jumped up, knocking over chairs and spilling ale all over the damn place. *What a fucking mess.*

"Grab her boots," he ordered to no one in particular.

Sage jumped to comply, still sober enough to follow orders.

"I swear if you don't—" Tink slammed a fist into his lower back.

Hook groaned. *Okay, that one hurt.* He grimaced, nearly snarling at people as they jumped out of his way, forming a narrow path toward the set of stairs he aimed for. More than one glanced to his hand, or lack thereof. *Fuck, fuck, fuck.*

"Lovers' spat. Give them space," Sage called.

"Lovers!" Tink shrieked but blessedly went still.

"Aye, love, you've had a bit too much." Way too much.

"Don't call me—ugh," she groaned as Hook took the steps two at a time. "So spiny."

"You're at the end of the hall. The rest of us are sharin' bunk rooms on the right." Sage slid around him, keys in one hand, Tink's boots in the other. "Do you want her—"

Fuck yes, I want her. "My room."

Sage bit back a grin but stayed silent.

The room was small—private, but small. And the bed...narrow, shoved against a wall, made for one. When the bloody hell was he going to get his bed back? He should have kicked Tink out of his room on the *Jolly Roger*, let her grab a spare cot with one of the crew. But he couldn't bring himself to. He didn't want to. And damn if he didn't want her here now.

Hook settled the too-quiet Tink on the bed.

Sage dropped Tink's boots on the floor with a dramatic thump. She jangled his key in the air until she had his attention, then tossed it to him with surprisingly good aim. "Anything else, Captain?"

"Dismissed."

She canted her head to the side. "Downstairs?"

He'd caused quite a scene, maybe worse than if Tink had exposed her bound wings—or her whole stunning self. "Drinks for the house." He tossed her a sack with the last of the coin not set aside for the witch. It'd keep the crowd happy if nothing else. It was a sailor's code to keep quiet when offered free ale, and it was sailors who favored this inn. His people. Maybe they'd keep their mouths shut for a few more hours at least.

"Aye, aye..." Looking from him to Tink, she wiggled her brows. "Captain."

18

*N*o sooner had Sage slammed the door behind her than Tink groaned, "Why is the floor moving?"

"You're drunk."

She frowned at him. "No shit."

"What were you thinking?" The anger he'd tamped down rose back to the surface. "Playing that game? Almost exposing yourself?"

Tink pulled the cloak from about her shoulders and stood wobbling. "I can expose myself to whomever, wherever I like! I was almost there. Almost..." Her hands fisted.

"Almost where?" To exposing them to rumors that would spread through half the city before dawn?

"It doesn't matter." She half-poured, half-spilled a cup of water from the pitcher on the nightstand. The darn thing wobbled almost as much as her.

She gulped the water and fumbled the cup back onto the small table. When she turned, she gasped, staring up at Hook with that face he saw in his dreams, his nightmares.

"It matters. You could endanger my crew. My—our—mission." He backed her to the wall, his arms caging her in on either side. This close, he could just smell the hint of ale on her breath. And flowers...something exotic that wasn't from the bar downstairs. The scent was entirely her. "Almost where? Tell me."

Her lips pursed. "To forgetting, okay?" She shoved ineffectually at his chest, but bloody hell, he loved it when she tried. "I wanted…" One hand fisted in his shirt, the other ran down his chest. His muscles tightened in response. Heat simmered under his skin. A pink tongue flicked out over her lips, and he almost forgot what she'd said.

"What do you want?" He leaned closer, his forehead nearly touching hers.

She stared at him. His gaze caught hers, savoring the desire simmering there, the sheen of lust looming just beyond the ale-induced blur. Would she taste like the drink he'd chugged or the sweet, floral honey he tasted the first time he'd claimed her lips?

"You."

Her lips pressed against his—tentatively, questioning. Breath caught in his throat. Time stopped. And then everything rushed back like the crash of waves on the shore. Soft lips crushed further against his, demanding a kiss in return. Lithe arms slid up his chest to wind around his neck.

He met her kiss, eager as a boy. *Honey. Fuck. Such sweet, delicious honey.* Hook groaned against her mouth. His good hand cupped her soft backside, lifting her into the air as her legs wound around him. Together they crashed against the wall. Tink jerked her head away with a yelp.

Wings. Damn. So delicate. The words slid away as she shot him a vicious grin and resumed their kiss. Hook stumbled back, the woman of his dreams clinging to him. His leg slammed into something. It didn't matter. Not with her lips on his, her taste in his mouth.

Bed. They needed—it didn't matter. Those legs wrapped around him, her hair tickling his face, her moans soft against him. Her tongue swept in his mouth, and the world spun. How he'd dreamed of this since the hot spring, to feel her, to taste her, to have her crave him again. He bumped something soft and tumbled backward, taking Tink with him.

She squealed as they fell. Breath fled his chest. Their heads bumped together.

"Ow." Tink slid back, grinding against his hard, needy cock. Bloody hell, why were their clothes still on?

As if she read his mind, Tink pulled the shirt over her head, tossing it away. Her breeches were already unlaced from earlier, exposing the beginnings of her underthings.

"In a hurry, love?" His voice was thick, hoarse. Gods, he loved the way she scowled when he called her that. It was one reason he kept using it.

She started to unwrap her wings and breasts. What a delight that would be, on both fronts. "Need some help?" He reached for the fabric with his hook, yearning to rip it asunder.

She swatted his hook away with a huff and set about her task. It took everything he had to sit still and watch, especially when she kept wiggling on top of him. Each move had his cock straining against his breeches. He ached to sink inside her, to feel her wet warmth wrapped around him.

He toyed with the edge of her breeches, rubbing his thumb along the soft material of her undergarments, savoring each slide of his fingers near the treasure below.

A soft sigh slipped from her kiss-swollen lips as the last of the fabric fell free. Her eyes closed, and shoulders drooped in simple ecstasy. Bloody hell, how would she look with a taste of real pleasure? Her breasts were larger than he expected, a perfect handful. *Aye, ripe for savoring.* And savor he would. The back of his good hand trailed up her stomach. She shivered, her gaze never leaving his as he palmed one soft globe in his coarse hand. *Divine.*

Her glassy eyes hooded. "Like what you've found?" Gossamer wings fluttered behind her, catching the light of the room. No, a light all their own. She glowed again.

"You're glowing again, love."

A sleepy grin spread across her lips. "Good."

"For me?"

Tink took his hand in hers, pulling it away.

Doubt settled hard in his chest. He shouldn't have mentioned the wings. Always he did that, and she pulled away.

But she didn't leave, didn't flee. Instead, she practically fell atop him, her breasts slamming into his chest as her mouth searched for his again. Their fingers twined against the sheets as he kissed her with all he had.

Hook followed as she pulled back, but she pushed him onto the sheets as she slid to his side on the bed. "I wa-want yous. You. I—" She tugged ineffectually at her breeches.

"Yous?" *Shit.* He'd forgotten how drunk she was. Did she even realize who she seduced?

The glow of her wings dimmed. "Please, Captain, I..."

Okay, she did, maybe. But her words splashed him in the face with cold reality. He couldn't fuck her, not tonight. His cock begged, strained. By all the seas and shores, he wanted her. But he had some shred of decency left, whatever the rumors about him said.

She started to remove her breeches, nearly tumbling onto the floor. He couldn't let her struggle like that.

"Hold still, love." Hook knelt. Slowly, he inched her breeches down, revealing a dark swath of fabric barely covering her treasure and pale legs that longed for the sun's kiss. His would have to do.

The moans that filled the room drove him on as he trailed kisses from the tips of her toes to the apex of her thighs. Her fingers wove through his hair, tugging, demanding, and almost painful. The sweetest pain. He'd kiss her delicate skin all day to have her crave him so for only a minute.

"Please."

Hook pulled away, striping down with vigor to only his breeches. Even those he unlaced, giving himself precious space. His cock fought a war with his brain as he worked, nearly winning, especially as Tink spread her legs on the bed, stroking herself through her underthings. He scrubbed his hand down his face. Gods she was wet. He could see it. Of all the times for him to commit to decency... No woman had ever tempted him half so much.

"Join me?" One delicate finger curled and uncurled, beckoning him over.

He intended to.

Hook slid into the bed, teasing and turning her until her back pressed against his chest. Delicate wings tickled his skin as they folded between them. The glow had brightened again, their light outshining the candles in the room. The whiff of floral scent from earlier wrapped around them, drowning out the ale and the musty odor of the room. It came from Tink —her body's own perfume.

Each stroke of his hand along the planes of her stomach tested his resolve. Each wiggle of her shapely ass against his cock blurred his mind. And each second that passed he risked claiming her. A lesser man might. But he couldn't be that man, not with her.

His hand slid down her underthings, venturing through her damp forest to her slick slit below.

"Yes, yes, please," she moaned.

Not touch her? Not have her? What was he thinking? Dipping his fingers in her inviting warmth nearly had him coming in his breeches like a boy. He'd never wanted a woman this much. Not even as a boy, when they were all tempting sirens.

Two stokes along her swollen clit, and she whimpered in his arms.

He wanted. Craved. Needed.

Couldn't.

He groaned low in his throat. "I can't fuck you."

Tink went completely still in his arms. Her legs clamped around his hand. The glow of her wings dimmed instantly.

"Why?" The crack of her voice stabbed him in the chest. "It's because I'm…I'm broken. I—"

"No." The ache in her voice slew him. He pulled her closer, careful of his hook and her wings. "You're perfect. But I won't be a drunken regret." It was the very last thing he would be.

"James," she whimpered.

He sucked in a breath. This woman knew how to work him. Using his name, one he almost forgot he'd given her. Hook rubbed his face in her hair, savoring her scent and the way it tickled his skin. "When I fuck you, and I plan to, I want you sober, eager." He stroked her again, slowly, deliberately. "When my cock slides into you—" He flicked his fingers against her clit. "—it'll be because you want it there, because you asked for it, and not because some drink made you think you wanted it."

"I do want it. So much I…" A moan cut off her words.

"Then you'll want me tomorrow." One rub of his fingers. "And the next day." Another. "And the next." And another. "Because one night with you will never be enough." Damn it, it was true, and he hadn't even admitted it to himself. Oh he was cursed all right, whether by magical means or not, he wanted this woman like no other, and no drunken fling would satisfy.

"Now. I want—" She ground against his hand.

He nibbled the edge of her earlobe before whispering, "You want to come?"

"Y-yesss."

With the last bit of his calm, he used his hook to tug down his undershorts, freeing his cock. Her wet core pressed against his fingers as he teased her folds. His pace quickened. Hook ground himself against her wiggling backside, savoring the slide of moist cotton against him. It wasn't the destination he longed for, but bloody hell, it would do.

Tink cried out, clamping down around his hand. He thrust against her eager warmth, wringing out her pleasure as she arched against him. Her wings fluttered, teasing his cock and showering the room in sparkling light. A moan tore from his lips as he came, jerking toward her soft and willing flesh. He palmed her wet mound, pulling her tight to him while they embraced the last of their ecstasy.

As the world solidified around him, he could swear he saw something drifting in the air. Dust, but more than the room held before. Something to do with her scent? He may as well lay with her in a field of flowers rather than the narrow bed.

"James..." His name was a raspy whisper on her lips as she twisted her head around to see him.

"Sleep, love." He kissed her cheek, finally relinquishing his prize to grab the nearby pitcher and a cloth to wipe them clean.

The glow of her wings dimmed as she heaved a contented sigh and settled into the bed.

He wouldn't sleep a wink with her near-naked body pressed against his. All the same, he wouldn't leave her. Not now. Maybe not ever.

19

The room spun. Something drummed a soft but steady beat at Tink's temple and refused to let up no matter how hard she squeezed the pillow over her head and willed it away.

"Ugh! Stop!" She flung the pillow, sitting up in bed.

Mistake. Still spinning. She pinched the bridge of her nose and scooted to the side table, grabbing at the cup of water there.

Blessed, sweet water. It had never tasted so good, nothing ever had.

Strong floral scents filled the room. If she closed her eyes she was almost at home, sitting in a glade in the vale, dust on her wings. *Dust!* Her wings twitched. She'd made dust! The witch hadn't lied. She could do it. She leaped to her feet, stretching, relishing the looseness of her body.

And froze.

Durin's beard! She was almost completely naked and—

"Oh shit."

Heat raced across her cheeks and up to the tips of her ears. She grabbed at the sheets, covering herself and searching the small room for Hook, but he wasn't there.

He'd...they'd...oh holy revered elders, they'd almost...

When I fuck you, and I plan to, I want you sober, eager.

Her thighs clamped together, but she couldn't escape the delicious feeling of him there. The stroke of his thumb across her clit, the thrust of his fingers... She flopped back onto the bed, ignoring her pounding headache in favor of more delightful reminders of the night before.

Hesitantly, her fingers wandered below her underthings, sliding through the moisture there. She bit her lip...hard. Hook could return at any moment. Would he still want her?

Holy Flora, she wanted him. She'd wanted to forget, to escape. Dice, it had started with dice. And too much ale. Had he carried her up here? A deep breath filled her lungs. He *had*. Then that kiss. And oh— She covered her face with her hands. She'd begged. *Oh no. Oh no, no, no.* She'd practically begged a filthy, no-good pirate to fuck her.

And he hadn't. The thought loosened the anxiety twisting in her chest.

If she were honest with herself, he wasn't filthy, and perhaps not even no-good, not with all she'd seen, all he'd done. Or not done, in their case. How poorly she'd misjudged him, all of them.

Titania forced them to ally with one another, but it wasn't because of the mermaid queen that she wanted to help them now. She owed them for the curse she'd placed on them. And their captain...

Even if it were only for a few days, only until they retrieved the scale of Leviathan and removed their curse, she wanted to be with him no matter whose ring he still wore. Today, tomorrow, the next. She'd been with him as long as she could.

He had to know it wasn't just strong ale fueling her desire.

Tink cleaned herself up and dressed in a hurry. A few benign motes of dust glittered from the sheets, the table, even the floor, but those weren't the good stuff, just a byproduct of its creation. The real pixie dust still clung to her wings, as it would until she chose to shed it. What was left in the room wouldn't be useful to her or anyone else, so she let it lie. Most humans would never know it from normal dust anyway, and there was plenty of that around too.

She flung open the door, only for it to crash into something on the floor that groaned. Not something—someone. She slid out the open crack to find Smee sitting on the floor outside the room, rubbing his head.

"I'm up...I'm up."

"What *are* you doing?" She braced her hands on her hips.

"Just took a little nap is all."

"Outside my door?"

He rolled his neck before pushing to his feet. "Outside the captain's door."

The tips of her ears burned.

"He asked me to make sure you weren't disturbed."

That was kind of him, and Smee. Sleeping against the door couldn't be comfortable. "Thank you."

"Always happy to help." A sheepish grin spread across his face.

He was, that much was obvious, loyal to a fault too. Hook couldn't have picked a better first mate. Tink smiled. "Do you know where the captain went? When he'll be back?"

"Didn't say."

A sigh caught in her chest. *Of course not.*

"I think…I'll go look for him."

He stretched his arms above his head. "Bed calling me back. So soft." He stifled a yawn. "We're to meet here before noon."

She nodded. "I'll be here." Hopefully sooner than that.

The hopes she held of finding Hook in the downstairs common room were dashed. It would have been so easy to drag him back upstairs and spill her heart. She was ready, prepared. But nothing was ever that easy, not for her.

The streets were busy that morning. A storm was coming, she overheard someone say. The sky was still clear, but far on the horizon dark clouds gathered. Tink wrinkled her nose as she caught sight of them. Hook wanted to get back to the ship as soon as possible, but being stuck here with him a few more days wouldn't be all bad.

Quick shopping in the market yielded new clothes, which she stored away in the backpack she carried. Finally, she'd have a shirt that fit, though she'd grown fond of Hook's. At least that was one chore done. She'd gotten so thoroughly distracted by her meeting with the witch yesterday that new clothes had been the very last thing on her mind.

The trill of a pipe drew her attention as she wandered back toward the inn. People clapped along to the lively tune, a small crowd forming in the cobblestone square. The musician was good, and she'd know. Pixies loved music almost as much as nature. They all had an instrument they favored, usually several.

Applause rose as the song finished. A few well-clad citizens cheered in appreciation. Tink caught a flash of red hair as she wove through the gathered people, aiming for a better look. She squeezed between two large men—Gamoreans by their uniforms—coming to the front of the circle of onlookers. A boy, standing on a box, raised a wooden pan flute to his lips and began a new tune.

Tink sucked in a breath. The tune was familiar, one she'd often played in the Crow's Roost back on Tortuga, but it was the boy who made her eyes widen. She hadn't been seeing things yesterday. Peter, the boy who stole her treehouse and handed her over to Hook, stood before her.

How in the scared plains did he get here? *Why* was he here?

She scanned the crowd for the rest of his gang. It'd be just like them to distract these people with a song while the little ones picked pockets. Though if they did, the kids did a great job of keeping out of sight. The only child in the crowd was a little girl with ribbons in her hair who stared at Peter in a gleeful trance.

If he'd torched her treehouse... Her foot tapped on the ground, completely out of rhythm with the song. Not that she'd need the treehouse anymore if their quest was successful. She could finally go home. *And leave the captain behind?* A traitorous voice whispered in her head. She swallowed. Well, there was time to figure that out later.

Tink stared at Peter, waiting for him to notice her. She was the only one not smiling after all. Shouldn't be too hard for him to spot her.

His gaze floated over the crowd as he bobbed along to the melody. Finally, his attention snagged on her.

Then moved on.

What the—

The music faltered. His focus snapped back to her, then away.

Oh yes, he noticed.

Moments later, he ended the song and bowed to the crowd. "Thank you, thank you."

Onlookers called for another, but he smiled and hopped off the box.

Peter snatched the little jar some people had tossed coins into and headed in the opposite direction from her.

Tink stalked after him. "Hey, wait!"

He didn't even look back, just picked up his pace, aiming for the buildings on the far side of the square.

"Peter!"

He stopped, going completely stiff. The boy twisted around to face her and shoved his flute into a belt around his waist. "What do you want?" he demanded.

"Why are you here?" she asked. "What did you do with my treehouse?"

"It's fine," he said. "Right where you left it."

She couldn't stop the eyeroll. "You take over my home, ambush me, then sell me off to a bloody pirate just to leave and come here?"

He crossed his arms. The coins had already disappeared from the now-empty jar. "Yep."

Something wasn't right. It just didn't make sense. "And the rest of your boys? You left those little kids on their own?"

"Course not. They're around."

Picking pockets, probably. Tink sighed. What a great role model he was for these boys. Still... "You couldn't play music in Tortuga?"

"I did." He shrugged. "Coin we got wouldn't last forever, and the boys needed to eat. Got a better offer to come here."

Tink pinched the bridge of her nose. Why was she wasting her time with this kid? She glanced toward the sky. More of the day had passed than she realized. "Stay out of my house," she said, determined to have the last word.

A shadow fell over them. "There trouble here?"

Great, just great. Tink squinted up at the shaggy man. "I was just leaving."

"Nope," Peter said at the same time.

"So long as there's not." A beefy hand landed on Peter's shoulder.

Tink forced a smile. "Farewell th—" The words stuck in her throat as the man's one eye widened.

Oh fuck.

Oh fuck. Shit.

He was one of Captain Blackbeard's crewmen. She hadn't realized at first, but that eye patch with the little skull on it was unmistakable. He'd *escorted* her below deck to meet the captain. Worse, he remembered her too.

Tink bolted, racing across the cobblestones.

"You! Stop!"

The gruff words only fueled her steps as she raced down a busy street, weaving around carts and people. One quick glance showed the man a few cart lengths back, pushing through a couple and spilling their goods on the street. Shouts and exclamations continued as she sped down an alley stinking of human waste.

Several blocks later, she finally slowed her steps. Her chest rose and fell as she sucked in heavy breaths. Sweat trickled down her skin, causing her clothes to stick. No shouts arose behind her. She couldn't spot the pirate or Peter, but she was far from safe. If there was one, there were more, and now they knew she was here. The *Kraken* hadn't been docked in the port this morning, but neither was the *Jolly Roger*.

She swallowed and ducked down another alley. Hook needed to know. They all did. She glanced at the sky. And Merrin's teeth, she needed to find her way back to the inn—quick.

Hook and his crew lounged in the inn's common room, eating an early lunch, when Tink barged in through the main door. She'd never been so happy to see pirates in her life.

The captain set down his fork, looking at her with an expression she couldn't quite place as she made a beeline for him.

"I need to talk to you. Now."

"I'm all—" he started.

"Upstairs. Quick."

Sage nearly spat out her soup.

Tink groaned. "All of you." She glanced between them, lips pursed. Leave it to pirates to think without their heads.

Hook pushed back his plate and rose. Others grumbled, but Tink didn't wait for them as she bolted up the stairs.

No sooner had the door closed behind them, sealing them all in Hook's freshly cleaned room—*thank all the elders*—than Tink spilled her news, "I saw one of Captain Blackbeard's men. Here. In town."

Smee nearly dropped the bowl he'd carried with him upstairs.

"Already?" Francis groaned.

Hook slammed his fist on the table. "Bloody hell."

Conversation flooded the room, filling it with the same thoughts that had chased her back to the inn.

"The *Kraken*'s in port?"

"Not that I saw."

"Where are they hiding?"

"Are you sure?"

"Absolutely. I recognized one of them, and—" She ducked her gaze. "He recognized me too."

"Shit," Sage replied.

Hook said nothing, emotions flickering across his face that she still couldn't place.

"That's not the worst of it," Tink continued.

That had them all sitting up straighter.

"Peter, the kid who stole my treehouse. You know, the one you bargained with to hand me over in exchange for a few coins?" She stared Hook down.

"The hell?" Sage said.

She could have sworn he flushed before he looked away.

"Well, he's here too, with Captain Blackbeard's men. And he saw me. If he tells them about our little encounter on Tortuga, then he'll know you're all here too."

"Home..." Francis turned ashen. "If the *Kraken*'s not here..."

Shit. She hadn't considered that. They could already be in trouble.

"We gotta go," Smee said, eyes wide. No doubt, he worried for his sisters.

"We can't." Hook hung his head.

"Captain?"

"We have to meet with the witch first."

Sage reared back. "But Coconut Cove. The ship, the crew, our families—"

"May be completely fine," Hook said, his voice eerily calm. "We came to see the witch, and we're not leaving without direction from her." He sucked in a breath. "Tink, Smee, we go to the witch now." His voice rang with command and confidence once more. His back straightened, the uncertainty from moments ago vanished in an instant. "The rest of you, pack and wait for us by the blue shack near the forest path. We'll meet you there as soon as we're done."

"Aye, sir." Sage's reply lacked her usual spark.

The heaviness in the room weighed on Tink, making her wish she could slide through the floorboards and escape. This was so not how she expected today to go, but they had to know. It was better they knew, right?

Hesitantly, she glanced to Hook, who gave her a nod. Were her thoughts so obvious? She flushed and looked away.

"Let's go." Hook gestured to the door.

Off to see the witch. *The witch. Oh, Merrin's teeth.* She'd never told him about the witch's offer. There hadn't been time. And now... The stiffness of Hook's shoulders and hard set of his jaw were as unwelcoming as a turbulent sea. Not to mention the storm going on behind his eyes. He didn't need another burden, not when she wouldn't be taking the witch's offer anyway.

20

*E*very person they passed was an enemy. *Look each one over. Don't rely on their clothes. Don't make eye contact. If they look at you, make them want to look away. Keep watch at your back. Look far ahead as well as close. Keep your hand on the dagger at your side.*

Those were the rules he traveled by as they made their way to the witch's shop. Dark clouds shadowed their steps. *Bloody curse.* It picked the worst times to send a storm his way. They couldn't afford to wait it out either. The rain better bloody well hold off until they made it back to Coconut Cove.

Blackbeard was here—or at least his crew was. Right under the Gamoreans' nose. Whatever information they may have on that crocodile's hideout would have to wait.

The witch's shop was just as stifling and uncomfortable as the day before. No, somehow it was worse. A slight burned scent mixed in with the hideous perfume emanating from the very walls.

"Ah, just as expected." The man behind the counter, the same as before, gave a too-bright grin. His face was painted again in the same shades of gold and green. With a dramatic flourish, he gestured to the curtains at his back. "Right this way."

Hook glanced back at his companions. Tink was rigid, her gaze flitting this way and that. She'd been on edge since her unexpected announcement. If Blackbeard or his men had laid a hand on her... He couldn't think about that now. That bloody bastard already had much to answer for. He'd made every one of their lives a misery in one way or another. No wonder she'd gone so pale when the *Kraken* arrived after their meeting with Titania.

With a shake, he turned and followed the shopkeep through the crimson curtains. The narrow hall beyond was almost pitch black. The place made it too easy for an ambush. His hand slipped from the pommel of his dagger, reaching back for the woman behind him. He nearly sighed when her hand slipped into his and gave it a squeeze. Tink twisted to glance up a flight of stairs ascending into the gloom as they strode down the hall toward the back of the shop.

Light bled in around them as the shopkeep pushed back another set of heavy curtains, revealing a small room. The witch sat alone behind a round table in the center, which sported bottles, bowls, and vials like those in the storefront. A grin lifted her lips, barely visible below the garish mask of green and gold she wore to cover her face. Dark hair streaked with silver spilled out around it, cascading over her shoulders and a dress of shimmering emerald.

"Captain Hook, is it?" She tilted her head. Hands decked in gold and jewels tapped on the tabletop. She wore a fortune—if it were real gold. The way it shimmered in the light spilling from the candles in the chandelier above said it was. He would know. "Please, have a seat."

The witch's gaze passed right over Smee—rarer than jewels that was— and settled on Tink. Her grin widened. Tink straightened at his side, her grip tightening in his. Reluctantly, he let her go as they took vacant seats across from the witch, each one different in style. Her shopkeep dragged the unused fourth, a gaudy mess of green velvet, to the heavy curtains caging them in. Curtains even draped from the ceiling above, cloaking wood and stone. So much garish fabric. What a waste.

"You brought payment?" the witch asked.

Hook tossed a bag of coins onto the table. It landed with a heavy thump. "That should be to your satisfaction."

"Mmmm." She pried open the strings holding the bag closed and let coins slip through her fingers. "Depends on what you have to ask of me."

Greedy witch. Though he had half a mind to call her another name if she tried to deny him. He already offered her a hefty sum of gold. An average merchant would take ages to gather so much, but perhaps she charged more to pirates.

Smee reached for a nearby bottle.

"Don't touch that!" the witch screeched, rising to her feet.

He snapped his arm away like the scolded child he was.

The witch's lips twitched as she regained her seat and smoothed out the falls of silk across her lap.

"Apologies for my friend." Hook gave a scathing look at the man, who dipped his gaze in apology. "He won't do that again."

"No," she said. "He won't. State your business or be gone."

Smee... Hook slid forward in his chair, letting his hook thump onto the edge of the table. "I need to know the location of the scale of Leviathan. Its precise location and how to get there."

Her eyes widened. "My, you don't want much, do you?"

"You've located things for me before. You can do it again." Memories from years ago tried to claw their way into his mind, to fester there as they once had—his mother, his hand. Blackbeard's smirking face. He slammed them back in their box.

"I remember. You went by a different name then."

"We're not here to discuss my past." *Not here. Not now.*

"As you will." She shrugged. "Executus!"

The shopkeep rushed to her side and gave a dramatic bow.

"My scrying bowl and the green, crystal jar, please."

He bowed again before sliding through the curtains behind her. Hook stiffened. Another false wall. Smee shifted on his seat, no doubt keeping a hand, or two, on his hidden daggers as he did. Tink was pale, her chest rising and falling. He should have given her one too, an oversight he wouldn't make again.

The witch's prying gaze looked them over as the silence stretched. No one dared to break it. Smee barely breathed. The witch knew too much about him already. He wouldn't give her another word. And she gave nothing for free.

The shopkeep, Executus—he committed the name to memory—returned carrying a heavy pot. A young boy trailed behind with a sparkling green vial, shaped like a teardrop and nearly as long as his arm.

"Careful, boy," she said as he set the delicate item on the table to her side. "Or you'll regret it."

Hook jumped as Tink grabbed his thigh. He glanced to her and the wide-eyed look she shot him. *The boy,* she mouthed. Yeah, he didn't like her threatening kids either. Never sat well with him. But they already risked the witch's ire after Smee's slipup. He had to know the location of the scale. Everything depended on it. He patted Tink's hand. When she dug her fingers into his leg again, he squeezed it in return. Later they could help the boy. Not now.

With a wave of her hand, the witch shooed her assistants away. "Now we begin. Hold very still." Bright, white teeth filled her grin. "Unless you care to be stuck here quite a while."

Tink pulled her hand away from his. He almost wished she hadn't.

Hook nodded to the witch.

The moment she pulled the stopper on a black vial, the light dimmed. One after another, the witch added ingredients to the cast-iron pot in front of her from the assortment on the table: one red flower, something that resembled a chicken bone, another that he tried not to look too closely at, a few drops of liquid red as rubies. Finally, she reached for the green, crystal vial. The substance that floated into the pot was grainy, like sand but lighter, and it glowed with a faint golden light. His stomach tightened. Like Tink's wings when he kissed her or... He shifted in his seat. *Can't think about that now.*

Absolute stillness settled over the room, except for the witch, who moved her hands in a smooth, fluid motion over the pot. The light expanded, swelling out of the pot. *Run. Run.* Everything in him cursed him for staying in his chair. Smee visibly rocked backward. Tink sat eerily still, transfixed at the sight in front of them.

The witch's eyes slid shut, and the light faded until near darkness swallowed the room. Hook leaned forward, hand on his dagger. Dark smoke rose from the cauldron as the witch began to speak in a slow, melodic voice that came from everywhere and nowhere at once.

"Follow the second star to the left.

Beyond the veil, the bearded man guides you in.

The wooden trident marks the path.

Fog confuses. Don't trust it.

Light in front. To the left. Right is right.

Up and up, higher still.

Hold your breath as you sway and swing.

Follow the eagle into the ground.

In shallow pool, the scale is found.

But only those bound two as one,

Can have the dragon's gift."

The witch opened her eyes and sucked in a deep breath. "My, you should have written that down."

That— Fury rushed under his skin as he slammed the point of his hook into the table.

"A riddle?" Tink gasped.

"That ain't—" Smee shook his head.

"This isn't what we agreed," Hook spat.

"Is it not?" The witch canted her head. "Follow the spirit's guidance, and it will lead you to what you seek. How else did you expect to find something in a place that no one knows?"

The chair clattered behind him as he stood. "If you lie..." He pointed his hook at her.

"You'll know where to find me." She merely shrugged and leaned back in the chair. "But you should know, my magic is always right." A slow grin stretched her lips. "James."

His name may as well have been a slap. No one called him that. Not anymore. He'd left it behind, buried it with his mother after the last time he called upon the witch.

No one. Except...

Tink grabbed his arm. "Let's go." She tugged him toward the door.

The stiffness in his jaw loosened as he met her determined gaze. *Right.* No time to lose. They'd get nothing more from this greedy bitch.

He glanced back across the table. "Witch," he said by way of farewell.
"Captain."

Hook gestured to Smee, who strode for the curtained entrance
without a backward glance. Hook slid his hand into Tink's and turned to
leave as well.

"Oh, Tinker Bell."

Tink froze, her hand stiffening in his.

"Have you thought about my offer, dear?"

Her offer? His brow furrowed as he stared between the women. Tink
had yet to turn to the witch, her eyes wide and wild, pleading with him in
silence. A deep flush raced across her cheeks.

A heaviness settled in his chest. "What offer?" he grated.

"Oh my, I am sorry," the witch said.

Hook nearly snarled. She wasn't sorry. But she would be.

"You didn't tell them, dearie?" the witch continued, her surprise as fake
as the mask on her face.

His stomach dropped. *Tell me what? What offer?* He pleaded with Tink
in silence, but she looked away. The world spun around him. He dropped
her hand as if it burned.

The witch knew her name. She hadn't given it while they were there.
Hook stared between them again, breaths coming short and quick.

"I do see you managed to make some dust." Her fingertips danced
across the tabletop as merry as her grin. "Took my advice, huh?"

Dust. Her glow. Of course... It was pixie dust the witch used. And Tink
had used him to make more of the precious, wicked substance. Once a
trickster, always a trickster. Didn't he know? *Bloody hell.* She fooled him.

Tink glanced over her shoulder. "I reject your offer." Her voice
warbled, but her pace was stiff as she fled the room.

"Pity," the witch said as the curtains closed behind the pixie.

"If you've played me..." He shook his hook at her.

"I gave you exactly what you wanted, Captain."

Worn nails dug into his palm. It took everything he had not to wipe
the serpentine smile off her face. One more moment and he would.

Hook stormed after his companions and brushed past the shopkeep
who said something in an all-too-pleasant voice. Cloudy drizzle greeted

him as he stepped out the door. A fierce wind whipped down the street, a match for his inner fury.

"You." He nearly shook as he stared Tink down.

Smee stepped back, taken unawares. "Captain—"

Hook silenced him with a look. His teeth ground together as he focused on the scowling pixie. "You met with her."

She crossed her arms and notched her chin higher.

"Without us. Didn't even tell me."

Smee looked between them, wide-eyed.

"Because I had so much time? I was drunk, then you…" Her cheeks flushed. "You were gone when I woke up! Besides, we've got bigger problems." As if on cue, thunder boomed.

They didn't have time for this. Loathe as he was to admit it, they did have bigger issues, and they demanded attention. Now. He couldn't put his crew—his family—at risk. They'd wasted enough time.

"There!" Tink gaped, pointing down the street. In a heartbeat she was sprinting past him, boots slapping on the wet cobblestones.

Hook grabbed her, nearly sending her slipping to the ground as he pulled her to a halt. "Where do you think—"

"The boy! We have to get him!"

He twisted his head in the direction of her frantic waving. A boy stood frozen, looking back at them, before he darted down an alley.

"Now!" she screeched, tugging against him.

Why take an interest in this one kid? "He's fine. We have bigger worries."

"No!" She wrenched free and glanced either way, her eyes wide. "He's one of Peter's. They're with Captain Blackbeard."

The words smacked him like an icy squall.

Fuck.

"If he heard the witch's instructions…" Her body shook.

Fuck.

Smee ran a hand through his damp hair. "We gotta—"

The world swayed under his feet. "No!"

Both of them stilled at his exclamation.

"We stick to the plan. The boy's gone. We can't delay." The *Kraken* wasn't here. But it could be. Any minute it could be. And they had to be gone, far from here. He'd want the scale. Who bloody wouldn't? And once he had the witch's words, he'd go after it.

Fuck.

He took off at a run toward the forest, not caring if anyone saw. "Come on! And don't think we won't talk about your little visit!" He shouted behind him.

Oh, he'd get to the bottom of that. *Little minx.* But she was right, they had bloody bigger problems. And she'd tried to warn him—her hand on his leg. Fuck all, if only he'd realized...

They had to find the scale first. With the power of Leviathan in his hand, Captain Blackbeard would rule the seas outright. Curse or not, Hook would be doomed. It couldn't happen. *Never bloody happen.*

He'd have his victory over Blackbeard. In this and more.

21

*S*torms sucked. They didn't have them in the Sylvanna Vale. Not like this. Pleasant rain showers? Sure. Foggy mornings? Those were the best. Rain that stung like needles and seemed to come from every direction at once? *Hah, no.*

"Eeep!" The drone of wind and pounding rain swallowed up her exclamation as she slipped...again. Her palms splashed into rocky mud. Her knee banged on a root.

If only she could sink into the mud and forget this horrid flight back to Coconut Cove. Everything was wet. Everything. And muddy. Her legs ached, she'd broken half her nails, and her hair... *Durin's beard, will it ever get untangled?*

But all that she could handle, maybe. It was Hook's stubborn silence and glares fiercer than lightning that were the shit drizzled on top of the rotting pie of a day.

Of course the witch outed her. *Bitch.* Everyone wanted her dust. Every—

"Come on." Sage grabbed her, helping her to her feet. "Almost there."
Okay, maybe not everyone.

She tried to blow the hair out of her face and failed. Tink swiped her muddy hand across her forehead, pushing the wet tendrils clinging to her skin away. What could a little more mud hurt?

"Clear!" Smee hollered, trotting back toward them on the path. He'd run ahead, desperate to check on his sisters. How such a big man had quite so much energy she'd never understand.

"Thank fuck!" Francis exclaimed, picking up speed as he passed her on the path. Or what was left of it.

Blackbeard hadn't found them. They were safe. For now anyway. The relief she expected didn't come. If he beat them to the scale, he'd have more power over the seas than ever before. Her way home would be gone. The curse on Hook and his crew wouldn't.

She gritted her teeth. One storm—magic or natural—wouldn't stop her from getting back to the Sylvanna Vale.

The homes dotting the hillside were nearly impossible to see in the storm, especially since night had fallen during their trek. With shutters closed and braced for the storm, the wind blowing any smoke away, and no moonlight on the water, the homes were just more shadows in the darkness. She'd have stumbled right past them and into the sea if someone hadn't thrown open a door and ushered them inside.

Tink made a beeline for the fire. *Oh, blessed warmth!* She let her pack slide off and thump wetly by her feet. If only she could shed her clothes too. Climb under a blanket…

"We all here?" Hook's commanding voice echoed through the room, conquering even the raging storm outside.

"Aye," a chorus of dripping pirates answered him.

"Rest, ready yourselves. First break in this bloody squall, we sail."

A more muted response greeted him. Rest? As if anyone could in this storm. She squatted on the floor near the fire, her wet clothes already forming a puddle.

"Rell, set a watch. Come straight to me if the storm breaks before dawn."

"Aye, aye!" the girl responded.

"Out! All of you," Hook ordered.

Tink groaned, shoving off the floor. She'd just sat down.

"Not you." Hook pointed in her direction.

A few pirates tossed pitying looks her way before dashing out into the storm. They worried for her when they were the ones braving that squall again, for however brief a time.

Tink dropped back on the ground and faced the fire. He ordered her to stay? *Fine.* She'd be warm while he yelled at her about the witch.

Something scraped across the ground. A chair? A heavy thump followed.

Her shoulders stiffened. Any moment now...

"I'm sorry."

"What?" She blinked at the fire. He was talking to himself, wasn't he? Ridiculous pirate.

"I'm sorry I yelled at you."

She spun around on the floor to face him. Hook hunched over the table, his head in his hand.

"You tried to warn me about the boy. You wouldn't have done that if you were working with the witch against us. Whatever she wanted with you, that's your affair."

That's your affair. She mouthed in echo. Did he get knocked with a tree branch on the way back? Drink too much rain?

"And she seemed...upset when you rejected her. Will that come back to hurt us?" He looked up, all the fire he'd shown before his crew gone out of him.

"Shouldn't." She crossed her arms. "She wanted my dust. I didn't think I could make any more outside my home. Seems I can." Her wings twitched, wet and miserable as they were bound up and stuck to her back. "She told me how. It worked. But I'm not selling it to her. Or anyone else." *Unless I have to. Again.* Her bracelet could only break once. It didn't break again the more she'd sold her dust, but why add to her sins?

"Pity. It's the drug of choice all across the seas. Could make us some coin."

She rolled her eyes. Of course the pirate would bring it back to money. Didn't he always?

"It was dust she used in her sight spell?"

Her brows arched. Observant pirate. "It was."

He scratched at the stubble on his chin. "So you can weave some magic."

Tink huffed. "No, her spells are not...natural." Not for a pixie, and she couldn't slide further down the path away from the vale. Their dust was meant to nourish the land, which fed and cared for them in return. The great circle of balance. Humans perverted that use, like so many other things.

He nodded, but his attention lay somewhere else. "And when your wings glow...that makes dust?"

If he hadn't looked away, he'd have seen her face turn red. Her ears heated. All of her might as well have lit on fire. The raging storm couldn't break the tense silence that hung between them.

"Pleasure." Her word was a hoarse whisper. "Happiness." When the cares of the world fell away and all that was left was something enjoyable, it could happen. Or when her body lit on fire, stirred into a kind of pleasure she'd rarely given herself, though not even that had made her wings glow in this human world. It happened with him. A bloody, filthy, thieving, handsome, loyal, delicious pirate.

Holy revered elders, I am in trouble.

Back home in the vale, dust came naturally. Her wings had been laden with it when she and Lily snuck into this world. But after she shed that at Blackbeard's command, little had come back. Then, none at all. Nothing about her wings worked right outside of the vale.

"I...um...I should find a place to sleep." She leaped to her feet and wrung water out of her hair, letting it splatter on the floorboards.

Smee's sisters had practically carried her off into their house when they'd pulled up to the dock—had that been only two days ago? That night she'd been so miserable among their happiness. It was great the way they invited her in, gave her a place to sleep, food, drink. They'd offered her clothes too, but their pretty dresses would've made her stand out too much in Rochland and wouldn't suit a trek to the Shrouded Isles. But watching the crew and their loved ones celebrate, the way they were so comfortable with one another like one large family, it wrecked her. It was too much like home, too much like the family and friends she'd lost. They even worked toward a common good for their community, sharing the work, the food, their treasures—just like pixies—rather than for themselves like many of the other humans she'd observed. The joy of it all choked her, until she'd fled into the night to be alone. But even that joyful misery would be better than lingering with this man who infuriated her in so many ways.

"Stay here." His gaze caught hers. "You can, I mean. There's an extra bed."

For the first time, she looked around the room, catching sight of the sparse furnishings: a table and chairs of simple wood, a few cabinets and shelves bearing books, trinkets, and small paintings, a cook pot resting on its stand near the fire. A home. Though not the lavish one she expected for such a man. "Your home?"

He rubbed the ring around his neck. When had he pulled it from under his shirt? "It was my mother's."

A thought struck her like lightning. "That ring...it was hers?" She'd been too afraid to ask before, too nervous he'd say it belonged to a lover he cherished, one who might be waiting for him in some port.

"It was." His attention dipped to the puddle forming on the wooden floor. "You'll need something dry." Without another word, he crossed the room to the narrow stairs and disappeared into the darkness.

His mother's... Knowledge slammed her in the chest. She'd pulled away before because she thought he loved another and carried her token around. But all that time, it was his mother's.

Idiot, idiot, idiot.

And so was this house. She swallowed, suddenly ashamed for dripping on her floor. Not that she was here to be upset about it, but still... She twisted the end of her sodden braid. Gone? Dead? She didn't have the heart to ask. It couldn't be easy having a pirate as a son, no matter how well he provided for his crew. Smee's house had all the trappings of a fine manor—not that she'd seen many others, and even then only through windows. One couldn't tell it from the outside, not with the simple façades half-hidden in the forest. This house, though... She ran her finger along the mantelpiece. Rustic, old, efficient, but not grand. A far cry from Hook's cabin on the *Jolly Roger*.

A faded painting stared back at her from a small frame, no larger than her palm. A young woman sat holding a little boy, their bodies stiff and straight despite the smiles painted on their features. She squinted, leaning in closer. They shared the same dark hair, hers bound in a bun, little tendrils escaping, the boy's a little too long, touching his ears and just aching to be brushed behind them.

Tink jumped away from the portrait as the steps creaked, alerting her to Hook's return. Her mouth dried as she took in the man warmed by the fire's glow. He'd discarded much of his clothing, leaving just that ring shining against the smattering of dark hair on his bare chest. Barefoot, standing there in just his wet breeches with clothing thrown over his arm, he could have been anyone…if she ignored the hook. Not that she minded. It only added to his persona, gave him that fierce, sharp edge that she shouldn't want but couldn't help craving. Her tongue flicked out over her lips. Damn, she really did want him. There wasn't any ale to blame it on this time either.

"Enjoying the view?"

She flushed, ready to join the puddle at her feet. That devilish smirk on his face was a taunt and a tease all at once. He'd come down like that on purpose. *Bastard.*

"In fact, I am." Why deny it? He already knew the answer.

His eyes widened.

"But if you give me the things you brought and point me to the spare room…" She placed her hands on her hips. "I'll happily look away."

"Well," he dragged the word out, letting it play across his tongue.

Tink stared him down as he strode across the room with slow, deliberate purpose, a slight swagger to his step. He didn't stop until he stood at the edge of her puddle, forcing her to gaze up into his smirking face. "If you're happy to leave, the bedroom is through that door." He bobbed his head backward.

"No father or siblings I'm going to interrupt?" She arched one careful brow.

Hook shook his head. "My da was claimed by the sea before I was born. Or so ma said. It's just me."

Just them, alone in this house. Together. Her nose wrinkled as she snatched the clothes off his arm.

He pulled his arm away in a flash, almost spilling some of the fabric into the wetness. Was he so self-conscious about the straps attaching his hook to his arm? She was intrigued, the desire to inspect it—all of him— pulling her a step closer.

One dark brow arched toward the ceiling as if to say, "Your move."

"Thank you," Tink replied, intentionally brushing against him as she aimed for the door. Would he follow? Call after her?

She threw open the door and glanced behind her. The smoldering look on his face knocked the breath from her lungs and fanned the fire burning in her core. One crook of his finger and she'd be his. But he stood still as a statue where she'd left him. His chest didn't so much as rise and fall.

She grinned. "Good night." *Your move, Captain.*

22

*E*very inch of her felt flushed, whether from desire or embarrassment, she couldn't say. *Both? Definitely both.*

Tink tugged at the ties on the waistband of the undershorts. *His* undershorts. They'd be comfortable if she could get them to stay on. But they were *his*. He'd worn them. Who knew how many times? His cock has rested against the fabric brushing her curls. She bit her lip at the warm wetness building between her legs. How was she supposed to sleep in these? How?

Her wings fluttered behind her as a shiver raced over her skin. The shirt he'd given her wouldn't do either. Well, it would, but ruining another one of his shirts just for one night seemed a waste. And she sure as heck wasn't binding up her wings again. *Nope, nope, nope, they need to breathe.* They ached so much these days from the constant binding. Wings weren't meant to be bound. She'd be lucky if they worked at all anymore with the way she treated them.

She needed to sleep. Weariness tugged at her. Her body still protested from the hike. She'd expected some bruises and scrapes when she'd carefully cleaned and wiped the grime from her body, but not as many as she'd found. Tree roots just loved to reach up and trip her. She'd always been a bit clumsy, and binding her wings only made it worse.

With a blanket wrapped around her—tucked under her wings but pulled up over her breasts—she carried the last of her wet clothes into the main room. The rest of her belongings already hung off the backs of the chairs near the fire in an attempt to dry them by dawn. She added the last few she'd stripped off. Rain and wind crashed against the house. Though if the storm didn't let up, the chances of them staying dry for long were poor at best.

Thunder boomed, nearly shaking the house. Tink jumped. The last of her clothes landed on the chair with a wet thump. She tugged the blanket closer and turned back for the bedroom.

But those stairs... *Damn.* She couldn't step out here without staring up into the gloom. She hadn't heard a thing since she'd retired to her borrowed room and taken her time brushing the knots out of her hair. Was Hook asleep? He must be. He should be given their exhausting trek and the days ahead of them.

Then you'll want me tomorrow. And the next day. And the next.

Those words haunted her. They'd slipped right through her drunken, lust-laden haze and imprinted on her heart. Had that really been only a day ago? It could have been a week for all that had happened. Damn if she didn't want him. Today. Tomorrow. *Right this very fucking minute.*

Because one night with you will never be enough.

She hadn't made that up. Couldn't have. She'd never expected those words from a filthy pirate, especially not *that* filthy pirate. The way he'd touched her... She shivered. If she closed her eyes, she could feel his hand on her, his breath on her neck, the way he set her on fire.

Her thighs squeezed together, pressing the material of his undergarments to her skin. *Holy elders.* He gave her those on purpose just to torment her. She stamped her foot, scowling at the stairs. That was the reason for his smirk. He knew what he was doing. He knew what she'd think of, how it would mess with her. Didn't he want her to get any rest?

After she'd retreated into the bedroom, she'd cleaned in a hurry, expecting him to knock or saunter right in any moment, eager to pick up where they'd left off the night before. Even as she'd sat there, stark naked and brushing out her hair, she'd half been holding her breath the whole time, eagerly awaiting him.

But he didn't show.

She slid one hand down the front of the borrowed undershorts. One quick rub across her clit, and she moaned into the little room. Her wings twitched and fluttered. It wouldn't take much, not much at all, but he'd started this and by Holy Flora she wanted him to finish it.

Tink pulled her hand free and stomped toward the stairs. Her courage slipped on the first step, but she forced herself onward, one careful footstep into the darkness at a time.

Choices were few at the top of the stairs, thank goodness. Stumbling around in the dark and earning more bruises wouldn't satisfy her needs. Thin tendrils of light crept out from under one door. That's where she'd find Hook.

Tink edged closer, listening intently. Knocking would be wise. Though if he were asleep, it would be rude to wake him, even if he'd added fuel to the fire of her desires.

Light, muffled sounds came from within. She leaned closer, nearly pressing against the door. The storm made the sounds indistinguishable through the wood. Tink gave a hesitant knock.

No reply came, but the noise continued.

She glanced over one shoulder, back toward the stairs. She could leave. Go back down and...no. She'd come this far. Tink cracked the door.

The captain lay on a large bed, covered in a sheet—one that wrinkled and moved where he wiggled underneath. A deep moan slipped from his lips and carried across the room.

Tink leaned into the opening. *What is he—*

"Y-yes," he moaned. The sheets bucked. "Tink."

She fell into the room and crashed onto the floor. The blanket fell away to puddle beside her. *Oh holy, revered, fucking elders.*

Hook jumped from the bed. "What the bloody—"

She dared a glance at him. His bare chest rose and fell. Her gaze dipped. *Oh, oh, oh no.* He wore not a scrap of clothing. His cock, flush and erect, jutted between them. An inferno engulfed her. He'd been...to thoughts of her...

Her mouth went dry. Beryl's wings, he was more divine than her imaginings. The sculpted muscles she'd admired on his chest adorned the rest of him too—chiseled calves, strong thighs. But she'd be lying if she said her attention wasn't glued to the impressive appendage between them. It took effort to pull her attention to his face, which he currently scrubbed with his hand.

"Tink." He sat on the edge of the bed, legs spread.

"Uh…hi." She waved from the floor.

Hi? Hi! That was the best you could come up with?

She wanted to sink into the floor, to crawl under the blanket.

"You woke me to say hi?" He arched one careful brow.

Woke him. She blinked. He'd been asleep? Asleep…and dreaming of her. "I…" She pushed to her feet, her breasts peeking out from the fall of hair over her shoulders.

Hook sat a little straighter on the bed.

No going back now. "I…just wanted to say that these don't quite fit." She tugged the string on the borrowed underthings, letting them slide to the floor.

His gaze raked her, crawling down every inch of her body in the most delicious and all-consuming way. He didn't say anything. Didn't need to. The look in his eyes said he'd woke from a pleasant dream to a better one, and he still couldn't believe it. Hook shook his head and ran his hand down his face again. "Well, love." His voice was thick and sweet as honey. "We'll have to do something about that."

A subtle glow lit the room behind her. Her wings. He didn't even have to touch her and they lit for him. *Wicked things.*

A glint of light on metal caught her eye. His hook lay on the side table, absent from his arm. She hadn't even noticed. Hook followed the line of her gaze and slid his arm behind him as if to hide it.

Now, now, we can't have that. Tink crossed the room to him. Each step was harder and easier at the same time. His inviting grin pulled her in just as it twisted the knot of desire tighter within her. When her legs nearly brushed his, she ran the back of her hand down his handless arm. "I like you just how you are, you know. Even if you are a pirate."

He leaned back on his good arm, as if he refused to touch her despite his obvious desire to. "Is that so, love?"

"It is. And I'll have you know, I'm completely sober this time."

Hook sucked in a breath as Tink straddled him, her knees on the bed to either side of his hips. Tink gasped as he grabbed her ass, tugging her close until his cock slid against her thigh and precariously close to her eager opening.

Her hands explored his chest, sliding over strong shoulders, up his neck, through his damp hair. Every inch of him was as wondrous as she imagined. No—better. Her skin tingled as she placed one hand over his racing heart and whispered, "I want you to fuck me, James."

The slow grin that stretched across his face, even as his eyes hooded, nearly had her coming right there. He leaned in. Stubble tickled her cheek before he took her earlobe in his teeth. Her core clenched, ass tightened in his palm. "Are you sure?" he crooned.

More than. Nothing had ever felt so right. She dipped her fingers between her lower lips, coating them in her wetness. "Yes," she whispered. Hook groaned as she ran them over his cock, spreading her moisture there. "And I'm more than ready for you."

He crushed his mouth to hers and pulled her further onto the bed. Their teeth knocked together, but it didn't matter, not with his taste in her mouth, his hand on her body. She wanted all of him, pirate or no. And she was ready to give all of herself to him. Today. Tomorrow. And the next.

A calloused hand teased her breast as he broke their kiss. A flick of his thumb over her nipple had her squealing in delight. "Do climb aboard, love. Or would you prefer me to captain our ship?"

Tink pushed him down onto the bed. "Filthy pirate."

"Aye." His eyes hooded. "But there's only one treasure I desire."

"Lucky you." She wiggled her brows with a grin.

Hook trailed his fingertips down her chest where she crouched above him, sliding across her belly, then lower... Gooseflesh broke out across her skin. Lightning flashed, the searing light slipping through the closed shutters. Thunder rumbled, and he echoed it with a rumble of desire deep in his throat. "Such a lovely forest." He flicked her clit, sending a bolt of desire straight to her core. Another flick and she bucked toward him, unable to withstand the taunt.

Tink swatted his hand. "Do you want me or not?"

He slid his hand behind his head and glanced meaningfully at his cock where it jutted between them. "What do you think, love?"

A soft golden glow spread behind her. Her wings twitched as she tentatively took him in hand. He was so warm. Hard yet soft. So delightfully thick and eager. Her thumb slid over the tip, finding a bead of moisture there and rubbing it down his length to mix with her wetness she'd painted on him.

Slowly, carefully, she lowered herself onto his length.

He sucked in a breath, cock twitching in her hand, as the tip touched her wet folds. *Nessa's flute, he is big.* She bit her lip and took him inside her, inch by tortuous, slow inch. Hook's gaze locked with hers, sure, steady, full of raging desire as they drew together. And oh, how he filled her, stretched her in the most delicious way.

"James," she moaned. His nostrils flared, and he moved, just the smallest twitch that lodged his cock deep inside her. Tink's back arched. Her core tightened around his girth. Her whole body tingled, that dam of pleasure so close to bursting open already. *And revered elders, he hadn't even moved.* Just the feel of him deep within her nearly took her over the edge.

Her hands trailed down his chest, savoring the hard muscle dusted with dark hair. He was glorious, and she looked her fill, savoring his strong jaw and the stubble that coated it, his slightly pointed nose, that wicked mouth that even now stretched into a contented grin, his dark, grey eyes, hooded with lashes that many women would envy. And his hair —how she loved to tangle her fingers though those dark locks.

"You're glorious, love." It wasn't just lust radiating from his face as he took her in. No, something else lay behind those stormy eyes, something that aroused her as much as it scared her.

"Am I?" she teased, raising her hips then sliding back down his length.

A low moan slipped from his lips as she repeated the motion, finding a slow, steady rhythm. "That and more." His hand trailed up her leg before settling on her hip. Calloused but gentle fingers teased her skin as she rode him, relishing in the feel of his hard length filling her, sliding in and out of her sodden heat. Completing her, bringing her to the edge of something wondrous.

He slid his hand along her belly, angling down until his thumb found the sensitive nub between her legs. One slide of his calloused finger across her clit had her clenching around him. "Ah! Don't!" Sweat broke out on her back and between her thighs.

"You don't like it?"

"I—" She loved it, needed it. But holy elders, what it did to her. He'd send her tumbling over the cliff of pleasure far too soon. He teased it again. She screamed, bucking against his hand, ramming down on his cock.

"Come for me, love."

That thumb, oh gods. Not yet, not yet, but oh— His cock surged in and out, meeting her rhythm pounding into her from below. He stroked her clit, faster, harder, bearing down.

"Come for—"

"James!" Orgasm tore through her. Her eyes rolled back. The room blurred. Everything was sensation, rapture, glowing white light that surrounded them until all she knew was the feel of James deep inside her, pushing her pleasure on, stoking the fire he'd started and watching her burn with it. His consuming gaze was locked on her as she returned, the sinful, gentle planes of his face lit by her glow.

He swore softly under his breath, his focus never leaving her face.

"James." His name was a plea, a bare, breathless whisper on her lips. She reached for him, falling toward him though they remained joined, her hips softly rolling against his like waves on the sea.

He sat, meeting her halfway, and pulled her against his chest until she was sitting in his lap. His lips crashed into hers. The kiss was everything, salvation and damnation all at once. Her arms slid over his shoulders. Her hands twined in his hair, gliding through it as she kissed him back with an intensity she could never have predicted. Skin on skin, his breath in her lungs, his manhood still lodged within her—and it still wasn't enough.

James pulled away from her greedy mouth, trailing kisses along her cheek, the line of her jaw. His stubble scratched her cheek as she took his earlobe in her teeth. "Tink." Her name was a hoarse whisper.

And then he moved in her again. Tink panted, her breasts pressed against his chest as he rocked against her, sliding in and out in gentle pursuit. A knot of desire began to twist tight within her core once again, building toward another explosion of pleasure. Oh, how he worked her, as if he'd known her body forever and knew just how to touch her, where to flick his tongue against her neck, how to tickle that spot on her back with a brush of his hand below her wings, and just how to slide his cock so it thrust against that extra-sensitive spot within her.

She'd been needy, eager to draw out their pleasure, but so close to release she couldn't stop from tumbling straight over the edge. But he was patient, diligent, forcing her to come on him, to relax, and join him in this slow, sensual joining that was just what she needed but didn't know she wanted.

But though a pirate loves the rock of the seas, he never takes his eyes off his aim for too long. James picked up his pace, fucking her with eager thrusts. She'd never get enough of him. The way his thick cock claimed and stretched her in the most delicious way. Each pump of him within her only pushed her pleasure higher, building it back to that precious precipice just out of reach. She wound her legs around him, shifting the angle of his penetration. She gasped at the new sensation. He moaned into her neck, nipping the sensitive skin there.

Tink met each thrust, rocking her hips, urging him deeper within her as she clutched him for dear life. Her hands fisted in his hair as another orgasm ripped through her. James slammed into her, wringing a screech of pleasure from her that echoed through the room. Then his hand was on her ass, grabbing her, lifting. He groaned as his cock slipped free with a wet pop. He gritted his teeth, his body jerking under hers as he reached his own thunderous peak.

Her core ached at the loss of him as the last of her orgasm subsided. He panted, his forehead pressed against hers, his fingers still digging into her soft backside as he clutched her to him. Steaming breaths mingled together as each of them slowly came back to the moment, recovering from a high stronger than pixie dust could ever deliver.

James placed gentle kisses along her neck and collarbone as their breathing evened. Only then did she notice the room was bright as day, with small particles of dust floating in the air. Her wings had never glowed so brightly. Never.

Only for him.

He collapsed on the bed, bringing her with him. Tink slid to his side, one leg still tangled over his. "That was..." Her hand trailed down his chest. There were no words.

James brushed a lock of hair back from her face, tucking it behind her pointed ear. "Perfection."

Tink smiled and placed a kiss on his chest. Perfection, yes, that was the word for it. Thunder boomed outside, as if echoing their sentiment.

"Am I going to be lost for days breathing in..." He gestured to the motes of dust in her slowly dimming light. "This?"

"I shouldn't think so." The real dust, the kind humans paid a fortune for, still clung to her wings. "This is..." Her lips quirked. Truly, she wasn't sure what to call the stuff. "Well, it's not *that* kind of dust."

Hook trailed his knuckles along her cheek. "Good. Because if I'm to be lost with you, love, I don't want to forget a moment."

23

Three days on the sea. Three days since he awoke with Tink curled against his chest.

Possibly the best three days of his life.

Storms loomed on the horizon, that crocodile Blackbeard couldn't be far behind, and they had only the witch's vague clues as their guide to finding Leviathan's scale. Even so...

Hook grinned as he spied Tink working with his crew on deck, showing them how to use the new device she'd conjured to bring in the sails with ease. Bloody hell, he could have stabbed a man when he was awakened from his delicious dream those nights ago. But there she was, nearly naked, more delightful and bewitching than any dream. It had taken everything to sit there and watch her, to wait and see what she'd do. *Worth it. So damn worth it.*

She wanted *him*. She called him James, that name he'd buried so long ago. She still used it when they were alone. Something shifted in his chest. James had died and been reborn for her. Only her. He glanced at Tink out of the corner of his eye. Sunlight gleamed on her hair, against her wings. She hadn't bound them since they'd left port, had even flown a bit to the delight of everyone. She was free, happy as she should be. She caught him looking and gave a cheerful wave. He grinned in return. His lustful pixie.

The more he had her, the more he craved her. It had been that way from the start, from her very first pixie-dust-laden kiss. She'd been the only face he'd seen, all he wanted. He'd thought it a curse then. Maybe it was, but this one he had no interest in breaking. Last night he'd restrained himself, only fucking her once, even when she'd whimpered and asked for more. They had to sleep sometime before they reached the Shrouded Isles. Wouldn't do any of them good if they were asleep on their feet. He looked away, out to the ship idling many lengths away, as he adjusted his breeches. It was one of the few merchant ships they'd spotted, one smart enough to give them wide berth. Not a concern.

They were close to the Shrouded Isles, he could feel it. They needed to come ashore before they were knocked off course by the looming storms, or worse. Even with all the risks, his crew had woken at dawn in the drizzly end of the storm the morning after they returned to Coconut Cove. To the last man and woman, they were with him. Pride swelled in his chest. They could have stayed behind. He'd offered. Though it would have been damn hard to captain the *Jolly Roger* without them.

That ship... He neared the railing, watching as the merchant ship sailed toward the dark clouds building to the west. Why would they...

A sharp whistle slipped down to him from the crow's nest. Boots thumped on the deck. Hook reached for his spyglass and took aim at the oncoming clouds to the east. *No.* He stiffened. Fog. And they were coming upon it quick. It had to be the Isles. That was the reason the merchant ship braved the incoming storms.

The second star to the left had led them straight here.

"Let out the sails!" Hook ordered. They needed to slow. Thick fog was more dangerous than a pit viper.

The wheel fought against him as he shifted course. The bitch liked to give him hell at times, but he always won.

Tink raced up the stairs toward him. "The Isles?"

"It must be." He could taste it in the air, a wrongness. He'd known the sea all his life, from living on its shores to fishing skiffs and on to bigger vessels. But this... He'd avoided this place all his life for good reason. The wheel fought against his grip. She didn't want to sail these waters.

The sails fluttered, spilling wind and slowing their pace. The fog seemed to rush toward them, faster than should be possible. It'd been a league away, but now it stretched toward them like a crone's hand.

Tink visibly shuddered. "No wonder the merfolk don't like it. This is...wrong."

He wasn't the only one who felt it then. The crew weren't as lively either—hesitant glances, no bawdy jokes.

"The bearded man guides you in," Tink recited the line from the witch's vision. "Can't be a real man, can it?"

That was the problem. He grimaced. No one lived on the Isles...that they knew of. "Any ideas?"

He'd put his crew to task coming up with possible solutions to the clues she'd given them. The stars were easy. Every sailor knew which to follow to reach the Isles—to avoid that path if nothing else. The rest... Best be ready for anything. This one seemed obvious—a bearded man. But finding him, that would be the trick. They wouldn't find a mountain in this bloody fog.

The temperature dropped as they slid into the mist, sending a chill down his spine.

"Keep an eye out." His voice sounded unnaturally loud, carrying through the sudden quiet. Hitting a rock or reef out here could be deadly. Help wouldn't be coming for them, and Blackbeard certainly would.

They held their collective breaths. Crew members leaned over the railing, looking for anything other than the grey that consumed them. Light drizzle spotted the deck, clinging to Hook's clothing.

"Land!" The call came from above.

Hook squinted at the horizon. As if someone had pulled back a curtain, the fogbank broke, spitting them out near a large island. Forested mountain peaks stretched toward the sky, cloaked in their own tufts of fog. The sound of waves crashing onto the rocky shoreline beckoned them near. A few larger rocks thrust from the ocean swells close to shore.

Hazardous, to be sure. They'd need to stay well away, take the rowboats in. But first, they needed a bearded man.

"Keep distance. Look for the bearded man, or any sign of life." He grabbed the wheel. No piers jutted from the shore, no buildings, no obvious trails, though it was hard to tell given their vantage.

He'd never ventured near the Shrouded Isles—no reason to risk it—but it lived up to reputation. More rock than sand lined the shore. The seas, typically clear and blue in the shallows, were dark and shadowed, as if someone had spilled a massive pot of ink that never faded. Even the trees were strange, almost muted in color rather than the vibrant greens, browns, and tans he was used to. Thick moss, or something like it, clung to trunks and branches alike, trying to drag them down into the rocks and sand. Beyond the shore, however...the peaks rising into the fog were green, lush—the opposite of the land near the water.

It was too much to expect to find the bearded man right away. But after an hour of drifting around the isle, the crew had grown antsy, Hook most of all. He paced back and forth, alternating between his spyglass and natural sight, searching for something, anything that might answer the witch's clue.

Tink slid next to him, placing her hand over his. All at once, he relaxed. He almost smiled just looking at her. She'd been less seasick this time. Perhaps she was finally getting used to the *Jolly Roger*. "They're called the Shrouded Isles, right?" she asked. "As in, more than one?"

Blast. He frowned. She was right.

Nearby, Smee rubbed the back of his neck. "But there's only one here—"

"Through the fog." He stiffened under Tink's touch, even as she scooted closer. "There may be more." And they might not be so lucky the next time. It'd be easy to run up on a reef, a rocky shoreline, shallow coves... A hundred terrible possibilities spooled out before him. "We'll go a little farther around this island."

Perhaps Lady Luck would smile on them yet.

Ten minutes later, and their luck had only gotten worse. Fog crept over the isle, sidling out over the shore. He dreaded taking them into more danger on these unusual seas. Perhaps they could find another way, something else Queen Titania desired. If there was a treasure to be had, he could steal it. Finding one in this place, however, was another story.

"Not even any fish," Smee lamented, leaning over the railing. None they'd seen anyway.

No birdcalls reached Hook's ears either. Other than the crash of waves on the shore and the comforting creaks and groans of his ship, it was eerily silent, as if nothing lived along the shoreline. His crew had spotted a few large birds in the distance, hovering near the forested peaks and sliding in and out of the fog, but nothing here. Not even one errant seagull.

"Is that..." Tink edged toward the side of the ship and leaned on the railing. "Smoke?" She glanced over one shoulder at him before gesturing back at the isle. "There. On the side of that hill."

Smoke? With the fog looming over everything it was hard to tell but... He raised his spyglass. A small stream of fog, a bit thicker than the rest, filtered up from the trees. He sucked in a breath. It had to be.

"Bring us in, Smee!" he called. "Ready anchor!" They'd almost passed it by, sailed on without noticing the slight oddity that Tink, his Tink, had spied. But who would live in such a wrong, lifeless place? Farther inland, where the trees at least looked alive rather than like moss-covered wraiths, perhaps, but near a fishless shore? It made no sense. Even so, the sign was too promising to be ignored.

"We'll take the rowboats in," he told Tink, taking her hand after he slid his spyglass into its holder. "You can stay here—"

She pulled her hand away and crossed her arms. The tap, tap, tap of her boot on the deck was answer enough.

He grinned, though a tingle of unease raced through him. It'd be nice to have her safe, protected here on the ship. But he loved her fire, that desire to push ahead no matter the odds. Hook held his arms up. "Or go with us."

"That's better," she said, letting her arms drop to her sides. "Of course I'm coming. Titania charged us both to find it, remember? I'm not missing out on my half of the reward." She winked before walking off.

She was oblivious to the dagger she'd just thrown his way. It slipped between his ribs, cutting deep, maybe worse than a real blade. She still wanted a way home. They'd find the scale for Titania, remove his curse, and fix her bracelet. Then she'd be gone. Back to her homeland. He swayed—he'd never swayed on deck. No matter how she consumed him, she wasn't his. The greatest treasure he'd found... But if he stole her again, locked her away, he'd lose her. And if he didn't...he'd lose her then too.

In removing the curse she'd unwittingly placed upon them, in saving his ship and crew, he'd lose the one thing he'd come to prize.

24

*L*ittle boats sucked worse than big boats. They moved more. Rising, falling, side to— Tink gagged, clamping her hand over her mouth as the rowboat sped them toward the shore.

Eyes glanced her way, though thankfully no one looked too closely. Well, other than Sage, who gave her a dramatic frown as she kept rowing.

Pirates with stomachs of steel didn't get sick on boats. But she was no pirate. Merrin's teeth, how she hated the sea...most of the time. Wrapped in Hook's arms, she could almost forget.

She leaned her head over the side. At least she could save them some mess. Then, something caught her eyes in the rock formations jutting out of the sea near the shore. Her fingertips dug into the side of the boat as she willed her rolling stomach to quiet enough so she could speak. "There." Tink pointed. "Look."

The boat rocked and swayed, sending bile rising up her throat, as pirates turned and shifted to get a better look.

"That..."

"A nose?"

"Aye, could be an eye...maybe two."

She clamped her lips closed, fighting a war with her stomach. *Oh, to be on land.*

"The bearded man." Finally, Smee arrived at the thing she'd seen.

"It is!"

"Aye. Whaddya know?"

Someone smacked her on the back, nearly sending her over the side. Tink screeched, her arms slapping against the sea. *No, oh no, please no.* The boat tilted. Saltwater splashed her face. She closed her eyes, bracing for the worst.

A strong arm wrapped around her, pulling her back.

"S' all right, love." James held tight, her back pressed against his chest.

She sucked in one breath after another, slowly prying open her eyes. Beat by beat, her racing heart returned to normal as she leaned into the safety of her lover. Somehow the boat's movement wasn't so horrid when he held her.

"You'd think you'd never been in the water," Smee said.

Tink glared at him. Her fingers dug into James's arm, refusing to let him release her. "I can't swim."

The captain stiffened around her. "You can't..."

"No," she snapped. "I can't." She couldn't swim, and she got seasick. She couldn't be a worse addition to the crew if she tried. And that didn't even include the curse she'd gotten them mixed up in when she stole from them. *Whoops.*

Want pirates quiet? Tell them you can't swim. Everyone stared. No one spoke. Sputtering, flailing, and gulping down seawater would have been preferable. Possibly even sinking down into the cold, wet depths.

James finally broke the silence. "Gonna let the waves do all the work? Row!"

The crew snapped back into action, turning their attention back to the shore and the task at hand. Several muttered to themselves.

"Ignore them," James whispered. His warm breath tickled her ear, raising the fine hairs on her arms.

He rose, pulling away. Reluctantly, she let him go. She wasn't moving. Not one inch until they pulled onto the beach. If she vomited, they'd just have to wash it out.

Finally, after minutes that felt like days, crew members leaped out the side of the boat and hauled it to shore. Even then, Tink sat hugging her legs...until James held out his hand to her. Her wings fluttered as she looked up into his grinning face. "Coming?"

With a deep sigh, she took his hand. Even with help, she stumbled as she stepped out onto the rocky, wet sand. It sucked at her boots, trying to pull her back as she trudged inland. What a miserable place. Dark water crashed onto a beach of grey sand that was more like little pebbles than the fine, sugary stuff gracing most of the shores of the Cerulean Sea. Some of the trees looked familiar. Palms, lofty figs, palmettos, and others she knew, but they were wrong...like life had been sucked from them, yet they still lived. And the moss hanging from their branches with little vines creeping through it? Everything in her rebelled against that. It wasn't right. Wasn't...natural. She shivered.

"So...if that was the bearded man," Sage said, pointing to the rocks. "Then who does the smoke belong to?"

It was easier to see now, rising in a column to mingle with the fog hanging over nearly everything. Dense trees and undergrowth—not to mention that horrible, stringy moss—separated them from the source, blocking the view of whatever or whoever was there.

"We're about to find out," James said. "On your guard."

He nodded to Tink, his gaze sliding to her thigh and the dagger strapped there. She patted it and forced a grin in return, letting her hand settle on the hilt. She wouldn't be a liability. *Nope, nope, nope.*

Machetes hacked a path through the overgrowth, cutting away branches and shrubs that had likely never seen a blade. Unfortunately, the island wasn't as lifeless as it looked. A thick, brown snake hissed at them from a tree. Bugs buzzed and hummed a chorus almost as loud as the crashing waves. A welt already rose along Tink's arm from a stinging bite.

It wasn't long, nor far, until James brought them to a halt. He gestured to his crew as he passed back down the line. "Camp ahead. Small," he whispered, just loud enough for her to hear.

What idiot would camp out here?

"Tink?"

The feminine voice made her heart skip a beat. Her eyes widened. Her back stiffened.

"Lily?" She spun around, peering into the jungle. It had to be a figment of her imagination. A trick of the mind.

But James's crew looked too, scanning the area, blades at the ready.

Then she saw it—movement from behind a thick tree, the flutter of wings, a swath of blonde hair tied back in a bun, the same color as her own but cut shorter. Tink swayed on her feet. Lily's eyes widened as she stared back at her.

"It *is* you," they said at the same time.

Lily reached for her.

Tink's eyes watered. How could it be? And here of all places. She stepped toward her cousin, ready to race to her side and throw her arms around her, but Hook blocked her path with an outstretched arm.

"Let me pass." Tink shoved at him.

He edged farther in front of her. "Could be a trick. Magic."

"It's Lily!"

"Tink." Her cousin raced forward, stumbling through brush. "You're here. It's really you!"

Smee and the others closed in around them, weapons raised. Lily slid to a halt, nearly falling.

"Stop!" Tink yelled, finally shoving past Hook. "Don't hurt her!" She sprang into the jungle, heedless of anything but her cousin. It was her. Those clear blue eyes, her lithe build—though the tight breeches and billowing shirt, so like her own, were new. Even her wings, with their slightly green hue, were just as she remembered. It was her, the cousin who'd been at her side since they'd first learned to fly as children. It had to be her.

"Oh Tink!" Lily threw her arms around her, pulling her into a crushing hug when they finally met among the underbrush.

Hints of citrus and jasmine teased her senses as she leaned into her cousin's embrace. It was her. A sob cracked from Tink's throat without warning. Impossibly, somehow, it was her. She was alive. She was all right. But... Tink pulled back. "Why are you here?"

She should be home. *Safe. Happy.* Tink had given everything for that.

"Why are *you* here? I've been looking everywhere." Lily's gaze shot up before she gasped and jumped back.

Tink felt him before she saw him. James loomed just behind her. Tink twirled around on the balls of her feet, lips pursed, arms outstretched. "Don't hurt her."

James frowned. She didn't fail to notice his fingertips drumming on the hilt of the sword sheathed at his side. "I know you want it to be her..."

"I won't hear it," she snapped. "It's her. Real as anything."

"I *am* real," Lily said. Tink didn't even need to see the wrinkle of her nose or her hands on her hips to know her cousin stared down the pirate in front of them.

"And just here, on the Shrouded Isles, where no one goes, and right where—" He cut himself off.

He didn't want to share the details of their purpose with her? *Fine.* But she sure wouldn't let him send her away, tie her up, or any of the other nonsense she could see brewing behind his pinched brow and stiff jaw.

"I can explain that," Lily said. "If you'll let me."

"Of course he will." Tink glanced past him to the rest of their companions. "They all will." Something slithered past, stirring up the brush at her feet. Tink screeched, jumping toward James, who had the decency to pull her close.

Lily sidestepped away. "Perhaps at my camp?"

25

*A*nother pixie. Tink's cousin. *In the bloody, weird forest. On an island everyone avoids like a plague.*

None of it made sense. Oh, she looked real enough. Could have been Tink's sister with their similar build and coloring. But there was something in her face, a twist to her smile, a glint in her eyes, that repulsed him. Too much like the woman he craved, and yet nothing like her.

The smoke belonged to a campfire she'd lit, the center point in a small clearing that sported a rough lean-to and a few half-rotted logs his crew attempted to use for stools. Attempted being the key word. Smee tumbled to the ground the moment he sat on one—half the side gave way, spilling him into the rotting leaves coating the ground. Nearly everything was damp from the foggy mist. How she got the fire lit was a mystery.

Lily clung to Tink, their fingers twined. She tugged her down on the one good log. "I was so scared," Lily said. "You were talking to that big, burly man, so I started talking to this handsome redhead. Before I knew it, I'd had too much to drink, and I was on a ship. There were all these men—"

"No." Tink clutched Lily's hand in hers. "They didn't...did they..." Her face flushed in a rush, the way only a pixie's can.

"No, no, they were nice actually." She shook her head.

Hook nearly snorted. *Not likely.* The Blackbeard he knew wasn't some noble gentleman. Neither were his crew. If he'd hauled her onto his ship, as Tink said, it was with reason, and he wouldn't be letting her go. At least…not until he had what he wanted. Something was missing here.

"They led me ashore, and I went back to the bar to find you, but you weren't there," Lily continued, sighing and fretting with dramatic flair. "The bartender said you'd left. I went all over town looking for you, but I couldn't find you. Beryl's wings, Tink! I was so worried. Distraught. Then I heard some men near the dock talking about how a pixie demanded to see Captain Blackbeard and left with him on his ship. It wasn't 'til then that I realized who they were."

Tink leaned in, her wings nearly touching her cousin's. "So, what happened then? How did you get here?"

"Aye, do tell us," Hook said. Both women turned to stare at him as he took a seat next to Tink, feigning a casual posture. Every muscle in his body was on edge. "Should be a rousing tale." His leg brushed hers.

Tink scowled at his tone, but he didn't let it dim his grin. He'd get to the bottom of this little mystery, and he'd keep her close while he did.

Lily glanced around at his crew, her shoulders hunching ever so slightly as she turned her attention back to Tink. Apparently, she warranted her focus where the rest of them didn't.

"I didn't know what to think. Why you'd gone. Where. So I went home."

Tink stiffened at his side. Hook slid his hand against her thigh in a show of support, but she didn't notice, or pretended not to.

"I'm so sorry." Lily pulled her closer, away from Hook. "I didn't want to leave you. I just didn't know what else to do."

Hook leaned around Tink. "Care to get to how you got here?"

Both women turned and scowled at him again.

Lily shook herself. A cloak of sorrow fell over her features again, everywhere but her eyes. She had the pout down, the set to her shoulders, but a person's eyes always told more than anything else. "Everyone was so worried about you. The elders, they went back to town to search…but…" She looked away.

His hook tapped against the log in impatience.

"Well, they heard stories about a pixie running off with pirates and… selling pixie dust."

"I did…" Tink's wings dipped as she raised her hand, letting her broken bracelet dangle from her wrist. "I did it to save you, so Captain Blackbeard would release you."

Lily gasped, her hand flying to cover her mouth. "You committed an unforgiveable sin to save me?"

Tink's shoulders drooped. Her wings almost seemed to dim. This wasn't the conversation he wanted them to have, not here in front of him and his crew. It was wrong, vulgar. Several of them had turned away, studying the surrounding jungle. Francis and Davies left completely. All the better.

"Tink is quite the woman. Brave. Selfless." Hook laid a hand on her knee, giving it a squeeze. Wrapping her in his arms would be better. Carrying her off and kissing away her fears, making her wings glow… what he wouldn't give for that. But she'd hate him for coddling her, for stealing her away. Again.

"Oh, no doubt!" Lily's head cocked to the side as she glanced back at Tink. "But then, where were you?"

Tink leaned back, folding in her wings until she rested against his shoulder. "They took me on to the next port. It took almost two weeks to get back."

And by that time her people had turned on her, learned that she'd sold pixie dust and was worthless to them. He ached to punch something. *Bloody pixies.* They had no idea what she suffered, the sacrifice she'd made to save her cousin. All she did was work to get home to the very people who'd exiled her. They didn't deserve her.

"I knew you couldn't have done it without reason," Lily said. "So I came back to find you. To help."

"Thank you." She moved away from him, back to her cousin. Reluctantly, he let her go. "You've always been right there with me. I knew you'd have done the same if the situation was reversed."

"Of course."

"Not to break up this love fest, but we do have *things* to do." Hook looked up into the fog, refusing to see another set of scowls. Every minute, Blackbeard gained on them. He could be nearing the island already, preparing to strike.

Tink stood, dusting off her breeches. "He's right, Lily, we have things to do. Come with us."

What? He snapped his head back toward them. "Perhaps she should wait on the ship." Something still felt wrong. Maybe she was real—the story matched what Tink had told him—but that didn't mean they had to trust her, not with something so important.

Hands on her hips, lips pursed, Tink said, "She should come. She could help and—"

Hook pulled Tink out of the way and faced down Lily. "How did you get here? Short version."

"Hey!" Tink shoved back, but he took her hand in his, giving it a squeeze. Someone had to get to the bottom of things.

Lily's nose wrinkled. "A mermaid told me who Tink was with and where you might be going."

"Which. One?"

The girl huffed. "Blue hair. Green scales. Didn't get the name."

A quick glance at Smee confirmed they had the same thought. Could be any of a dozen merfolk they knew, but none that were in Titania's inner circle. The queen wouldn't have been so free with the knowledge of their quest.

It was a lie. He could almost taste it in the bitter air. However she'd discovered Tink's whereabouts, that wasn't the whole story. No way she just happened to make camp right here, at the bloody bearded man rock. Not to mention the campfire. She wanted to be found. He knew a trap when he saw one.

"Come on," he called to his crew. "Let's give these ladies a moment." He turned to Tink. "*Just* a moment. Then I'll expect you on the beach."

Fisted hands landed on her hips as she straightened. "Aye, aye, Captain."

Great. She's bloody pissed off. Hook turned on his heel and gestured to his crew with a flick of his fingers. They hopped up and scuttled away without a word.

Until they reached the beach.

"She—"

He raised his hook in the air, silencing whatever torrent Sage planned to spew. "I know."

She paced back and forth, kicking up damp sand. "Every minute we stand here—"

"I know." *Gods, don't I.*

"We should be searching for—"

"I bloody know, all right!" His hand fisted at his side. He grimaced, fighting the urge to apologize. It was a fine line being their captain but also a friend—no, family.

"We'll split up," Smee said. "I'll take the ladies on a trek down the beach, then...uh..."

Hook rubbed his forehead. "No, we've split up enough already." He didn't like dividing his crew between land and sea. It put them all at risk. But leaving the ship unmanned was an even worse option. He'd already left Barley in charge of others onboard. They'd guard the ship, make ready to get away from this island as soon as their quest was done. Sending more back? He glanced toward the foggy peaks. *No.* There was no telling what danger awaited them. He couldn't spare more taking a pixie back to the ship, and they had no time to lose waiting around for them to return. "We'll bring her with us."

Groans and grumbles answered him. His raised hook requested silence. "Tell her nothing. Or as little as possible."

If Tink didn't tell her everything herself. He'd have to talk to her, get her alone and make her see reason. The witch's clues came at too steep a price to give them away for free, especially to someone he didn't trust.

"All right." Smee stepped forward. "Let's find that second clue."

Hook met his gaze, giving him a firm nod. When everything went to shit, Smee was always there. Solid, reliable, a stalwart friend to the end.

"The wooden trident marks the path," Anne said. The woman had a mind like a book. Tell her something once, and she could almost always remember it. She tossed her auburn braid over one shoulder. "At least, that's what you told me. Wooden...like a carving?"

There'd be no shortage of wood on an island like this, but who would have carved it?

"We'll know when we find it," Smee said, ever the optimist. "Like the bearded man."

Davies coughed, drawing their attention, and tipped his head toward the trees. Tink and Lily appeared on the pathway—hand in hand.

Hook's lips thinned. He'd never been so jealous of a woman before. Cousins or not, their closeness rankled.

"Well?" Tink asked.

The crew stood stone-faced, staring down the approaching pixies. He had to give it to them, they could be intimidating when they wanted. Hook glanced from one to another. "She can come with us. But—" He raised his hook, advancing on the newcomer. "I'm the captain here. You follow my orders. Answer my questions. Obey my crew. Got it?"

Lily visibly swallowed. Her focus flitted around as she nodded. For a moment, she looked much younger than her years, though Tink claimed they were almost the same age.

Fine. "Now spread out, but stay in sight of one another. You know what we're looking for."

"What are—"

Hook shot Lily a glare, silencing her question. The pixie flinched.

Tink frowned but kept her mouth shut. *Good.* "Spare a minute, Captain?"

Now it was his turn to frown. Nothing good ever followed his title. "Fine, come with me." He gestured toward the tree line opposite the shore. "Lily, stay with Sage." He pointed for the pixie's benefit.

Sage's eyes glittered with mirth. Oh, she'd keep the girl in check all right. Wouldn't hesitate to knock her out and tie her up if needed either, not like one of the men might.

"What's going on?" Tink said in a screechy whisper as they neared the trees stretching up toward the sun over the grey beach.

"I don't trust her."

She gaped.

"I know. She's your cousin. The one you saved. But out here?" He gestured around them. "You can't tell me that makes any bloody sense."

Her wings fluttered in what could only be annoyance. Color raced to her cheeks. She glanced back at Lily, who walked with Sage down the shoreline.

"She shouldn't be here, love. We can't risk our mission, lifting our curses, my crew. Give us time to see what she's about." His hand settled on her waist, and she relaxed...a little. "We'll keep her safe, just...protect us too."

Tink glanced up at him, her gaze softening. "Bloody pirate."

A laugh burst out with his grin. "You're starting to sound like me, love."

She rolled her eyes. "I wonder why. But she..." She glanced back at her cousin. "It *is* her. She's okay," her voice cracked, and she shook her head. Fighting away tears?

"She is." He gave her a light squeeze. For her benefit he'd say it, even if he didn't fully believe it himself.

Tink sighed. "Let's just find this scale and go home."

Home. The word cut at him and forced his grin to falter. Her home...or his?

26

*O*kay, *he's right.* It was weird that Lily was on the Shrouded Isles of all places. On the beach near the bearded man, near a fire that she wasn't trying to hide... And a mermaid telling her? It didn't feel right. But it *was* her. She'd seen her face every day for pretty much her whole life. Tink knew that voice, the way her eyes crinkled, the shade of her wings, her smell. It was all too real to be an illusion. Her story checked out too, much as it hurt to believe it.

Captain Blackbeard and his men hadn't hurt her, not physically, but they weren't the kind she'd have gone off with on her own—no way. They were the epitome of wretched pirates. Why would Lily go with them? And without telling her? She couldn't ask. For some reason, the words just stuck in her throat. A heavy feeling in her chest told her she wouldn't like the answer. But this was Lily. Her Lily.

She shook her head. Later. They'd get the scale, then figure it out. "Where are we supposed to find this trident anyway?" Tink gestured to the heavy-laden palms leaning overhead. Her hand swiped some of the strange moss, and she shivered. Wiping her hand on her breeches wasn't enough to totally remove the lingering soiled feeling.

They were supposed to find a wooden trident on an island made of trees covered in this terrible stuff? It could be anywhere. Any size. Any wood. Probably hidden behind more of…whatever the horrid stuff was. The witch had not been specific, not at all. The bearded man was totally different than she expected, so it stood to reason the trident would be too.

"Aye, that bloody witch wasn't worth the gold we paid her."

No, the bitch wasn't. Tink sighed. Yet another person who wanted her dust. Sunlight slanted through the palm fronds casting dancing shadows across James's strong jaw. Funny, the one person who inspired her dust told her to keep it for herself. She'd offered it to him on the journey to the Isles—compensation for the jewel she'd stolen. He'd just laughed and said he'd stolen a better treasure instead.

Her cheeks flushed, and she turned away. Oh, the effect he had on her. "Yes, well, that trident. Where in all the—" She blinked, stunned into silence.

"Love?" James was at her side in a heartbeat.

Just down the beach, an odd palm split into three about two feet off the ground. It couldn't be seen from the beach, not with the angle of the trunks, but from where they stood it was visible between its brethren and the mossy drapery. "Look at that." She pointed to it. "Do you think…?"

She hurried down the beach, as fast as one could in the mix of grainy sand, small rocks, and old fronds that littered the ground. James ran a few steps ahead of her.

"There's a path!"

Could it be? Her wings fluttered, nearly lifting her off the ground. Sure enough, there it was—the barest hint of a trail winding up into the foggy mountainside about fifty feet from the trident. A few branches hung low over it. Ropes of mossy vines zigzagged it, nearly hiding it from view, and a whole tree lay across the path just before it bent, but it was there.

"You think we should…?" She glanced at James.

The storm clouds that darkened his face when they'd discussed Lily vanished. Instead, he beamed with hope and pride.

"Only one way to find out."

James called over the crew, and they hacked their way to the path. They were careful at first, stepping in each other's footprints, trying not to leave much of a trail for anyone to follow. But after the bend the path narrowed considerably, until it was nothing more than a vague trail skinny as her. Each step took forever as they cleared limbs and debris out of the way. The witch's vision hadn't included a route back, so if everything went well, they'd be coming back through there again. If it didn't…well, it wouldn't matter.

Rocky sand gave way to soil strewn with old leaves and thorny bushes. Palms grew sparse, yielding to a variety of thicker trees, many laden with leaves. Some even held fruits that she had no name for. The vegetation was unlike any that grew in her homeland, and that blasted moss liked it just as much as the plants near the shore. Fog hung heavy ahead. Its tendrils crept down the hill to wrap around their boots and disguise much of the ground.

"The fog," Tink whispered. It was the next clue.

James sheathed his blade and took her hand in his. "Stay close."

"It's like this all over," Lily said, just behind her. "The slope near my camp too. I wouldn't go in it. It just felt…wrong."

A shiver raced down her spine. No kidding. The temperature had dropped. They still couldn't hear any birdcalls, and even the hum of insects had faded to the occasional, annoying buzz. The land near the shore had been wrong enough—cursed maybe. The looming fog was even worse, as if it had a ghastly life all its own that even the mosquitos were wise enough to avoid.

"Captain…" Smee paled as he pointed into the fog.

Tink followed the angle of his arm. There, among the trees, a small flame glowed. Gooseflesh raced across her skin. Fog swirled around the flame, but she couldn't see the handle of a torch or anything hanging from the trees. It floated on its own, an eerie specter.

"Another one," Sage said, pointing off to the right, the opposite direction the path wove.

"Might be a third there too." James gestured to the left, just off the pathway ahead.

Light in front. To the left. Right is right. The witch's words echoed in her head.

James looked down the line at each of them. "We go right."

"Right!" Lily screeched, causing Tink to jump. "But the path goes left. We can't go into the fog."

"Care to go back?" James asked.

James... She silently reprimanded him, but he ignored her pointed look. He wasn't wrong. It was either go back or follow the witch's words, not that Lily knew.

"We're with you." Smee laid a heavy hand on Lily's shoulder, causing her to stiffen. "Right?" He grinned at the double entendre.

"I just don't think..." Lily protested.

"We're going." Tink squeezed James's hand as she stared Lily down. She couldn't blame her cousin. Every bit of her wanted to run back down the path to the shore, but they couldn't give up now.

Lily sighed, then nodded.

Tink held her breath as James led them into the fog. Not that she could hold it all that long.

Whispers teased her ears, turning her skin clammy and causing her hair to stand on end.

It isn't them, can't be them. But oh, by Holy Flora, it sounds so real—like her parents might step out from behind a tree at any moment the way Lily had. Everything in her urged her to run into the dense mist. *Go to them. They wait for you!*

"Tink?" her mother called. "Are you there, darling?"

Mom! She bit her lip, holding in her cry. Her heart crumbled in her chest, leaving her aching, lonely, and longing for home. It was just like that time she got lost in the woods as a youngling. She'd gotten turned around somehow. Injured her wings and couldn't fly. Tears had streamed down her face as she called for help in the fading light of day. It was her forest, her home. She was safe there, or safer than out in the world, but her young mind hadn't understood that yet.

Hook's hand tightened on hers, almost painfully so. Their connection brought her back to her senses. *Not them. It isn't them.*

Tink stared up at the solid man in front of her. His shoulders were stiff, jaw set hard. Other voices called for him, no doubt. His mother too?

A glance back down the line confirmed the others fared just as poorly —spooked looks, jumpiness, hands clasped together for dear life. Anne bodily jerked Davies back onto the path despite her slighter stature. Lily whimpered. Limbs of the trees and thorn-laden bushes pulled at their clothes as fiercely as the voices calling to them.

"The fog confuses. Don't listen."

Ahead of them, the floating flame still flickered in the fog. Though they'd trekked for minutes, it was no closer than it had been, as if it moved with them or they'd gone nowhere at all. There was no path, no markers, only a hazy cocoon encasing them within the nearby trees and underbrush.

Worry slid around her middle, making her chest grow tight. Another tendril grabbed at her throat and squeezed. They were trapped here. No matter how they walked, where they went, they'd never get out. Other voices whispered to her now, ones she didn't know. Unlike her parent's reassuring words, these were mocking, teasing, jeering. A branch scratched her cheek, another seemed to reach for her.

Tink tugged her hand, tried to pull it away from James to slam her palms over her ears. A scream rose to the tip of her tongue.

"It clears ahead," James said. "Almost there."

Light cut through the mist, slicing a path ahead of them. The underbrush seemed to pull back, creating a path of packed dirt. Her whole body tingled with the desire to run. Her wings fluttered behind her, stirring up the last traces of fog. The whispers faded away completely.

James sighed, his grip loosening on hers.

And then they were out, standing in a clearing with cloud-dotted skies and sun overhead. Three mountain peaks speared above the canopy. Two were flush with vegetation, one brown and rocky. Colorful birds squawked from the trees. Even the air itself greeted them with a strong perfume of flowers from the red blooms hanging on vines in the trees. This part of the island was everything the land near the shore wasn't.

Sage brushed at her clothes. "We're finding a different way back."

"That was...something." Smee shivered.

"Those voices." Lily paled further.

"The fog confuses," Smee echoed the witch's words.

Tink looked back. The fog lingered thick as ever, and there was the eerie flame still floating at the edge of sight. A chill slid down her spine.

They'd never passed it, nor had it grown closer. "You think we can follow it back?"

"Told you, we're going another way," Sage said. "That—" She pointed back at the fog. "—is one big nope."

"We may not have a choice." James rubbed at the scruff on his chin.

A cloud moved to block the sun, leaving them in sudden shade. Not just any cloud, a dark one. *Just great.* Their curse would choose to rear its head on the Shrouded Isles of all places.

"Of course," Sage sighed, staring up at the sky.

"Come on," James said. "We've got to beat the storm."

The path grew wider. Clear, packed dirt and smooth stones guided them up into the mountains. Someone made this path. Maybe they maintained it even now. How else would it be clear when so much else wasn't? But who? They hadn't seen a soul. Nor any evidence of a person living here except Lily. She claimed not to have seen anyone either, and on that score, Tink believed her.

"People avoid the Shrouded Isles for a reason," Anne said. "Many reasons. But none of the stories I've heard mention anyone living here..." She ran her hand along a smooth stone where she knelt on the path. "Making trails like this."

"Ghosts," Sage said.

"Maybe."

Tink swallowed. If skeptical Anne agreed, it might just be true.

Rain pelted the crew by the time they made it up the mountainside path to a clearing. A rickety, old rope bridge swayed in the wind over a gorge. If Tink didn't know better, she'd bet the ground had cracked in two like an egg long ago to form those steep, rocky cliffs. Too bad she'd seen spiderwebs sturdier than the poor excuse for a bridge holding the sides together.

"Hold your breath as you sway and swing," Smee said, an echo of the witch's guidance.

"Nope. Not happening. No way." Sage threw her hands up in the air.

James rubbed at the stubble on his chin. "What choice do we have?"

Lightning lashed at nearby tree. Tink screeched and crouched on the ground. James was at her side in an instant. Thunder crashed and rumbled, louder than a cannon blast.

"We can't stay here!"

Tink looked around James to see Lily clinging to Smee. No, they couldn't stay there, but the bridge... She glanced back at the rotting conundrum.

"I'll go first," James said.

"No!" Tink latched on to his hand.

"We've got to do something."

But that bridge...there's no way they'd all make it.

"Let me go," Anne said. "I'm lighter than you."

Tink swallowed. But she was still human, taller and heavier than a pixie. There were two people lighter than Anne, but Tink could never risk Lily, not again. "I'll do it. I'm the lightest."

"No." Now it was James's turn to step in front of her. "Captain's orders. It'll be me, or we turn back right now."

Rain soaked through her clothes. Her wings and hair were already drenched. Even her boots squished.

"We could make a new bridge," someone offered.

But that would take time they didn't have. Blackbeard might already be hunting the Isles for them.

James clapped Smee on the shoulder. "If the worst happens..."

"Aye, Captain."

Tink swallowed. "James—"

Heads turned toward her. *Shit.* "Er, Captain..." She looked away, her boots sliding in the mud.

The rain stopped stinging her skin. James loomed over her, his face unreadable. Then all at once, she was in his arms, his lips pressed against hers. Stubble scraped her chin, her boots slipped in the muck, but it didn't matter. His kiss was all-consuming, passionate, a promise, and a...

Her chest clenched as he pulled away. Tink stumbled, barely keeping her balance as James turned and ran onto the bridge.

27

"No!"

"James!"

"Shit!"

"Captain!"

*T*he chorus of voices chased him. His boots slipped on the wet, rotting wood. *Bloody hell, what a terrible idea.* Wind howled through the gorge below, sending the bridge, and him, swaying and wobbling.

One glance over his shoulder nearly shattered his resolve. Tink stood at the end of the bridge. Smee had one arm on her shoulder, probably the only thing keeping her from running after him. Her cracked, pleading voice almost had him turning back. Almost.

But they had to finish this. The storms wouldn't stop until they did, and the damn things would ruin him—all of them—if they kept up.

Hook clutched the frayed rope of the low railing. It wouldn't hold if he stumbled and fell into it. Splintered boards creaked under foot.

The next two boards were already missing, challenging him to stretch across. Wind whistled. His friends had gone deathly silent behind him.

Just a few more planks.

A sharp crack split the air. The rope in his hand went slack.

His stomach dropped as his heart lurched into his throat. *Shit.*

"James!" Tink's scream nearly rent his soul.

He lunged for the cliffside in front of him as the bridge dropped. Breath fled his lungs as his chest slammed against the boards between him and the cliffside. His fingers slid on wet wood. His hook dug into the soft fibers, wrenching his arm. And his feet… Only crumbling cliffside met the tips of his boots.

Fuck.

Rain poured from above, dragging him down into certain death. He'd never make it. He'd—

"James!" Dainty hands hooked under his arms, tugging him upward.

His heart nearly stopped. "Tink?"

"Up!" Her wings buffeted him with frenzied gusts.

Shit. She'd flown…with her poor wings, in this rain. She couldn't die because of him. Never. With a renewed burst of strength, he pulled at the boards and stretched his hook to dig into the cliffside.

"There," she gasped. "Just…a little…"

His hand closed around a jagged rock at the top of the cliff, the edges biting into his skin. But he had it. Let it cut him, let him bleed—he'd give his one hand just to get them onto the cliff.

"Up! Now!" he yelled at Tink as she helped to pull him up. He needed her safe, couldn't concentrate with her in danger.

Another burst of effort had his elbow over the cliff edge. Leverage. He sucked in a breath.

With a rasping gasp, Tink crawled onto the cliff next to him. Her wings collapsed across her back, limp as wet cloth. Hook's boot found purchase on the last remnants of the bridge, and he pushed himself onto the cliff.

"Captain!" Smee's shout reached across the gorge between them.

He glanced back over his shoulder. His crew stood along the edge of the far cliff. *All there. Safe.*

Lightning struck another tree, causing them to jump and crouch in the downpour.

Maybe not so safe.

"Get to cover!" he called.

They wouldn't be crossing the gorge in this weather, especially not without a bridge.

Hook cupped his hands around his mouth. "Meet here after the storm!"

Whenever that would be. He didn't wait for confirmation. They'd carry out his orders—so help them, they better. Last thing he needed was more of his crew in trouble.

"Tink!" He scrambled to the woman still lying on the ground. His heart nearly pounded right out of his chest. If she'd—

"James," she gasped, pushing up on her arms. Rain soaked her like a wet rat. Bright red lips stood out against too-pale skin.

Tension slipped from his limbs as he pulled her to him. "What the bloody hell were you thinking?"

"I...I had to—" A shiver wracked her body.

Cold—too cold. And soaked.

They needed cover, shelter. Trees ringed the narrow clearing. Narrow paths wound off in two directions. "Come on." Hook pulled Tink to her feet, linked his hand with hers, and took off down to the right.

Right is right, the witch had said.

A previous clue, but now was no time to search for the next. The eagle could wait. Such a proud bird wouldn't be out in this squall anyway.

Just down the path, a shadowed opening loomed in the cliffside through the trees. "This way."

Tink followed, stumbling along after him, her hand still too cold in his. His bruises and scrapes were long forgotten, shoved deep down in favor of his worry.

Hook's arm brushed the sword at his side. He'd fight a bear to get her warm and sheltered. Mountain lion too.

The forest spat them out at the entrance to the cave, with just a few small boulders lingering between them and safety. Hook dropped Tink's hand to leap one boulder, then reached back over for her. "Give me your hand. Careful."

His voice echoed back at him from the recesses of the cave as Tink took his hand and slid over the stones. Her wings were still plastered to her back, wet and limp as the rest of her.

"Is it...?" She looked past him into the gloom.

His gaze followed hers, but nothing stood out. Barely any light filtered in, and soon there'd be none when night fell—storms or no. Dry branches littered one side of the cave. "We need a fire. Help me gather these."

The fire took forever and no time at all. He never went anywhere without flint—it could save a man's life. Tink hugged her knees to her chest near the flames as Hook picked up a lit stick.

"James, I..." Hair clung to her face as she glanced up at him.

"Stay here, love. I'm going to check out the cave."

Very slowly, his heart returned to its normal rhythm. He rolled his shoulders as he picked his way into the darkness. His muscles, even his bones, groaned in response. Crashing against the bridge had bruised his ribs. The climb had wrenched his arm. A cool chill seeped into his skin, but he was alive. And Tink... He rubbed an arm across his face. Reckless, foolish, bloody courageous woman. He had half a mind to yell at her for what she'd done. Would have if she hadn't been so cold and weak, but part of him was grateful. Without her help, he might not have made it up. She'd saved his life.

What he wouldn't do for her. Once they got the scale and got out of there, back to sea... His chest constricted. His boot smashed into a stone, causing him to stumble.

Shit. Once they got the scale, she'd get her reward from Titania. She could go home. Away from him. Back to her people where she belonged. He kept forgetting that. Every smile or touch wiped that horrible truth straight out of his head.

He swung the torch this way and that, scowling at the stalactites. He had half a mind to forget this quest. But his crew... He swallowed. He was a captain. Had a responsibility. He couldn't budge on that, not even for the woman he craved.

No bears jumped from the shadows. The rumbling growls of a predator he expected didn't come. The cave was one long tunnel, like the butt of an oar punched into the mountain. Water dripped from somewhere above to a shallow pool at the back. There was no way out—that he could see.

Tink stood near the fire hugging her chest when he returned. Half her clothes were off, laid over nearby boulders to dry.

She glanced up at his approach. "James."

The whispered word slipped under his skin, reigniting all the emotion that had cooled on his short trek.

"You..." *Foolish, wonderful, brave woman.* If he didn't already crave her every moment of the day, the sight of her in only sodden underclothes clinging to her every curve would make him wild. She was his own special drug, one he could never get enough of. And in that moment, there was only one thing that would satisfy his hunger.

28

The captain's gaze was unreadable in the dim firelight. Rain soaked him as much as her, but it only added to his fierce look. He was the sea, and the sea was him. The two could never be separated. She knew that, knew he was a captain before all else and could never be hers, but when she'd seen him fall...

"I..." She looked away from his intense, hard gaze. "I had to. When I saw you fall...I couldn't, I just couldn't not save you. I had to try."

Let him be mad at her, but she couldn't lose him, not like that. If they went their separate ways, it would suck—worse than anything—but he'd be alive, out there somewhere. Maybe someday they—

A calloused finger traced the line of her jaw, tipping her face toward the pirate at her side.

"Jame—" Tink's eyes flew wide moments before his lips crashed against hers.

Heat raced under her skin, warmer and more luxurious than their little fire, even as he pulled her tight against his wet body. His kiss devoured her. It demanded all her thoughts, her worries, her fears, until they vanished into the darkness of the cave. Her arms wound around his neck. Her fingers slid through James's wet hair, along the firm muscles of his neck, then down the stiff fabric of his coat.

His lips parted, an invitation and a request. Her daring tongue flicked against his, and he met it with gusto. Tink's wings fluttered to life behind her, the strain and ache from pulling James onto the cliffside no longer important. For him, they trembled and glowed, sore or not.

Tink squeaked against his mouth as James lifted her off her feet. She wound her legs around his middle, pressing further against him until they were one statue in the rocky cave.

With a moan of mixed pleasure and pain, James broke their kiss and stumbled across the stony floor. Cool, smooth rock kissed her skin through her thin underclothes as James set her upon a boulder. The look in his eyes as he gazed down at her stole her breath and made all thoughts of the cave vanish.

"You saved me," he said.

She swallowed, her mouth suddenly dry at his raspy words. "You'd have done the same for me."

"Yes." He leaned in, an arm on either side of her. "But I'd rather die than lose you."

His words crashed against her like a wave. She wobbled on the stone. *He'd...he'd die...for me?* But then, she'd almost done the same for him, and she would again. Somehow, this pirate had managed to steal something she never planned to lose—her heart.

James shed his jacket, tossing it over a boulder. His shirt followed, then a boot. But all the while he shed his clothes, his scalding gaze never left Tink. Instead, it roamed across her—slowly, intensely, every intention clear in his features.

"I need you." A thick slur clung to his words. His hand scrubbed down his face. "Not the place I'd—"

Tink spread her legs.

James froze, his breeches half off.

Biting her lip, Tink trailed her fingers along her underthings—no longer wet just from the rain. "I'd have you anywhere."

He blinked before sucking in a deep, shaking breath. Tink would swear fabric ripped as he shed the last of his clothes to stand naked before her.

She'd never tire of that sight. This proud, glorious man, confident inside and out despite the scars and injuries crisscrossing him, body and soul.

Tink stroked herself through her clothes and inched her legs wider as he sauntered near. James knelt between them until their faces were level with one another. Her tongue slipped out to moisten her lips, eager to resume their kiss.

James moved her hand to the rock at her side. A wicked grin spread across his face to join his hooded gaze.

A shiver raced across her skin as the metal of his hook slid under the hem of her underthings and pulled. Tink arched her back and raised her hips, letting the fabric fall free. Her head tipped back as cool air tickled her sensitive skin.

James guided the fabric down her legs, giving them a gentle, tingling caress as he went. Between the drumming of rain outside and the whisper of his touch, Tink was in paradise. The cold, the rock, her bruises—nothing could dim the moment. It couldn't possibly be better...until James's hot mouth pressed between her legs.

Tink gasped and jerked upright. The captain knelt between her legs, lapping, devouring. *Holy revered elders on high!*

The shadow of a beard on his cheeks grazed her sensitive skin, a contrast to the soft, slick movement of his mouth. He nudged her legs wider, and she complied, inching them farther apart. He wasted no time deepening their connection and wresting a moan from her parted lips.

Each flick of his skilled tongue had every inch of her humming in delight. A soft glow filled the cave behind them—her wings. Motes of benign pixie dust floated in the air.

"James." She kneaded his head, unable to hold still under his ministrations.

He glanced up, his eyes ravenous and intent—a true wicked pirate captain who never failed in a conquest and wasn't about to start now.

A calloused finger slid deep in her channel. "Oh!" Tink moaned.

He curled it inward, seeking that magical place inside her. Each thrust and flick had her nearly bucking off the rock. She abandoned her hold on him, all focus given to staying upright amid the delicious torment he wreaked upon her.

A second finger joined the first, and Tink screamed. Her vision blurred. Stars danced before her eyes.

"Aye, love." James's whiskers teased her thighs as his fingers pumped, wringing out her pleasure, making it last until she was nearly crying in pleasure and didn't know which way was up.

Tink whimpered when he pulled his hand away. She'd shut her eyes amid the storm of sensations, and when she opened them, he filled her vision.

James licked his lips before wiping away the wetness from his face. Hers.

Molten fire settled low within her as her thighs clenched, only to hug his hips. The tip of his cock nudged against her entrance. She'd barely pressed her lips against his when he thrust inside of her, one powerful, all-consuming stroke.

Her body embraced him like a missing piece. A shudder had her shivering against him as she savored the fullness—completeness—of him inside her.

James tugged her hips forward until he was buried so deep it almost hurt. And then he pulled back, beginning a seductive rhythm she'd begun to know and enjoy so well. He was insatiable—but then, so was she.

Metal scraped stone as he steadied himself with his hook. His hips shifted, and he pulled out. Tink reclined on the stone, her lower back against the cool surface—a contrast to James's warmth. Her wings fluttered free past the stone's edge. The perfect bed for them despite the hardness.

At this angle, he filled her in new ways that sent her head spinning all over again. *Clever pirate.* Her bare legs wrapped around him to steady herself and urge him on. Her heel ground into his rock-hard backside, and he groaned in pleasure.

Tink was helpless but to cling to him as he thrust in a fierce but careful pace. His every move demanded her submission, and she gave it. He captained their ship on this voyage, and he'd take no orders from his mate.

Screams echoed in the cave, ones Tink dimly recognized as her own. They rocked together on a sea of pleasure, utterly lost in one another.

In that moment he was everything, all-consuming, and she relished it.

No amount of time with him would ever be enough. She'd never tire of his lips against hers, the feel of him inside her, or the way he stared at her as if she was the greatest treasure he'd ever stolen.

With one hard thrust, Tink hurtled over the edge of pleasure once more. Her nails dug into his shoulders. Her legs squeezed tight. She clenched his shaft, begging it to stay lodged deep within her despite his own desire to move.

James thrust into her tightness, his breath hot and quick against her neck. "Ah, love, I—"

He shuddered against her. With one last, deep thrust, he stilled.

Her breathing slowed, and the sound of the rain returned. It—and the whole cave, other than the rock they reclined on—had vanished so completely during their lovemaking.

The glow of her wings, bright as ever, illuminated the sheen of sweat on his skin. They clung together, joined as one in the last lapping waves of their release.

Eventually, James settled them both on a mostly smooth stretch of rock near the fire. He insisted Tink be closer to the flames.

"You think I'll freeze in the night?" she teased, tracing a scar on his arm.

He shifted against her, twining his bare legs through hers. "I'm sure I can keep you warm, love. But this way, I can see you better."

"Oh, like there's anything you haven't seen?" She grinned despite the rush of heat creeping across her chest.

"Who would tire of such a view?" He gave her a once-over for good measure.

She rolled her eyes and shoved his chest, earning a chuckle in return. "Are you going to sleep with that on?" Tink tilted her head toward his hook.

He lifted his arm into the light, letting it dance across the cloth and leather straps. It had to chafe, wet as it was.

"Not if you'll help." He eased a little space between them. "It's hard when it gets wet like this."

Of course. No matter how well-made, it surely wasn't meant to be that wet. Why hadn't she thought of that before? Her attention drifted back to the rock they'd occupied. *Okay, well, there were reasons, but still...* She felt bad for not offering him aid.

Slowly, carefully, she removed the contraption from his arm. The stump where his hand used to be was puckered at the end, jagged, even though the injury clearly happened years ago.

Her fingers trailed across it, and James made to pull away. Instead, she grabbed his arm and placed a kiss upon the end. It was part of him, and she loved it all.

Loved. Her breath hitched.

Could she? Did she really? *A pirate, a man of the seas, a human for Flora's sake!* But...

"That repulsive?"

His words jerked her back. "No!" She leaned closer and placed another kiss for emphasis. This time she held his gaze as she did, watching his shoulders relax before she snuggled back against his chest.

"I was just thinking..."

"About?"

She swallowed. *Love.* It was too big. Too much. "You. I..." *Shit.* She glanced away. "You never told me how you got your hook."

"Ah."

Way to go, Tink.

Regret settled hard in her chest, but it ebbed as he pulled her close with both his arms.

"That is a long story."

"I think we have time." She glanced toward the cave entrance where rain still poured and the occasional boom of thunder rumbled.

"Aye." His forehead pressed against hers. "We do."

29

$\mathcal{H}$ is hook.

Now that was a story he hadn't thought about in years. One he'd never fully told. *Figures she'd ask about it eventually.* He'd taken it as his name after all.

He sighed and lay his head on the stone, staring up at the stalactites above. With Tink's soft warmth curled against him and contentment from their bout still flowing through his veins, it was as good a time as any to face those old memories.

"Ah, where to begin." He slid his fingers through her hair. "My ma got sick. Salt fever. It dries out the body slowly, over weeks, until a person is a husk of themselves and lets go. Lots of people got it that year, and the doctor's stores of violet root had run out. It was the only cure for the slow disease that ate away at her. I was still on the edge of a boy, scraping by with what I could make working the fishing boats. It took everything I had and then some—my first steps into piracy—to get the witch to use her spells and direct me to violet root. It grew on another island, a few days' journey by boat. Didn't have my own ship then. Thought to steal one, but captaining it on my own during the storm season was a fool's mission. Couldn't help Ma from the bottom of the sea."

Tink propped herself up on one elbow. "I thought you and Smee were friends since childhood."

"Aye, we were. But he was watching after Ma for me, along with his own family. One of us had to. His ma was pregnant, and his da, well, he'd been older when they settled down. Could barely get around back then and passed not too long after. Smee, as the oldest, always had a lot to do. Even then he was happy to help. Loyal. Always optimistic."

His lips pulled into a grin at the thought of his first mate, his first friend, and really his brother if ever he had one. They'd gotten into such trouble as boys before obligation to family encouraged them to straighten up...and before they sought any means they could to provide for those they loved. Hook shook his head, his smile vanishing. "Anyhow, I heard of a ship going toward the island where the violet root grew."

A soft gasp whispered across his skin. "The *Kraken?*"

Hook nodded. "I begged that bastard, begged him on my knees, to let me join him just until they reached my destination. I still remember how he grinned at me, one golden tooth gleaming through his thick, bushy beard. Then he clapped me on the shoulder with his beefy hand and proclaimed me one of his crew. It shouldn't have been so easy, but I was too relieved to be wary. Too young and dumb.

"It'd be a lie to say he didn't scare me. And his crew... In so many ways they reminded me of the worn, rugged fishermen I knew. Hard workers. Bodies worn by the elements. Always singing a bawdy tune. But there was a dark edge to them, a look in their eyes that said they wouldn't hesitate to slit my throat and throw me over the side if I stepped out of line. So I worked hard. Scrubbing the deck, cleaning the cabins. All the chores no one wanted." A phantom burn heated his skin, a memory from when the sun had blistered his skin from days at sea in shabby clothes. Fishermen were done by noon, selling their catch in the shade. Not Captain Blackbeard.

"We finally reached the island, and I followed the witch's directions to find the violet root. She was more direct that time. It was easy to find the field where they grew. Things were finally looking up. I picked extra to sell in the port, planning to buy passage on the next ship home." His missing hand tingled, yearning to close into a fist though a hook now took its place. "I didn't get the chance. Blackbeard's men found me and dragged me back onto the ship."

He could still see it, the grain of the wood that they tossed him down on in front of Blackbeard. The faint scent of jasmine. Blackbeard's polished boots thumping into his line of sight. "Thought ta sneak off, boy?" Blackbeard had jerked him to his feet by his shirt, ripping it in the process. "A little rat, scurrying away."

Hook's cheek stung at the memory of the backhanded slap that came next. "Ya'll leave when I say ya can."

Something soft and warm brought him back to the moment. Tink cupped his cheek. Firelight flickered across her face and caught in her wings. "You don't have to tell it."

No, he didn't—but for the first time, he wanted to. "I haven't answered your question yet." He covered her hand with his before tucking her closer into his side.

"You don't—"

"I know. Even Smee doesn't know the whole story."

She jolted against him. "What?"

The hint of a grin pulled at his lips. "That's right, so listen close, because I may never tell it again. Where was I?" he asked, for dramatic effect. "Ah, yes. Captain Blackbeard was furious that I tried to leave, even though we'd only agreed on me joining them for that one leg. He thought to teach me a lesson." He glanced at his hook, a lump in his throat. "He cut off my hand." It was a mercy he did it quick. He'd barely understood what was about to happen before one of the crew stretched out his arm, and Blackbeard swung the blade—a cutlass—he pulled from a crocodile skin sheath.

Tink kissed his cheek. The soothing motion of her hands over his bare skin kept him grounded. Without her... *Gods, without her, I'd be lost.*

"He threw me in a cell. Left me there to clean and stitch my own wound in that filth-ridden place. Most of it was a blur." A lie. He'd never forget those days, hovering on the brink, laying in his own mess. Every moment was etched in the darkest part of his soul, the part that vowed vengeance. It had festered there, a disease of sorts that no amount of time healed. If anything, it only grew worse until all he could focus on was revenge. At least, that had been the case until he met a certain pixie in a bar. He brushed a hand through her hair again. "But one day, Blackbeard arrived at my cell. He threw a polished metal hook in with me. A way to end myself if I wanted."

Those cold, uncaring eyes still haunted his nightmares. "Fisher boy," he'd said. The man wouldn't even use his name, though he knew it. "Gut yerself or git yerself together."

A shudder of anger passed through him. "I lived, and they let me off at the next port." Dumped him on the dock was more like.

"Boy might become a man after all," Blackbeard had laughed. His bushy eyebrows pinched together as he stared him down like he was a fish that flopped on his boots. "I'll be watchin' ya, boy."

And Hook would be watching him. He'd made a vow that day. He'd rise, make a name for himself, and take away from Blackbeard the one thing he loved—the seas. Killing him would be too easy, too quick. Better that he suffer by seeing the boy he'd nearly destroyed rise to become a better pirate than he.

"That was the hook?" Tink glanced at the offending object.

"I've had it with me every day since. He thought to bring me low with it, and so I used it to make a name for myself."

She kissed his chest before grinning up at him. "And here I always thought you just lacked creativity."

Leave it to her to find a way to make him smile.

"At least it's better than being named for what your parents do and their favorite flower." She pouted.

Tinker Bell. "I always wondered about your name," he said. Such an odd one it was.

Her face flushed, and she dipped her head. "It's pixie tradition. You have family names, we have job names. Our job name comes first, then our given ones."

Interesting. "Can't change jobs?"

"Oh, you can. Then your name changes too. I thought about it. I like music, but tinkering and making things are what I'm best at. Like my old treehouse," she sighed. "Besides, the elders may have thrown a fit if I'd asked for a formal change."

"And Lily? She's a…"

"Tinker. Tinker Lily."

His lips quirked. "So why don't you go by Bell?"

"It's too…" She waved her hand up in the air.

He understood. Bell was a beautiful name, maybe too gentle for her wild nature and fiery heart. No wonder she'd chosen to go by Tink instead. It fit. Even so… "You could change it if you hate it, love. Humans don't have such rules."

One finger slid down his collarbone. "I'll think about that." She took the silver ring on his necklace between her fingers. "She'd be proud of you, I think."

He glanced at her from the corner of his eyes. "I doubt that."

"What…" She shook her head. "No, never mind."

Hook swallowed down the knot lodged in his throat. "What happened to her?"

She looked away. "I don't want to…" Tink blew at the lock of hair falling across her face. "Well, I guess I've already ruined the mood."

"You could never ruin anything." He tilted her face back to him. "It hurts to speak of her, I can't deny it, but my vengeance against Blackbeard isn't just for me." He pushed the lock of hair behind a pointed ear. "I finally made it home two weeks later. By some chance, I'd managed to keep some of the violet root. But it didn't matter. She'd passed two days before I returned."

He took Tink's hand in his, closing her delicate fingers over the ring against his chest. "If Blackbeard had let me go, I'd have made it in time. She could have gotten better." He wouldn't have forgiven Blackbeard for what he'd done to him. He'd have still sought revenge, at least for a time, but maybe that would have faded over the years. But his mother's death? That he could never forgive.

Tink leaned impossibly closer. "When we're done here, once we've retrieved the scale and lifted your curse, I want to help you stop him."

He sucked in a breath, turning to face her fully.

"What about your home? Lily?"

"She can go back and tell everyone I'm okay. Her bracelet is still intact, so we just need to get her back to one of the doors. Once Blackbeard is defeated, I can use the pearl to fix myself and go back later."

So she'd still leave him. A deep ache rent through his chest. *Should have known.*

"That is..." She released the ring, her fingers trailing down his skin. "Unless you don't want me to," she rambled on, clearing noticing the change in him no matter how he tried to hide it. "He's hurt you worse than me, I just want to help—"

"You do help. I'd love your help." And so much more. But he couldn't ask it. She hated the sea. *Bloody hell, she can't even swim and retches up everything in her stomach half the time.* And he couldn't leave his crew...or the sea... They were part of him as much as the air in his lungs. "We'll figure this out."

She nestled into his side with a soft sigh. A murmur slipped from her lips, too quiet to hear. Despite the troubles that no doubt awaited them, in that moment he had everything he desired.

30

"Good morning, love."

A rock dug into her leg. At some point she'd rolled on a wing, and it ached something fierce. But as she cracked open her sleep-heavy lids and gazed into James's smiling face, none of that mattered. One leg was twined with his, so much warmer than the other. Color raced to her cheeks as she registered the hardness pressed against her thigh. James's arm flexed around her waist as he tugged her closer.

"Good morning." She bit her lip, holding in a sheepish smile. It didn't matter how many times they woke up together, each time was a wonder, a joy, a moment she wanted to last forever. The damp cave had to be one of the worst places she'd ever slept, yet she had no desire to leave.

Birdcalls teased her ears. Light spilled into their dwelling, reflecting against the wetness of one wall. "The storm passed?"

"Looks like it." His legs rubbed hers, eliciting a small whimper.

Tink glanced toward the entrance. The crew would be looking for them. The flood of light said it was past dawn. She sighed and dropped her cheek to his chest. "I wish we could just stay here."

Calloused fingers trailed up her side, leaving gooseflesh in their wake. They twisted a lock of hair, traced one ear. "Me too, love. Me too."

Slowly, reluctantly, he slid out from under her. Cold rushed into the vacated space.

Tink twisted around, watching with unabashed interest as Hook inspected their clothes. His tight ass could inspire sonnets. Not to mention the strong arms, powerful legs, and lean hips. Her thighs squeezed together as she took stock of the man before her. She had half a mind to drag him back down to the hard, rocky ground and have her way with him.

James looked back at her over one shoulder, an upward twist to his kiss-bruised lips. "Little minx."

She grinned in return. Why deny it?

"Still a little damp." He balled up her clothes and tossed them to her.

A little damp was an understatement. They'd barely dried at all.

Tink sighed and glanced back toward the cave opening. At least the sun would be warm. Already it crept along the cave wall—

"James!" She jumped to her feet. Her wings gave a slight flutter.

"What?" He whirled around, still stark naked, searching for a danger that didn't exist.

"Look!" she nearly squealed.

"Aye, it's sunny today."

"Not that." She rushed toward the carving she'd spied, not caring about the hard rocks under her soles. "There!" She flung out her arm toward the cave wall.

"Wha—" His eyes flew wide. "The eagle."

Laughter spilled out as she bounced with glee. The clue. It had to be.

James's chest rose and fell before he whipped around toward the back of the cave. "There's a pool back there." He turned back to her. "A shallow pool."

"In shallow pool the scale is found," she repeated the witch's words.

James grinned like a man who'd just been declared king of all, and he waved her to him.

Tink fluttered across the ground, her toes barely touching. He'd already hefted a torch from the remnants of their fire. Its smoke curled up toward a narrow opening above that dripped rainwater into the cave.

Still naked as the day they were born, they picked their way over the rocky ground toward the back of the cave. What did clothes matter when the object they sought was within reach? Besides, the witch said it would be in the shallow pool—no sense getting everything wet or stripping down yet again.

Cool air raised gooseflesh along Tink's skin, but she barely noticed, not with the tingle of excitement already running through her veins and joy practically pouring off the man at her side.

A pool of clear water stretched toward the edges of the cave at the end of the tunnel. Narrow strands of light filtered in from a crevice in the roof.

"It's deeper than before." James frowned as he wedged the torch between two nearby rocks.

The storm's fault, no doubt. Of course it would make this last part harder too. Didn't it always?

Small pebbles littered the bottom of the clear pool. "How will we find the scale in all this? Do you even know what it looks like?"

James shook his head. "No idea." He looked her up and down. "Though it might be a good thing we left our clothes behind."

Heat rushed to the tips of her ears. As if she needed another reminder of his nudity. She'd stubbed her toe twice on the short walk there because she'd been too preoccupied with her view of James. Their goal within reach or not, he was a huge distraction. Even the cold didn't detract from that…too much.

Water splashed as James stepped into the pool. "Bloody cold!" he yelped.

Tink sighed. They were going into the water. *Of course. Why, oh why, do I always have to get in the water?* She stuck a toe in and nearly shrieked. *Bloody cold is right.*

Calm pool. No waves. Not that much different than the streams at home, she repeated silently to herself, trying to calm her racing thoughts. But the streams at home were warm and much less deep. Shallow pool, her ass. Maybe it had been—before the rain.

Her foot slipped. Tink yelped as her arms flailed in the air and her wings beat behind her, barely keeping her upright.

"Got you." James grabbed her arm, steadying her.

Tink gasped, but it wasn't just his touch that had her heart racing and the cold melting away. Out in the deepest part of the pool, something glowed a pale, eerie blue. "Look."

He followed her line of sight. His eyes widened, and he stepped in front of her.

"The scale?" She peeked around him.

"Don't know." His voice held a hard edge, as if an enemy had just dropped from the roof. "Stay here." No sooner had he let her go to venture into the deeper water than the glow vanished.

"Bloody—"

"Where'd it go?" Tink splashed forward, heedless of his words or the water rising up her thighs. She brushed against James, and the glow flared back to life.

Breath caught in her throat. "Every time we touch..."

James turned toward her. "Two bound as one." The last of the witch's words. He took her hand in his. "We have to get it together."

Tink swallowed the sudden tightness in her throat. She'd have to go into that deep water with him.

"And one more thing..." He glanced down at the stump of his hand where he'd yet to reattach his hook.

Her stomach dropped. "If you're holding my hand, you can't pick up the scale."

"Aye."

"I could hold your arm...maybe..." She looked away. Blast it, that water would be over her head.

He pulled her close in a comforting embrace. "I'll swim for us and get us down there. You just have to grab it."

Easier said than done.

Tink practically clung to James like a monkey in a tree as they walked out into the depths. True to his word, all she had to do was hold on. And hold her breath. James plunged below the surface with Tink wrapped in his arms.

The icy water closing over her face nearly made her screech out all the air she'd sucked in before he dove.

Water everywhere. Can't swim. Lungs burning.

James gave her a little shake.

Scale. Right. Get it together.

Small stones littered the pool floor, but only one emitted the eerie blue glow that surrounded them. *The scale?*

Tink grasped it, but the slimy sensation she expected didn't greet her fingers. It was smooth and flat, like a triangle-shaped rock. Before she could wonder at it more, James kicked off the bottom and hauled them to the surface.

"Perfect, love. Don't drop it."

She barely heard him over her gasps for air. They'd only been down there a moment, but it could have been a lifetime.

When they reached waist-deep water, James set her on her feet. She shook the water off her wings. Tink unfurled her hand to reveal the small object she'd clutched for dear life. "It doesn't look much like a scale." Not that she had a ton of experience with fish, but she was pretty sure scales weren't stones.

"Aye, but it fits the witch's words."

Tink frowned. "Unless she led us to a rock."

"Something like this..." James picked up the stone whose glow had faded. Out of the water, Tink could see finely engraved marks across its surface. "It has to be what Titania wants."

Please, please, let it be. "Then we can lift your curse," she said, in an effort to be optimistic.

A sad smile touched his face. "And you can go home."

Her chest ached. *Home. Right.* She could no longer meet his gaze. James placed the scale back into her palm and turned away.

"Wai—" Tink reached for him, but he dived back into the pool.

A minute later, he returned bearing a handful of the other rocks. "Just in case," he said, shaking the water from his hair like a dog.

Tink raised her arm against the splatter. "In case what?"

He shrugged. "Well, we didn't know what it looked like. I'd wager no one else does either. Can't be too careful with treasure."

His grin sent a whole mess of feelings sloshing inside her that she couldn't deal with, especially as his gaze dropped to her chest, barely hidden by her sodden hair, then lower. Tink coughed and turned away. They needed clothes. *Now.*

Sliding the cold, wet garments over her skin was more of a travesty than diving in the pool. *Well, almost.*

James slid the fake scales into his pack but brought the real one back to her. "I want you to hold onto this."

"Me?" Tink squeaked, rocking onto the balls of her feet.

He took her hand and pressed it into her palm. "I like to have the things I value most in one place." The look in his eyes nearly stripped her bare—again.

Words failed to reach her tongue. All she could manage was a soft "oh" as her skin heated in a rush.

The stone was oddly warm in her hand as she slid it into one of the little inner pockets sewn into the waistband of her breeches. No one would get it there...except maybe James. Damn, if she didn't look forward to his attempts to seek that plunder. Spending so much time without their clothes had not dulled her desire to see him without them again—not at all.

Tink blinked against the bright sunlight and shielded her eyes as they emerged from the cave. *Blessed warm, beautiful sun!* The storm had passed all right, leaving blue skies above. A haze of fog lingered just below them on the mountainside that the day had yet to burn away—if it even could on this cursed island. Birds chirped and squawked. A monkey chittered off to her left. But the crew was nowhere to be found.

"Maybe they camped a ways down the path," James said as if reading her thoughts.

"Maybe," she echoed, but something felt wrong. The scene was too happy. Too...normal. And wouldn't they have come right back? "You think they went for supplies to repair the bridge?"

"Maybe. Come on." His words were clipped, but it wasn't frustration. He was worried. The stiff set of shoulders gave him away, even as he held his hand out to her.

She took it, following him over the uneven rocks until they reached the narrow section of gorge she'd nearly plunged into the day before.

"If we find a thick vine, we might—"

"No, I've got this." Her wings fluttered. She stretched and rolled her shoulders.

He'd argue against it. She'd told him how weak her wings were outside the vale. Yesterday it'd taken all she had to haul him up the cliffside in the pounding rain. Dust had returned. So much of it, more than she dared hope, and she hadn't shed a bit of it to use for other purposes. It was because of him, their time together. Despite the hardships, she was happy in his arms, his presence. Each smile...

His jaw shifted, and she rushed to explain. "I can—"

"I trust you."

Her eyes widened. "You..."

"I trust you," he repeated.

"All right. I can do it," she added, more for herself than him. "I'll just, um..." She stretched on her tiptoes, lacing her arms around his neck. "Lift me—oh!"

James palmed her ass, lifting her up and pressing her tight against him as she wrapped her legs around his waist. He tipped his forehead against hers. "You have my life in your hands again, love."

No pressure or anything. One deep breath filled her lungs, then another. "Back to the edge of the cliff."

One careful step after the other, he complied.

Wings, don't fail me now.

Lifting them was easy. There was solid ground below their feet. Flying out over the gorge, breeze battling against her wings, was another story. Each beat and flutter ached. Pain raced down her back. James was utterly still in her arms. She didn't dare look at him. Or speak. Her heart thundered in her chest. Sweat broke out on her neck.

Almost there. Almost...

Tink cried out in a mix of pain and relief as James's boots touched the other side. Immediately he leaped back from the edge and spun her around to safety. She sagged against him, her feet sliding to the ground and her wings folding against her back. They'd made it. *Thank all the holy elders.*

James tilted her face up as she heaved in one breath after another. "Brilliant, love."

A humorless laugh bubbled out. She could do without trying to lift her lover over another deadly drop. "Let's go." She turned away, unwilling to confess how hard the flight had been. "They've got to be close."

Twenty minutes of stumbling down the rough pathway, and they'd seen nothing more than a scrap of cloth on a branch—which could have come from their trek up.

Tink halted. "Maybe we should go back."

"Smee!" Hook called. Only the birds answered. "You're right, let's—" He turned, his eyes widening.

A beefy hand clamped over her mouth.

31

*B*lood raced in her ears. She kicked, hit, cried as the man—it had to be a man—crushed her wings against his body. "Too late now, *Captain*," the deep voice rumbled from behind her.

James pulled his sword. "Let her go."

The man raised his own blade to Tink's neck. She went utterly still, frozen by fear. "Think not."

That voice. She knew that voice. James's eyes locked with hers across the space between them. Raw fear lingered there.

Captain Blackbeard. Her stomach plummeted, her knees shook dangerously. Other men emerged from the dense jungle, their own blades raised.

"What do you want?" James demanded, ignoring the others.

"Ta take ya to yer crew, of course." He chuckled. The edge of the thick, curved blade nearly scraped her skin. Her vision blurred, but she could swear he gripped a handle wrapped in some kind of reptilian skin.

"What have you done with them?"

"They're waitin' just ahead."

Lily.

Her heart nearly beat out of her chest. *Had she gotten away? Did he have her too?* A tear slipped down her cheek as Blackbeard ushered her forward.

Everything she'd sacrificed was to get her home safe, and now Blackbeard probably had her again. She'd gotten James and his crew cursed, put them in danger, and for what?

"Drop tha sword," Blackbeard ordered, angling the blade of his own against her throat for emphasis.

James didn't take his eyes off her. "If you hurt her..." He tossed his blade away.

"Ye'll what?"

A bulky man with long, greasy hair kicked the back of James's legs, knocking him to the ground. A grunt of pain slipped out as he slammed into the dirt. Tink yearned to run to him, but Blackbeard held her steady. One move, one ill-timed lunge, and his sword would cut her throat.

Another man, short and lean, punched James in the face, knocking him to the ground. "Fish bait," he spat.

In moments, they bound his arms behind his back and hauled him to his feet. Blood dripped from a cut on his lip. She ached for him, hurt worse for his wounds than her wings screaming in pain, trapped against the bulk of Captain Blackbeard.

The pirates pushed James down the path ahead of her. Deadly quiet reigned until they entered a small clearing. Even the birds and other animals made themselves scarce in the presence of these monsters. Blackbeard removed his filthy hand from her mouth, but what could she say? There could be no reasoning with this monster. She knew to even attempt it would mean wasting her breath. Hook's crew was bound and gagged, tied together in little clusters with Blackbeard's men on watch.

A tight knot bobbed in her throat as Tink scanned each of the crew, taking stock of injuries—bruises, a little blood, nothing fatal that she could see. But...

Lily. Her heart skipped a beat. "Where is she?" she blurted, before she could think better of it.

Smee looked away. Sage snarled against her gag. Why...?

"Looking for me?"

Lily strolled out from between two of Blackbeard's men, none the worse for wear. Tink's brows scrunched. Her mind tried to work it out and failed.

Blackbeard lowered his sword and shoved her forward. Tink floundered like a fish, mouth agape, and fell to the ground. Her knees barked in pain even as her wings sighed.

"Tink!" James lunged for her, only to be jerked back.

"Bind 'er." Blackbeard ordered.

She scrambled to kneel, blinking at Lily, before her arms were wrenched behind her by two brawny men. "You're..." Reality choked her. Truth stabbed her in the gut.

"With them?" A feral grin crossed her cousin's face.

No.

Acid crawled up her throat.

No. It can't be.

"I loved you. I saved you," she gasped. "I gave everything." Tears burned the corner of her eyes, but she refused to cry, not for her. Rope bit into her wrists as the man behind her pulled the bindings tight.

Lily sauntered over and crouched before her. "Your mistake."

"My—" Breath left her. She hunched as if kicked in the stomach. A cold sweat broke out on her skin.

"I *wanted* to go with them that night." She grinned at the only decent-looking man among Blackbeard's crew, who blew her a kiss in return. "I planned to come back...eventually." She shrugged. "But then you had to be all perfect and heroic. Little shining star Tinker Bell, off to save the day."

Tink reared back at the sarcasm in her voice. *Perfect? Shining star?*

"They told me what you offered for them to send me back to shore. And you know my first thought? Freedom. Finally. No more being Tinker Bell's shadow. Always overlooked and unappreciated."

Each word struck worse than a blow.

"No more being compared to Little Miss Goody-Goody. I could finally shine. Me!"

"I never..."

"No, you never knew what it was like to be me. Not as pretty, not as smart, not as skilled. Every day my parents compared me to you. Why can't you be more like Tink? Even the elders just had to go on and on about you and pretend I didn't even exist!"

Tink dry heaved. They'd always been together. They played together, studied together, shared secrets. Lily was her friend. Her best friend. "You asked me to go with you. Always. You said you trusted me, wanted me with you." Any time they snuck away to the human lands, Lily had insisted she come. Who could she trust better than her very best and closest cousin? Who else could she possibly want with her? Tears streamed down Tink's cheeks.

"Of course." Lily blew a lock of blonde hair out of her eyes. "If we got caught, you'd make sure we didn't get in trouble. They just *loved* you so much. And..." She shrugged. "I kinda hoped you'd like it. Maybe stay? Get lost? But you have to do everything *so well.*" Her laugh, once so comforting, grated like coarse sand.

Lily wanted her to be cursed and cast out. Her own cousin. Someone she'd loved, given everything for... Tink stared at the ground, unable to look at her. "You never even went back." No wonder no one came to look for her. They never knew where she'd gone.

"Oh, of course I did."

Her head snapped up. "Then...what did you—"

"Say? See, I know you so well. Though apparently you never knew me, did you?" She bared her teeth. "They were distraught. 'Poor Tinker Bell,' they said, 'we must find her at once. We have to help her.' None of them cared a whit about me. *Taken hostage* by pirates." She gasped in feign shock. "Barely escaped in time. I might as well have been invisible. So...I might have given them the wrong location." She rolled her eyes.

"You—"

"Oh, and told them you sold your dust on purpose and *asked* the pirates to take you away."

Her body shook. They couldn't believe that, her parents, the elders. Everyone she'd ever loved...

"They were dubious, of course, but when they couldn't find you. Well?" She stood and flipped her palms to the sky.

The move shifted something in her. Changed the tide from sorrow to fury. "You bitch."

Lily straightened, her smirk vanishing.

"I gave everything." *Home. Family. My way of life.* "Everything! And you —" Her nails cut into her palms. "You'll pay for this!"

The other pixie threw her head back and cackled. "Everything? You think this is everything?" she mocked. Lily ripped the pixie bracelet from her arm.

Tink gasped as the beads joined the dirt. *That shouldn't...* They didn't break so easily.

"A fake." Lily shrugged.

"Then you..." She'd cursed herself too.

"Of course. Who wants to stay where they're not wanted?"

"You're the one who sold dust to the bartender in Tortuga." Hook's icy words cut through her haze of fury.

Lily smirked. "There and half this side of the Cerulean Sea. Had to make sure my story would check out for anyone who came looking."

Tink shook. That's why James was confused when she told him she hadn't sold dust in months. He'd come across Lily's. It had led him to her.

"Enough." Blackbeard stomped his way to them. "Ye've had yer fun," he snapped to Lily.

Lily's nose wrinkled, but she stepped back as Blackbeard circled near. He looked just as he had that awful night—tall, stalky. Jet-black hair tumbled from under a black hat to graze the back of his neck. Streaks of silver highlighted it, especially in his overgrown beard that covered the lower half of his face. From the way he wielded his cutlass with practiced ease, the man was still muscular beneath the thick, black jacket that covered him neck to boot.

"Now." He twirled his curved blade and walked to James. "We've a few things ta...discuss."

Tink blinked away her tears as she gazed at James where he knelt on the ground a few feet from her. The look on his face said everything: fury at Lily's betrayal, heartache for her. And a promise—she hadn't lost everyone who cared for her.

32

*L*ily would pay for hurting Tink. He'd known something wasn't right from the moment she showed up. Everything screamed trap. *And it was. It bloody was.* But he never expected her to be in league with that bastard.

Several possibilities had come to mind when he considered the pixie. A phantom conjured by the island? *Possible.* Paid off by one of the Gamorean royals? *Maybe.* An idiot out for her own good? *Definitely.*

His fist tightened where it was tied behind his back. She'd pay for betraying them, but most of all, for hurting his Tink. Watching her cry, body shaking, heart visibly breaking…torture. If he didn't hate the bloody crocodile stalking toward him so much, he'd thank him for shutting Lily up.

Blackbeard pointed his sword at Hook, glaring down its length. "Where's tha scale of Leviathan?"

"Haven't found it," Hook snapped back as he stared intently at the monster looming above him.

Blackbeard tipped his head to one of his men. The lanky man advanced.

Hook loosened his jaw, tilted it just so… Pain flared in his cheek as the man's fist smashed into him. He let his head swing, gritting his teeth.

Fucker.

Tink cried out, "Stop!"

Blackbeard ignored her.

From the corner of his eye, Hook saw his crew squirm and wiggle. A nice gesture, but it wouldn't help. *We're right fucked.* And it was his fault. He'd led his crew into this mess, ignored his gut, chased a damned treasure. Not that he really had a choice. They needed it, but he could have gone alone, insisted they stay on the ship far from this bloody island.

Hook spit blood onto the dirt near Blackbeard's boots. "You acted too soon, you old crocodile."

Blackbeard stepped forward. The tip of his sword grazed the underside of Hook's chin, forcing him to crane his neck back. The same sword he'd used to cut off Hook's hand. All these years and he still had it, handle freshly wrapped in new croc skin. "Ya never learn, fish boy."

The old taunt raised his hackles.

"Can't give ya what we don't have, croc," he taunted, mimicking the man's voice.

Blackbeard snapped his attention toward Lily, a question clear on his face.

She winced. "We'd only found half the clues so far."

Fury radiated from Blackbeard as he went utterly still, letting his sword dip ever so slightly. If looks could kill, the pixie would be dead.

"This was the best chance, I promise," Lily rambled. "With the storm, the fog. It was the only chance I had to sneak away, to tell you."

How she pandered to him. *Disgusting.* Tink wouldn't even look at her cousin. She didn't seem to look at anything, staring at the ground, her features pale. And her wings... He hadn't noticed until now how one bent awkwardly. Hook struggled against his bindings. If he could rush Blackbeard, dodge his sword, find a way to—

"Nuh uh," Blackbeard tsked. The sword point dug into the soft skin under his chin with a sharp prick. "Ya confirmed the clues?" he asked Lily.

She placed her hands on her hips. "Of course."

Blackbeard's gaze landed on him again, cold as iron. "Men, take this lot to tha *Kraken.*"

Hook hazarded a quick glance at his crew before two men hauled him to his feet. *Don't do anything stupid.* Steady looks from his crew confirmed the silent order. He shifted his focus to Tink... *Bloody hell.* The raw fear and panic in her gaze cut sharper than Blackbeard's sword.

He had to find a way out of this. For all of them. At least they didn't have the scale yet. *Don't give it to them, love.* It wouldn't save them. Blackbeard would sooner kill them all than let them walk free. Once he had what he wanted, nothing would stop him from doing just that. He yearned to tell her. They wouldn't give him the chance, and he couldn't risk mouthing it. *Please, love.*

Tied together in one long chain of prisoners, there was no way to escape. Hope slipped further away with each step toward the rocky beach. He could see it now, the *Kraken* looming just offshore near the *Jolly Roger*. The tightness in his chest worsened the closer they got. What happened to the men he left behind? Barley with his new baby on the way, the others... If Blackbeard hurt them—

No. Hook shook himself. He couldn't let his emotions take over. They'd never win then. He had to wait for it, that perfect moment to turn the tides against him. At least a dozen times the odds had been just as stacked against them, and they'd won. He wouldn't lose today. Not to Blackbeard or anyone else. He'd put that bastard in his place and claim his vengeance. There was no other option.

A few small figures waited near the rowboats on the beach. Hook nearly tripped. Children? Why the bloody hell would Blackbeard have children with him?

Not just any children. Hook's eyes narrowed as they neared. He remembered that redhead, the one he'd bartered with at Tink's treehouse. Hot fury raced under his skin. *Little brat.* And that short one near him, definitely the kid from the witch's shop. He barely paid him any mind, but the scrappy kid hadn't even changed his clothes.

Why work with this lot?

"You!" Tink crowed ahead of him. He could barely see her, just the slightest flash of blonde hair as she strained against the ropes that linked them all together.

"It's that pixie!" the brawny boy exclaimed.

"*Why* are you here? All of you?"

Good question, love.

"He pays good," the redhead said.

"Peter, you idiot! He's evil," she screeched as one of Blackbeard's men forced her into a boat. She squealed again, nearly spilling into the water.

The boy stood a little straighter. At least two had the decency to look away, and the smallest one tugged on Peter's shirt.

The whole ride to the boat, Hook waited for a chance that didn't come. Or maybe he missed it. He couldn't take his eyes off Tink, who had been forced into the rowboat ahead of his—along with too many of the bastard's crew. She vomited into the boat, earning groans and outcries. They deserved much worse than filth-splattered boots.

"Which one a' these things doesn' belong." Blackbeard's words poured over him like an icy fog.

Hook snapped his attention to the captain, who grinned smugly toward the boat carrying Tink.

He looked away, but the damage was done. Blackbeard knew too much. *Bloody crocodile.* "Where's my crew?" Hook demanded as they rowed past the *Jolly Roger.* It bobbed like a toy boat, its anchor pulled up and tow lines attached to it from the *Kraken.* A few unfamiliar faces—Blackbeard's crew, no doubt—leaned over the railing.

"Should worry 'bout yerself, *Captain,*" Blackbeard mocked.

A dark haze clouded Hook's vision. His breaths came faster. He could tackle Blackbeard right now, wrap his bound wrists around his neck and drag him under. Blackbeard might be free, but Hook was stronger. Younger.

A strong gust of wind smacked him in the face. But the sea would take them both, and if it didn't, Blackbeard's crew would finish the job. He'd never see Tink again. Or Smee. Or anyone else he loved. It would be a last resort. If all else failed…

The *Kraken* loomed as fierce as its namesake as their rowboats neared. Larger than the *Jolly Roger,* but fast, with extra sails that were ready to be hoisted at a moment's notice. The exquisite hull gleamed with strength— well repaired after their battle days ago. Where they found the time, he could only guess. If he didn't hate the man so much, he might have been impressed. The old croc even bothered with little flourishes—engravings around the portholes, a kraken masthead whose tentacles wrapped around the front railings—and he'd bet the interior was even finer. *Fucking bastard.* The whole thing mocked him. Though if it had belonged to anyone else, he might try to commandeer it. But the croc's taint was something that could never be scrubbed clean. No, this ship belonged only one place—lost, deep in the sea like its namesake no one had seen in decades.

Onboard the *Kraken*, Hook spotted the rest of his crew—bruised and bound, but no worse than the rest of them. *Thank all the gods.*

"Set sail, mates. Tow tha dinghy."

Dinghy? Hook grimaced.

"Sail?" one sailor balked.

Blackbeard snarled him into silence.

"The scale," Lily whined.

"We'll get er. But this. Ah, I've waited so long. This I plan ta savor. Little fish boy finally rounded up with his minnows." Blackbeard's boots thumped against the deck as he paced in front of him. "Ya should'a stayed on land, boy."

"Tick tock, croc," Hook mocked. "Your time is running out."

He laughed. "We have all tha time in tha world."

The sea was his friend, his love, his life. But today it failed him, letting the *Kraken* tow his ship without a struggle. No storm came to blow them apart, not this time. Even the fog seemed to part for the croc and his crew, spitting them out into blue skies and gleaming seas.

A nearby spit of land, not worthy of a name, loomed just beyond the fog bank, a last rest before the Shrouded Isles.

Blackbeard blocked his view. The grinning bastard waited, still as a statue, until Hook finally met his eye. "Tha last rest of the *Jolly Roger.* Couldn't a picked a better spot if I tried," he bellowed, pleased with himself. "Unless…"

"What do you want?" Hook spit.

"Join ma crew."

He swallowed the acid in his throat. "And my crew?"

"They 'n join too. These decks could use a swab."

Nearby, members of Blackbeard's crew snickered.

Memories from years ago threatened to drown him. Blackbeard wouldn't be a gracious captain to his crew. He'd work them to the bone, just as he'd done to him.

But life might be better than death. At least for some of them.

"Let them speak their choice."

33

*B*lackbeard narrowed his eyes. Silence reigned, punctuated only by the creak of wood and the call of gulls from the nearby rocky spit of island. Finally, he waved one gloved hand.

Blackbeard's crew swarmed his, ripping free gags with little care. His narrow gaze never left Hook's. "Who'll join me? Speak now."

Hook braced for the inevitable. They'd served well, loyally, for years. This wouldn't be a betrayal. Not really. Their legacy would live on. Someone needed to protect the families at the cove.

"Do it," Hook snapped, craning his neck to try to see his crew. Those he could see stared back, faces hard and resolved.

"With ya 'til the end, Captain," Smee said.

Fuck. He hunched in on himself, struggling against the bindings.

"A little persuasion?" Blackbeard marched to the side of the ship. "Ready tha' cannons. Light tha' arrows. Bring us round. Beach tha *Jolly Roger*...there." He thrust a finger toward the rocky islands before turning back to Hook. "Let all who see 'er remains know what happens ta those who tangle with tha *Kraken*." Blackbeard laughed as he strode away to see to his commands.

"You idiots," Hook railed at his crew.

"Won't leave ya now," Barley said with a wince as he rolled his injured shoulder.

"Your wife, your kid!" Hook protested.

Barley stiffened his jaw and remained silent.

"Together 'til the end," Sage said.

He twisted frantically, trying to stare each of them down. "You have families!"

Anne looked away, suddenly pale. She wouldn't leave her child. The boy was only three. She couldn't. "We knew what we signed up for." Slowly, she raised her face toward him. "You pulled us up from death before. This won't be the end."

Idiots, every one. He fought against the ropes. Their coarse strands cut into his already raw and bleeding skin. If only he could angle his hook a little more...

A deep thump and woody groan struck him like a boot to the chest. His ship, run aground. He couldn't bear to look. *Fucking bastard.* More cracks and crashes reached his ears as the waves battered the ship, likely canting her onto the rocks. It'd take forever to fix.

But she was a ship. His baby, but repairable, replaceable. His throat constricted. His crew, his love...they were not.

"Tink."

His call snapped her from whatever veil of shadow she'd fallen under. She looked up at him, eyes red, cheeks flushed, damp hair matted to her face.

"Go with Lily."

Her eyes widened. Her mouth puckered with distaste. "No. I won't abandon you." She glanced over his crew then back to him. "None of you."

Fury surged through him, mingling with pride. He didn't know whether to yell at her or rejoice. *Crazy, beautiful pixie.*

"Begin!" Blackbeard called.

The *Kraken* groaned and shook as a massive cannon heaved its contents straight into the *Jolly Roger*'s hull. Wood shattered. Another booming cannon fired, the sound ringing in his ears. Fragments clattered onto the deck near them. This time, Hook couldn't look away. Flaming arrows zipped through the air, catching the sails, landing on deck. They must have spread oil or tar. Fire caught fast, licking at canvas, turning it black as night. *Bastard.* He planned this before they'd even given him an answer. He never planned to spare Hook's ship, no matter what they said. The acrid smoke wafting into the air confirmed his suspicions. The blast of the cannons continued to echo through his body, jarring his teeth where he gritted them at the horror unfolding.

His ship was a goner. There'd be no coming back from this. The attack was overkill—a punishment for him. Of all the things he'd stolen, his ship hadn't been one. It'd taken years for Smee and him to save and steal enough for her. Custom built, just for him. Their home on the sea.

Already the waves lapped into the splintered side. The bow dipped, settling into the rocky sea. Burned pieces of canvas let free and drifted down to the sea.

"Now then." The words crawled up Hook's spine as Blackbeard approached. "Any takers?" He scanned the crew, circling them like a butcher choosing a goat for slaughter. The croc's crew were even worse—snickering and leering. If he'd been free, he'd have cut one's eyes out just for the way he looked at Tink.

The cannons ceased firing. Blackbeard's crew stared at his, watching, waiting.

No one spoke. They wouldn't betray him, not even to save themselves. *Shit.* He had to do something. Anything.

"Drop them at the next port, and I'll join you." Him for his crew.

"No!" Tink yelled.

He caught the flail of her blonde braid as she lunged for him.

"Pathetic," Lily sneered, having re-emerged from somewhere. Her boot connected with Tink's legs, knocking her to the ground. Tink screeched in pain.

"You bitch!" Hook yelled.

Lily whirled on him.

"Enough!" Blackbeard roared. He snarled in annoyance. "Take tha boys below."

"But—" she sputtered.

"Now." It was perhaps the only act of mercy he'd ever offered.

The youngest lad whimpered at the sight of the sinking ship canting over onto the rocks. *I feel ya, boy.* The anguish cut deep, enough for him to yearn to sink below the waves with his ship. It'd be better than whatever Blackbeard had in store. But he couldn't, not until he saved Tink and his crew.

When the kids had been hustled away, Hook repeated his offer. "Take me. I'll serve. But let them go."

"Captain—" Sage began.

Hook snarled, demanding silence.

Blackbeard toyed with a section of his greasy beard, rubbing the black ribbons tied through it. Slowly, his impassive face broke with a grin. Golden teeth glittered between their rotting siblings. "Aye, a fine addition. We'll let them go."

He sagged in relief. Adrenaline ebbed, making his raw and bleeding wrists and bruised face all too known.

"Now then." Blackbeard unsheathed his curved blade and stalked toward Tink.

"No!" Hook roared. "Stop! What are you doing?"

Tink went pale and still, her bound hands stretched before her.

"Don't!" Rope dug into his wrists, burning worse than fire.

Blackbeard swung.

Tink screamed.

The rope binding Tink with the others fell away.

She panted for breath as she opened her eyes.

Okay. She's okay. He didn't hurt her. Hook repeated over and over to himself. His ship he could lose. It hurt, worse than the aches of his body, but a ship could be rebuilt. Losing Tink?

Impossible.

He'd rather lose his other hand. His own head. Anything.

Blackbeard slammed his sword back into its sheath. "Milady." He held out a hand to her like the gentleman he wasn't.

Fear clutched at Hook's throat. If he did anything to her...

Tink looked at him, her eyes wide.

He gave the slightest nod. It'd be to her best interest not to anger him.

Reluctantly, Tink reached her bound hands toward Blackbeard. He grabbed the ropes that tied them together instead and jerked her forward. "Bring out tha plank!"

No. He shuddered. A scream lodged in his throat.

Tink looked at him, confusion written on her face. She didn't know. *Bloody hell.* She had no idea.

"You said you'd let them go!" Hook yelled.

"Aye," Blackbeard replied. "I'm letting em' go." He pulled Tink across the deck to where his men readied the plank.

She saw. She understood. Her heels dug in. She wrenched herself backward, to no avail. He strained, the rope biting deep.

"What do you want?" Hook screamed. "I'll give you anything."

His crew chimed in, but he barely heard them. He could barely hear himself over the rush of blood to his ears and the pounding of his heart.

Blackbeard laughed. "Looks like I picked tha right one ta start."

Two men grabbed her by the arms, hauling her up on the plank. Tears streamed down her face. Her body shook. With her bent wing, she wouldn't be able to fly, not far enough.

"What do you want?"

Gold teeth glittered through the other captain's beard. "I have it all."

"The scale of Leviathan!" Tink blurted.

Blackbeard froze. His whole crew looked at Tink as if she'd sprouted a second head.

"Ya have tha scale," he said at last, barely a whisper.

"Let us all go, and we'll give you the scale," she said again.

Smart girl. Brave girl.

"That's right, let my crew off safely, and I'll give it to you."

He stomped over to Hook. "Why? When I have tha clues."

Hook notched his chin higher. "It's not there."

"You?" Blackbeard cocked his head.

Hook's lips thinned. He looked past him to Tink, begging her, pleading in silence for her not to speak. She couldn't give him the real scale. No matter what. A fake, he could give him that. He'd have to hope it worked, and it bought them time.

He toyed with the ribbons in his beard. "For 'er? Why?"

Hook looked at Tink. "Because I love her." *Bloody hell, I do. Fuck all, I love that thieving pixie.*

Her lips parted. She sniffled.

"Well now," Blackbeard said as he wandered over to the plank. "Isn' that something?"

His heavy black boot slammed onto the plank. The board wobbled. Tink swayed. Time seemed to slow as her balance faltered. A deep, roaring bellow filled the air. Hook's own. Her eyes widened, locking with his.

And then she fell.

Her scream reached through the air, ripping out his heart, shredding his soul.

Water splashed.

Blackbeard looked over the railing before he turned and grinned. "Who's next?"

34

The sea dragged her into a cold and dark oblivion. Water invaded her mouth, consumed her scream. Salt seared her wounds. Tink bucked and thrashed, but everything was the same. Up was down, and down was up.

This was it. The end.

He loved her, and she hadn't been able to say it back. Oh, how she wanted to. It'd been on the tip of her tongue the night before, lingering right there. Why hadn't she told him? *I love that stupid, filthy pirate.*

Tears didn't come, or maybe they did. The water burned her eyes and choked her lungs. Pain stabbed her everywhere.

A light? The sun?

Something brushed against her. *Maybe.* Something hard pressed against her chest and her back.

Water rushed around her.

And then she saw James staring down at her. He smiled and touched her face. She wasn't in pain anymore. Everything was warm, happy. He pressed his lips to hers.

Darkness crept in around her, but she wasn't scared anymore.

I love you.

35

*M*emories, dreams, thoughts… Everything and nothing rushed through her mind. Each image escaped before she could grab ahold. Her body jerked. Water spewed from her mouth. She gasped, sucking air into her raw and aching throat.

Everything hurt. *Ev-er-y-thing.*

If this was the afterlife, it sucked.

Sight returned slowly, everything around her blurry and spinning.

"—alive. Easy now"

She beheld pale pink against dark grey lit by a blue glow.

She pulled in another breath, just as painful as the first.

"I'll be back." A splash followed the musical voice.

Tink moved. She could—somehow. She tried to sit and failed, collapsing onto the rocky ground in a fit of coughs. Sharp rocks jammed into her back, just one more pain along with the searing burn in her wings, the throbbing headache, and her general state of shit.

A cave? Her sight cleared as she searched from her position on the ground.

Reality finally smacked her in the face. She'd drowned. She was dead, and this was some shitty afterlife. The elders always said the next life reflected the actions of the past one. Had she really been so terrible as to deserve this? She'd made her mistakes, but most of them were small: cutting out of class early, playing pranks on friends. Or her bad habit that lingered from childhood of stealing extra dew candy from the storehouse. Was it because she was cursed? All this for selling pixie dust?

A splash echoed through the cave, followed by sputtering and a heavy thump.

Tink sat up successfully this time.

"Smee?"

He lay on the rocky ground next to her, half his body still in the water. A naked, pink-haired woman leaned over him. A soft, blue glow illuminated them in the darkness.

No, not a woman... A navy tail flicked in the water below her. She sliced at the ropes around Smee's wrists with her claws—swift but careful at the same time. She twisted to Tink. "Up. Good. See to him." She backflipped into the water and disappeared into the depths.

"Tink," he wheezed.

"You're here." Such a stupid thing to say, but it was all she could think of. He was here. That was a mermaid, one she'd seen before. They weren't dead. She'd saved them. *Holy fucking revered elders, I am alive.*

No wonder she hurt so bad.

Tink scooted across the stones. They were on a small, rocky beach hidden within a cave. Some kind of blue coral grew on the walls and down into the water, providing illumination—like the moon on a dark night. It was stunning really. That might have snagged her full attention if not for her revelation moments ago.

The ropes fell away from Smee's wrists as he tugged the last bits apart.

"We're not dead." Tink just couldn't stop staring at him. *Real, he is real.* And alive, just like her.

"No," he said. "Captain..." He shook his head. "Never seen him like that. He thought you—"

James! He was still out there. She had to get to him. She had to save him. Tink tried to rise and stumbled, falling into the water. Her fingers clutched at the rock. Her boots kicked open water.

"Got ya!" Smee grabbed her arms, pulling her with him onto the safety of land.

She shook. One wrong move, and the sea had almost claimed her again.

"Shh, I got ya." He wrapped his arms around her as if cradling a child—size-wise she was, compared to him. "So glad you're alive. When you didn't surface..." He shook his head.

Another mermaid emerged with a sputtering Barley. Smee released her and scrambled to his friend. Another friend made it, but how many more?

"Take me back," Tink demanded, voice raw.

The mermaid whirled on her. "No." Not a mermaid, a merman, one with an angular face and hair draping down his body like dark kelp.

Before she could say another word, he was gone, disappearing down into the deep water that had nearly drowned her a second time.

One by one, the crew appeared in their cave, hauled in sputtering or unconscious by the merfolk. Every time, Tink begged their aid, asked to be taken back to the *Kraken*. How could she leave James?

Each time one of the merfolk broke the surface, she hoped for one face. But he never appeared, and they never took her back with them.

"Where is he?" Tink demanded. She paced the rocks, near hysterical.

The pink-haired mermaid—Adella, Smee called her—had reappeared in the pool and, this time, did not leave to fetch another sailor. There were no more. All members of the crew of the *Jolly Roger* were accounted for—except its captain.

"*He* was not in the water." Her hair floated around her like a bright cloud, catching the light of the bioluminescent coral.

Tink's hands fisted in her own hair, nearly yanking it out by the roots.

Barley wrapped his arms around her to stop her pacing. "Captain's strong. He'll be okay."

"Okay?" A humorless laugh bubbled into the air as she pulled away. "Captain Blackbeard has him tied up on his ship! He just tried to drown us all. He burnt the *Jolly Roger*!"

"I know," Barley said, ever the level-headed one.

"We all do," Smee said. He sat with his arm around Anne, who looked paler than usual.

She heaved a sob, fighting against the tears that threatened. She'd never cried so much in her life. Barley took her in his arms again. Sage joined them. "We'll figure out a plan. Soon as we get out of here," she said.

"Speaking of which..." Barley glanced at the merman who'd joined them.

He bobbed idly in the water. "She comes," his deep voice echoed through the cave.

"She?" Tink asked.

The water seemed to swell and expand. A moment later, a pale head draped in violet hair burst through the surface. Titania's bone-white crown bore a twist of green kelp. Necklaces of baby pink pearls were draped over her bare chest.

"My, you all look wretched." She appraised them one by one with her too-intent gaze.

"Thank you for saving us." Smee stood before bowing to the queen. He was truly the first mate in that moment, taking on the mantle of leadership.

"Thank my consort and his sister." She waved her hand at the other two.

Consort? Tink raised her brows before dipping a respectful bow to the green-haired merman and his cheery sister.

"Queen Titania," Tink burst out before she'd fully raised her head. "Captain Blackbeard has James, er, Captain Hook. We have to get him back."

The queen lifted one lavender brow. "Asking another favor of me?"

"Yes." She'd taste the lie if Tink tried to deny it.

Titania blinked. "You love him."

It wasn't a question. Even so, she answered, "Yes."

Standing there in her truth, her soul bared, she'd never felt more comfortable. She loved him. His crew might as well know—they'd heard his confession after all.

Titania nodded, thoughtful. The haughty air that hung about her dimmed until she looked almost normal, relatable, friendly. It wasn't a real change, more a softening of her features. "I cannot risk my people. Not even for love."

Tink's stomach dropped. That was it, their chance to save James. Sharp nails bit into her palms. Titania could save him. She didn't say she couldn't, just that she wouldn't. "He got caught because of you!" She threw an accusing finger at the queen, her voice going sharp. "We're here because you wanted the damn scale of Leviathan!"

The temperature in the cave dropped.

"Tink." Sage grabbed her arm in warning.

Titania's eyes narrowed. Her tail stirred up waves.

"You're here because you wanted something from me." She bared her fangs. "My people saved your life!"

The words hit like a slap to the face. Her shoulders fell. She was right, of course. It wasn't the queen's fault. They'd asked for a way to remove their curses. Tink had gotten James and his men cursed when she stole from them, after Blackbeard had taken the jewels to begin with. It was Blackbeard's men who seduced Lily, who accepted Tink's dust in trade for her, even knowing she was there by her own will.

Blackbeard. It all came back to him. He was the source of all their pain, and now he held James's life in his hands—after trying to end all of theirs.

"I'm sorry," Tink croaked, holding back a sob.

"She's upset," Smee said at her side. "She didn't mean it. Not really."

Titania's tail fins slapped against the water. "I know." She crossed her arms. "I believe you have something for me?"

Tink sniffled and wiped at her face. "How did you know?"

She grinned, revealing her sharp fangs. "Magic such as that...I feel it." Titania glided forward through the water, nearing the drop-off of the rocky beach. She unfurled one clawed hand to reveal a black pearl.

Tink sucked in a breath. Her entire focus narrowed down to that one shimmering object. *Finally*. Her way home.

But the joy she expected didn't come. It'd be a relief to let her family and friends know she was all right. Sleeping in her hammock, eating the sweet fruits they grew...it would be like a dream after so long away. But those joys were fleeting. They satisfied the body but not the soul.

"You don't look pleased," the queen observed. "It's what we agreed."

"Yes, yes, it is." Tink fished in her pocket and pulled forth the scale.

"You found it," Barley gasped.

"Thought Captain was lying," Smee added.

Tink shook her head. "He wasn't. We found it in the cave when we escaped the rain." She looked around at the crew. The people who'd become friends, companions, gathered round to glare at the stone scale in her hand.

Leaving wouldn't just mean losing James. It would mean losing all of them too.

The queen's eyes widened as Tink held out the scale. They met at the drop-off, Titania raising her torso out of the water as Tink sloshed to the edge, trying to forget that she was one step away from falling into the depths.

The exchange was simple—unremarkable. One small, precious item for another.

Titania looked past Tink. "Your captain's pledge is fulfilled. The storms will chase you no more."

"Thank you, your highness," Smee said, as if he were a gallant, royal courtier and not a pirate.

He must have done something, because Titania's eyes twinkled with mirth. "I do like you all. You've been a friend to the merfolk."

Anne rose to her feet and stepped forward. "Then why did one of yours tell Blackbeard where we'd gone?"

Titania froze. The temperature in the cave dropped again. The other merfolk gasped.

"They..." The queen shivered, and the temperature returned to normal. "I taste your truth." Her tail splashed water, sprinkling them with droplets. "Always someone seeks my crown... I am sorry you suffered for this."

A claw-tipped finger tapped against her cheek.

Hope ballooned within Tink's chest. The queen might help now. Someone had tipped off Blackbeard's crew, given Lily the chance to get there ahead of them and set her trap. Tink rocked on the tips of her toes, then scrambled back from the edge.

"Still, I will not attack Captain Blackbeard for you. It risks too much for my people, especially if some of mine ally with him." The rising tide of hope ebbed. "But..." She glanced to her consort and his sister. "I believe some friends are nearby?"

One sharp nod confirmed her question.

Titania shifted her attention back to Tink and the others. "Rest here. My people will bring food. When Captain Blackbeard has gone, they will take you to the surface."

"Friends?" Barley asked.

The queen only grinned. "You shall see. We did not save you to strand you here." The sharpness faded from the queen's face—the briefest lowering of her imperious curtain—and she winked. A moment later, she was gone.

36

*T*he last time Hook lay in the *Kraken*'s cell, he vowed revenge. Over and over, he'd visualized the day he'd repay that bloody crocodile Blackbeard for taking his hand and delaying his journey home. He'd fought the duel a hundred times in his mind, seen himself stab Blackbeard through the chest with his blade, toss him from a cliff, drown him in the sea. For a few weeks, his fantasies of revenge had involved the creative use of a cannon.

For years he'd worked to build his crew, hone his skills, grow his reputation. Anything to dethrone Captain Blackbeard as the most notorious pirate on the seas. He'd take his title, beat him at his own game. And then, only then, would he challenge him to that fateful duel.

But now...

Now...

What did revenge matter when he'd lost everyone he ever loved?

Emptiness consumed him. Tink's final scream haunted him, echoing in his ears as if it would continue forever. Smee had looked to him before he was pushed off the plank, giving him one last warbling smile.

One by one, over and over, he watched as those he loved were bound hand and foot and sent to the depths—laid to rest with the *Jolly Roger*.

He stared at his hook, no longer bound behind him. Who needed bindings when locked behind iron bars? More than that, though, it was a mockery of the last time he was here. Personal. Intimate. Blackbeard gave him that hook to end himself. It was tempting. Perhaps that's what he wanted—why he'd had him untied. Hook pressed the pad of his thumb against the point, watching blood well and drip down his hand. All those years, he worked toward his revenge, only to end up right back where he started.

Perhaps this was the end.

Even if he got his revenge, what did it matter anymore?

A door slammed open.

Lantern light flooded the dim room, illuminating the soiled hay and refuse lingering in the other cells—and his.

"Capt'n wants to see you," one of the men slurred through his missing teeth. "Yer ta come with us."

He narrowed his eyes at the men. "Or what?" What more could they do to him?

The two men looked between one another. "Er...well..."

Idiots. Hook looked at the crimson painting the tip of his hook. He'd plunge it into Blackbeard's neck before the night was done. Even if it cost his own life—and part of him prayed it did—that bastard would get what was coming to him.

He raised his brows and held his hands out in front of them. "Better be about then."

They looked between one another again, as if having a silent argument about who would venture into the cell first. They were of similar height and coloring. Brothers? Cousins? Not that it mattered.

The loser of their silent challenge clasped iron shackles on Hook's wrist and led him, smashed between himself and his likely relative, to Blackbeard's cabin.

The room was a gaudy affair of crimson, black, and gold. Velvet, jewels, and carved mahogany adorned the space. It was all too like his own if he were telling the truth, not that he would admit it. Another reason the bastard deserved to die.

Blackbeard sat with his legs propped up on his desk while he toyed with a braided section of his beard. With a wave of his hand, he dismissed his men, leaving Hook shackled in the center of the room.

He slid his boots from the top of his desk and stood. The croc had a satchel clenched in his fist—Hook's. They'd wasted no time going through his crew's things, the ones they stripped off them when they'd been brought onboard, or the ones on the *Jolly Roger*. Hook bit the inside of his mouth as he spied a stunningly crafted clock that used to reside in his cabin…right next to the bed he'd shared with Tink. The invisible knife lodged in his chest twisted.

Blackbeard upended the satchel and spilled its contents across his desk. Small, smooth rocks tumbled out in a heap.

"Which one's tha scale?"

He nearly laughed. He'd fallen for his ruse, assuming one of the other clever rocks to be the scale, not that it mattered now. "None of them."

The other captain crooked one bushy, dark brow. "Tha pixie lied?"

"No." He swallowed the tightness in his throat. "You sent it to the depths with her," he grated, barely getting the words out.

"Ah." Blackbeard rounded his desk. "Ya did love her."

Hook snarled.

"Or ya lie?" He drummed on the hilt of his sword.

Always with the insults. "Ask the witch."

Blackbeard narrowed his gaze.

"Seems you two are on terms. Had one of those boys working for her after all." Or didn't he know?

Gold teeth glimmered in the gap of his beard. "That witch—" He may as well have said a different word. "—charges ta much."

"Afraid of the truth?" he goaded, anything to get him to take a few steps closer.

Alas, Blackbeard held his ground. "Never. Mayhaps I will…James."

His jaw slammed shut as he squared his shoulders. How dare he use his real name?

"Crocodile," Hook shot back.

"Hah!" His hand fingered the crocodile pommel of his blade. "Still upset about tha hand, eh?"

A snarl ripped from between his gritted teeth. With all the horrible things he'd done that day alone, he thought it was the hand that bothered him?

Blackbeard stepped closer. "I made ya, boy. Yer name." He pointed to his hook. "Yer reputation. Ya wouldn' have that without me."

No. He would not claim that too. He would not take away the very last thing he had. "You gave me this hook to end my life. I used it to forge a new one."

"Did I then?" His boot slid across the rich carpets.

A few more steps and Hook might be able to reach him. He relaxed his stance and shifted his weight, hard as it was to concentrate with the fury thrumming through his veins.

"I'd call it a mercy. Gave ya a way out. Ya were a weak boy. Simpering. Soft. Knew ya wouldn't take it. Too much like yer father, ya are."

"My fath..." He floundered. How would he know? His father had been a simple fisherman. He had died at sea before he was born.

"She never told ya then?" He scratched at his beard. "I wondered."

The pit of his stomach bottomed out completely. Suddenly he was drowning on land. He couldn't get enough air.

Blackbeard grinned.

His knees gave out, sending him crashing to the floor.

"Marianna never could accept tha pirate life."

"Don't!" His breath came sharp and ragged. "You don't get to talk about her."

He neared, crouching just out of reach. "She was a beaut. Ya got 'er eyes. But tha pirate in yer blood, that's all me."

Everything became hot and cold at once. Chills and sweat beaded on his skin. His vision blurred. "You're not my... I could never be like you!"

He clucked his tongue. "But ya are."

No. Fuck. It couldn't be true. "What proof do you have?" As if that bastard could produce anything to make him believe his filthy lies.

"That ring round yer neck. 'Twas Marianna's?"

Hook ached to reach for it, to feel the comforting silver slide under his fingertips, as it had a million times.

"I gave it ta 'er. There's an engraving..."

Blood turned to ice in his veins. His mother's ring, the one she'd always worn. Not from bloody Blackbeard. It couldn't have been from him. But there was an engraving, one worn so smooth he could hardly make it out anymore.

"Endless as the seas." Hook whispered the words in silence as Blackbeard said them aloud. What a joke. As if Blackbeard could love anyone but himself.

"See there. And yer just like me. Proud. Ruthless. Skilled on tha seas. Born leader. Almost good as me." He stood. "Almost."

"You cut off my hand." His head snapped up, staring at the man before him with all the hate he could muster. "Nearly killed me!"

"I killed tha mewling fisher boy," he sneered. "That weak child couldn' be part a' my crew. My heir."

His eyes widened. "Your—"

"Why did ya think I let ya live? You think I couldn' a tracked ya down, snuffed out yer little *crew* before ya became a threat? Really, son, I expected better."

"Don't ever call me son."

"But ya are. Was there tha day ya were born." He looked away. The slight gleam in his eye turned Hook's stomach more than the sea in a squall. "Planned to raise ya meself. I'd make those royal rats cower on tha seas, become a king over 'em all on the waves, and pass on tha crown to my heir. They wouldn't look down on us. Never again. But no, Marianna wouldn' have it." He glanced back at Hook. "Thought I'd lost ya, 'til ya showed up on that dock. Knew right away who ya were. Too much like tha face I saw every time I closed my eyes."

Blood dripped from his fist. He didn't even feel the pain. "She's dead."

"Aye."

"Because of you," Hook snarled.

He had the gall to look shocked, to take a step back in surprise. *Bloody good actor too.* "I never saw 'er after she left. Came lookin' for ya both a year or abouts later after our little rendezvous. Thought maybe by then she'd a changed her mind. You too. Heard she'd passed and ya were up and vanished."

The tip of his hook slammed into the floorboards. "When I boarded your ship, I was hunting for violet root. For her! To heal her!" When he didn't respond, Hook continued. "You dropped me on that bloody, remote dock, and it took weeks to get back. She died two days before I got back with her medicine. Two. Bloody. Days!" He smashed his hook into the ground again. "She died because of you!"

Blackbeard wouldn't quite look at him. Kept staring just beyond his head.

"You think I'd ever sail for you? You've destroyed everything I loved! First my mother, now my crew, my ship, my..." His Tink. Tears hadn't come. Not when his ship burned. When he watched her fall, or watched his crew, his family, meet their fates. He wouldn't give Blackbeard that, not when he took everything else. But now. Now... They tingled at the edges of his eyes, forcing their way free.

Fuming silence hung in the air between them. Eventually, Blackbeard broke it. "Good thing I thought ta make a spare. He's already tough. Harder than ya were years older."

He... *A brother.*

When he'd thought the last lash had fallen, there was always another. One more to bring the stinging pain of the others roaring back to life.

"Who?"

He had someone left. Family that might not be dead, or dead to him. He could find him, save him...

The answering smirk told him all he needed to know.

The shape of his face. The calculating twinkle in his eyes.

The boy. "Peter."

A half-nod confirmed his fears. "Just picked him up. He and his...*crew.* Tough ones ta find, let me tell ya."

That's why they were here, on this ship, in his service. Blackbeard had found another son. Had he abandoned this one, or had Peter's mother stolen him away too? Whatever happened, the boy was on his own now with his gaggle of friends. Or he had been.

"Does he know?" Had it gutted Peter the way it did him?

"Not yet. Gotta get a measure of him."

What he didn't say spoke volumes. If he didn't like what he saw, he'd leave him stranded on the docks somewhere, maybe without a hand, or two, or some other grim reminder. And his friends... Hook shuddered. Those boys didn't deserve that.

"Let the boys go. Safely. On land. At a port." He couldn't save the rest of his family—he'd be damned if his request would be misconstrued again.

"You'd deprive them a bed? Food in their bellies? Coin in their pockets?"

"They had all that." The memory kicked him like a horse. They'd had Tink's treehouse—for a while. The food she'd no doubt stored. Coin he'd given them.

Blackbeard laughed. "Begger boys they were. But if ya agree ta sail with me..." He twisted his beard.

The mere thought burned his throat like acid.

He neared. So close. Another foot and Hook might be able to snare him. "Well?"

Hook stared him down, daring him to step closer, to demand his answers. But Blackbeard rocked back on his heels with a huff. A moment later, he'd passed him, headed for the door to his cabin. *Fuck.*

The door swung open with a clatter. "See fisher boy here ta his cell."

Hook twisted around, peering as the brothers returned for the quarry.

Blackbeard laughed. "In a few days, maybe he'll be Captain Hooks."

37

The merfolk thought fish were perfect for feeding humans. The crew agreed. But no matter how her stomach gnawed at her in that damp cave, Tink couldn't bring herself to eat them. Certainly not raw and wiggling the way the merfolk preferred.

The queen's consort, Neres, brought her oysters. Somehow those were even worse. *Slimy, goopy balls of...yuck.* Though Smee loved them, slurping down one after another like they were the best thing ever.

Kelp wasn't food, Adella had insisted when Tink asked for some, and the strands she brought did somehow look even more revolting than the fish. It didn't matter anyway. How could she eat when James was a prisoner—or worse? She hung her head in her hands on the rocky shore.

They'd been there for hours. Probably over a day, Barley figured. They had no fire. The crew worried about suffocating themselves with the smoke. *Smart,* Tink figured. She wouldn't have thought of that. Alone, she might have gotten herself killed after the merfolk's daring rescue.

At least they had the glowing coral, and it was breathtaking. Several of the crew wagered it would be worth a fortune—if the glow held. Davies tried to break off a chunk, only to earn curses and a swipe of sharp claws from the merfolk. Defacing their cavern was not allowed.

Tink had tried to slip through a small crevice at the back, one that undoubtedly let in enough fresh air to keep them alive, but even her lithe form couldn't squeeze through. What would it matter anyway? Inside or outside, they were stuck.

Most of the crew were feeling better physically, especially thanks to some impressive mermaid medicine. Even her wing hurt less, though it still had a bend to it that needed to be set. Mentally...they were all about as rough as her.

A brunet merman surfaced, one of several who'd joined the others over the hours. "They arrive."

"Excellent!" Adella clapped her hands together, her claws clicking.

They'd still yet to say who or what they'd lured to their little cave.

Adella twirled around. "We'll take you to them. Who's first?" She blinked innocently.

Water. Oh no.

Tink's lungs burned at the memory of them filling with seawater. Panic closed in around her like the wet darkness that had swallowed her. She stumbled back in a daze, even as those around her moved toward the merfolk appearing in the pool. Her heel caught a rock, sending her stumbling.

Strong arms caught her. For the briefest moment, she deluded herself into believing it was James. He was safe, there with her.

"Got ya." Smee's voice jolted her from the daydream.

A hiccup turned into a sob. Her vision blurred. All at once, the tears she'd held back broke free.

"Shh, now." Smee pulled her closer, tucking her cheek against his chest as his big hands cradled her head. "We'll get you home."

Home? She missed her family terribly. That ache would never leave, but the thought of leaving them, leaving James? Impossible. All they'd endured, and here Smee was coddling her like a child again. She sniffed, looking up into his broad face. He forced a smile, but it didn't meet his eyes. The lovable first mate held deep sorrow just behind his sea-blue eyes. He'd known James all his life, yet he kept it together. Tink pulled back and rubbed at her eyes. Smee let her go.

"I can't go home. We have to get James back."

"Aye. We will, or die trying."

"Aye!" the crew echoed in agreement.

Tink whirled around to find them all staring at her, several knee-deep in water. No one judged her tears. Instead, she got nods of encouragement, weak smiles: Sage and Barley, hand in hand; Anne, with her hands on her hips; Francis and his crooked, gapped grin. And all the rest too. Even the merfolk looked mildly intrigued.

She pulled herself higher and turned back to Smee. "Or die trying."

Tink sputtered and gasped as she crawled ashore. A wave crashed against her back, twisting her wings and knocking her face-first into the sand. The sea tugged at her, trying to drag her back. Saltwater invaded her nose—again.

Suddenly, she was plucked from the sea.

"It's a good thing you're small," Sage joked as she tossed her over one shoulder, knocking wind and water from her lungs. "I swear—" She sat her carefully on dry sand. "Once this is over, I'm teaching you to swim."

"I'm never," Tink sputtered, "going in the water again."

Sage slapped her on the back, sending up another coughing fit. "We'll see."

"You all are a sorry lot." Captain Cressida stood on the beach, hands on her hips, and half a dozen of her crewmates behind her.

Tink blinked, shielding her eyes from the too-bright sun. That's who the merfolk got to help them?

Smee emerged from the surf, shaking water off him like a dog. "Cressida!" he called, his voice too jovial for the situation. He'd been the last to leave the cave. The captain, or temporary captain, couldn't go before his crew.

She cocked her gaze to him. "That's Captain Cressida. And from what I hear, you're Captain Smee?"

That sobered him up. Everything about his face turned hard, his shoulders stiff as he stomped onto the shore. "Temporarily."

"How do you know he's alive?"

"They'd have dumped his body in the sea," Smee said solemnly.

Cressida gave the slightest nod.

"The merfolk searched. They didn't find him," he added.

"Well..." Her gaze slid over Tink and the others gathered on the beach. "Best of luck trying to retrieve him once I drop you in port."

In port? Drop them? *Further from James.* Conversation became an inaudible buzz in her ears. How far away would Blackbeard be by the time they got to port? Then they'd need a new ship and have to track the bastard down. He could do terrible things to him by then. He likely had already. If they got there too late...

"No!" Tink shoved to her feet, kicking up powdery sand.

Cressida raised her brows and glanced past Smee to Tink.

"You're helping us get him back. Now. Right now!"

"Tink," Sage grabbed for her, but she pulled away, stomping toward the pirate captain.

"Why would I do that, little pixie?" Cressida crossed her arms and tilted her head to the side. "Interesting that you hid your identity before." She glanced to Smee, who shrugged in return.

Tink ignored the question in her statement and came to a halt next to Smee. "If you let Blackbeard get away, who do you think he'll come after next? You attacked him too, remember? And we may not be there to help. We certainly won't if anything happens to James, er, Captain Hook, because of you."

Cressida's gaze darkened in the shadow of the wide hat upon her head. "She speaks for you?" she asked Smee.

Smee draped an arm over Tink's shoulder. "Aye. I support the words of my crew."

His crew. Her heart swelled. Her chin jutted higher.

One of the women behind Cressida leaned forward and whispered something in her ear. From the corner of her eye, Tink caught other members of their crew coming near. It was becoming a standoff, Cressida's crew versus them. They had the numbers, but her crew was healthy, rested, and most importantly, armed. All the *Jolly Rogers* crew's weapons had been stripped from them aboard the *Kraken*.

"You have a point," she said at length. "But the *Siren* can't take the *Kraken* alone, and I assume you don't have an extra ship floating anywhere around here."

"No." Smee rubbed the back of his neck. "But we—"

Tink sucked in a deep, fortifying breath. "Yes."

All eyes turned to Tink. *No turning back now.* Cressida was right. One ship alone couldn't beat the *Kraken*, even if they caught it unawares. But two...they might have a chance. She reached in her pocket and pulled forth the black pearl.

"No." Smee wrapped her hand back around the treasure. "Captain wouldn't want that."

She'd underestimated him, thought him a bit slow. Maybe he was, sometimes, or just distracted. But he'd known exactly what she planned when he saw that pearl in her hand.

"He'd understand," Tink said. "'Til death, right? Besides, a person can have more than one home."

His chest swelled. For the briefest moment, she thought she saw a sheen of wetness in his eyes. "Aye."

"Care to explain to the rest of us?" Cressida asked, her boot tapping in the sand.

Tink glanced at the captain. "Watch."

Water lapped at her calves as she waded into the sea and, for once, didn't fear it. It'd be giving her something today, not taking it away. *Merfolk never lied, right?* She held up the pearl, watching it glisten in the sun. Well, she'd put the claim of their treasure to the test.

Please, fix the Jolly Roger. Good as new. Let us save James.

At first, nothing happened. A hard ball of doubt started to form within her chest before the air around her pulsed, rippling out through the sea. Tink gasped, nearly dropping the pearl. Exclamations rose behind her, but she dared not look away. Merfolk who'd lingered just offshore sped off. The pearl began to glow, shimmering gold and silver, brighter than any shiny new coin.

The ground rumbled. The sea bubbled like a pot of boiling water. Then, the water offshore swelled like a great wave that would wash them all away.

Curses and accusations filled the air, but she ignored them. Suddenly, a mast stabbed through the wave, accompanied by sails that puffed and billowed as if dry. Seconds later, the rest of a ship emerged, spit out by the sea. It blocked out the sun, bobbing on soft waves.

"The *Jolly Roger!*" Smee exclaimed, wading into the water beside her.

A pirate ship had never looked so beautiful. Had anything? Tears of joy slipped down her cheeks unchecked. James's ship was reborn. They could save him.

"Damn," Barley whistled.

"Look at that," someone said. "No patch in the hull!"

"Like she's good as new," Smee whispered in awe. He turned back to the shore. "Well?" he asked Cressida. "Will she do?"

Tink looked back over her shoulder.

Cressida nodded, an easy smile on her face, accompanied by something perhaps like wonder. Her attention slipped to Tink. "Aye. She'll do."

38

*D*arkness stared back at him, his only companion in the bowels of the *Kraken*. He rubbed his mother's ring, Blackbeard's ring, between his fingers.

Endless as the seas.

How long had it been since Blackbeard shattered him completely? A day? A week? Eternity? He ached worse than when the bastard had taken his hand. Lying there, bleeding out in the cell, would have been preferable. At least then he could give in this time. But no. Not yet. He still had one thing to do, a spark of vengeance he kept burning in the ruins of his heart.

He wouldn't sail for that bastard. The least he could do was rid the world of him, or die trying. Finish off that cursed bloodline for good.

Except your brother, his thoughts taunted him.

But the boy never had to know. If he dragged Blackbeard with him down to the depths, the secret would die there too. He'd wasted his chance to hook the foul man in his cabin, if he'd had one at all.

The door creaked open.

Perhaps his chance was closer than he thought.

Hook lay on the floor, waiting for a glimmer of lantern light, jeering laughter, the thump of boots, anything.

He imagined it. Just like he imagined Tink's face. Already her spirit came back from Davy Jones's locker to haunt him, just as it had in life. He saw her face in every shadow, heard the whisper of her voice in every sway of the ship. And each one sliced him open anew. She was dead because of him. To never see her, kiss her lips—

Someone struck a match.

Hook jolted upright as an oil lamp blazed to life. He shielded his eyes and blinked against the glare.

A young, beardless, redheaded Blackbeard stared at him through the iron bars—Peter. The boy's nose wrinkled as he took in Hook where he sat on the floor.

"You look terrible."

Hook groaned. Why'd the boy have to remind him of himself too? "Why are you here?"

"Tootles and Curly worried about you."

Tootles and Curly. He barely stifled an eye roll. Two of the other kids, no doubt. No pirate would go by such a name. "Aye, and why's that?"

Peter shrugged and shoved a flask through the bars. "Here."

With a dubious glare, Hook slid forward and took the offered item. His mouth was dry. They'd barely given him any water or food, and he couldn't die yet, not without his revenge.

"You know what happened to my crew?" If Peter did, he was just as heartless as Blackbeard, standing there all stern and stone-faced. He'd delivered his gift. Why linger?

"Left at an island," he said, too quick to be anything but what he thought was the truth. "It's what Tinker Bell said."

Breath left him in a whoosh. Peter might as well have punched him in the chest. Something skittered and scraped in the shadows, causing Peter to jump and his lantern to swing. He barely noticed, didn't care. It was probably a rat.

"Who?" he gasped.

"The pixie. Tinker Bell."

He'd seen her fall. Heard the splash. Unless… "Describe her."

"Wings. Blonde hair." He looked away, a touch of color on his cheeks. "Pretty."

"How'd she wear it? Her hair," he asked urgently.

Peter glanced back at him, recovering his wits. "Like a ball behind her head."

Hook's shoulders dropped. His chest loosened. Relief and sorrow warred together within him. Lily. She was using Tink's name. But why he couldn't say. Did that bitch even know what happened to her cousin? After all she'd done, she probably didn't care.

The rat, maybe more than one by the sound, knocked into something. Leave it to a cocksure fool like Blackbeard to let his ship get infested.

"Why'd they keep you?"

Hook unscrewed the top on the flask. The sweet, familiar caramel of good rum tickled his nose.

"Rum?" He raised a brow at the kid.

He shrugged again, looking back toward the sound. "It's what the men were drinking before they passed out."

Figures. He grunted. Still celebrating the end of the *Jolly Roger* and her crew. A wave of sickness washed over him that he hurriedly tried to block out. He should down the rum and pray it was strong enough for him to pass out. He squinted at the flask. It'd take more than this though. "Think you could get me a second?" he asked.

Peter ignored him. "Why'd they keep you?" he asked again.

He leaned forward, letting his hook clink against each bar in turn as he trailed it back and forth. "Torture," he said.

Peter stepped back.

"Know how I got this hook?"

The boy shook his head.

Hook mustered the most menacing grin he could. "It's how they initiate boys to the ship. Maybe they'll give you one." The lantern shook. "Or take your leg. Maybe an eye…"

"Y-you're joking." He set the lantern down with a clatter. "Trying to scare me."

His hook arm slipped through the bars, snagging the boy by the front of his faded green shirt. To his credit, he didn't scream. "Oh, I'm trying to scare you all right. Get off this ship, Peter." He nearly shook him as the boy stared wide-eyed back at him. "First chance you get, take your boys and run."

Peter shoved away from him. "This the best place we've had. Plenty a' food. Soft beds. Coin to spend."

Hook retreated. "Ain't worth it. Mark my words, kid, you and your boys are better off as far from this crew as you can get." He expected the boy to run, to turn and flee. Instead, he stared back at him like a bizarre puzzle he was trying to solve.

Now it was Hook's turn to shrug. He frowned at the small splash of rum that escaped the flask to drip down his hand. *What a waste.* He tipped the rest to his mouth, ready to fade away.

"Stop!" The urgent whisper stabbed straight through his heart.

She'd come back to haunt him already. Her ghost wouldn't even let him drown himself in rum and escape. He didn't deserve to. What captain led everyone he loved to their death?

Peter stumbled back as a hand clamped over his mouth. "Don't you dare scream."

Lantern light highlighted her blonde hair, the smooth planes of her face, her skinny arms, and the shiny dagger she pointed at Peter's face. *So perfect. So...*

"James." The hint of a sob caught in her voice.

Something burst within him like the wind of a squall. "Tink." The flask tumbled to the ground as he lunged for the bars, throwing his bruised body against them as if he could leap straight through to her. She was alive. His Tink. *Surely the gods wouldn't fuck with me this badly.* "You're..." *Real. Here. I love you.* "How?" He'd never been at such a loss for words.

"Long story. We've got to go."

Peter's gaze darted between them, at least as much as he was able to manage without moving. The boy barely breathed in Tink's grip. *Damn.* She looked good holding a dagger.

"Promise not to move or scream?" Tink asked the boy, inching the dagger tip closer for good measure.

The slightest, shaking nod was his only response.

"Good." She dropped her arms. A moment later her empty hand was back, but this time clutching something he couldn't see that she shoved into Peter's face. His eyes widened before fluttering shut. His limp body collapsed to the ground, knocking over the lantern. Tink righted it.

Unexpected panic for his half-brother surged through him. "What did—"

"Pixie dust." Tink grinned at him. "He'll be fine."

His heart swelled. "Clever girl." Of course she wouldn't hurt a kid.

She leaped over the boy's body and slammed against the bars, clutching at him for dear life the best she could with the metal between them. Breeze from the flutter of her wings ruffled past his face just before her lips crashed against his through a slit in the bars.

The touch of her skin gave him life, lit up the darkness that had nearly swallowed him whole. If he had any doubts left, her kiss erased them. Impossibly, she was there, with him. If the bars weren't between them, he'd have her half-undressed and pressed against him already, even with his brother's sleeping form nearby. All too soon, she pulled back.

"I love you too."

He blinked, barely able to process the confession. "You would confess to me when I can do nothing about it," he smirked. Gods, what he wouldn't give to take her in his arms that very moment.

Her gaze hooded, as if she could read his thoughts. Then she cocked one perfect brow. "Filthy pirate. Now..." She shook herself. "Time to go. We've got to get back to the ship." She fumbled with a ring of heavy keys.

"Ship?"

"The *Jolly Roger*." She tried one key, huffed in frustration, and tried the next. "It's back. The crew is safe."

He nearly laughed. Maybe he had died in his cell. It couldn't be real. It was too good, too much. "How—"

Tink fumbled with the keys, trying yet another on the lock. "Like I said, long story. Mermaids saved us. I used the pearl to fix the ship. The merfolk might have told us which direction the *Kraken* went. Oh, and the *Siren* is here too."

Of all the things she rambled off, one stood out among the rest. "You used the pearl."

She stilled and stared up at him. "Yes."

"It was your way home."

A sad smile touched her lips. "Home isn't just a place, it's a people, and I could never be truly home without you."

The key clicked into the lock. As soon as the door swung open, he pulled Tink into his arms, savoring the feel of her against him, the soft touch of her lips, the flutter of her wings—wonderful, magical sensations he never expected again in this life.

"We have to be quick and quiet," Tink said when she pulled away ever so slightly.

Reluctantly, he let her go, his hand trailing down her arm. "How did you get here?"

She glanced away. "I flew."

His heart skipped a beat. "Over water?" She couldn't swim. A strong gust of wind, a cramp in a wing, an arrow shot by Blackbeard's men...so many things could have hindered her flight.

"Yeah. Smee volunteered, but someone had to captain the *Jolly Roger*. Besides," she said, placing her hands on her hips. "Could you see him trying to sneak onto this ship?"

He held back a laugh. No, he couldn't. Smee would have the attention of everyone on the ship the moment he set foot on deck, if not before. Speaking of... "How did you get past the crew?"

Her wings fluttered, a slight glow illuminating the room. "Oh, just a bit of pixie dust...in the rum."

"That's why you told me to stop."

"It worked. A few sips, and they could barely stand. It was easy to grab the keys and slip down here. Besides, I couldn't have you falling down drunk like those idiots when we set this thing ablaze."

He gaped. "We?"

"That's the signal. They've been anchored here a while, or so our merfriend said. Should be dry enough. And there are plenty of oil lanterns around." She twisted the end of her hair. "I get you, we steal a boat, I set the sail on fire as we leave, and a few minutes later the *Jolly Roger* and the *Siren* move out of the fog and unleash hell."

"And if you got caught?"

"Then they unleash hell in a little bit anyway, so we need to move." She grabbed his arm, tugging him toward the door.

"Wait." Hook glanced at Peter where he lay on the floor. "We have to save the kids."

eryl's wings. In her elation at reuniting with James, she'd totally forgotten about the kid on the floor. Annoying, two-faced thief or not, no one deserved to be stuck on a sinking ship, especially not a kid.

"We'll take him on deck, put him in a rowboat," she said.

James already had the boy off the ground and cradled in his arms. "Got to get the others too, love." He gritted his teeth. An angry bruise still marred part of his face. Bloody scabs ringed his wrists.

Tink swallowed the tightness in her throat and focused on the task at hand. They'd completely forgotten the kids when they made this plan. Surely the crew would save them when the fighting started...but no, this was Blackbeard. He would probably use them as pawns rather than ensure their safety. Tink nodded. They had to get the kids. "I don't know where they are."

Great idea, knocking him out, Tink. So great. The one person who could aid them would be asleep for hours with the amount of pixie dust she shoved in his face. "Somewhere below deck," she continued. "But we'll have to be quick and quiet."

"Lead on, love."

Lucky door number three opened to a small cabin lit by a dim lantern.

Child-sized forms slept in narrow bunks. One of the boys rolled over, rubbing his eyes. "Peter?"

Oh, Holy Flora. Now what to do?

Other boys yawned and shifted.

James stepped around her. "Come with us, quickly."

"Peter? What happened to him?" another boy asked, his voice entirely too loud.

"He's asleep," Tink replied in an urgent whisper. "He wants you to come with us, now."

"Why would we trust you?" the biggest one asked.

James shifted Peter with a soft groan. "Because he's my brother."

Tink's mouth dropped open. *No way. Why didn't he tell me before?*

He flashed her a look that promised he'd tell her later.

Fine. Okay. But holy Nessa's flute, James has a brother!

The boys looked between one another, silent conversations happening in shrugs and shakes of their heads. The biggest one stepped forward. "Peter's brother is ours too."

James and the boy shared a nod.

Too trusting, kids, Tink wanted to say, but their fault worked in their favor—this time.

The boys grabbed their packs and followed them up the creaking stairs and onto the deck. Two pirates snoozed nearby, likely victims of her dust. *Thank Flora.*

"Grab those lanterns," Tink whispered as she pointed to the glowing objects on deck. "Douse the flames, spread the oil. Be quick about it."

The boys rushed to obey, obviously more used to following orders than questioning them.

"Over there." Tink pointed to a small rowboat ready to be lowered into the tide where they were anchored near Skull Rock. Heavy fog, as bad as that near the Shrouded Isles, hovered around them, cloaking the ships hopefully still waiting nearby.

They crept in across the deck. James deposited Peter in the bottom of the boat and helped the boys and Tink with the lanterns. She didn't miss the way he winced, the tight set of his jaw, or the slight sheen of sweat just visible on his skin. Each mark on him cut at her heart. Soon, so soon, they'd be away from here. He was alive. Wounds would heal, she reminded herself.

The plan took little time, but every second was one closer to danger. Each one ticked by like a gonging bell in the back of her head.

In minutes, they were helping the other boys into the boat.

"You're next, love." James held his hand out to her.

Tink shook her head. "You first, I have a job to finish."

James grabbed her wrist and pulled her close. "I can't lose you," his voice cracked. "Not again. I can't."

Something broke in her chest before healing even stronger than before. "You won't." She covered his hand with hers and stared in the face of the man—*the bloody pirate*—she loved. "Lower them down. I'm coming."

Tink pulled away and sprinted across the deck on light feet. She snatched a flickering torch from its stand. Damn, they couldn't have picked a lighter wood, could they? Probably should have saved a lantern. She hefted it above her head, letting the flame lick at the mainsail that had been pulled in while at anchor.

"Freaking misty fog," she mumbled. Her wings fluttered, pulling her off her toes and helping the fire climb higher. Finally, the area she'd tried to douse in oil caught. Joy crept through her as the fire crawled across the sail and sparked onto the rigging. She grinned.

Someone barreled into her, knocking the wind from her lungs and sending the torch tumbling away. Tink screeched, her wings screaming in pain far louder than her voice. Her body crashed against the deck, face slapping the hard wood enough to rattle her teeth.

"Tink!" James leaped from the lowering boat back onto the deck.

Other voices reached her. Hair nearly ripped from her scalp as someone jerked her off the deck by it. "You just can't go away, can you?"

"Lily?" Tink wheezed. Lily... It wasn't enough Blackbeard tried to kill her. She twisted around, bringing her boot into Lily's side.

The other pixie screeched and released her. Once, she would have pulled her punches. No more. Her cousin tried to kill her, her friends, and left her James to rot or worse.

Yells taunted her as the crew became aware of the scuffle on deck, or the fire. *Probably the fire.* Slurred exclamations rang in the air.

Tink pulled the dagger sheathed at her leg and pointed the tip at Lily.

Lily's eyes flew wide as she followed the angle of Tink's weapon toward her. "You'd—"

"Yes."

Lily jolted as if slapped.

"Your *captain* tried to kill me and those I love, so back off, bitch."

"Kill you..." Lily stumbled back a step.

"Oh, missed that, did you?" Tink swatted at the strands of hair the breeze blew in her face.

"Get to the boat!" James called.

Tink twisted toward him. He'd grabbed a sword from somewhere...or someone. A pirate stumbled toward him, and he knocked the man back.

She'd get to the boat, but not without him. Tink raced across the deck, flecks of burning fibers floating down around her. Others emerged from below, hardly noticing the fight as the fire drew their focus.

"James!" She barely held herself back from leaping into his arms as he backed to the railing. He waved the sword in front of him, warding back the advancing pirates.

"You'll have to jump. Fly."

Tink twisted around, sparing a quick glance into the darkness where she could just make out the little rowboat on the water. The boys grabbed at paddles, shoving away from the side. She turned back to the pirates, adjusting the dagger in her grip. "Not without you."

An imposing figure rushed onto the deck, blade already drawn. Tink sucked in a breath as Blackbeard turned their way.

"See ta tha ship, boys." He pointed his sword at James. "This one's mine."

40

*P*irates rushed away to tend the flames as Blackbeard sauntered his way with slow, determined steps.

"Go, Tink. Now! Fly!" He needed her out of here. *Now. Right now.*

"Not. Without. You!" She tugged his arm.

He stiffened his shoulders and shrugged her off. He couldn't turn, couldn't look at her pleading eyes that no doubt matched the frenzied crack in her voice. He'd cave. He'd go with her.

But then Blackbeard would escape. Again. He'd fix his ship and come after them. Again. They'd never be safe as long as he lived, nor would his brother. He couldn't save his mother. Damn if he was going to lose anyone else to this monster.

"James!" Tink squealed again.

"Sorry, love." He sucked in a breath, then shoved her—hard.

She fell with a screech off the side of the boat. The act nearly gutted him, bled him out on the deck. But she could fly. She would. The boys would take her away in their boat. She'd be safe. He had to believe that.

Had to. Hook locked those thoughts away as he adjusted his stance and focused on the man in front of him.

Fragments of burning rigging drifted around them, fluttering bits of light in the dark night.

"Ya can still join me, boy." Blackbeard lowered his cutlass ever so slightly.

Join the man who tried to kill Tink and his crew? Who took his hand? Who doomed his mother? Who made his life a living hell? Father or no, he'd rather die a thousand deaths than serve that bastard.

Hook spit onto the deck.

Impossibly, Blackbeard's countenance darkened further. As if summoned, a burning piece of sail landed on his beard and charred a section an even darker black. The brim of his hat dipped to hide his steely gaze as the smoke curled toward his nostrils. "So be it."

The captains met in a clash of blades. The sting of the blow rang up Hook's arm. Only thing he could thank this bastard for was not taking his sword hand.

"Ya think ta' beat me?" Blackbeard taunted with another blow. "Look at ya. Bruised. Bloody."

Hook gritted his teeth and adjusted his grip, doing his best to tune out words meant to distract and harm.

Wood creaked and groaned nearby as their blades met again.

"I'm bigger than ya, boy."

Hook dodged a swing. "You're slow, ya old croc."

He was. Blackbeard might have him in size, but not speed. Hook kept his back to the railing as best he could, lest someone sneak up behind him. He wouldn't go down that way, not unless he could take Blackbeard with him.

One parry and swipe after another, they circled in a deadly dance.

Hook's heart hammered in his ears as he anticipated Blackbeard's next swing. The other man's weight shifted. Hook adjusted his aim. With a quick slash, he caught Blackbeard in the arm.

The captain lurched back with a howl of pain, teeth bared amid his beard. "Ya won't get so lucky again."

Hook smirked. He would, and then some. The old man was slowing.

A boom sounded across the water.

Fuck.

He barely had time to brace before the cannonball struck the *Kraken*, sending both he and Blackbeard spilling to the deck.

His crew.

A surge of pure adrenaline raced through him as he pushed to his feet. An explosion lit the air in the distance as another cannonball let loose and sailed their way, this one missing. In the foggy dark, he could barely make out his ship. But that shadowed form—*aye, I'd know my baby anywhere*. It was true. The *Jolly Roger* lived. Tink told him, but he'd barely dared believe it.

A groan made him twist back to see the captain rising to his feet, sword in hand. Blood leaked down his face from a cut somewhere above his bushy brows. The broad hat he wore was long gone.

"Cannons!" he bellowed to his men. The fire and fury glowing in his eyes burned hotter than the charred sails.

Blackbeard lunged at him with renewed speed. Hook's eyes widened. Breath caught in his throat as he barely blocked the strike in time. Before he gathered his senses, Blackbeard swooped in for another strike. Then another.

The blade sliced his shoulder. Hook stumbled back amid the stinging pain.

But Blackbeard didn't let up. He attacked like a man crazed. A cold sweat broke out across Hook's skin. This wasn't the captain of moments ago. The fall, the cannon, something sparked an unholy fury that transformed the aging man into the fearsome pirate of his youth.

The black braids and charred hair of his beard mocked him. His gold-toothed grin promised pain and death. And his eyes...they vowed to devour his very soul.

Hook's blade sliced the other man's leg, drawing blood, but he didn't even slow.

Their swords clashed, locked. Blackbeard had the advantage, his curved blade caught against Hook's hilt. He pressed. Hook bowed back, giving it everything he had as the edge neared his throat.

Another cannonball rocked the ship.

Hook lost his footing.

His head slammed against the deck. The sword flew from his hand. *Fuck all.*

Stars swarmed before his eyes as he rolled to the side. *Sword*. He needed—

The tip of Blackbeard's blade hovered in front of him. The captain's heavy boots thumped on the deck.

"Didn' want ta' do this, boy. Ya leave me no choice."

41

*T*ink screeched as the water raced to meet her. Her wings flapped with all their might, struggling as she tumbled toward the sea. With one pained flutter after another, she leveled off just above the surface of the water.

A glance over her shoulder showed the towering *Kraken* behind her.

James was up there.

James had pushed her!

To save her, but still…

"Pixie!"

She whirled toward the voice.

The boys bobbed in their boat a few feet away. The biggest one reached for her, leaning out over the edge. *Oh, revered elders, a boat. Safety.*

She flew in their direction until her feet dipped to the sloshing sea, and they pulled her in with them. She nearly sobbed in relief as her boots settled on the bottom. Burning bits and cinders floated down from above, landing on the water then going out. Tink sucked in one breath after another as the boys picked up the paddles and began to furiously row again. The *Jolly Roger* was near. They'd see the signal and begin the attack. They had to get away from here.

Tink looked back over her shoulder. But how could she leave James?

A figure leaped onto the railing. Tink gasped at the familiar, slight form.

Lily took flight, soaring through the air directly toward them.

"Wait. It's Tinker Bell!" called the boy who'd taken charge.

Wait, what? Her gaze darted around the boys. "I'm Tinker Bell."

"Huh?"

Nessa's flute. Before she could get to the bottom of it, Lily hovered just above their little dinghy.

"How dare you!" she screeched.

"Me? How dare you say such a thing after all you've done," Tink shot back.

"It's on fire!"

No shit. Tink's lips thinned. It'd be splintered ruins soon, if her plan worked out. She glanced past Lily. *James...*

Lily barreled into her. Breath fled her lungs. Her calves knocked into something hard. Outcries rose from the boys around them. Then her feet slipped, and they went tumbling end over end. Her wings cried out in pain. Lily screeched. Tink's hip crashed into the side of the boat, and they plunged into cold darkness.

Tink choked on seawater. *Dark. Cold. Burning.* Just like before.

This was it. The sea would get her after all.

The merfolk weren't coming. Not this time. They'd left hours ago after pointing them to the *Kraken*.

She stilled, giving in to the embrace of death.

But as she did, James's face flashed before her eyes. Her captain. Her love. He was fighting, struggling for vengeance for all of them. How could she quit now?

Tink clawed through the water, kicking her legs, wiggling her body. Her lungs screamed in pain, ready to burst.

The water parted. She gasped for air, choking on the water in her lungs. Small hands grabbed at her, trying to pull her from the water.

"Got her!"

"Pull!"

Salt and panic seared her eyes. She choked and gasped, desperate for

life-giving air. Her wings pinched against the boat as the boys hauled her
—none too gently—back in.

"Are you all right?"

"Miss pixie—"

The boys crowded around her. Tink hacked up seawater, wheezing
for air.

"Row left!" the one in charge commanded.

Tink looked up through the wet hair sticking to her face. Lily was
wrong. Tink wasn't better at everything. Lily could swim—a skill she'd
never learned.

Lily adjusted her form in the water and fluttered her wings until she
began to rise. The boys jumped back as Tink sent her own into motion,
flinging seawater all over the little dinghy.

"Go back, Lily!"

"Lily?" the boys echoed.

Water dripped from her cousin as she floated in the air above the
churning sea. Her hands balled into fists. "Not yet!"

Tink pursed her lips. She couldn't let Lily damage the little boat. The
boys rowed furiously across the water, giving it their all. Peter, still
unconscious, leaned against the side. If it sprang a leak—or worse, if Lily
tipped it over—these boys could die. She couldn't let that happen.

Tink stepped up to the edge of the boat and vaulted into the sky.

"Wait!" the boys screamed, but she ignored them.

Sorry, kids.

"You got what you wanted," Tink yelled. "Leave us alone. Let us go!"

"No." Lily pushed wet hair from her face. "I can't let you get the scale.
You can't go home!"

The two pixies hovered a few feet apart in the dark night. Tink bared
her teeth. It was too late for that anyway. "Why? Too worried people will
learn the truth?"

Lily reared back.

She'd struck her target right on. "Using my name now too, huh?" The
boys had given her away. "Too afraid to commit your crimes in your own
name? Truth always outs in the end. They'll know. They probably already
know! I'm the good one after all, remember?"

Lily squealed with fury, just as Tink predicted, and hurtled toward her. At the last moment, Tink folded her wings and dropped, dodging her cousin's bared claws. The other pixie hurtled into the water, unable to stop herself in time.

No sooner had she gone under than her blonde head emerged, coughing and scrambling to regain her senses. The sea wouldn't keep her down, not long. Nearby, men ran across the deck of the *Kraken*. Her heart lurched as she caught sight of James, locked in combat with Blackbeard.

No.

Where was the *Jolly Roger*?

A high-pitched groan snagged her attention as Lily escaped the grasp of the sea and flew back into the air—straight for Tink.

"Lily, stop! Let's talk about—"

A boom rang through the night. Something whistled through the air.

The cannonball clipped Lily's wings before sailing past and crashing into the side of the *Kraken*. The pixie screeched in pain as she spiraled toward the sea.

"Lily!" Tink yelled and dove through the air toward her cousin, but stopped short just above the water. When Lily didn't immediately re-emerge, her stomach dropped. Her skin tingled as bile rose in her throat.

Her cousin had done awful, terrible things, but part of her still remembered the young pixie she'd grown up with—her best friend, her favorite cousin. She filled almost all her memories. To lose her to something as horrid as the sea...

Lily's head broke the surface. Tink's heart leaped. A pale hand reached toward her. And then she was gone again, lost in the depths.

"Shit. Boys!" Tink screeched.

"Row, row, row!" the one in charge yelled. But they fought against the current in their little dinghy. They wouldn't make it, not in time.

Tink swallowed. *Now or never.* Without a second thought, she dove toward the water.

Lily surfaced again, and this time, Tink was there to grab her. Her wings strained and screamed in pain as Tink tried to haul Lily back into the air. Her cousin was barely conscious, her eyes opening and closing as her head lolled to the side.

"Up! Don't die here!"

The sea wouldn't relinquish its hold. It was all she could do to keep Lily's head above water.

Cannons boomed. One missed the *Kraken* and crashed into the sea nearby, sending a wave that tugged them down until Tink's legs were caught in the deadly water.

"Boys!"

Close, so close, just another minute—

One boy jumped into the water and swam toward Lily. Together, they hauled her into the boat and laid her near Peter. She'd fallen completely unconscious. And her poor wings… The sight nearly had Tink spilling her stomach over the side. They'd heal, but it would take time.

"Take them and go." Tink perched on the edge of the boat, giving her wings a brief rest. Everything ached, but she couldn't stop. Not now. "Get out of here!"

"What about you?" the littlest asked.

She glanced back at the *Kraken*. "I have someone else to save. Now row! You have to get them to safety." Tink pointed to Lily and Peter.

Before they could protest, Tink launched into the sky.

42

*H*ook stared past the blade an inch from his face at the captain looming over him. The boat rocked, but not enough to unsteady the sure-footed man.

"Say hello ta' Marianna for me."

Hook bared his teeth. "How dare you speak her name!"

Blackbeard cocked his head to the side, his sword arm never wavering. "I loved her first."

"You killed her!" He hadn't swung the sword, but it was Blackbeard's fault his mother died. Every ounce of his body vibrated with rage. He couldn't fail now, not before he avenged her.

Blackbeard stiffened. What little emotion he had fled his features. "Farewell, son."

"Stop!" came a sweet, familiar female voice.

Tink. Tingles raced across his skin. *Wonderful, reckless woman.* A flush of adrenaline swept through his body.

Blackbeard turned toward the voice. "Who tha—"

Hook yanked the sword to the side with his hook and rolled. In one quick move, he kicked out his leg and connected with the older man's shin.

Blackbeard stumbled forward in a grunt of pain. The tip of his sword stuck into the deck.

With renewed strength, Hook leaped to his feet. The pain burning in his shoulder, his wrists, his legs—all of it fled in a surge of hope. His own sword might be gone, but he had another weapon always at his side. Literally. The croc had seen to that.

But first... He twisted to look over one shoulder. Tink perched on the railing, wet but alive. His chest swelled. "Stay there, love."

"We have to get out of here!" she called, but he'd already turned back to his opponent.

Not before he finished this. For good.

Blackbeard yanked at the hilt of his blade, but the decking held it firm. Members of his crew raced up. One tossed him a blade, but he waved them back. "Tha' ship, man!"

Flames had caught and licked at some of the boards. The ship canted as a boom split the air, and they returned fire on the *Jolly Roger*. *Hold strong.*

No sooner had the blasts echoed than more fired in the distance.

"A second ship!" one of the crew called.

Hook stiffened as Blackbeard looked past him out to sea. *Cressida?* But as long as they were friendly, it didn't matter. "Your fight is with me, croc."

He adjusted his grip on the borrowed sword with a grunt. "Ya should have run, boy."

Never. "Let's end this." His hook would be enough. It had to be.

"With pleasure," Blackbeard smirked.

They circled each other in the flaming wreck of the ship, stepping over ropes and debris. Tink tried to join him—he waved her off. Blackbeard did the same to two of his crew who refused to leave. This was their fight and theirs alone.

Every breath centered his focus on the other man—his father. The battle faded away. He caught the moment the old croc shifted his weight and turned the blade ever so slightly in his hand. Blackbeard lunged in a furious swipe.

Hook ducked, feeling the breeze of the blade as he slid close and slashed with his hook. It caught on Blackbeard's jacket—dug deep. A roar bellowed overhead. Hook yanked it free, jarring his arm, but it was worth the pain. Red painted the tip and splattered onto the deck.

"Incoming!"

A cannonball zoomed just past them and crashed into the mainsail mast. *Fuck.* His arms flew to cover his face as wood cracked and splintered. Debris buffeted him.

"James!" Tink screeched, but pain didn't lace her voice—panic did. Along with worry for him.

He glanced up to see Blackbeard advancing. Close—too close. He jumped back, but too slowly. The blade slid across his side. Fire bloomed, and he roared in pain. He needed space, time to think.

A deep, cracking groan sounded behind him.

"She's coming down!"

From the corner of his eye, he caught sight of the main mast breaking free and tumbling his way.

Hook lunged as the huge beam crashed right where he'd been standing. The entire ship cracked and canted. No time. *Can't—*

Dainty arms slid under his, hauling him up.

"We. Have to," Tink groaned. "Go!"

He gritted his teeth, pushing to his feet with her help. He hurt everywhere. And his side—not a deep wound, but it burned worse than fire coral. "Not yet. I have to—"

"Live!" She grabbed his face between her hands, forcing him to look at her. "You have to live!" Tears formed and fell. "With me. Don't leave me. Not again."

His heart nearly cracked in two. *Bloody hell.* She was everything, and he'd let her stay here, on this burning wreck about to sink into the depths, because of his hate, his anger. He'd almost lost her to the sea once. *Not again.* "Okay." He sucked in a deep breath. "Okay, love."

With one last look over his shoulder, he caught sight of Blackbeard. He struggled on the deck with his leg pinned below the mast. Groans and bellowed curses slipped out into the night. The old pirate didn't spare a glance for Hook, not as he tried to move the massive beam without success. Fire crept across the deck near him. The pirates who'd lingered to aid him were gone—fled or felled.

He could end this. Right now.

Blackbeard's sword lay on the deck, having fallen loose from the wood when the mast fell. It would be so easy to pick it up, plunge the wicked blade into Blackbeard's dark heart once and for all, and fulfill years of dreams and longing.

His shoulders drooped. But it would be a hollow victory, a mercy more than revenge. He took Tink's hand in his. The simmering coal of hate lodged in his heart dimmed. What he needed was ahead, not behind.

The deck tilted. Tink yelped as she tightened her grip. He stiffened. The *Kraken* was taking on water. They needed to get clear before she went down.

"Abandon ship!" someone called from beyond the ruined mast.

"Right. Let's go, love." He sprinted across the deck with Tink.

"Bloody fuck!" she screamed, leaning over the railing.

He couldn't stop the grin that spread across his face, even amid all the chaos. "Sounding like me, love."

She pursed her lips and swatted his arm. He hissed in pain.

"Oh!" She jumped and winced. "I'm sorry, I—"

The ship groaned and rocked. "No time. We have to go." He stepped onto the railing, pulling her with him.

"But—" She clutched at him. "I can't. My wings. Not both of—"

He pulled her to him. "Don't let go."

With a hope and a prayer, he flung them into the sea.

Tink screamed. Water closed over them. Salt seared his wounds and nearly made him lose his breath. Tink slipped in his grip. He wouldn't lose her. Never again.

Hook already kicked them away from the sinking ship by the time they surfaced. Tink coughed and sputtered but looked no worse for wear, from what little he could see above the water in the dark night anyway.

"Kick your legs. We have to get away." If the ship sank while they were too close, it would pull them under with the wreckage. A horrible way to die.

Slowly, painfully, Hook swam across the sea with Tink's help as the ship splintered and came apart.

"The boys..." Tink said, twisting this way and that in his arms. The little boat he'd loaded them into was nowhere to be seen.

"I'm sure they're safe." He was far less than sure, but he couldn't risk negative thoughts. Speaking them, even in one's mind, often made them true.

Neither spoke as Hook continued to swim into the darkness with her in tow, watching the *Kraken* sink.

Father. He'd always wondered. Always wanted to meet the man who'd sired him, but now... He slowed his pace, letting them bob in the water. They were far enough away from the wreck, and his strength was already flagging.

"Peter is your brother?" Tink whispered into the silence.

"Aye." Stars above, the pain in his side was killing him, almost as much as the pain in his chest he pretended didn't exist.

Tink's panic had faded, her chest rising and falling in even breaths where she clung to his back with her arms around his neck. "He told you that?"

"No." He sighed. "Blackbeard did."

"But how would he know?" He could almost see the pinch of her brows, the way her head no doubt tilted ever so slightly to the side.

Time for the fun part. "He's our father."

Tink was silent for a moment before her screech rang through the air. "What?" She flailed, her arms slipping.

"Tink!" He grabbed her arm to help her regain her hold.

"Sorry. Sorry." Her arms wrapped around his neck, and she nestled close, nearly pushing him under. "I just...wow. I never..."

"Me neither." Exhaustion tugged at him, willing his eyes closed. His skin had gone cold. He could barely feel his legs.

Hook had gone days with little food and water and lost too much blood. He wouldn't make it much longer. But he had to try. Had to be strong.

For her.

"Captain! Tink!"

His heart swelled as his eyes snapped open. He'd know that voice anywhere. "We're here!"

"That way!" Smee's voice carried across the water.

Clouds parted, and moonlight illuminated the *Jolly Roger*. *Bloody hell, has there ever been a more glorious sight?*

A rowboat bobbed their way, his stalwart first mate and best friend at the helm. They really were going to live.

Beyond, the moonlight caught another ship. He squinted into the night. The *Siren?* He nearly groaned. He'd owe Cressida a fortune.

"Almost there, Captain. Hang on!"

"We're safe. We made it," Tink whispered, almost too quietly to make out.

Aye, we did. Against all odds, his love, his crew, his ship, they were safe. He'd give a fortune for that. His good hand. His own life.

As Smee and Barley pulled them into the boat, Hook took one glance in the direction the ship had gone down. Perhaps Blackbeard lived. But the burning coal that had lodged in his chest all those years didn't burn quite so badly. He had everything he needed, everything he loved, and no specter of his past would make him lose sight of that again.

43

lear skies, calm seas, and no sign of unfriendly pirates were just what the doctor ordered. Or Tink, in this case.

"Sit still and let me get this bandage on." She smacked James on the arm as he tried to pull away from her ministrations.

"I'm a bloody captain, not some child in need of coddling," he whined for maybe the millionth time.

Tink rolled her eyes and blew at the lock of hair trying to fall across her face. "Just...let me..." She tied off the end of the bandage covering the vicious wound on his side, one he claimed was a little cut. *Nonsense*. The deep gash nearly had her spilling her stomach the first time she got a good look at it. "There."

He shook his head, frowning at the cloth bound around him. "Smee's going to take my job if I'm not careful."

Tink huffed as she carried the dirty bandages away and went about cleaning her hands. "He's just about the last person that would ever commit a mutiny. Besides, if you don't rest and that wound gets infected, then he really might have to take over for you—permanently."

She jumped as Hook slid his arms around her. "Well..." He placed one kiss on her shoulder, then another. "Can't let that happen now, can we, love?"

"Insufferable pirate." She glared at him over one shoulder.

"Mischievous pixie." He slid his hand down her side, raising gooseflesh across her skin. "Got me half undressed. Care to finish the job?"

She shoved at his chest, but it was a gentle move—playful. Oh, how she wanted to indulge his wishes. There was nothing she wanted more. But breaking open his wound was out of the question. "Not until you're better." Tink kissed his jaw as he sighed in resignation.

It'd been days since their escape from the *Kraken*, and he was on the mend, but she wouldn't risk him, not for all the treasure on the Cerulean Sea. She bundled up the last of the used bandages in a soiled cloth and turned back to the pirate idling behind her.

"Speaking of Smee," she said, "we should get on deck. We should be nearing home soon. Might even be able to see the cove by now."

"Home?" His wide-eyed stare had her mirroring his expression.

The word had just slipped out. "Home," she said again, rolling the word around on her tongue, tasting it. "Yes." Something blossomed in her chest, and she smiled up at him. "Home."

She'd struggled for months to make it home to the Sylvanna Vale, and though it was still out of reach for her, she'd managed to find another one —completely different, yet home all the same.

Together, once Hook had dressed, they ventured out onto the deck of the *Jolly Roger*. Friendly smiles greeted them, waves, a wink from Sage.

All their friends—their family—had made it through the battle with the *Kraken*. Tink beamed at the crew, savoring the sight of their happy faces, of people who cared for her, loved her even. That sight never failed to bring a grin to her face. Her chest swelled as she took them all in.

Barley struck a chord on the mandolin, much like the one Tink had played at the bars to earn some coin. "This is a new one I heard in Tortuga," he said to the crew members gathered around. They all celebrated their victory and voyage home. Rum flowed as freely as their smiles. As Tink and Hook ascended to the helm, Barley began to sing.

"There once was a girl named Ella. Who caught the eye of a fella. A prince, no less. Saw her distress."

Someone gave a dramatic, swooning sigh.

"Poor dear. Bullied and shamed. Her stepsisters to blame. She rose from cinders and soot. A beauty from head to foot."

A chorus of whoops and whistles rang out behind them.

"Queen she became. A rise to fame. But the prince was not wise, which spelled his demise, for he believed all of her lies."

A wry grin pulled at Tink's lips. What wild stories humans told. After the events of the last few days, maybe someone would write one about them.

Smee lowered his spyglass as they joined him at the wheel, hand in hand.

"The cove?" James asked.

"Aye, Captain." Smee beamed with a smile broader than the horizon. "Care to take her in?" He stepped back from the wheel, offering it to James.

James slid his hand from hers to join his first mate. Hook grinned, skimming his fingers across the spindles of the wheel. But then he halted and clapped Smee on the shoulder. "Sail on, Captain."

Tink gasped. Smee went utterly still.

"Might as well finish out this voyage before you return command," James finished with a wink.

Smee's deep laugh rumbled across the deck. "Aye, aye...James."

The two men smiled at one another, something unspoken passing between them. Tink's heart swelled. A prickle of tears stung the corner of her eyes before she blinked them away. They were brothers, not by blood, but by choice. A bond stronger than iron.

James returned to Tink and drew her toward the railing. Land graced the horizon. Sunlight glimmered across the water, leaving a trail of sparkles guiding them in.

"Home," James echoed again, as if he were still in awe of her words.

Color raced across her cheeks. "If you'll have me there, that is." She fought the urge to cover her face with her hands. What an assumption to make. He'd told her he loved her, and she him, but he hadn't exactly invited her to stay.

Deep laughter only inflamed her blush. "If you thought to leave me now, I might tie you to the bed again."

"Filthy pirate."

"Aye, but you love me anyway."

"So cocky." She rolled her eyes as she bumped her hip against his. "But you're right, I do."

His fingers brushed her cheek, trailing across her skin and tipping her face up to his. "Good, because I love you, Tink, and I'd have you stay with me." He swallowed, his gaze flittering. "I know you want to go home, to your home, but I'd hoped…"

She covered his hand with hers. "I'd like to visit. To see my parents, the elders, the rest of my family." Feel the soft grass between her toes, the perfumed breeze in her hair. There was no place in Neverland quite like Sylvanna Vale, and though she'd once considered it perfect, it wouldn't be anymore, not without the man in front of her. "I want to tell them that I'm safe. I'm happy."

"Are you, love?" He brushed a strand of hair back from her face.

A soft glow emanated from behind, just visible out the corner of her eye. She urged it brighter, let the warmth in her heart slip out to her fluttering wings. "You tell me." She grinned.

He pressed his forehead to hers. "Good. But we'll keep searching for a way for you to return to the vale, if only to visit. Besides…" James stepped back, flashing her a wicked smile. "There's not a treasure in Neverland that the great Captain Hook can't find."

She giggled. "The great Captain Hook, is it?"

The humor slipped from his gaze like a retreating wave. "Do you want to find…her?"

There'd been no sign of Lily, Peter, or the boys. They'd searched for the better part of a day. It should have been easy. They couldn't have gotten far. But even so, their whereabouts remained a mystery. They had seen a few of Blackbeard's men though, scrambling away in little dinghies and pulling to shore on a narrow spit of land. By Hook's order and agreement from Cressida and her crew, they let them go, let them choose a new life, a better one. Though they might just slip a few hints to the Gamoreans in Rochland. At least it might appease them for a time.

Of the *Kraken*'s captain, they saw no sign. Hopefully, the sea had truly claimed him as its own at last.

Tink gave herself a little shake. "I...yes. I think so. Peter and the boys too." She looked out across the sea and hugged her arms around herself. With any luck, they'd gone back to her treehouse, or would eventually. He was James's brother after all, even if the ties that bound them were dark ones.

"They're fine," James said, placing an arm around her shoulders and pulling her close. "I'm sure of it."

"You're right." She heaved a sigh. Somehow, she was certain of it too. They'd meet again, all of them. "We'll find them."

"Aye, pirates always bring home the treasure they seek."

She arched one careful brow. "Do they? I'm afraid you're coming into port a bit empty-handed this time."

"Oh?" He slid his arm down her back, pulling her close until they were nearly pressed together. "We're less one curse. And I might have just found the greatest treasure in all of Neverland."

The greatest treasure... She tilted her head to the side. *By all the revered elders, when did he find something like that?*

"You, Tink."

A flutter raced through her chest. Tears welled in her eyes. "James."

Beyond her tears, his dark gaze held wonder, joy, but most of all, love. "The last treasure I'll take for myself, and the only one I need."

His lips claimed hers in a soft kiss full of promise. Many adventures lay ahead, but no matter where the tide would take them, they'd journey there together. Though not the destination she originally had in mind, Tink found the home she sought—in the arms of a filthy pirate.

Thank you for reading! Did you enjoy? Please add your review because nothing helps an author more and encourages readers to take a chance on a book than a review.

And don't miss more Reimagined Fairy Tales coming soon, and find more from Megan Van Dyke at www.authormeganvandyke.com

Until then, discover THE WITCH COLLECTOR, by City Owl Author, Charissa Weaks. Turn the page for a sneak peek!

You can also sign up for the City Owl Press newsletter to receive notice of all book releases!

SNEAK PEEK OF THE WITCH COLLECTOR

BY CHARISSA WEAKS

Under the bruised light of early dawn, I sneak through the rear door of the baker's hut, swipe two loaves of fresh bread off a cooling rack, and slip into the silvery fog creeping through our sleeping village. No one sees me. No one hears me. I've been quiet and stealthy all my life, used to being the overlooked witch without a voice. But I've never been a thief, and I've never been a murderer.

People change, I suppose.

With the bread bundled inside my apron, I rush into the empty cottage that I share with my mother and drag my pack from beneath the bed. That sweet yeast-and-honey aroma makes my empty stomach grumble, but I must stay focused. The stolen bread might save us in the coming days.

The last few weeks have given me reason to believe that those I love can have a different future than the one that has stretched before us for so many years—one of fear, dread, and loss. Finally, we can leave Silver Hollow and this valley, find a new life far away, someplace safe from the heavy hands of immortal rulers. I just need to kidnap the Frost King's right-hand man first, force him to guide me through the forbidden Frostwater Wood, ambush the kingdom's guarded castle at Winterhold, kill my enemies, and take back my sister.

Alone.

Once I've added the loaves to the other items I've prepared for our flight, I shove the pack back to its hiding place. Most young witches in the village are probably huddled with their families, worried about being taken, while I'm plotting a one-woman uprising.

But unlike the other witches in the vale, I've never feared being chosen. Witch Walkers sing their magick, in Elikesh, the language of the

Ancient Ones. Born without the ability to speak, I learned to weave magickal constructions by translating Elikesh using the language Mother taught me—a language of signs spoken with hands.

Creating magick in this way is a difficult skill. Sometimes, I get it wrong. A word here, a refrain there. That struggle, and the fact that not a single witch's mark lives on my skin, has made me invisible for the choosing. The chosen Witch Walkers help protect the northernmost borders and Winterhold itself. What would Colden Moeshka, the Frost King, want with an unskilled witch like me?

A grin tempts my lips.

If only he knew all that I can do.

A hard *thud* smacks the door, and the sound reverberates through my bones. At first, I think it might be Mother, her arms overloaded with apples as she toes the door for me to let her inside. But the unmistakable scent of death wafts beneath the threshold. The smell is weak, but it's there.

When I drag open the door, a dove lies on the ground, its wings splayed and unmoving. With a gentle touch, I cradle the bird in the bend of my arm, trail my fingers over her head and breast, and carry her inside. Her neck looks damaged, but she's still alive, though barely. I have a few minutes to save her, but that's all.

More often than not, the chance to help passes me by. It's safer if no one knows that I'm a Healer. I've never dared tell my parents or anyone else. Not even my friend Finn. Only my sister, Nephele, knows that I have this skill. She always said to be thankful that I have no witch's marks, because the power living inside me makes me valuable.

And valuable things get locked away.

As the scent of death grows sharper, I sit in Mother's chair near the hearth and nestle the dove in my lap. Her death smells like pine needles and damp moss mixed with a hint of chilly rain. On a deep inhale, I close my eyes, absorbing that scent, and watch as the shimmering, coiled strands of the dove's life unravel like a spool of thread.

I'm not sure this is my wisest decision given what I must do today. Healing can be tiring, depending on how near death is and the size of the life I'm weaving back together. A tiny dove should be a small effort, though. I can't just let her die.

Concentrating, I imagine the dim strands becoming a gleaming braid, and the dove soaring over the valley. This is the first part of every rescue —to manifest a vision of my will. Next, I drudge up the ancient song I've known since the first time I saw the threads of life in a dying doe and form the lyrics with my hands.

"Loria, Loria, anim alsh tu brethah, vanya tu limm volz, sumayah, anim omio dena wil rheisah."

The strands glow and tremble, drawn together like iron to lodestone. I keep singing, repeating the words until the strands have entwined and the gilded construct of life is once again solid and resplendent.

The dove's wings flap and ruffle. When I open my eyes, her heart pounds so hard that her breast moves with each beat. Her little eyes open too, and she's up, flying from wall to wall. I shove open the shutters and watch her take off into the cold, vanishing in the distance near the forest's boundary.

I'm a little tired and dizzy, and cold sweat slicks my brow, but I'll recover. The strangest part of healing a life so close to its end is that the stolen death coils inside me like a shadow. I only have a handful of deaths tucked away, but I feel the tiny darkness of each one.

I begin to close the shutters, but instead, I pause and take in the view of morning in the village—possibly my last. To the west, where Frostwater Wood curves over the hills, the midnight shift of Witch Walkers moves along the forest's edge near the watchtower, gliding through the gloom like ghosts. And in the mist, just beyond the village green, a few women appear from the east. They carry baskets of apples on their heads, surrounded by clouds of their own breath. All else is calm, for now, a village on the cusp of waking for the most dreaded day of the year.

After stoking the fire, I exchange my cloak for a shawl and head to my worktable. The sun is almost up, which means that Finn will wake soon, and like the others carrying their apples, Mother will return from the orchard any moment. There's work to do, a plan that I must see to the end, though it's hard to imagine leaving all I've ever known.

But I cannot stay. We live in a world where wars simmer between two of Tiressia's continental breaks—the Eastland territories and the Summerlands to the south. For centuries, every eastern ruler has tried to conquer the southern lands, longing to claim the City of Ruin—a citadel believed to hold the Grove of the Gods, and the burial ground of Tiressia's deities.

Or so says the myth.

To the Frost King's credit, I've never known war. The Northlands have remained neutral, but our citizens—whether protecting the coast, the mountains, the valley, the Iceland Plains, or the king himself—must live according to the Frost King's wishes, guardians above all else. I believe I have the power to change that, to end his immortal life and make us a free land governed by its people, free to live as we choose.

And that's what I aim to do.

Father's old whetstone sits at the bottom of his trunk. I gather it from beneath his other work tools and scoop a cup of rainwater from the wash bucket for the grinding task. Just as I sit to work, Mother bursts into the cottage carrying a bushel of apples. She kicks the door shut, but not before a bitter wind out of Frostwater Wood follows her inside. With a grunt, she drops the laden basket.

The cold wraps around me, and I tug my shawl tighter, the colorful one Nephele knitted ages ago. Lately, her memory is everywhere. Even the rime-covered apples at my feet make me think of her. Nephele loved the orchard and enjoyed the Collecting Day harvest. She also didn't mind living on the Northland break of Tiressia's shattered empire, nor was she bothered by the touch of winter that clings to our valley after every harvest moon.

I'm the opposite. I hate living in the Northlands. I hate the Collecting Day harvest, and I hate this time of year. Each passing autumn day is another reminder that the Witch Collector is coming and that Silver Hollow, with its rolling green hills and sun-washed flaxen fields, will soon be buried beneath winter's suffocating frost.

Mother wipes a strand of graying hair from her brow and props elegant hands on her wide hips. "I know you'll think me foolish," she says, "but this will be a good day, my girl. I feel it in my bones."

Mother's witch's marks are few, her magick simple. The swirls of her ability glisten under a fine sheen of cold sweat, faint silver etchings curving along the tawny skin of her slender neck.

Setting the cup of rainwater aside, I force today's first smile. My fingers are stiff with cold when I sign. *"I am sure you are right. I should get to peeling."*

A beat later, I spin on my stool, turning away from her and those knowing eyes.

My smile vanishes as I light the candles that illuminate my work area. I want to avoid this conversation. It happens every year, and every year the Witch Collector proves Mother's intuition wrong.

Still, I would never call her foolish. Though a dreamer with her head in the stars, my mother is the wisest person I've ever known. It's just that this day is never good, and this year it might be worse than ever before.

Because of me.

I unlock the worktable drawer and retrieve our salvation, the reason I've found such bravery for taking back our lives: Father's old knife. *The God Knife*, he called it, said to have been fashioned by an eastern sorcerer from the broken rib of a long-dead god. It had been missing since the winter after my sister was chosen, lost in the snow-covered fields the day Father's heart stopped beating.

A few weeks ago, a group of farmers found the blade during harvest, half-buried in the soil of a soon-to-be fallow field. One of them, Finn's father Warek, recognized the knife by its unusual white granite hilt, strange black blade, and the amber stone set into the pommel. He made sure the farmers returned the find to my mother.

"What's so special about a God Knife?" I asked one night when I was still small enough to sit on Father's knee. My father carried that knife everywhere he went. There was no question that it was important.

He'd just come in from harvest. I still remember the way he smelled— like musk and field. I traced the veins in his hand, following his witch's marks—the marks of a reaper—that branched like tree roots over his knotty knuckles.

"The God Knife is a god remnant," he answered. *"God bone, fashioned by the hand of Un Drallag the Sorcerer. It harkens to the soul of the god from whose*

body the bone was taken. It can kill anyone and anything, the blessed and the cursed, the forever living and the risen dead—even other gods."

"Yet you keep it," I'd said, not understanding the depth of his words or the fact that they would one day change my world.

His only reply had been: *"Yes, daughter. I keep it. Because I must."*

Like Nephele, thoughts of my father are never far from my mind. Why he went to the fields the day he died—in the dead of winter—will forever remain a mystery, as will the question that might haunt me until my last breath: If the blade is so all-powerful, why didn't he use it to save us? To save Nephele?

He had possession of the knife for years—a god killer, an immortal slayer, a divine weapon. Never once did he use it against the Frost King to change our circumstances.

Mother leans over my shoulder and unties her cloak as she eyes the knife. The scent of cloves, fallen leaves, and smoky coldness floats from her skin and clothes.

"You're sharpening that old thing?"

She holds no faith in Father's tales of finding the God Knife along the Malorian seashore. Though she's kept the blade hidden away since its rediscovery, Mother still doesn't believe in its myth and claims it has no power.

But I believe. Because I feel it.

In answer, I hold the dull, black edge to the candlelight. I need this knife sharp enough to penetrate sinew and bone, and I only trust one pair of hands to make sure that it can.

Unfortunately, those hands aren't mine.

"Carry on, then," Mother says. "But we have better knives for peeling apples, Raina."

I need to get the knife to Finn. He usually works with iron mined near the Mondulak Range, but his hands are the hands I trust. I just need an excuse because Mother is right. We have other blades for the day's work. I've no reason to be so focused on this one, none that she'll believe anyway, and it's not like I can explain my plan. Something tells me she wouldn't be too keen to learn that her daughter means to kidnap the Witch Collector today at knifepoint.

Mother hangs her cloak by the door and crosses to the hearth to pour a mug of mulled apple cider. When she returns to my side, she watches over my shoulder as I position Father's whetstone on a piece of oiled cloth. She says the knife isn't made of bone. What bone is black as night and cold as ice?

But it's bone. God bone. Not flint or steel. I'm so sure of it. Something deep inside that old marrow vibrates with every pass, as though I'm bringing it back to life.

More sweat beads on my brow as I work, sliding the edge along the stone with careful measure. What if I damage it? Can god bone *be* damaged? And what if the Witch Collector bests me today when I hold this blade to his throat?

My hands tremble at the thought of standing against him, enough that I falter in my work. Bone catches against stone—a nick of my fingertip. I gasp and suck the wound.

Gods' death. Only *I* would accidentally kill myself with the very weapon that could save me.

"Raina, careful." Mother sets her mug aside and studies the cut. She touches my chin, love softening her eyes. "I know you consider this knife a connection to your father, but maybe Finn should have a look at the blade if you're so determined to use it. I prefer your beautiful hands intact."

My pulse quickens. I feel like a child again, a little girl hiding something from her mother. But this is the perfect moment. I couldn't have designed it any better.

"Finn is probably on his way to the shop," I sign. *"I will take it to him, and I will finish the apples long before noon. I promise."*

"Go." She smiles. "But don't be long. The harvest supper won't prepare itself."

I throw on my cloak, wrap the knife in a piece of animal skin, and head for the door.

"Daughter."

I glance over my shoulder, and Mother crosses the small distance between us.

"You try so hard to hide it," she says, "yet a mother knows her child better than all else. Do not let your loathing lead you—or us—to trouble, Raina. If you're going to promise me anything, promise me that."

Her sharp, indigo eyes dart to the bundled knife like she knows my every intention, and guilt and shame squeeze my heart for what I'm about to do. What I *must* do.

I lean in, kiss her soft cheek, and lie anyway.

"I promise," I sign, and slip into the cold, gray light of day.

Don't stop now. Keep reading with your copy of THE WITCH COLLECTOR, by City Owl Author, Charissa Weaks.

And don't miss more Reimagined Fairy Tales coming soon, and find more from Megan Van Dyke at www.authormeganvandyke.com

Don't miss more Reimagined Fairy Tales coming soon, and find more from Megan Van Dyke at www.authormeganvandyke.com

Until then, discover THE WITCH COLLECTOR, by City Owl Author, Charissa Weaks!

Every harvest moon, the Witch Collector rides into our valley and leads one of us to the home of the immortal Frost King, to remain forever. Today is that day—Collecting Day.

But he will not come for me. I, Raina Bloodgood, have lived in this village for twenty-four years, and for all that time he has passed me by. His mistake.

Raina Bloodgood has one desire: kill the Frost King and the Witch Collector who stole her sister. On Collecting Day, she means to exact murderous revenge, but a more sinister threat sets fire to her world. Rising from the ashes is the Collector, Alexus Thibault, the man she vowed to slay and the only person who can help save her sister.

Thrust into an age-old story of ice, fire, and ancient gods, Raina must abandon vengeance and aid the Witch Collector or let their empire—and her sister—fall into enemy hands. But the lines between good and evil blur, and Raina has more to lose than she imagined. What is she to do when the Witch Collector is no longer the villain who stole her sister, but the hero who's stealing her heart?

Please sign up for the City Owl Press newsletter for chances to win special subscriber-only contests and giveaways as well as receiving information on upcoming releases and special excerpts.

All reviews are **welcome** and **appreciated**. Please consider leaving one on your favorite social media and book buying sites.

Escape Your World. Get Lost in Ours! City Owl Press at www. cityowlpress.com.

ACKNOWLEDGMENTS

There are so many people to thank for this book becoming a reality, but I have to start at the very beginning of it all with my parents. Words can't properly express how thankful I am for all of your love and support throughout my life. You embraced and encouraged all my weird and gave me the courage to be myself and share my wild stories with the world. Thank you for all the many trips to the library, the swap shop, and Barnes & Noble, and for never saying no when I wanted a new book. Thank you for letting me play video games, watch sci-fi movies, and all the other things that inspired my imagination to grow and thrive. I know I wasn't always an easy child, but your love and support mean more than I'll ever be able to clearly express. You embraced my early stories, from my very first days attending the Young Authors program in elementary school to the messy first drafts of the books I wrote as an adult. I appreciate every subtle, and not so subtle, piece of encouragement you've given me to keep writing and pursuing my dreams. I couldn't have wished for better cheerleaders in this or life in general.

To my husband: Thank you so much for giving me the push to follow my dreams and encouraging and supporting me every step of the way. You asked me once what I'd do if time, money, skill, etc. were no barrier. I said I'd be a writer. You said, "So why not do it?" A great question. I had many excuses, most involving a lack of time, but that question lingered so strongly that I knew I had to start seriously following my dreams. I haven't stopped since. Thank you for putting up with the many nights and weekends where all I wanted to do was write. You comforted me through rejection and when I felt like my dreams were dying. You supported our family so that I could follow my dreams of being a mom and writer.

Thank you for every nightly prayer, for every word of encouragement, and mostly for your love and just being you. I love you.

To my son: Thank you for taking good naps and letting mommy write. You are the brightest star in my life, and I love you. Someday I might let you read this book, but not for many years yet.

To all of my family, especially those who took the time to read my work and support me on this journey: Thank you, thank you, thank you! Each word of encouragement means so much, and you really are the best family anyone could ask for.

The idea for this book popped into my head just when I needed it. It was the start of the pandemic, shortly after a cross-country move, when I felt like all my book dreams were falling apart, and I was doing my best to try to raise a one-year-old. I shared the ridiculous idea with my writing friends. They loved it and encouraged me to write it, even if it was just for myself. So, a huge thank you to all of my Oceans 11 ladies: Abby Glenn, Christy Dirks, Jen Davenport, K. J. Harrowick, Lauren Hazan, Maha Khalid, Melody Carabalo, Sanyukta Thakare, and Talynn Lynn. This book wouldn't exist without you, and I doubt I'd even still be pursuing my dreams if not for all your love, support, and encouragement. You've cried with me, cheered for me, helped me learn and grow, and been the best blessing I never knew I needed. From the bottom of my heart, thank you!

A huge thank you to my editor Heather McCorkle, and the entire team at City Owl Press, for seeing the potential in this story and making my dream a reality. I really feel like I found the perfect home for this story with you all, and I appreciate all of your dedication to bringing my fun, sexy, reimagined fairytales to the world.

So many people have played a role in my journey so far, and I would never have gotten to this point without every single one of you. Thank you to everyone involved with #WriterInMotion, #RewriteItClub, #RevPit, #TeamOptimism, my 2019 mentee class, my #22Debuts class, #QuokkaCrew, No Drama Writing Lemurs, #FridayKiss, my #CampRevPit cabins, my fellow Owls, and especially the following individuals: Bonnie Swanson, Carly Bornstein-Hayward, Jeni Chappelle, Kat Turner, Maria Tureaud, Maxym Martineau, Megan Records, Paris

Wynters, Paulette Kennedy, Rebecca Fryar, Rochele Smit, Sami Ellis, Sara Sellers, and S.M. Roffey.

You've all been instrumental in helping me learn and grow, being a shoulder to cry on, and encouraging me to keep going. Thank you for being a part of my story. I can't wait to see what the future has in store for all of us.

Finally, thank you to all of my readers. Without you, I'd just be sharing my stories into the void. I hope you enjoyed this book and you'll give me the privilege of sharing more tales with you in the future.

ABOUT THE AUTHOR

MEGAN VAN DYKE is a fantasy romance author with a love for all things that include magic and kissing, especially fairytales and anything with a happily ever after. Many of her stories include themes of family (whether born into or found) and a sense of home and belonging, which are important aspects of her life as well. When not writing, Megan loves to cook, play video games, explore the great outdoors, and spend time with her family. A southerner by birth and at heart, Megan currently  lives with her family in Colorado. Be sure to sign up for her newsletter so you never miss a minute!

www.authormeganvandyke.com

instagram.com/authormeganvandyke
facebook.com/AuthorMeganVanDyke
twitter.com/AuthorMeganVD
tiktok.com/@authormeganvandyke
bookbub.com/authors/megan-van-dyke

ABOUT THE PUBLISHER

City Owl Press is a cutting edge indie publishing company, bringing the world of romance and speculative fiction to discerning readers.

Escape Your World. Get Lost in Ours!

www.cityowlpress.com

facebook.com/CityOwlPress
twitter.com/cityowlpress
instagram.com/cityowlbooks
pinterest.com/cityowlpress
tiktok.com/@cityowlpress

CPSIA information can be obtained
at www.ICGtesting.com
Printed in the USA
LVHW040151040723
751506LV00006B/67